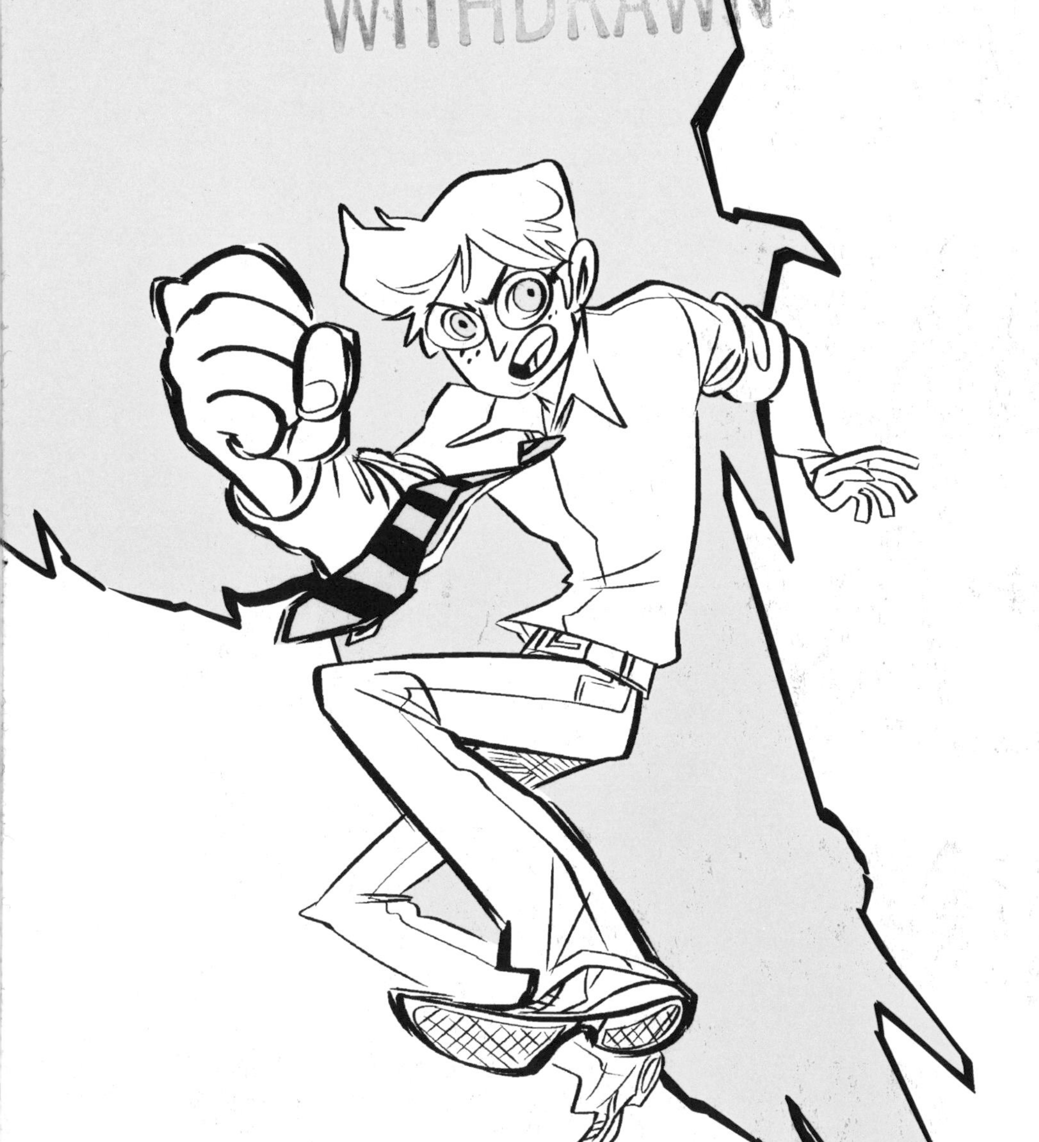

ONI PRESS

An Oni Press Production

WRITTEN BY

ANANTH PANAGARIYA

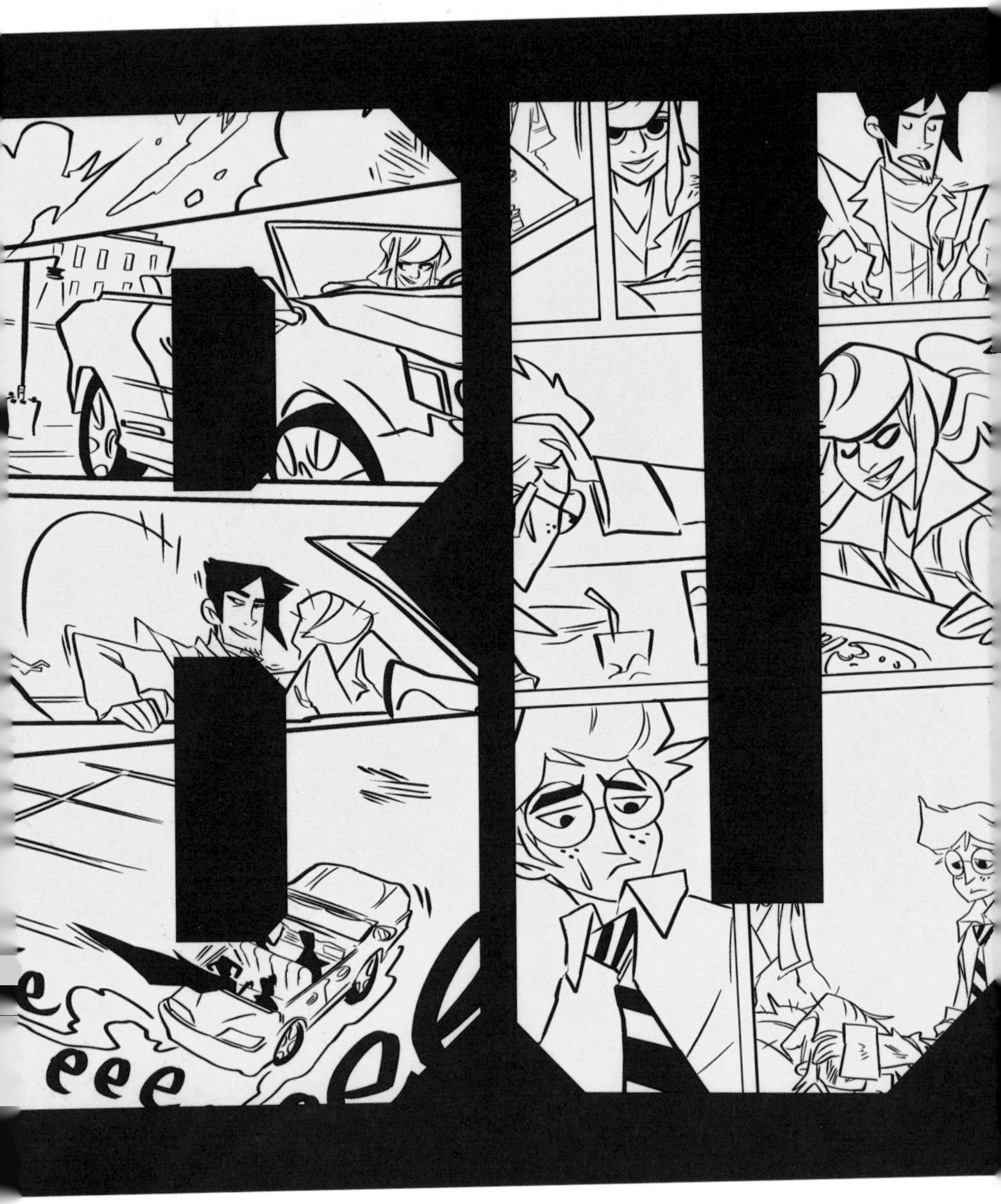
eee

DESIGN BY

Jason Storey

ILLUSTRATED BY

TESSA STONE

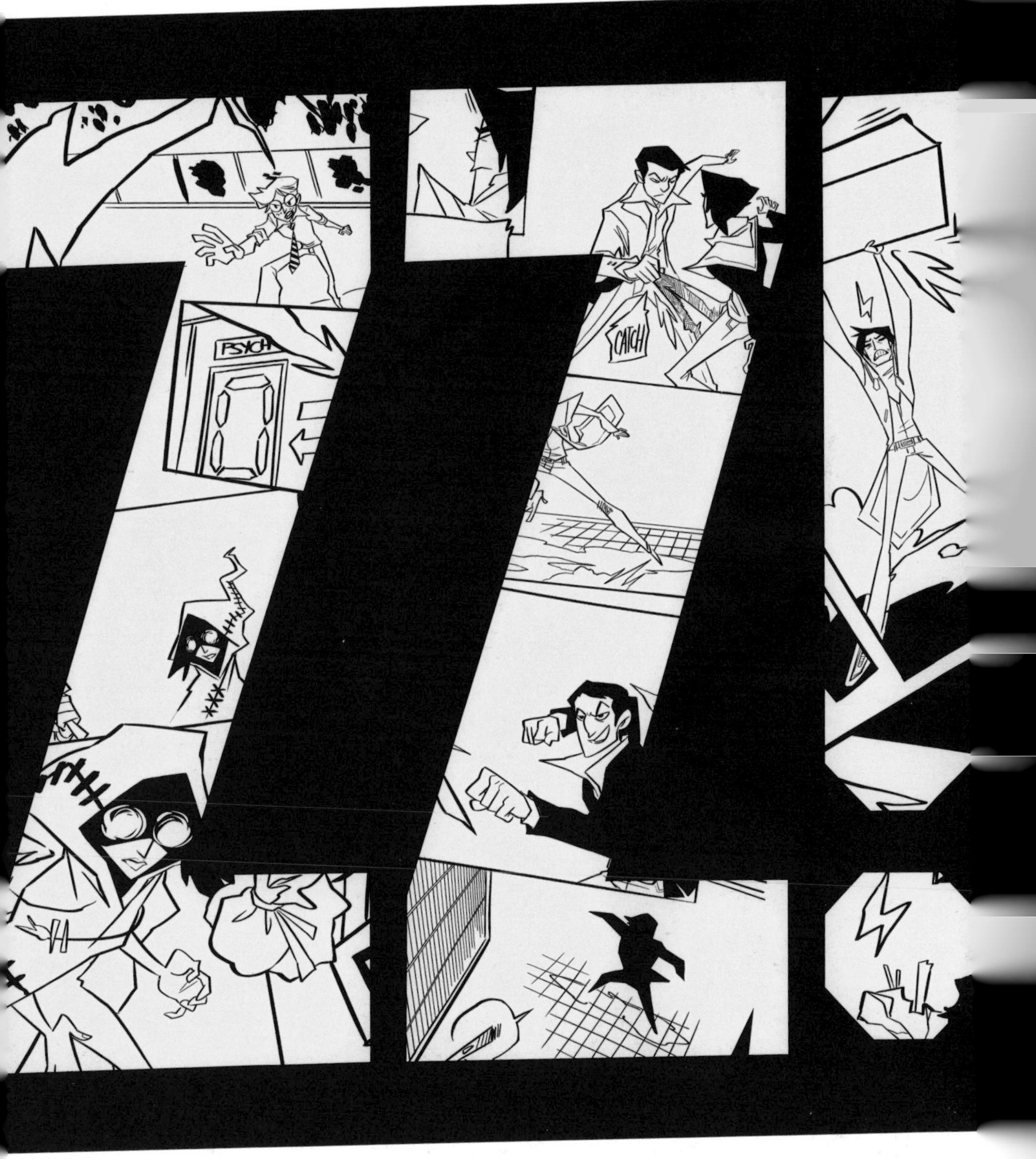
PSYCH
CATCH

EDITED BY

James Lucas Jones

Oni Press, Inc.

Publisher, **Joe Nozemack**

Editor in Chief, **James Lucas Jones**

Art Director, **Keith Wood**

Director of Publicity, **John Schork**

Director of Sales, **Cheyenne Allott**

Editor, **Jill Beaton**

Editor, **Charlie Chu**

Graphic Designer, **Jason Storey**

Digital Prepress Lead, **Troy Look**

Administrative Assistant, **Robin Herrera**

Oni Press, Inc.

1305 SE M.L. King Jr. Blvd.,

Suite A,

Portland Or 97214

USA

www.onipress.com

facebook.com/onipress ⚡ twitter.com/onipress ⚡ onipress.tumblr.com

First Edition: November 2013

ISBN 978-1-62010-088-2 ⚡ eISBN 978-1-62010-123-0

1 2 3 4 5 6 7 8 9 10

Library of Congress Control Number: 2013944648

Printed in China.

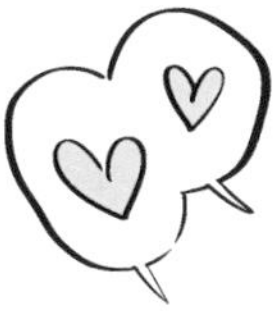

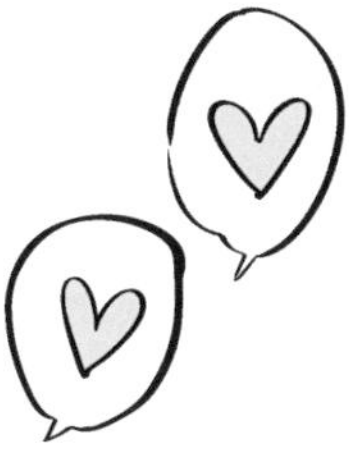

For Yuko.
And heartfelt thanks to Tess for her dedication, hard work, and vision... a comic can't live on words alone. You're a total pro, buddy.

-Ananth

Cheers to my friends, family and anyone who has ever believed in me and still does. May I never let you down! And to Sarah, because face it, you're one hell of a sister. I can drink to that.

-Tess!

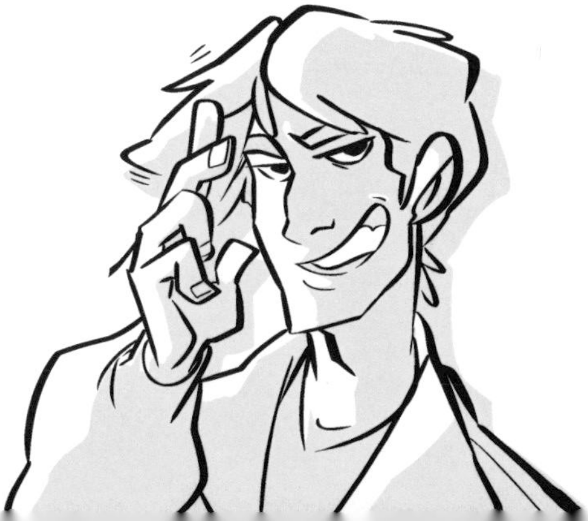

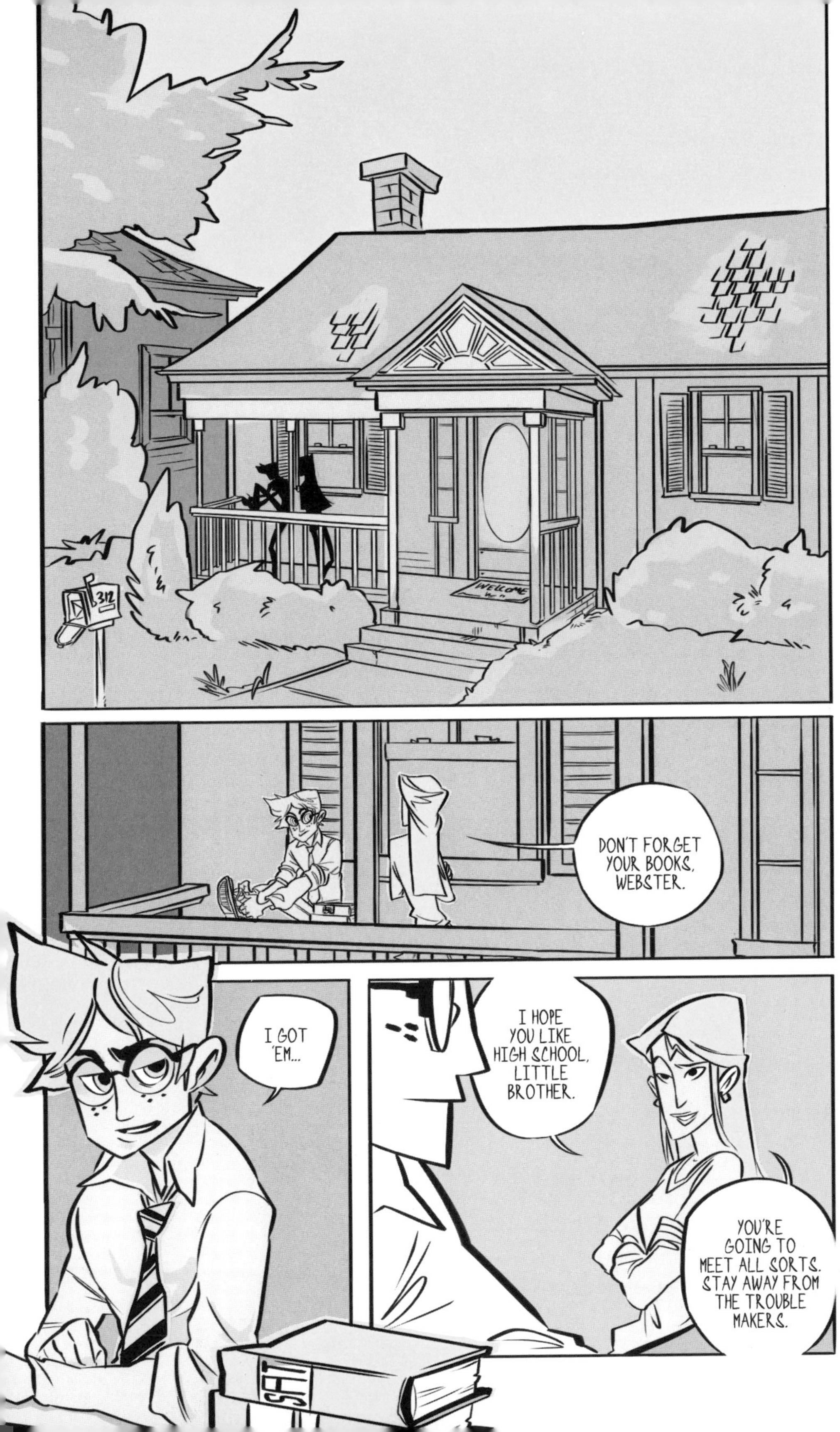
312
WELCOME
DON'T FORGET YOUR BOOKS, WEBSTER.
I GOT 'EM...
I HOPE YOU LIKE HIGH SCHOOL, LITTLE BROTHER.
YOU'RE GOING TO MEET ALL SORTS. STAY AWAY FROM THE TROUBLE MAKERS.
SHS

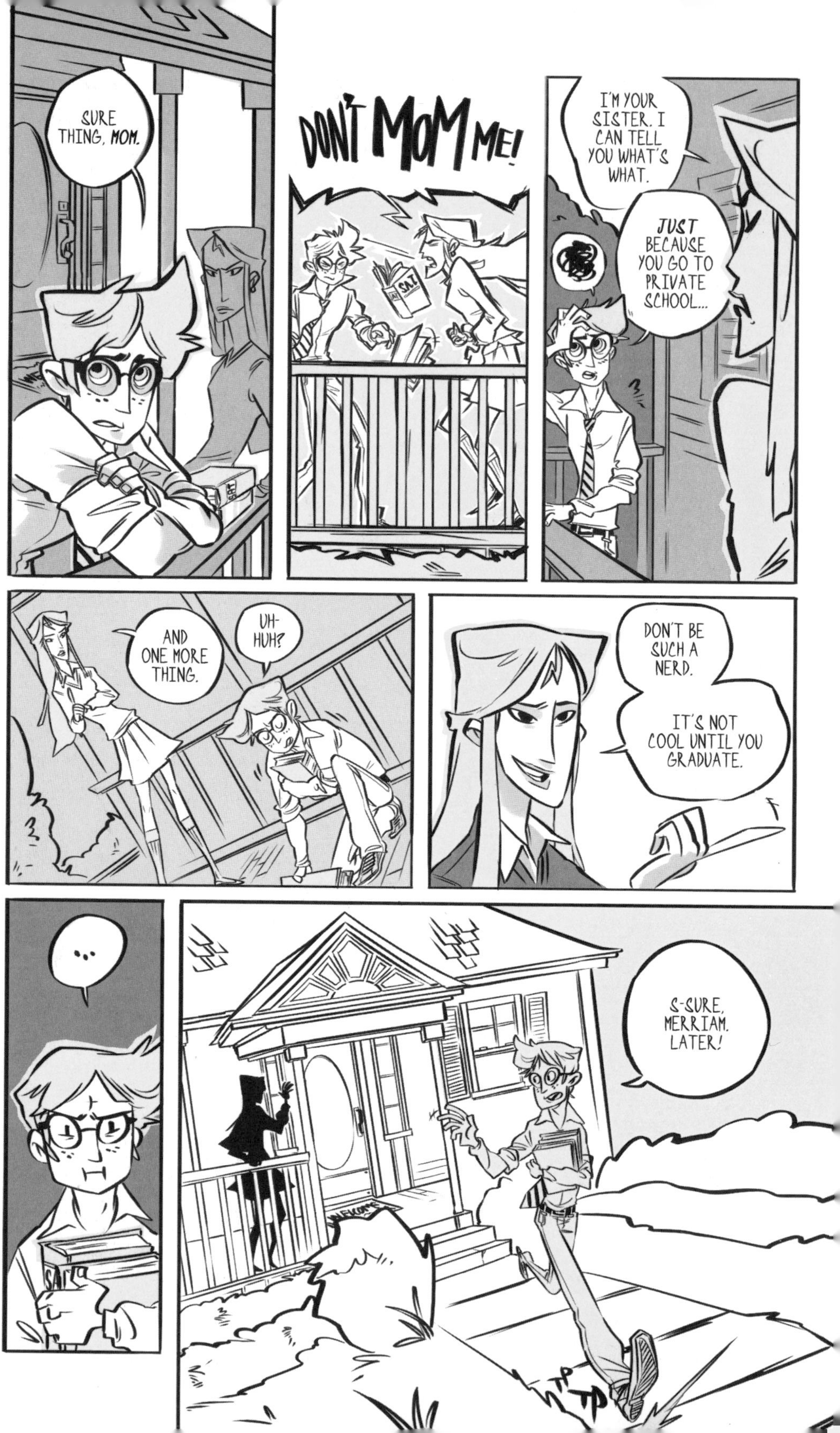
SURE THING, MOM.
DON'T MOM ME!
I'M YOUR SISTER. I CAN TELL YOU WHAT'S WHAT.
JUST BECAUSE YOU GO TO PRIVATE SCHOOL...
AND ONE MORE THING.
UH-HUH?
DON'T BE SUCH A NERD.
IT'S NOT COOL UNTIL YOU GRADUATE.
...
S-SURE, MERRIAM. LATER!
TP TP

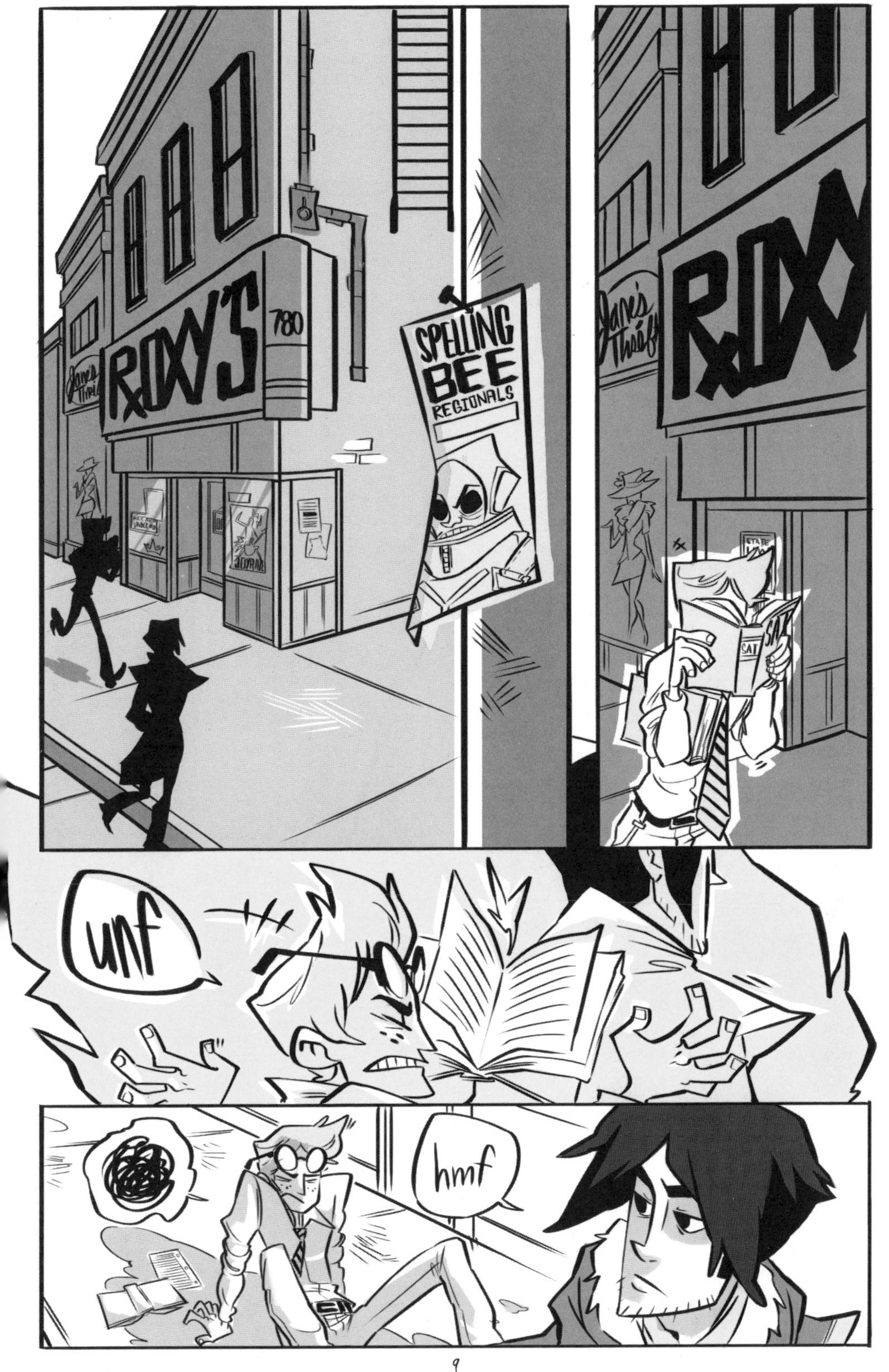
ROXY'S
780
SPELLING
BEE
REGIONALS
SAT
unf
hmf

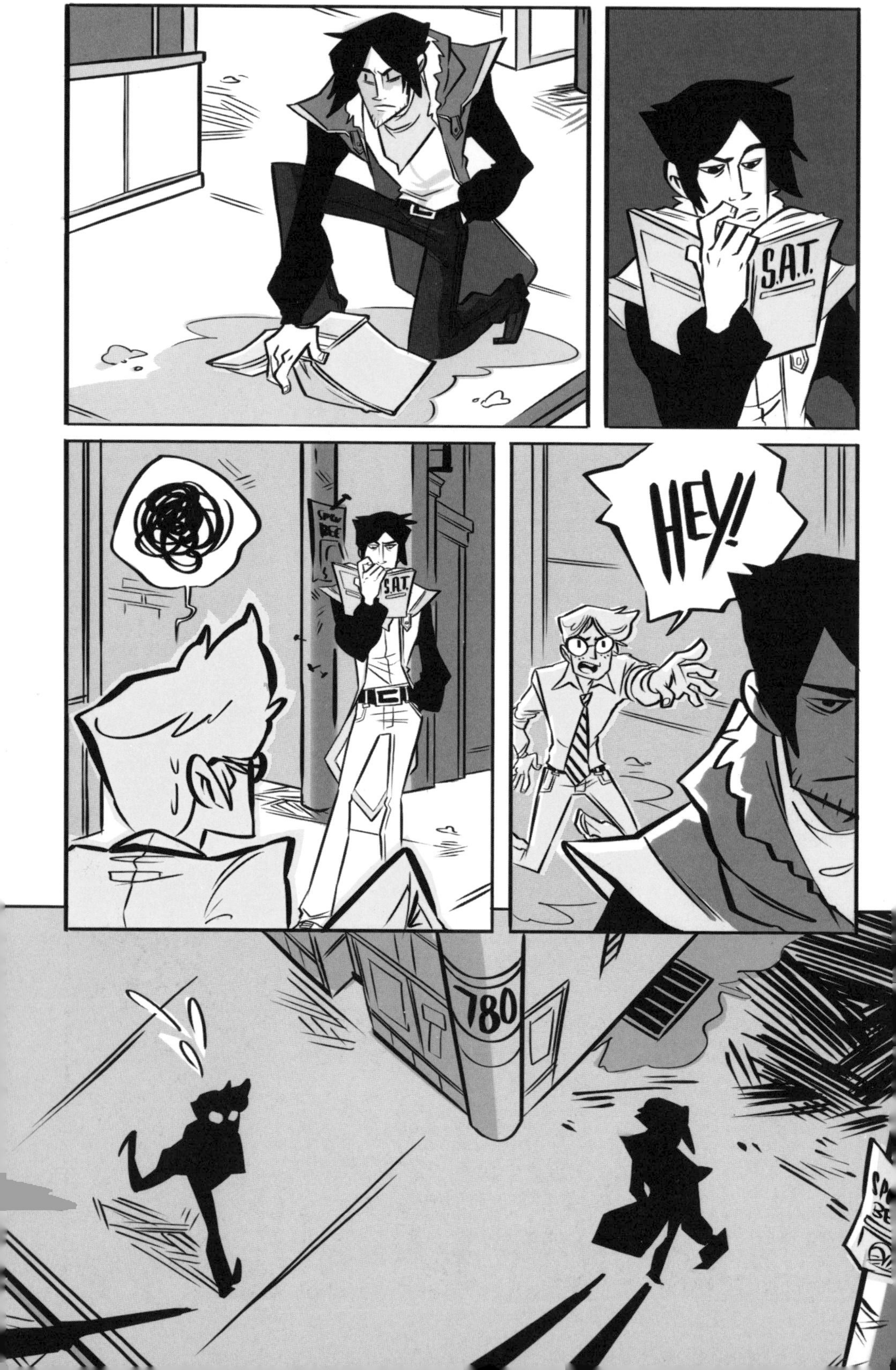
S.A.T.
S.A.T.
HEY!
780

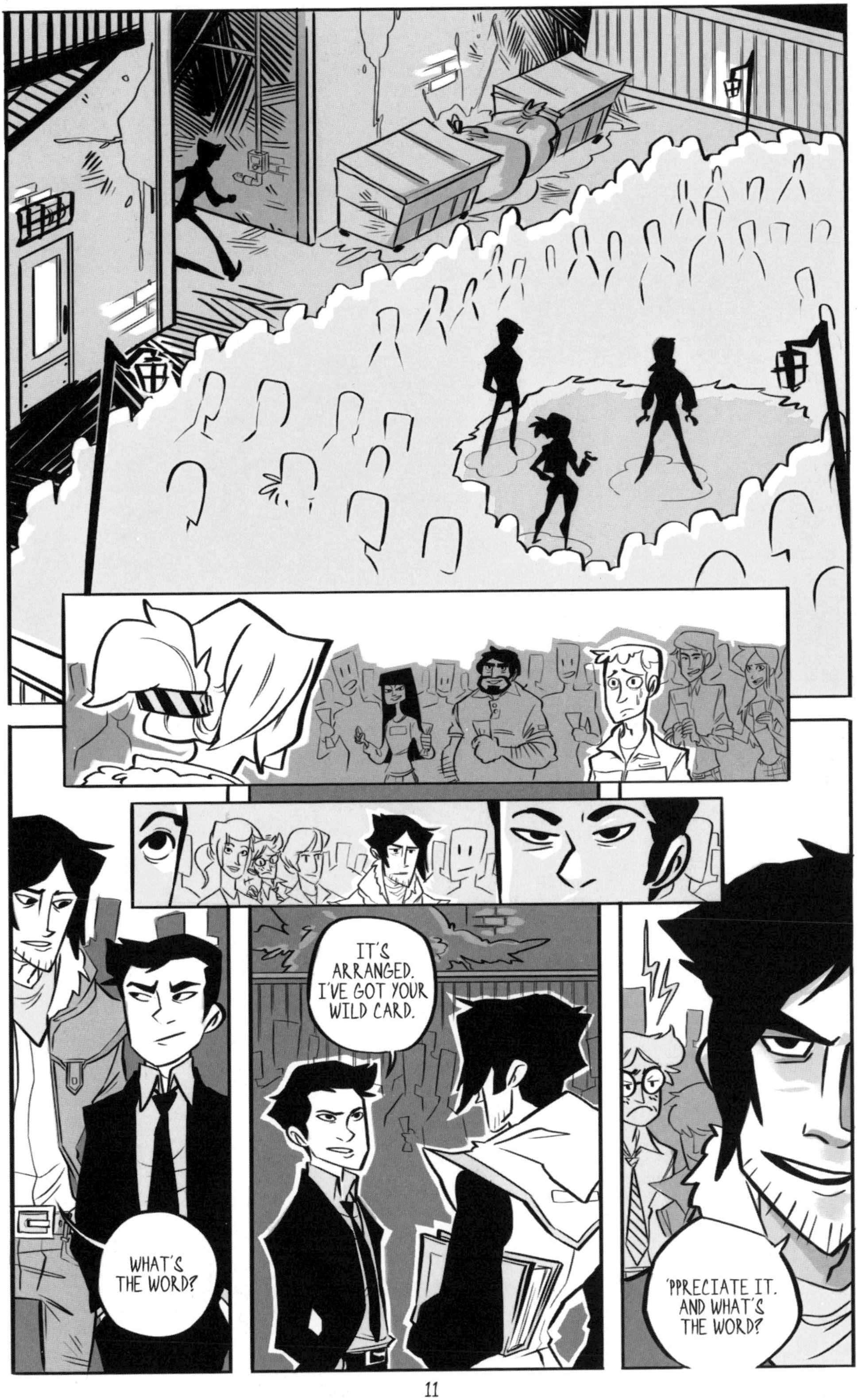
WHAT'S THE WORD?
IT'S ARRANGED. I'VE GOT YOUR WILD CARD.
'PPRECIATE IT. AND WHAT'S THE WORD?

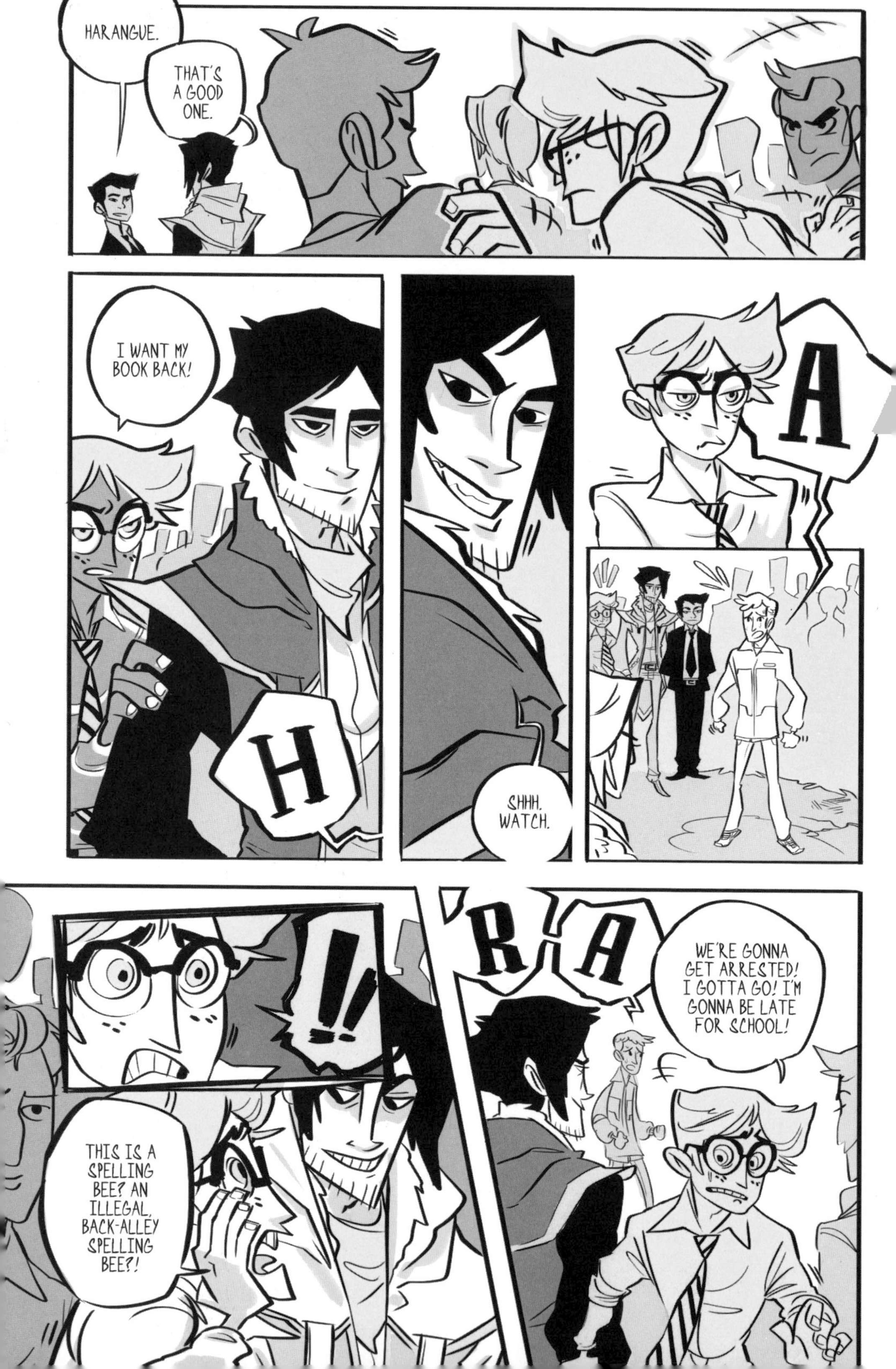
HARANGUE.
THAT'S A GOOD ONE.
I WANT MY BOOK BACK!
H
SHHH. WATCH.
A
!!
THIS IS A SPELLING BEE? AN ILLEGAL, BACK-ALLEY SPELLING BEE?!
R
A
WE'RE GONNA GET ARRESTED! I GOTTA GO! I'M GONNA BE LATE FOR SCHOOL!

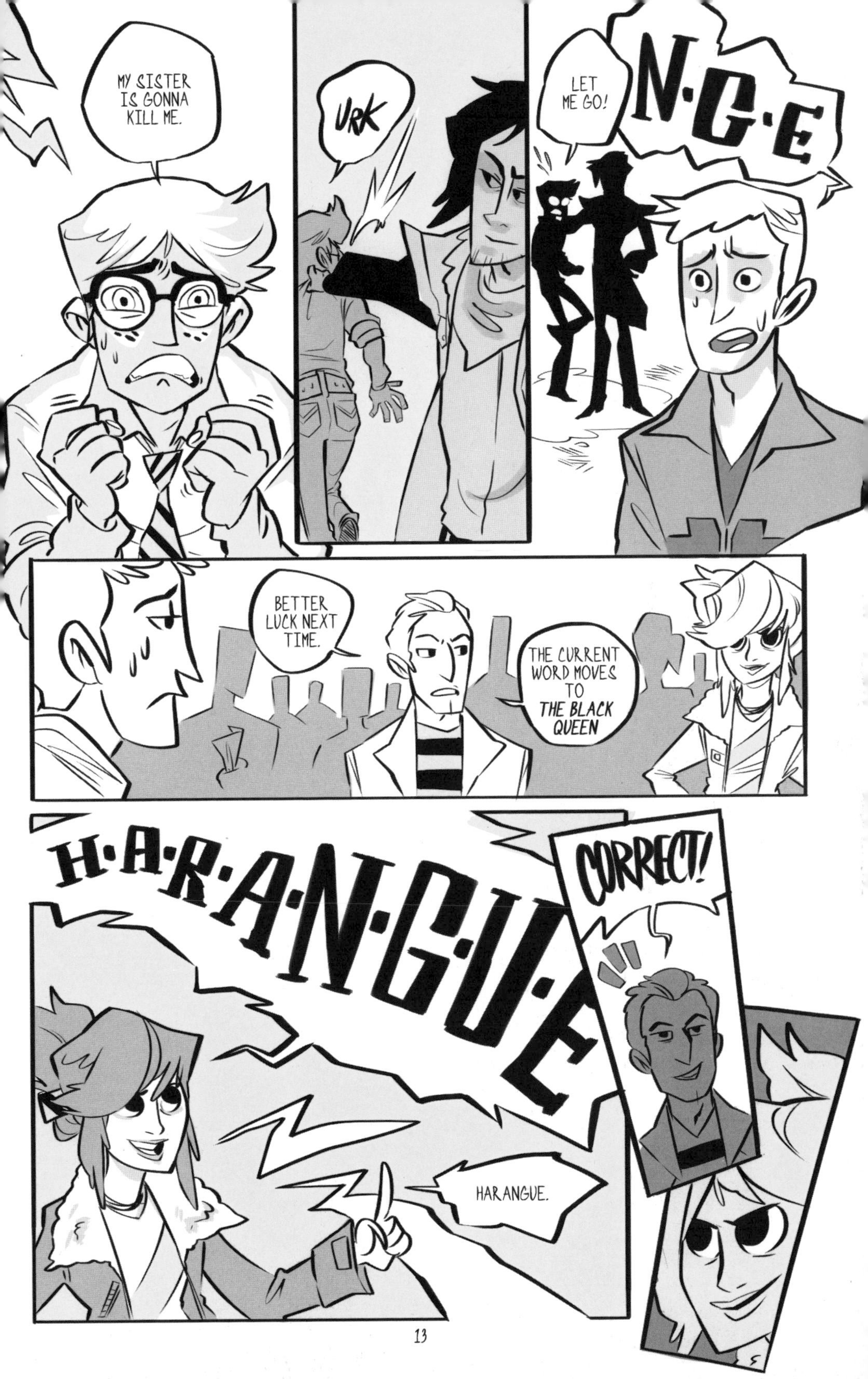
MY SISTER IS GONNA KILL ME.
URK
LET ME GO!
N·G·E
BETTER LUCK NEXT TIME.
THE CURRENT WORD MOVES TO *THE BLACK QUEEN*
H·A·R·A·N·G·U·E
CORRECT!
HARANGUE.

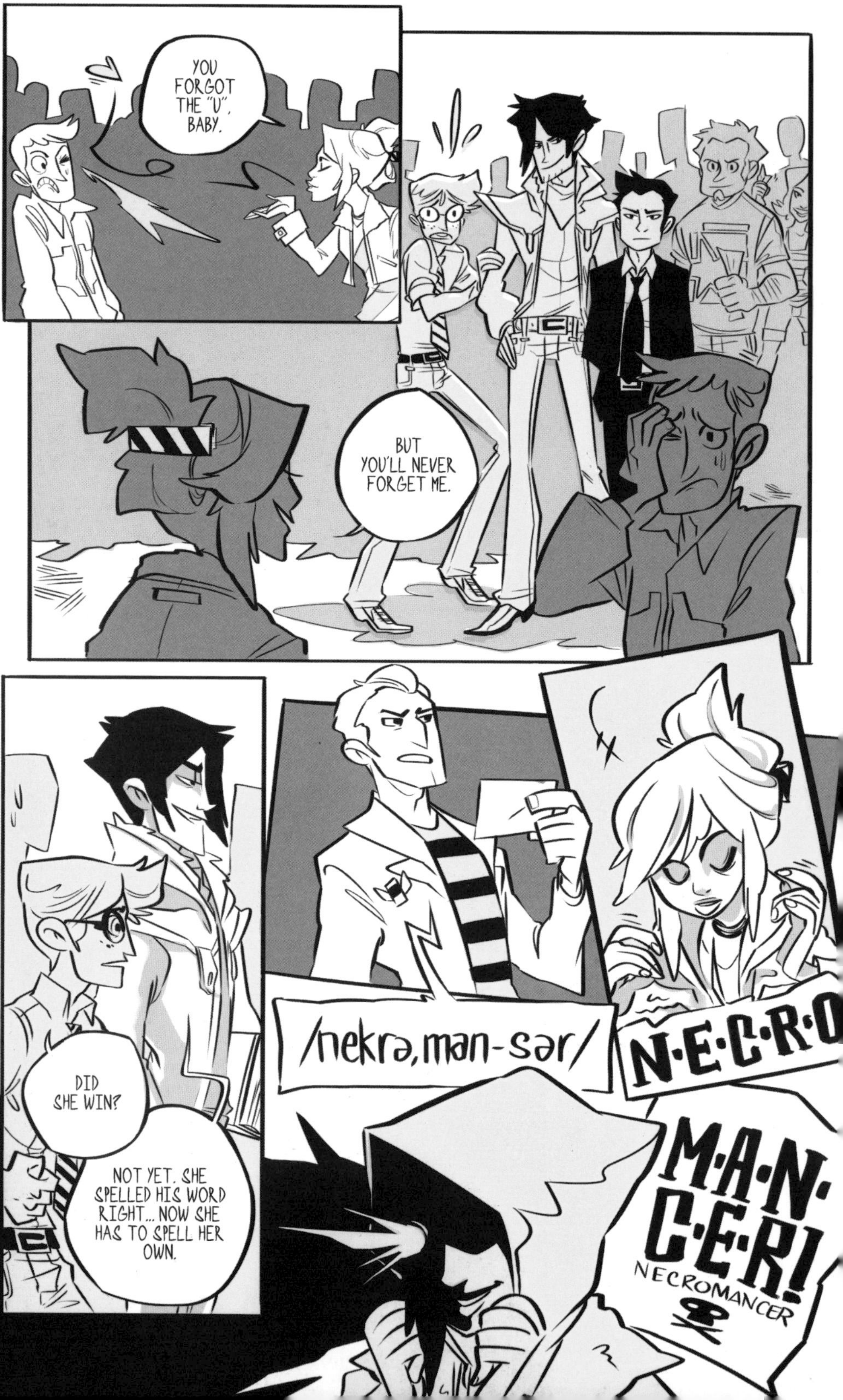
YOU FORGOT THE "U", BABY.
BUT YOU'LL NEVER FORGET ME.
DID SHE WIN?
NOT YET. SHE SPELLED HIS WORD RIGHT... NOW SHE HAS TO SPELL HER OWN.
/nekrə,man-sər/
N·E·C·R·O
M·A·N·C·E·R!
NECROMANCER

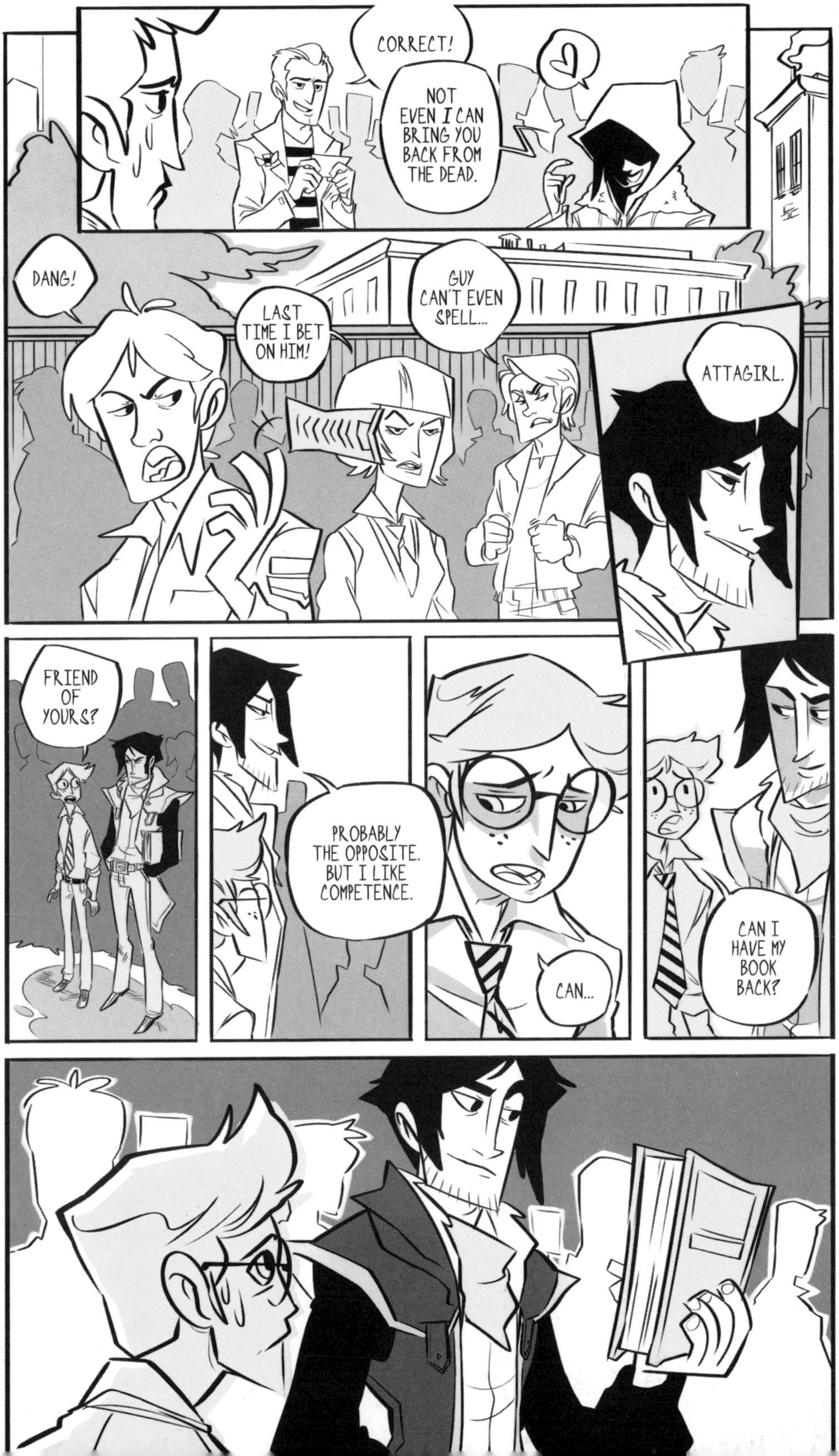
CORRECT!
♡
NOT EVEN I CAN BRING YOU BACK FROM THE DEAD.
DANG!
LAST TIME I BET ON HIM!
GUY CAN'T EVEN SPELL...
ATTAGIRL.
FRIEND OF YOURS?
PROBABLY THE OPPOSITE. BUT I LIKE COMPETENCE.
CAN...
CAN I HAVE MY BOOK BACK?

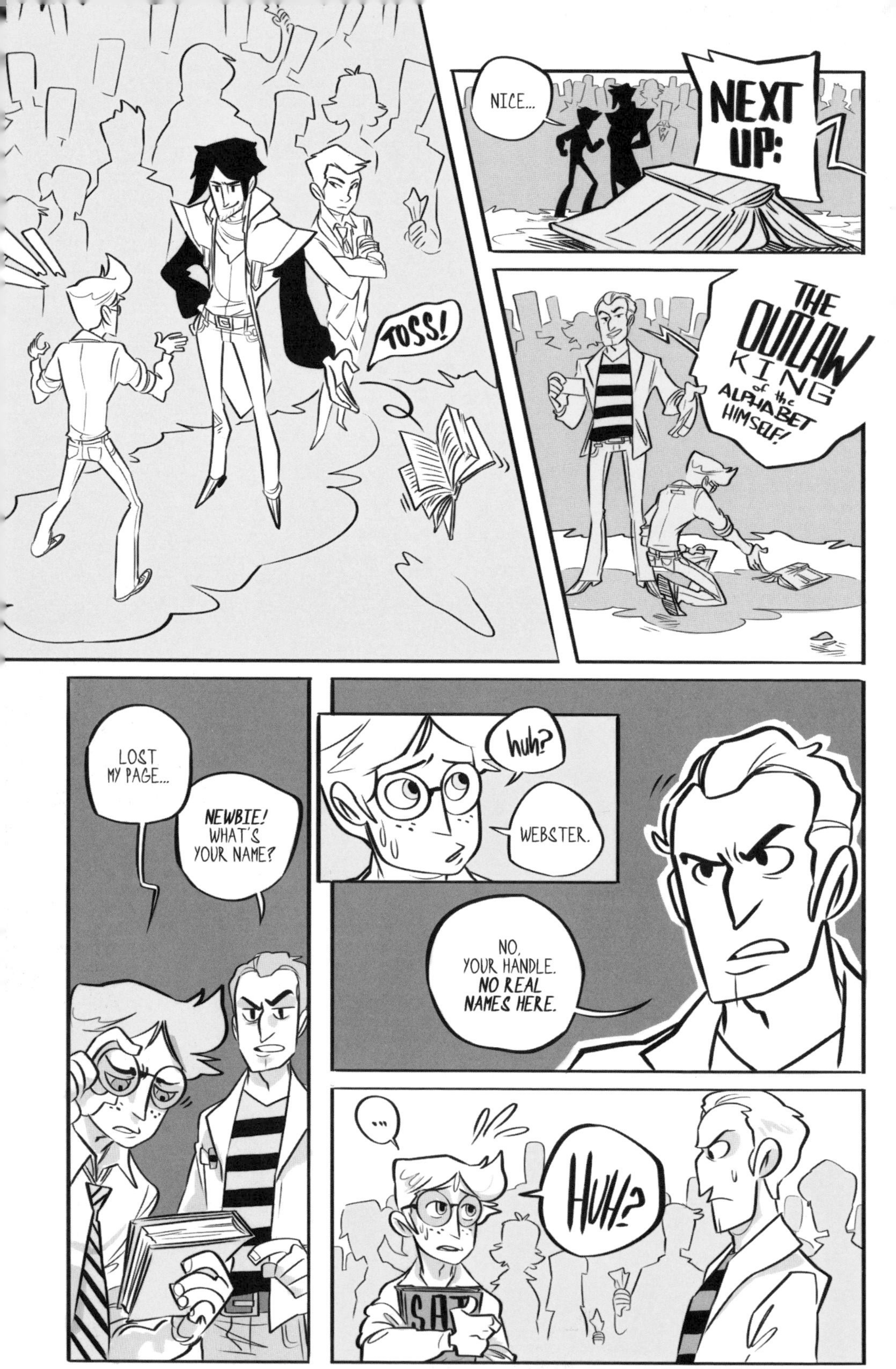
TOSS!
NICE...
NEXT UP:
THE OUTLAW KING of the ALPHABET HIMSELF!
LOST MY PAGE...
NEWBIE! WHAT'S YOUR NAME?
huh?
WEBSTER.
NO, YOUR HANDLE. NO REAL NAMES HERE.
...
HUH!?

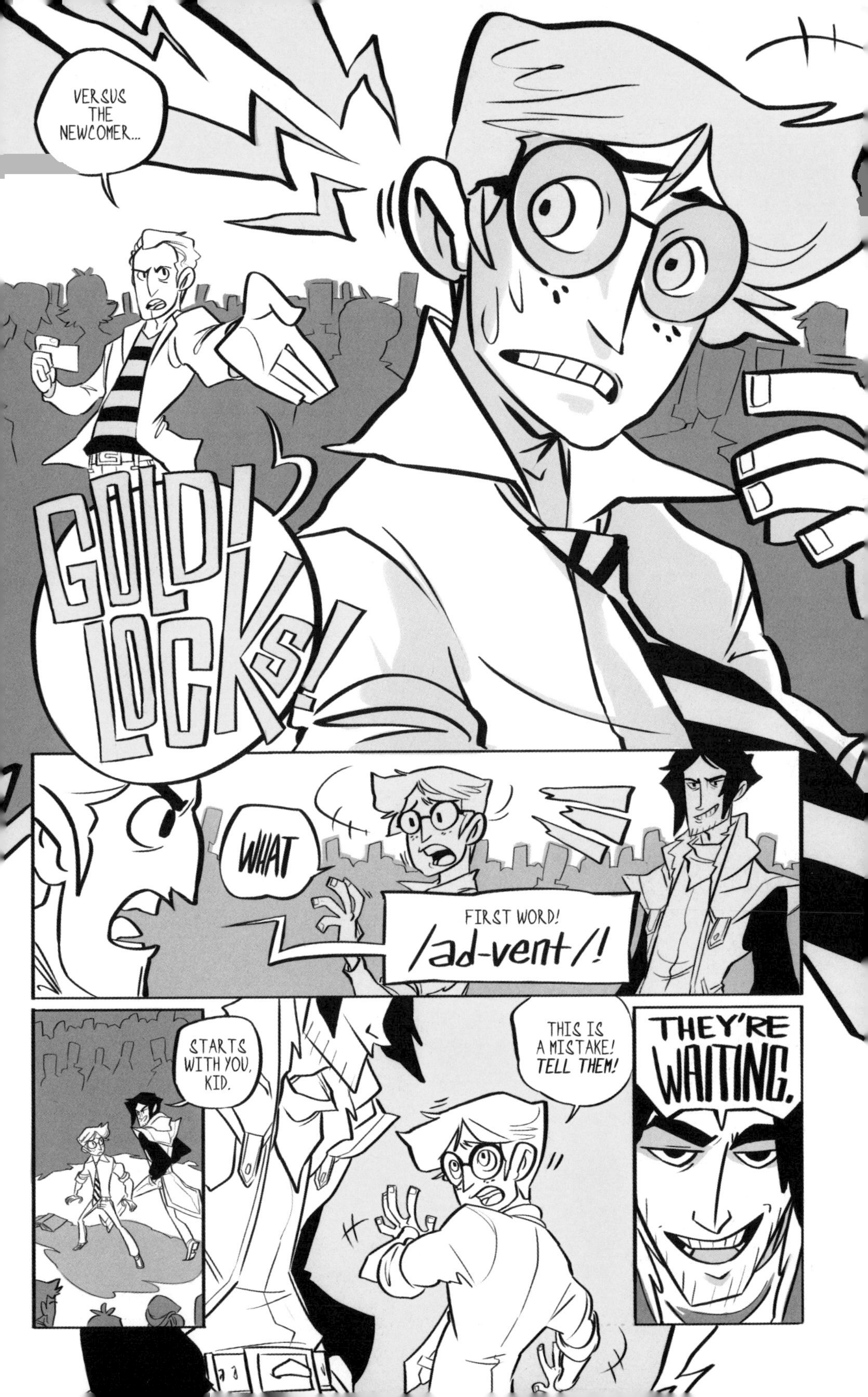

VERSUS THE NEWCOMER...
GOLDILOCKS!
WHAT
FIRST WORD! /ad-vent/!
STARTS WITH YOU, KID.
THIS IS A MISTAKE! TELL THEM!
THEY'RE WAITING.

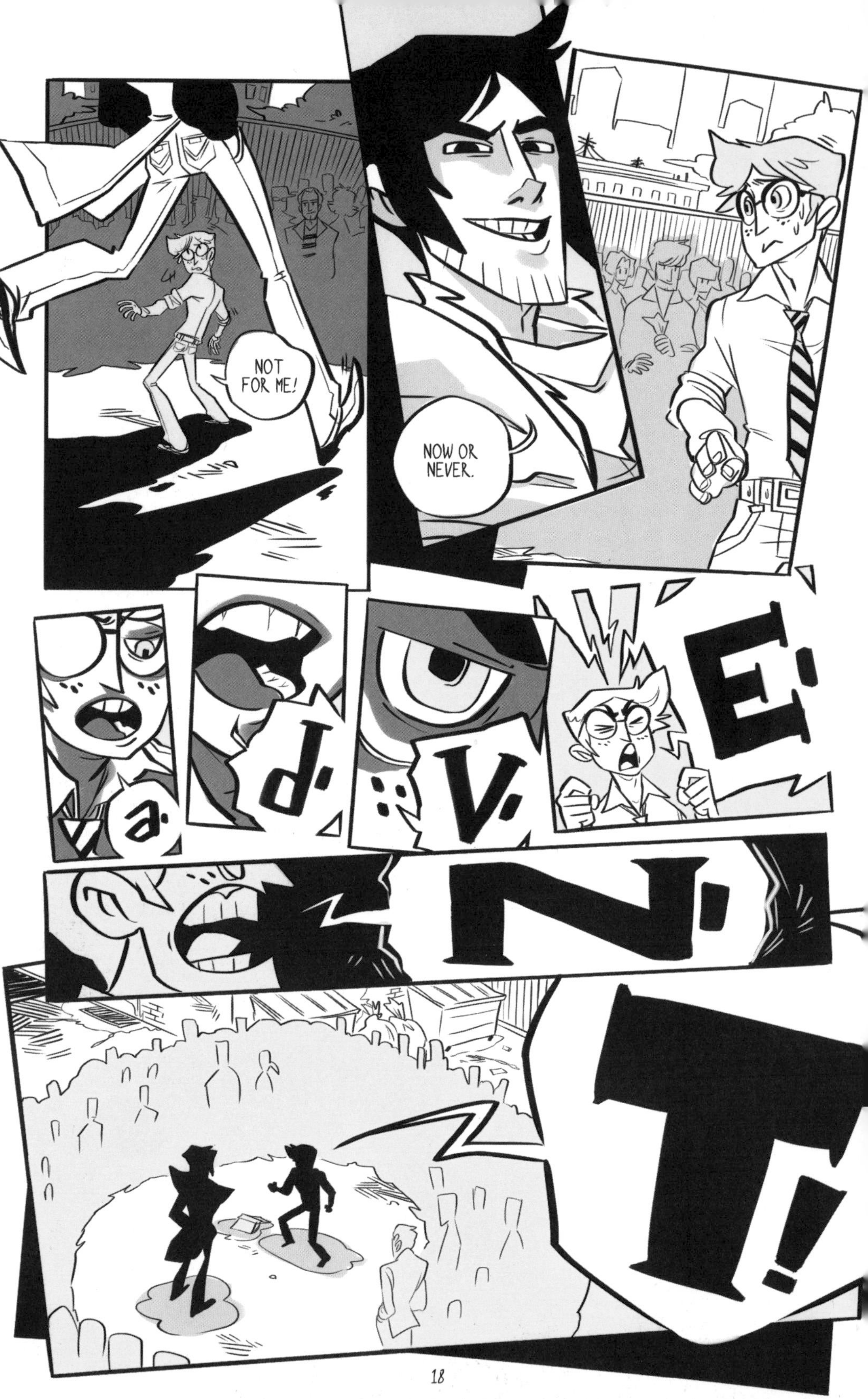
NOT FOR ME!
NOW OR NEVER.
a.
d.
V.
E.
N.
T!

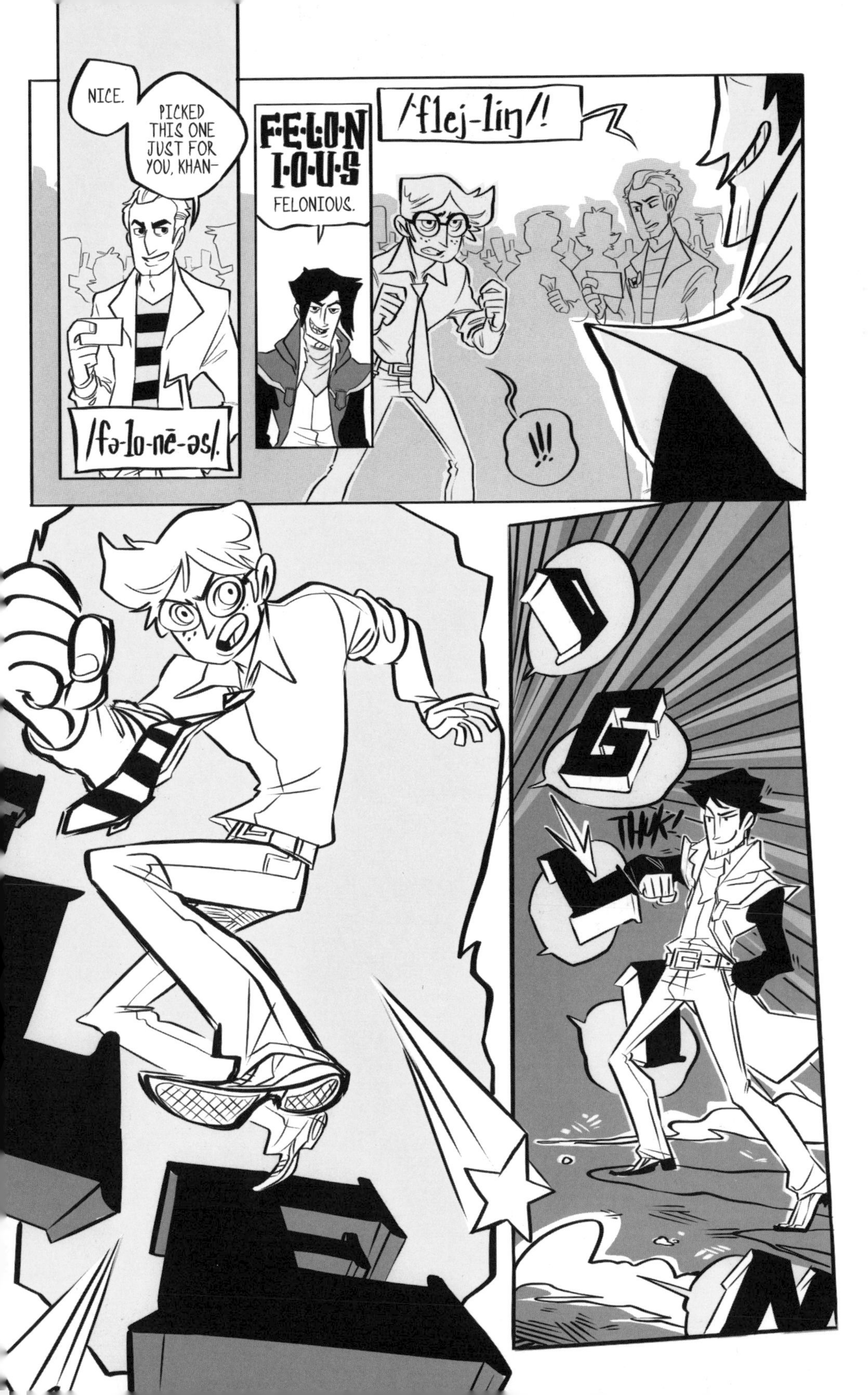
NICE.
PICKED THIS ONE JUST FOR YOU, KHAN-
/fə-lo-nē-əs/.
F·E·L·O·N I·O·U·S
FELONIOUS.
/ˈflej-liŋ/!
!!!
THUK!

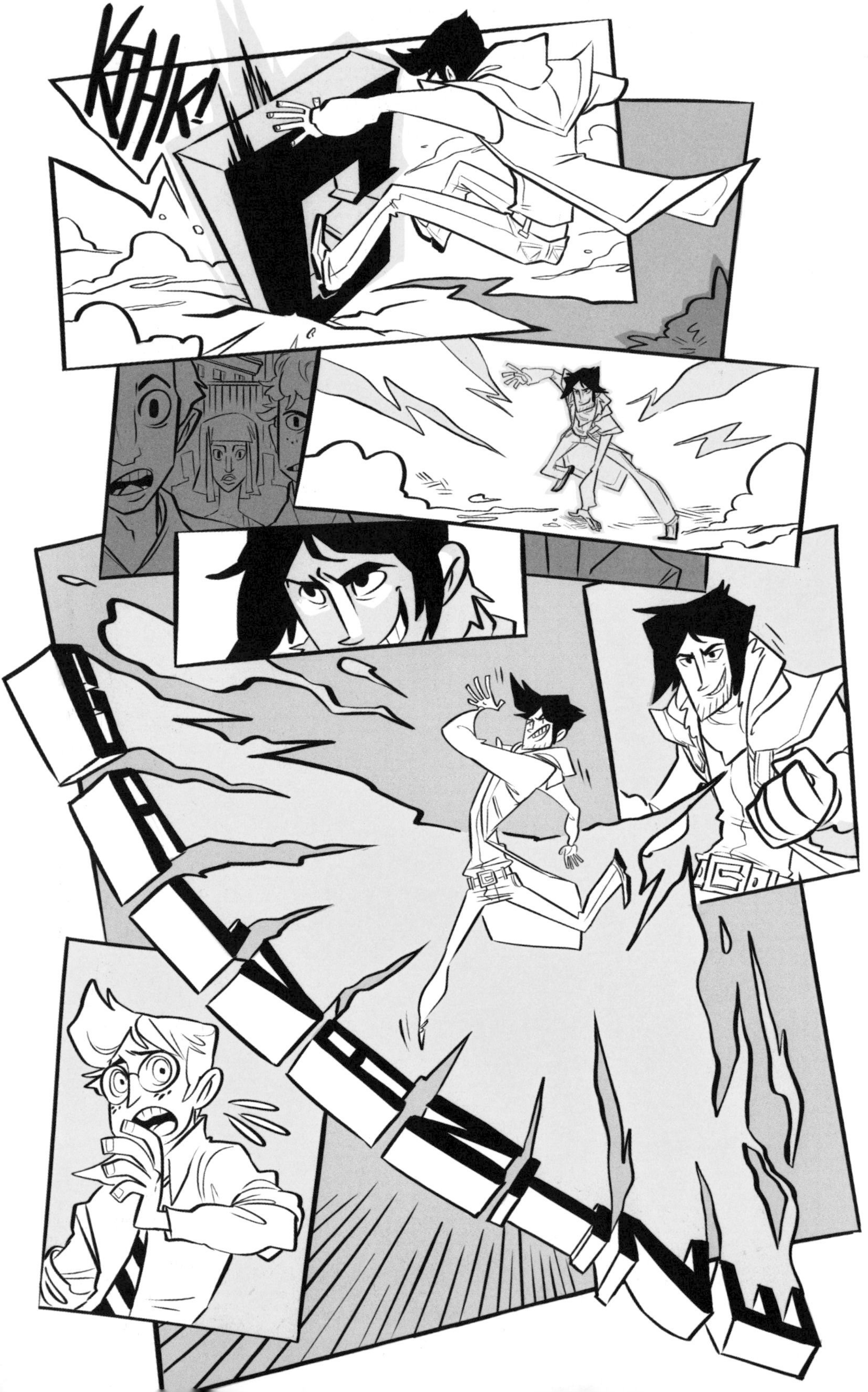
KTHK!

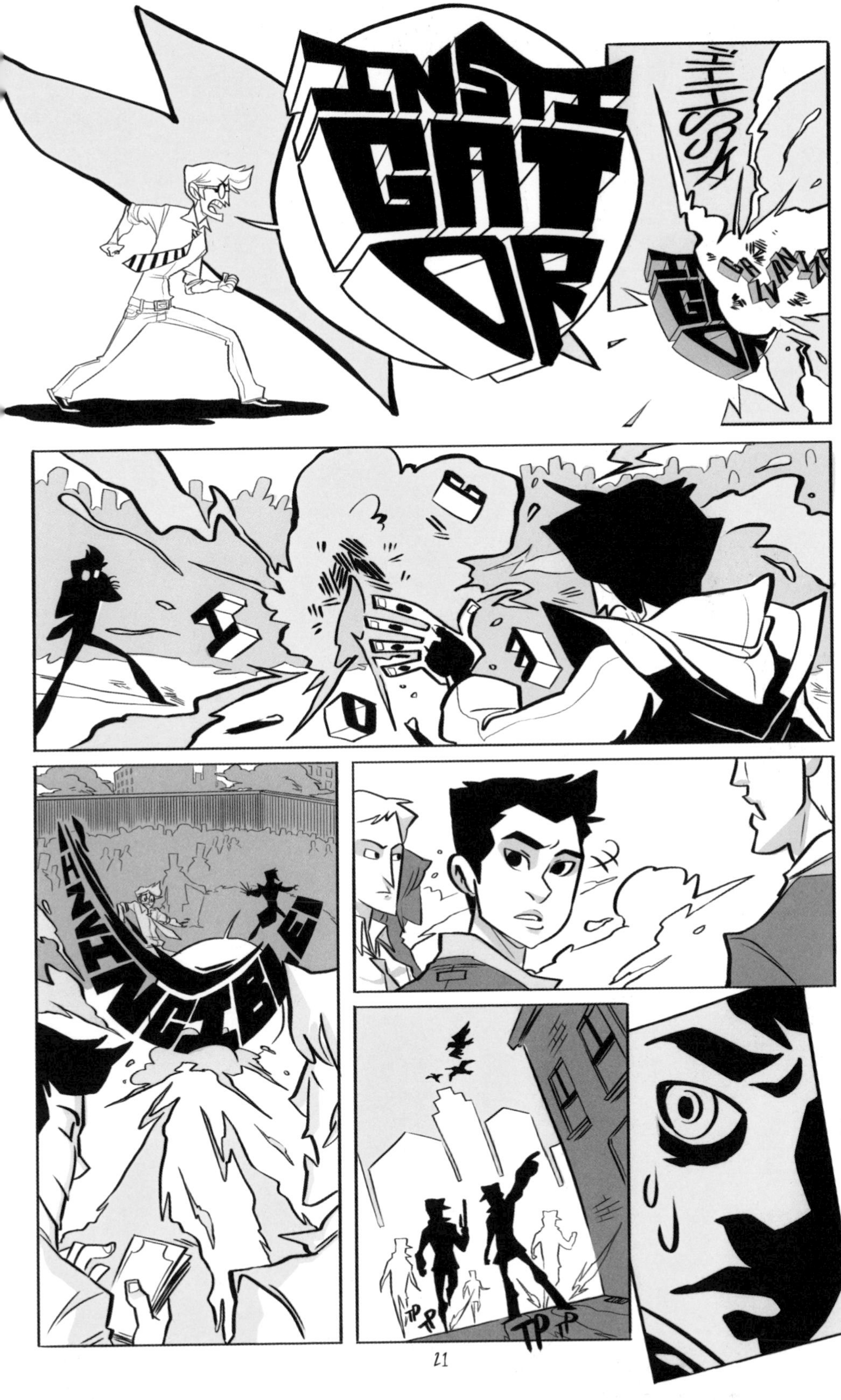
INSTIGATOR
GALVANIZE
INVINCIBLE
TP TP
TP TP

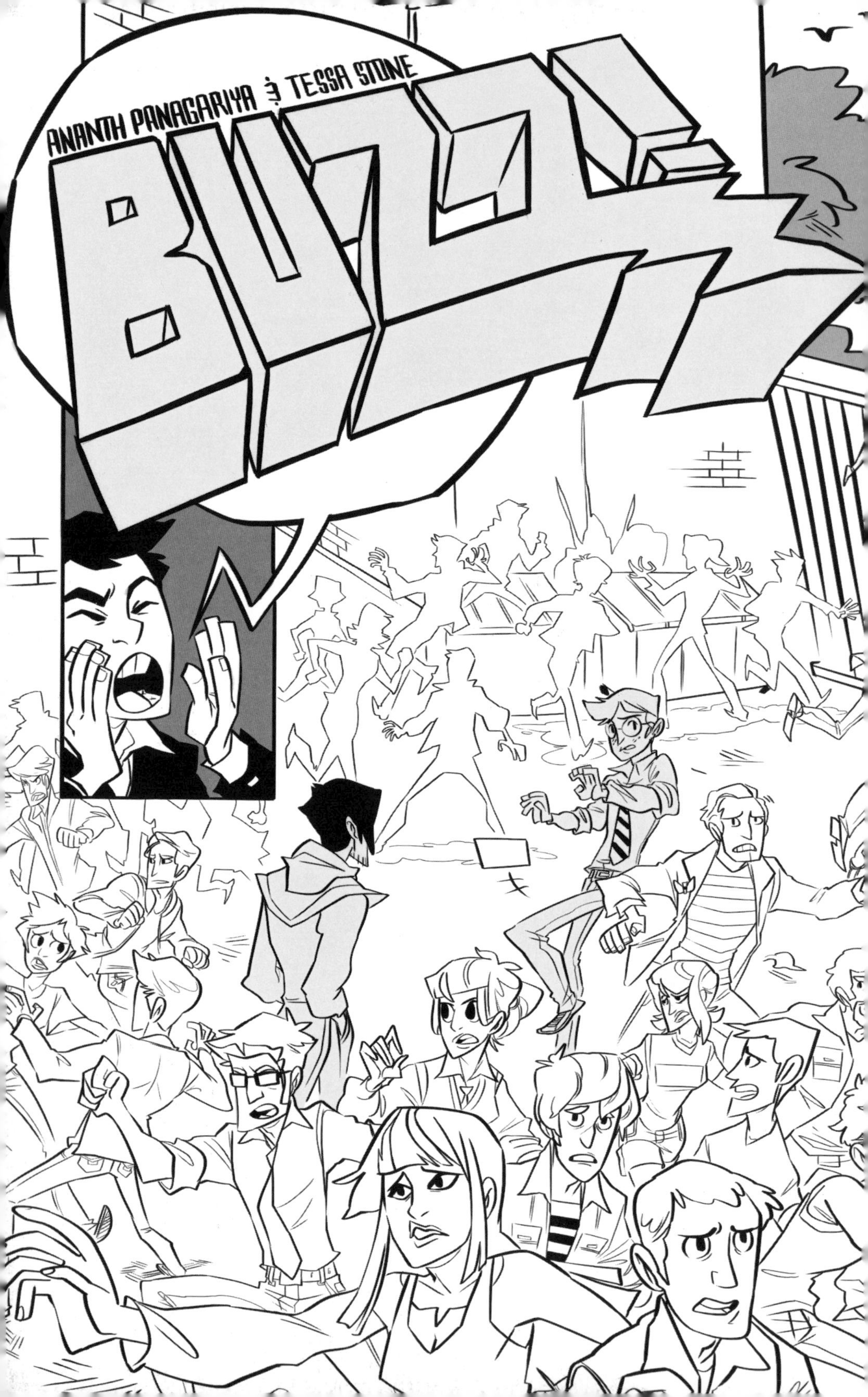
ANANTH PANAGARIYA & TESSA STONE
BUZZ!

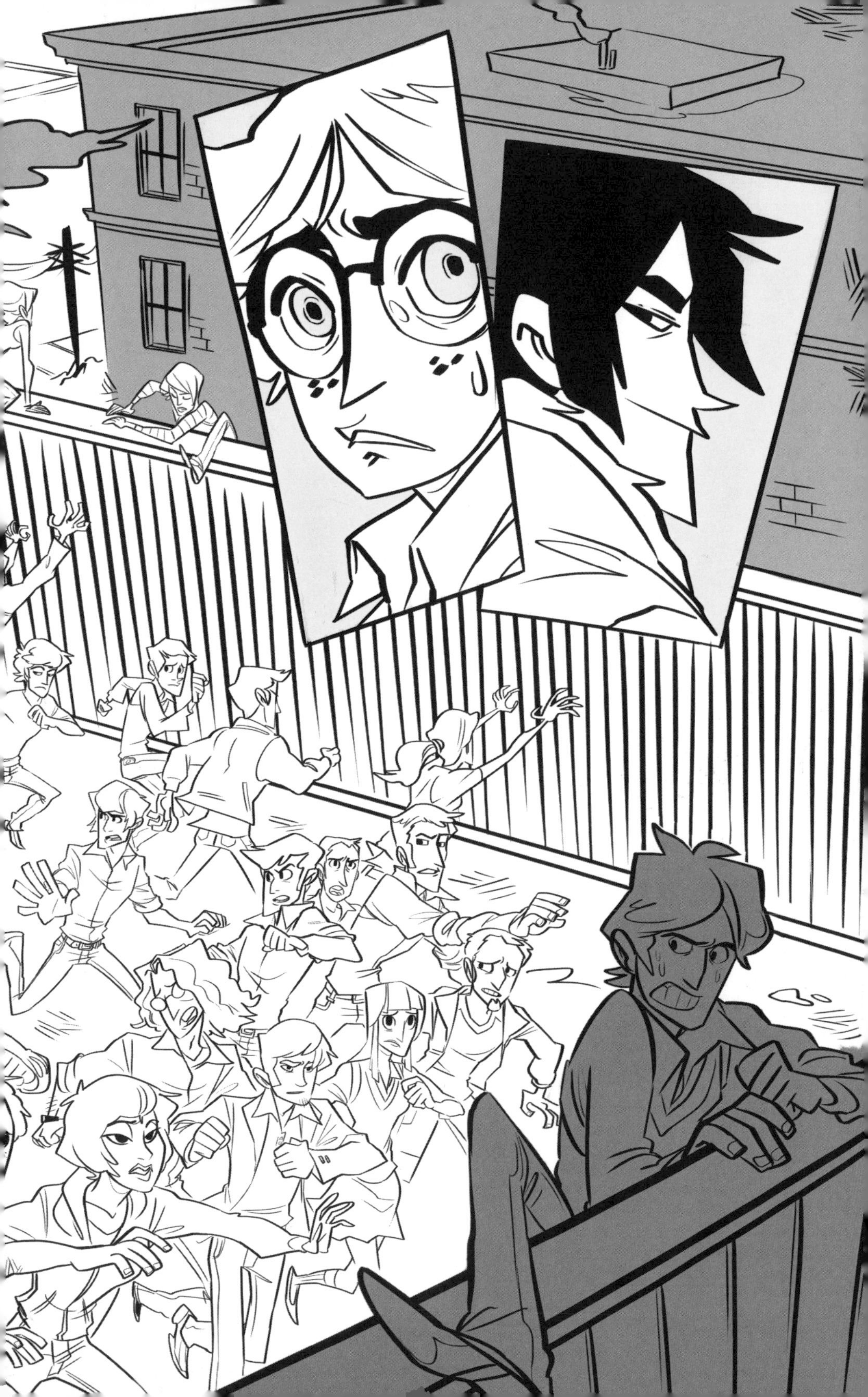

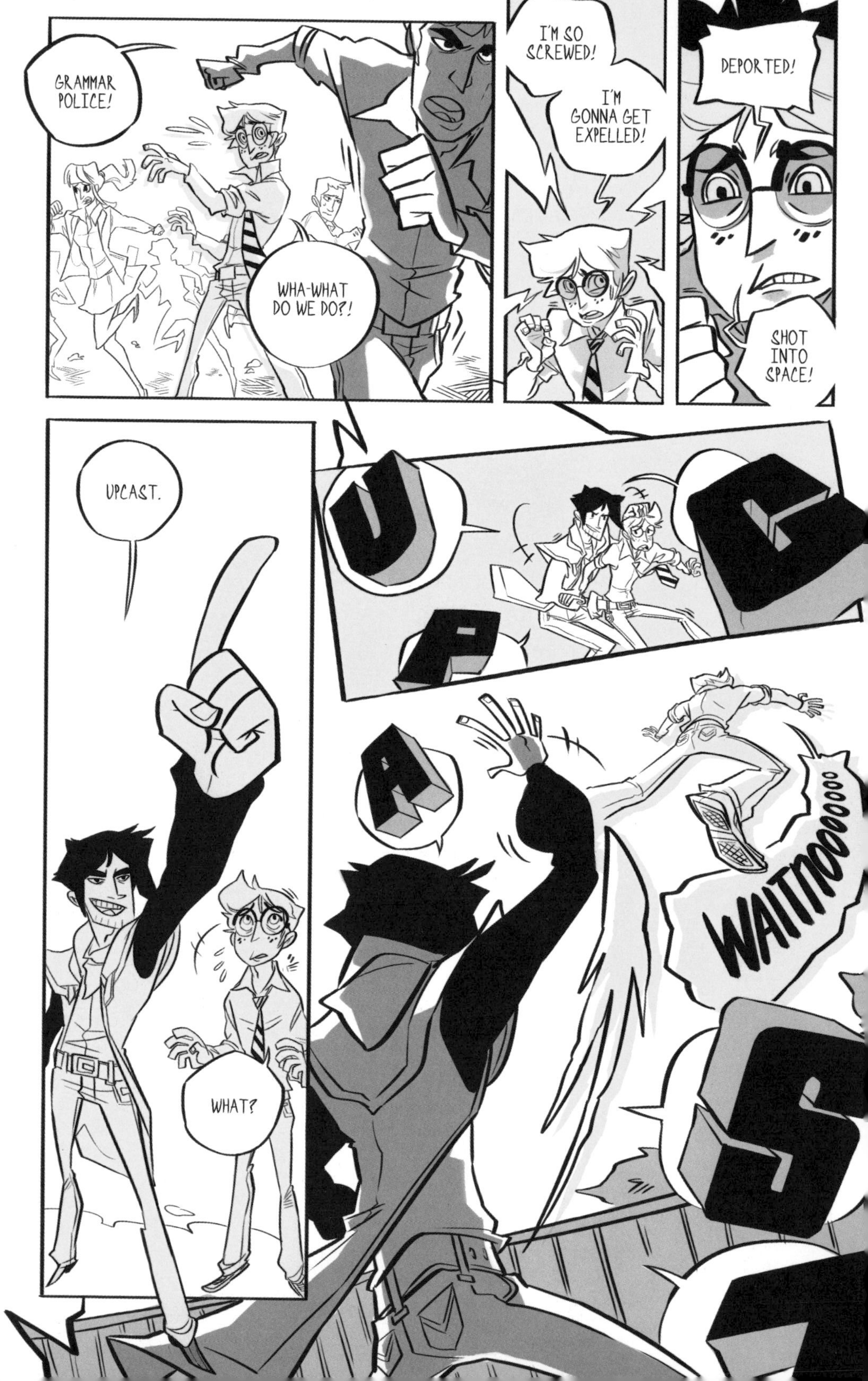
GRAMMAR POLICE!
WHA-WHAT DO WE DO?!
I'M SO SCREWED!
I'M GONNA GET EXPELLED!
DEPORTED!
SHOT INTO SPACE!
UPCAST.
WHAT?
U
P
C
A
WAITNOOOOOOO
S

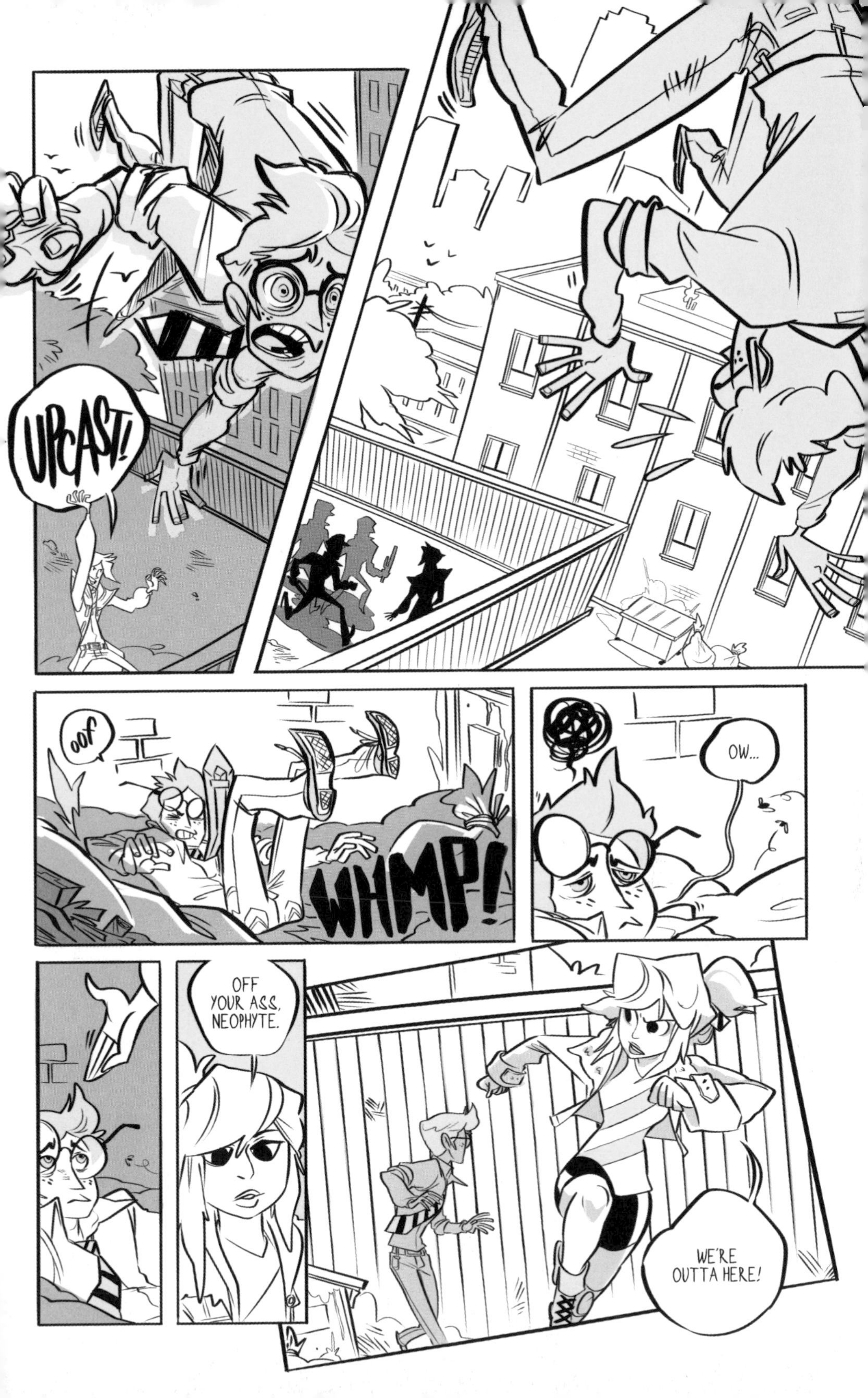
UPCAST!
oof
WHMP!
OW...
OFF YOUR ASS, NEOPHYTE.
WE'RE OUTTA HERE!

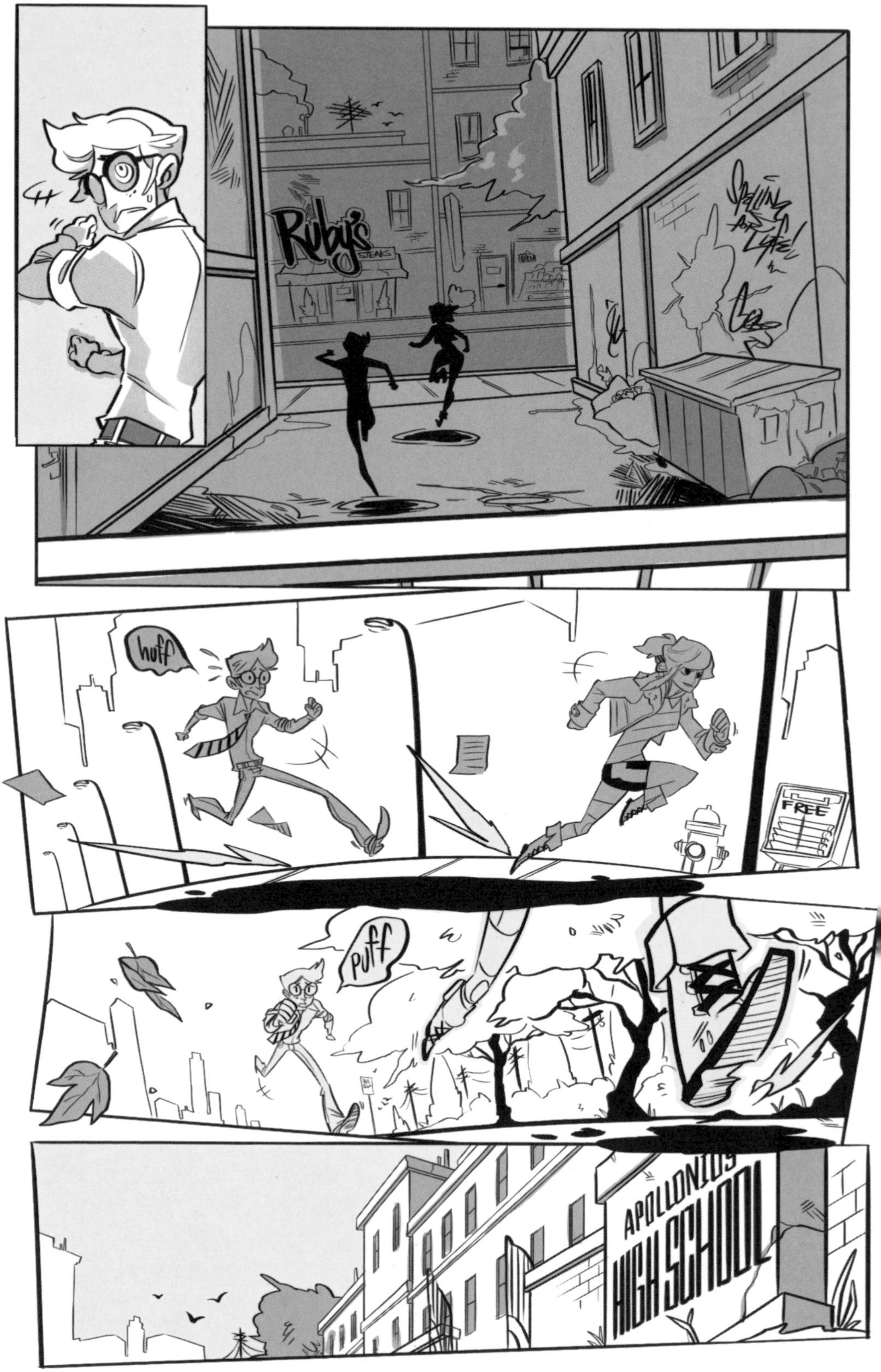
Ruby's
STEAKS
huff
FREE
puff
APOLLONIUS
HIGH SCHOOL

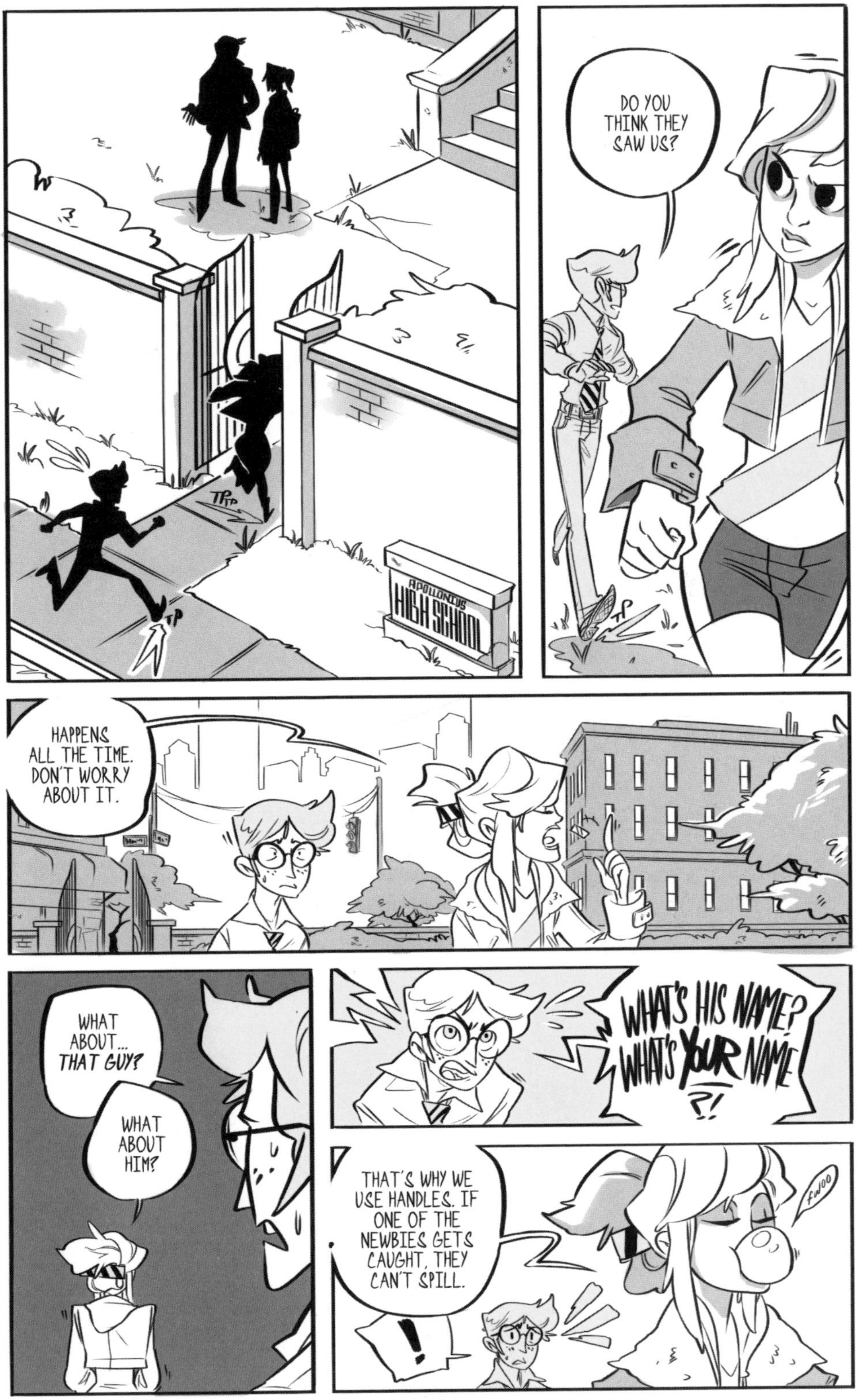
TPTP
TP
APOLLONIUS HIGH SCHOOL
DO YOU THINK THEY SAW US?
TP
HAPPENS ALL THE TIME. DON'T WORRY ABOUT IT.
WHAT ABOUT... THAT GUY?
WHAT ABOUT HIM?
WHAT'S HIS NAME? WHAT'S YOUR NAME ?!
THAT'S WHY WE USE HANDLES. IF ONE OF THE NEWBIES GETS CAUGHT, THEY CAN'T SPILL.
fwoo
!

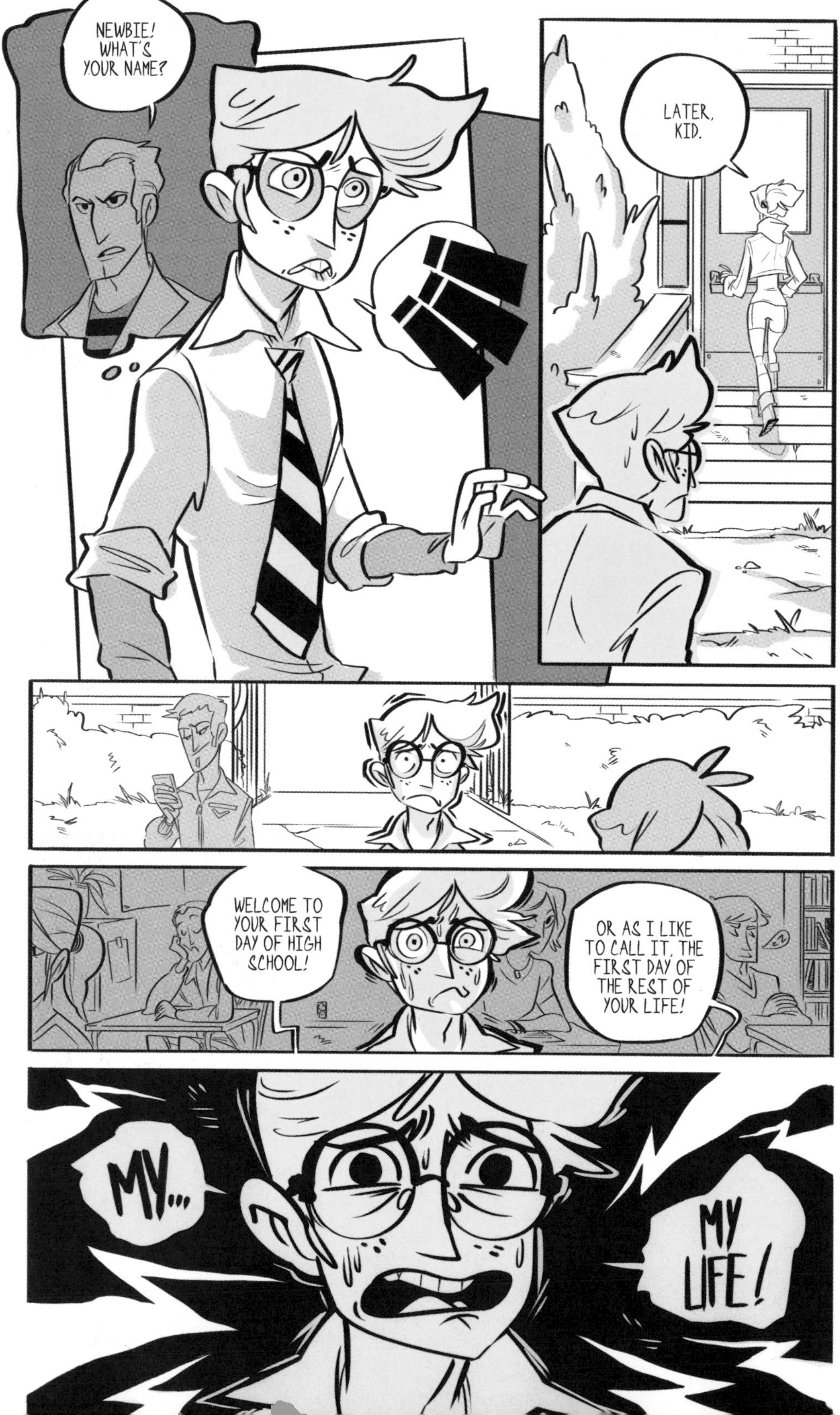
NEWBIE! WHAT'S YOUR NAME?
LATER, KID.
WELCOME TO YOUR FIRST DAY OF HIGH SCHOOL!
OR AS I LIKE TO CALL IT, THE FIRST DAY OF THE REST OF YOUR LIFE!
MY...
MY LIFE!

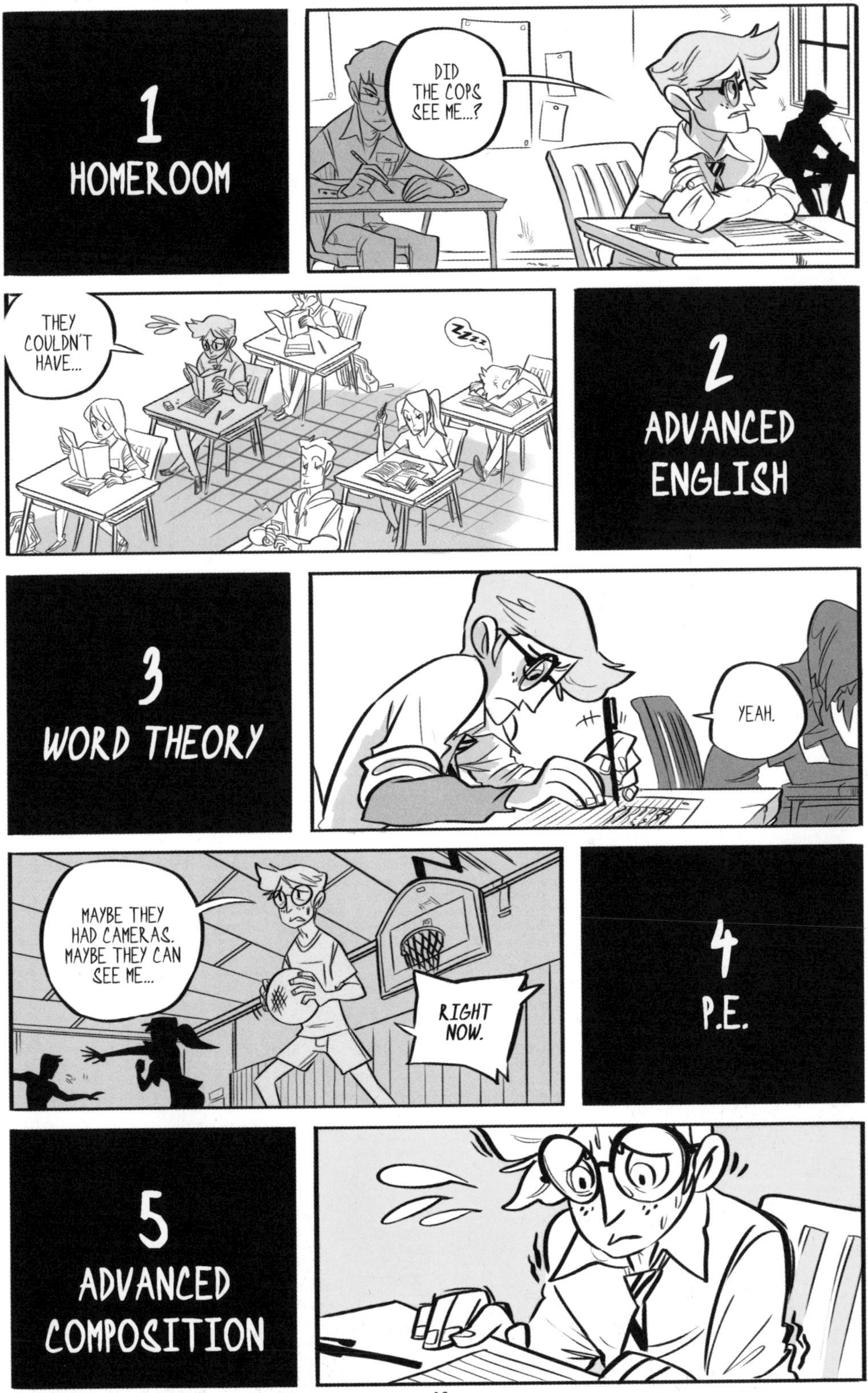
1
HOMEROOM
DID THE COPS SEE ME...?
THEY COULDN'T HAVE...
ZZZZ
2
ADVANCED ENGLISH
3
WORD THEORY
YEAH.
MAYBE THEY HAD CAMERAS. MAYBE THEY CAN SEE ME...
RIGHT NOW.
4
P.E.
5
ADVANCED COMPOSITION

6
DEAD LANGUAGES

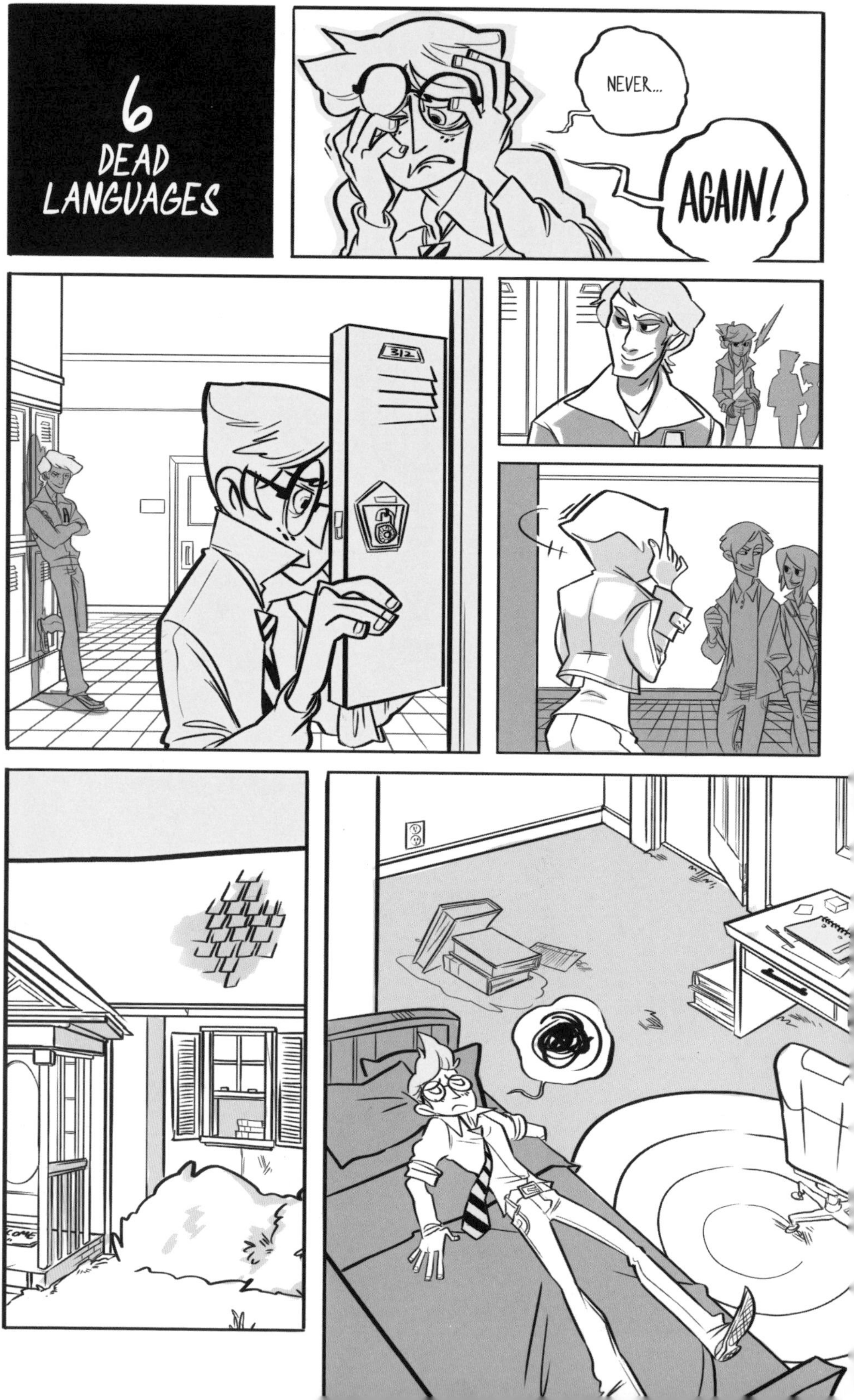

NEVER...
AGAIN!
312

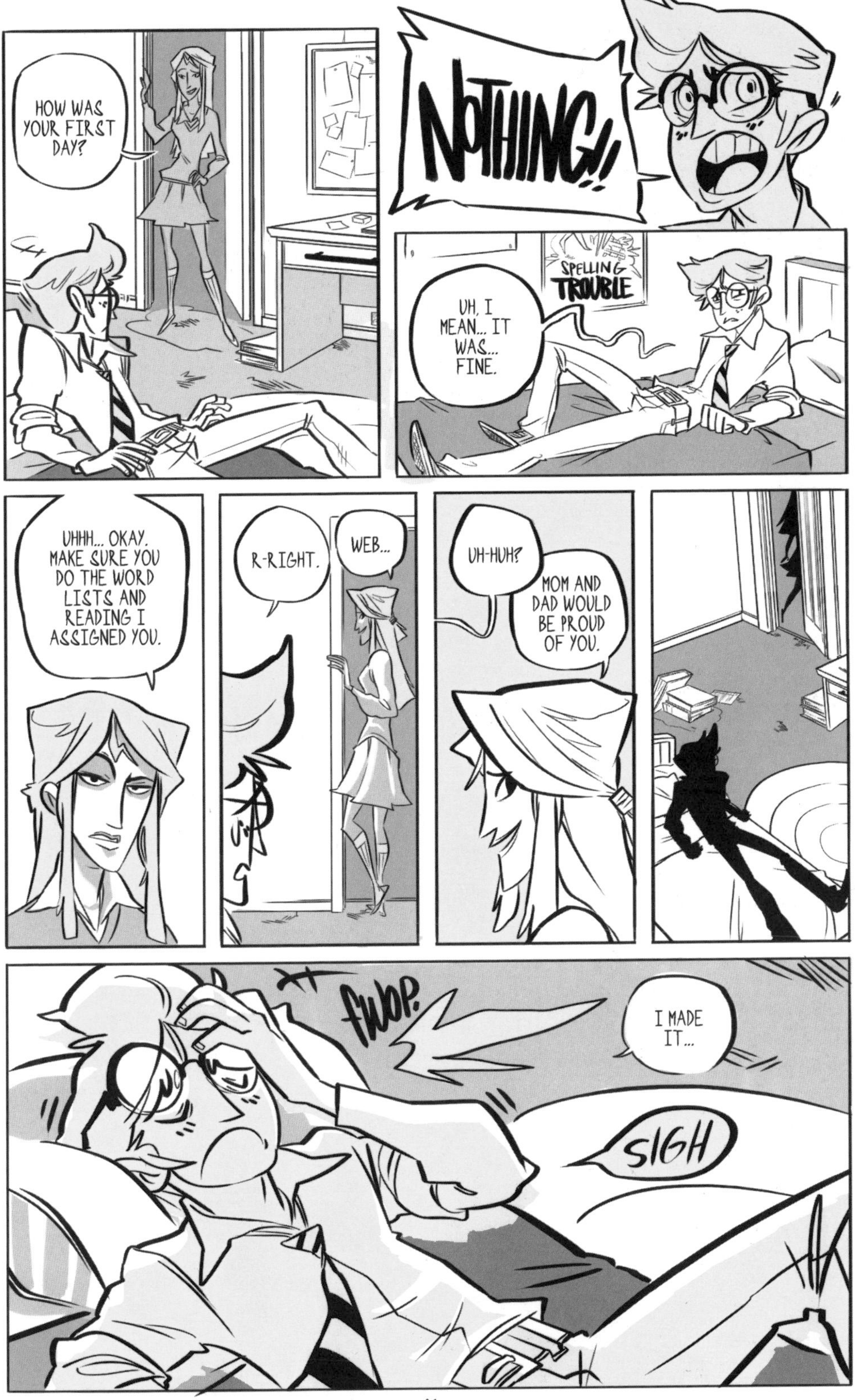
HOW WAS YOUR FIRST DAY?
NOTHING!!
SPELLING TROUBLE
UH, I MEAN... IT WAS... FINE.
UHHH... OKAY. MAKE SURE YOU DO THE WORD LISTS AND READING I ASSIGNED YOU.
R-RIGHT.
WEB...
UH-HUH?
MOM AND DAD WOULD BE PROUD OF YOU.
FWOP.
I MADE IT...
SIGH

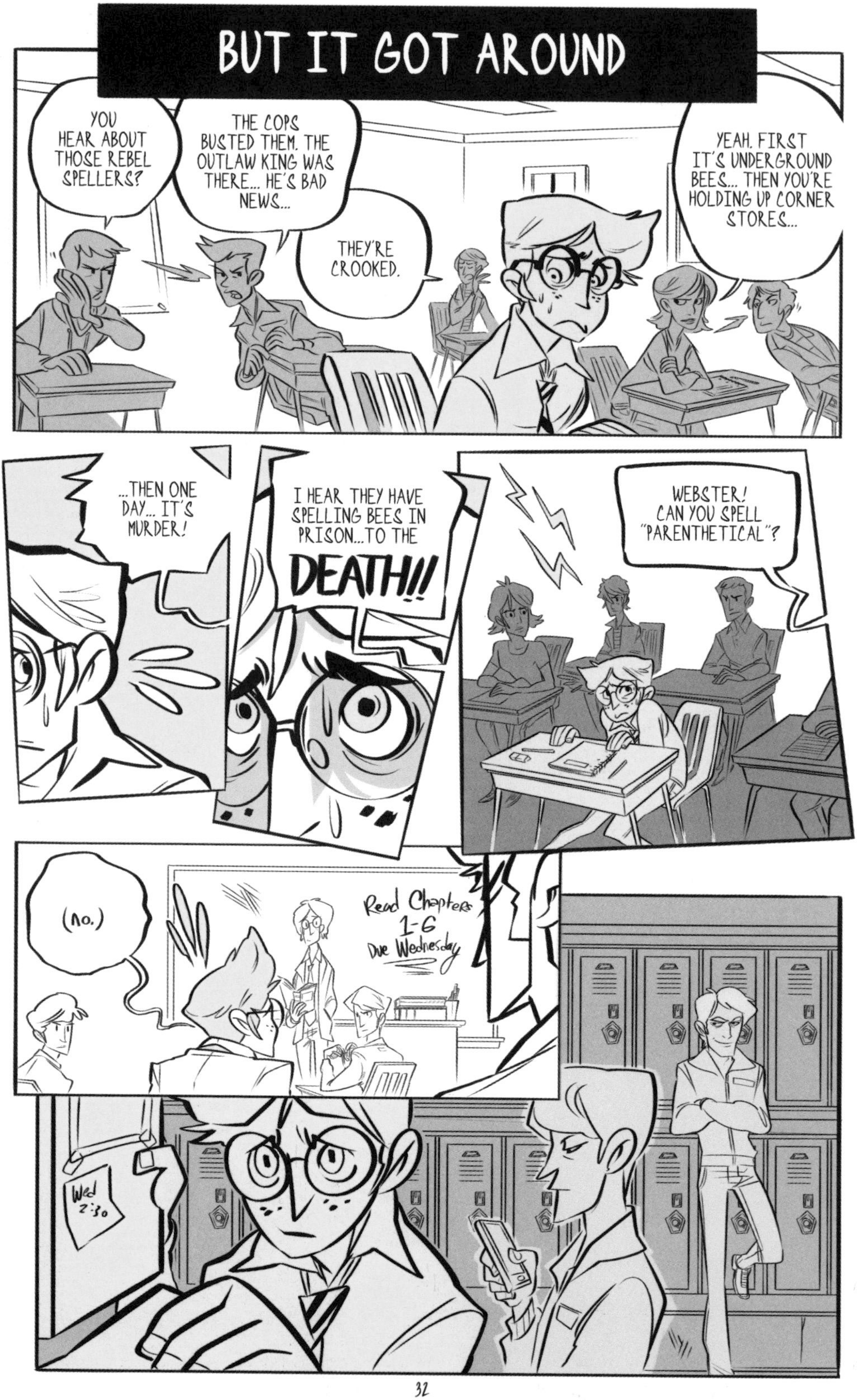
BUT IT GOT AROUND
YOU HEAR ABOUT THOSE REBEL SPELLERS?
THE COPS BUSTED THEM. THE OUTLAW KING WAS THERE... HE'S BAD NEWS...
THEY'RE CROOKED.
YEAH. FIRST IT'S UNDERGROUND BEES... THEN YOU'RE HOLDING UP CORNER STORES...
...THEN ONE DAY... IT'S MURDER!
I HEAR THEY HAVE SPELLING BEES IN PRISON...TO THE DEATH!!
WEBSTER! CAN YOU SPELL "PARENTHETICAL"?
(no.)
Read Chapters 1-6 Due Wednesday
Wed 2:30

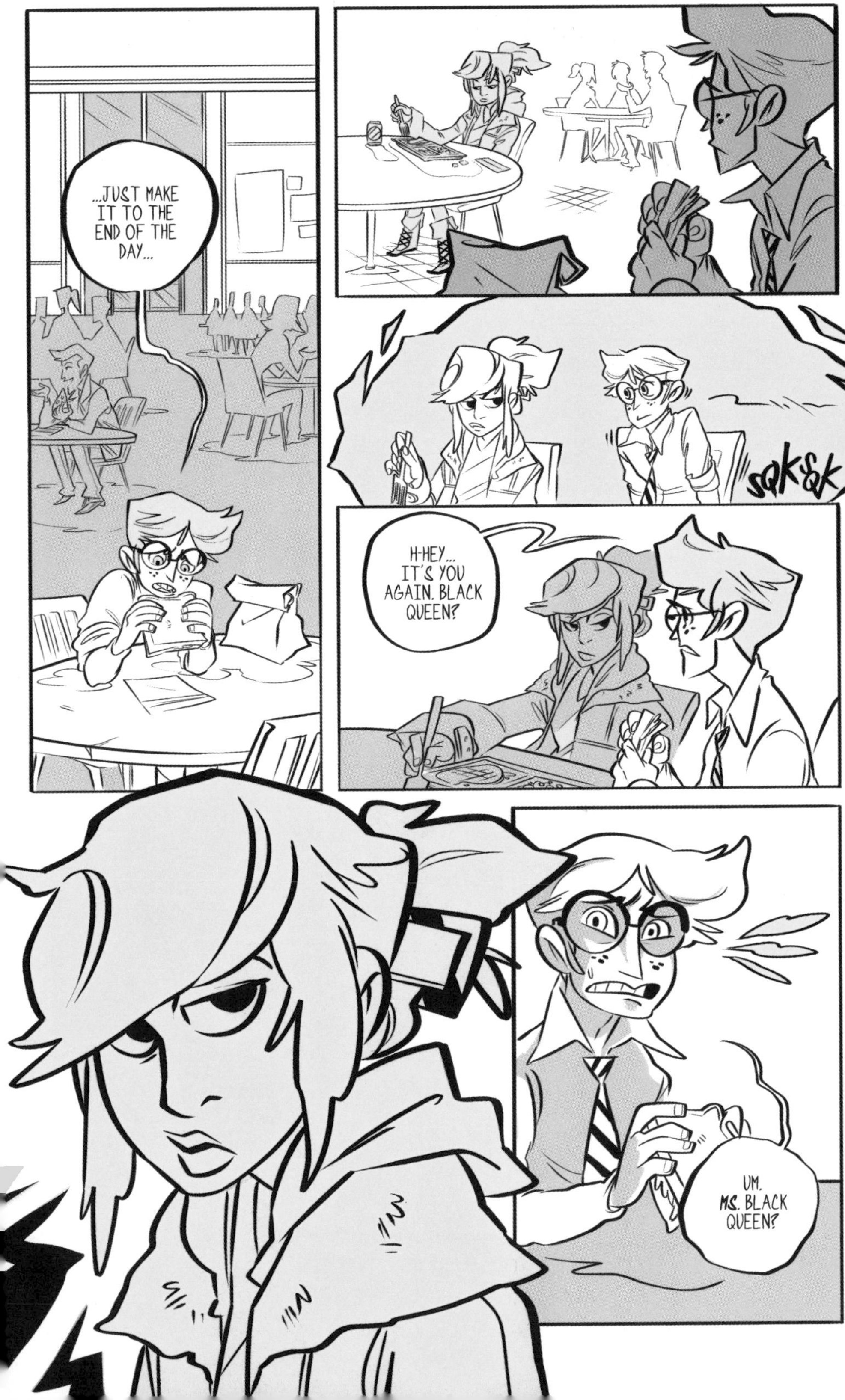
...JUST MAKE IT TO THE END OF THE DAY...
SQK SQK
H-HEY... IT'S YOU AGAIN. BLACK QUEEN?
UM. MS. BLACK QUEEN?

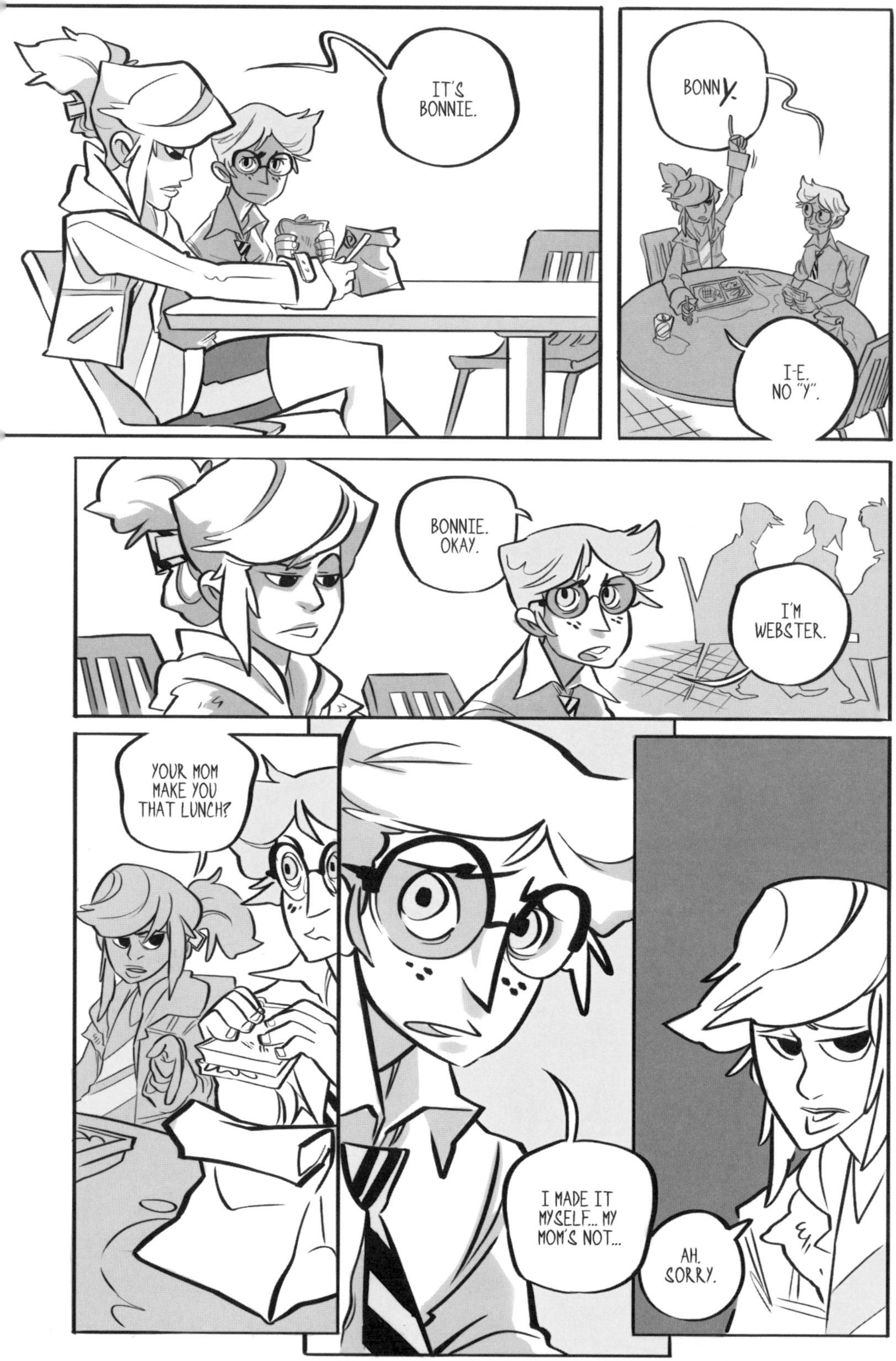
IT'S BONNIE.
BONNY.
I-E. NO "Y".
BONNIE. OKAY.
I'M WEBSTER.
YOUR MOM MAKE YOU THAT LUNCH?
I MADE IT MYSELF... MY MOM'S NOT...
AH. SORRY.

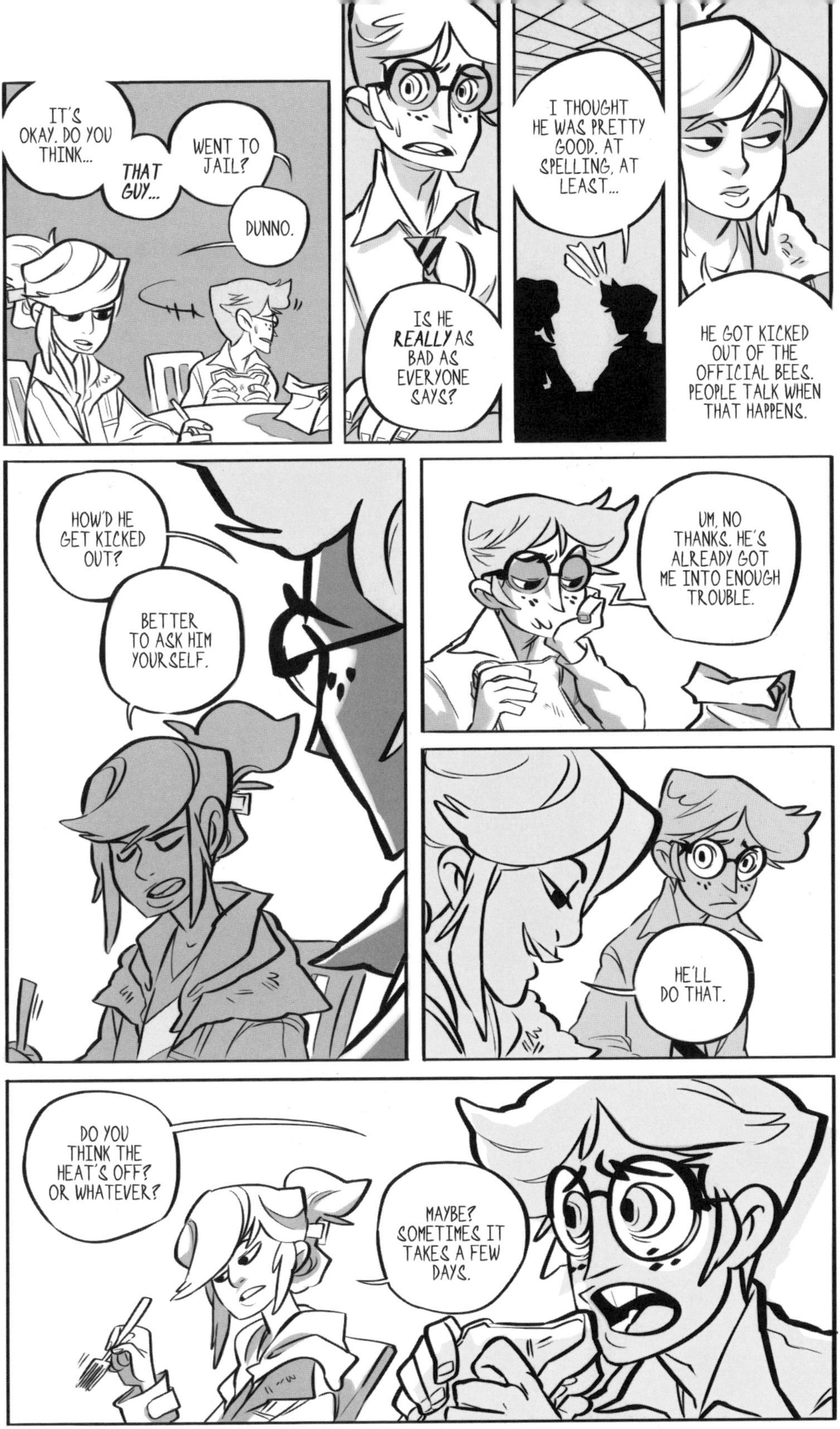
IT'S OKAY. DO YOU THINK...
THAT GUY...
WENT TO JAIL?
DUNNO.
IS HE REALLY AS BAD AS EVERYONE SAYS?
I THOUGHT HE WAS PRETTY GOOD. AT SPELLING, AT LEAST...
HE GOT KICKED OUT OF THE OFFICIAL BEES. PEOPLE TALK WHEN THAT HAPPENS.
HOW'D HE GET KICKED OUT?
BETTER TO ASK HIM YOURSELF.
UM, NO THANKS. HE'S ALREADY GOT ME INTO ENOUGH TROUBLE.
HE'LL DO THAT.
DO YOU THINK THE HEAT'S OFF? OR WHATEVER?
MAYBE? SOMETIMES IT TAKES A FEW DAYS.

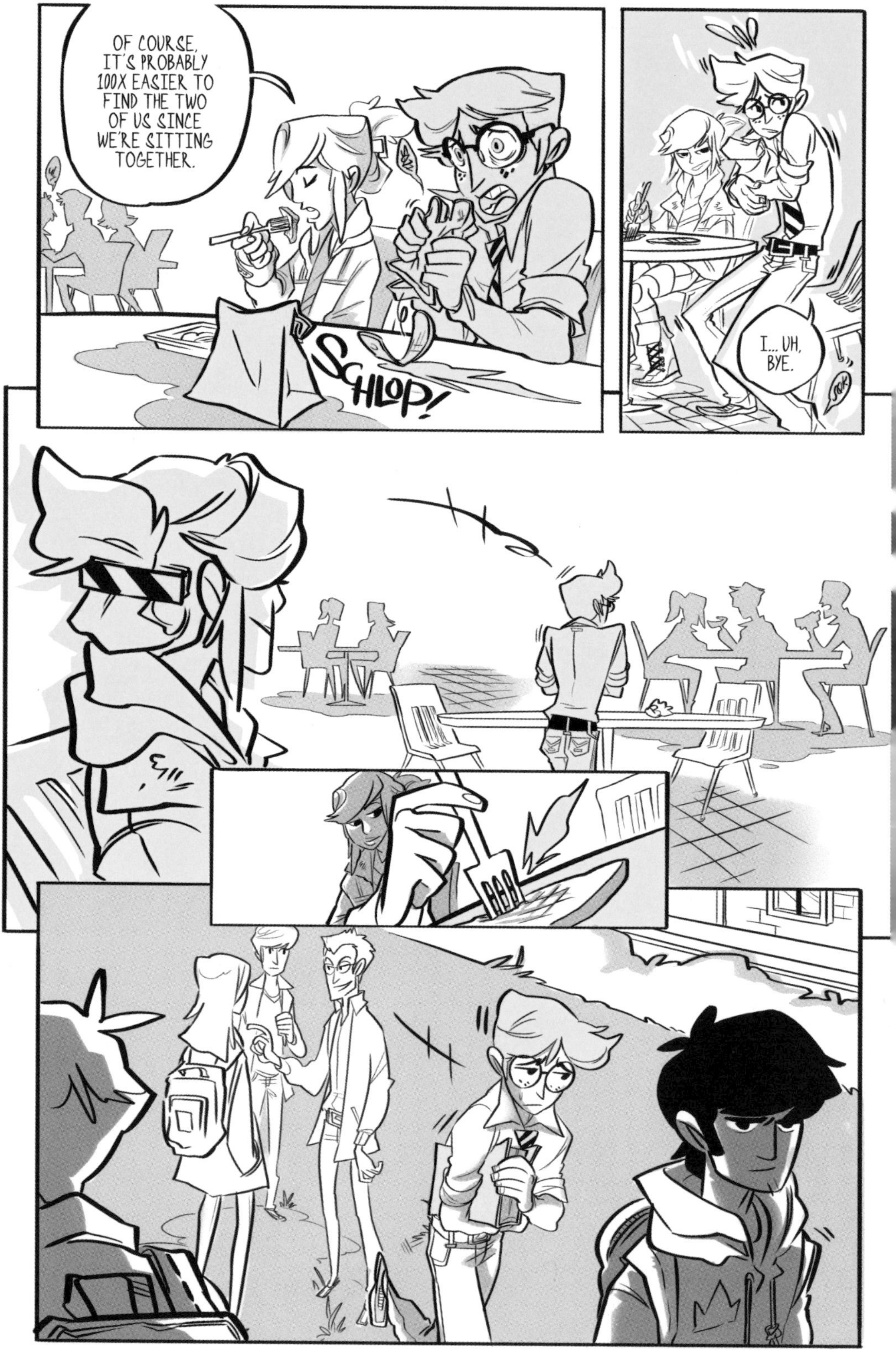
OF COURSE, IT'S PROBABLY 100X EASIER TO FIND THE TWO OF US SINCE WE'RE SITTING TOGETHER.
SCHLOP!
I... UH, BYE.

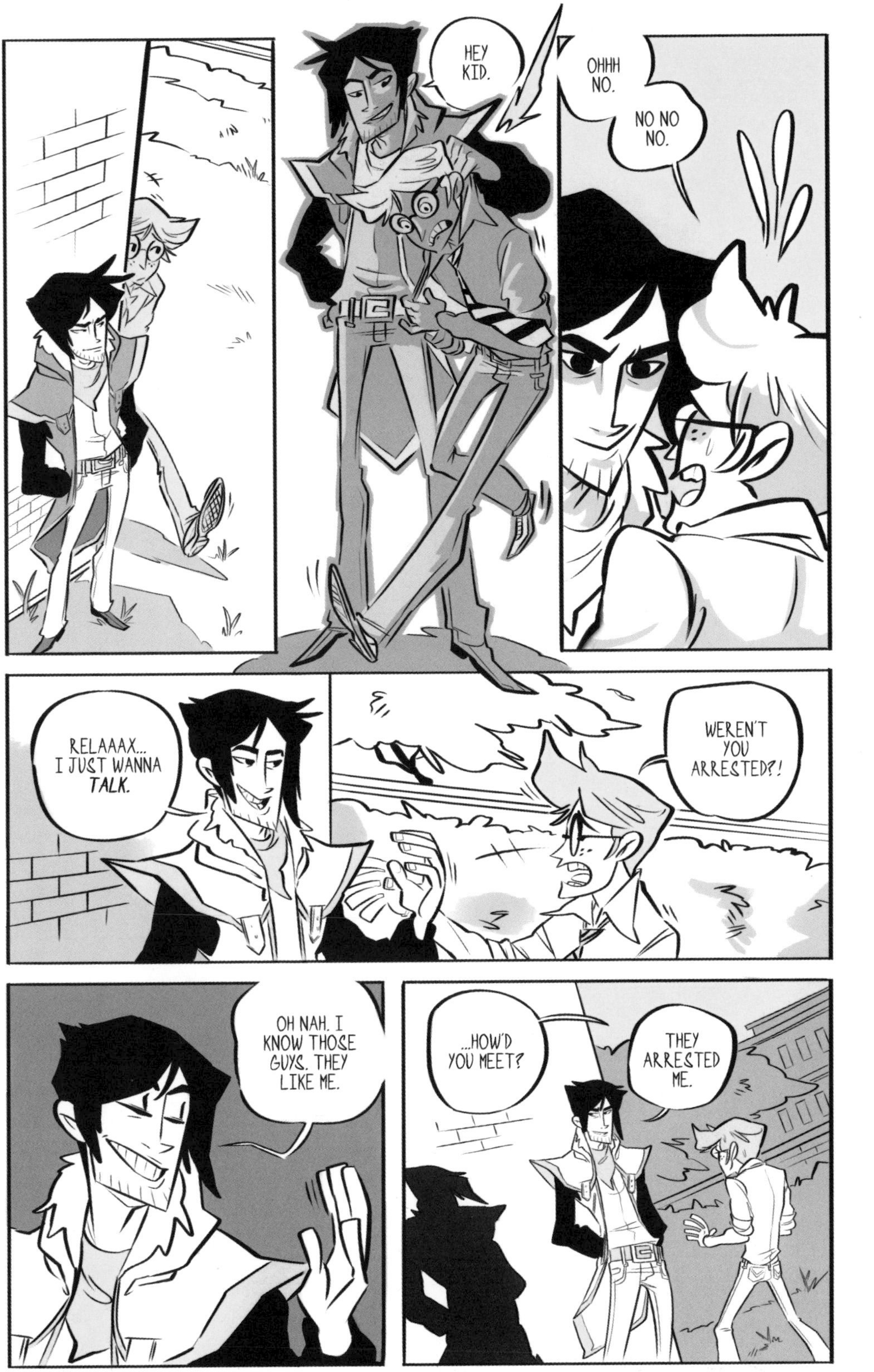
HEY KID.
OHHH NO.
NO NO NO.
RELAAAX... I JUST WANNA *TALK.*
WEREN'T YOU ARRESTED?!
OH NAH. I KNOW THOSE GUYS. THEY LIKE ME.
...HOW'D YOU MEET?
THEY ARRESTED ME.

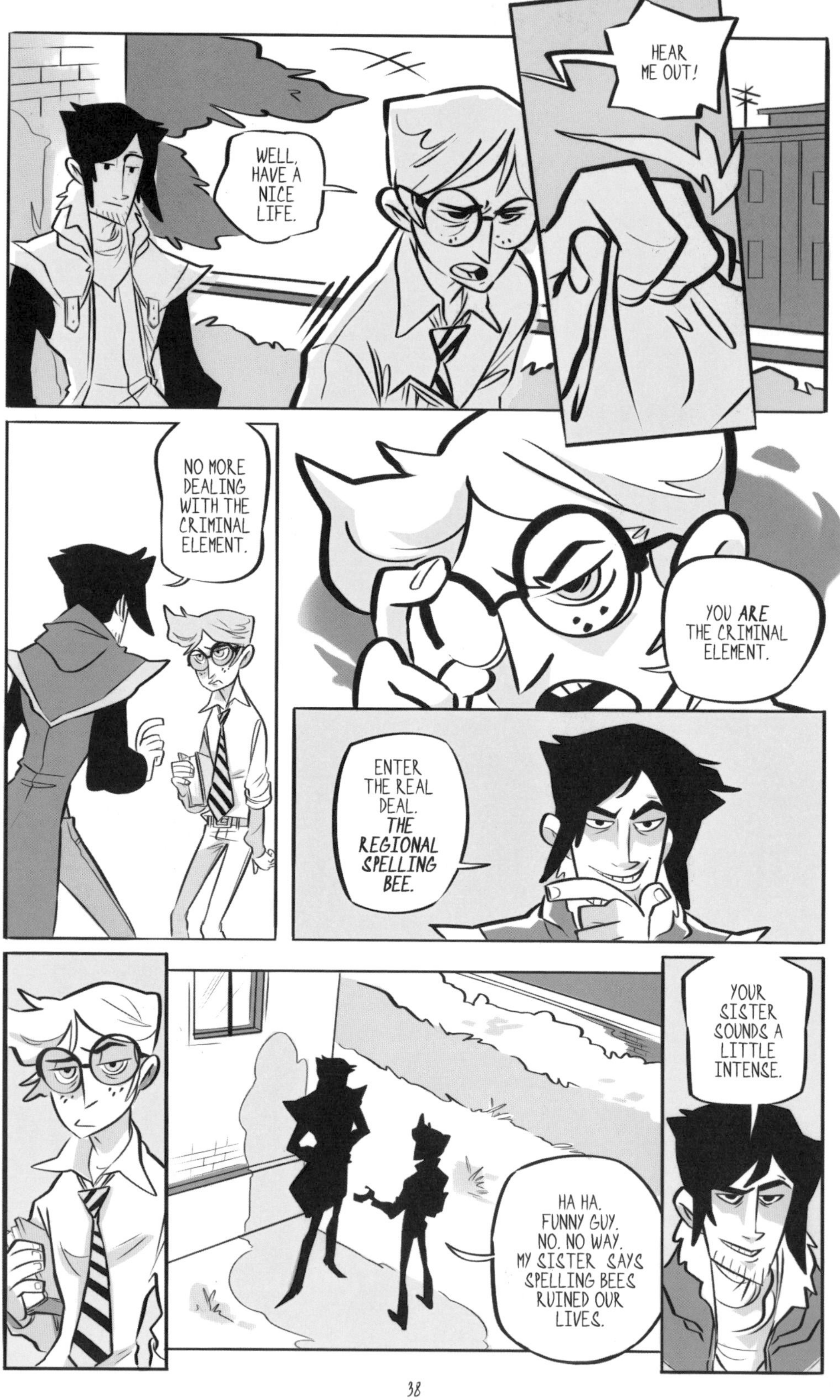
WELL, HAVE A NICE LIFE.
HEAR ME OUT!
NO MORE DEALING WITH THE CRIMINAL ELEMENT.
YOU **ARE** THE CRIMINAL ELEMENT.
ENTER THE REAL DEAL. ***THE REGIONAL SPELLING BEE.***
HA HA. FUNNY GUY. NO. NO WAY. MY SISTER SAYS SPELLING BEES RUINED OUR LIVES.
YOUR SISTER SOUNDS A LITTLE INTENSE.

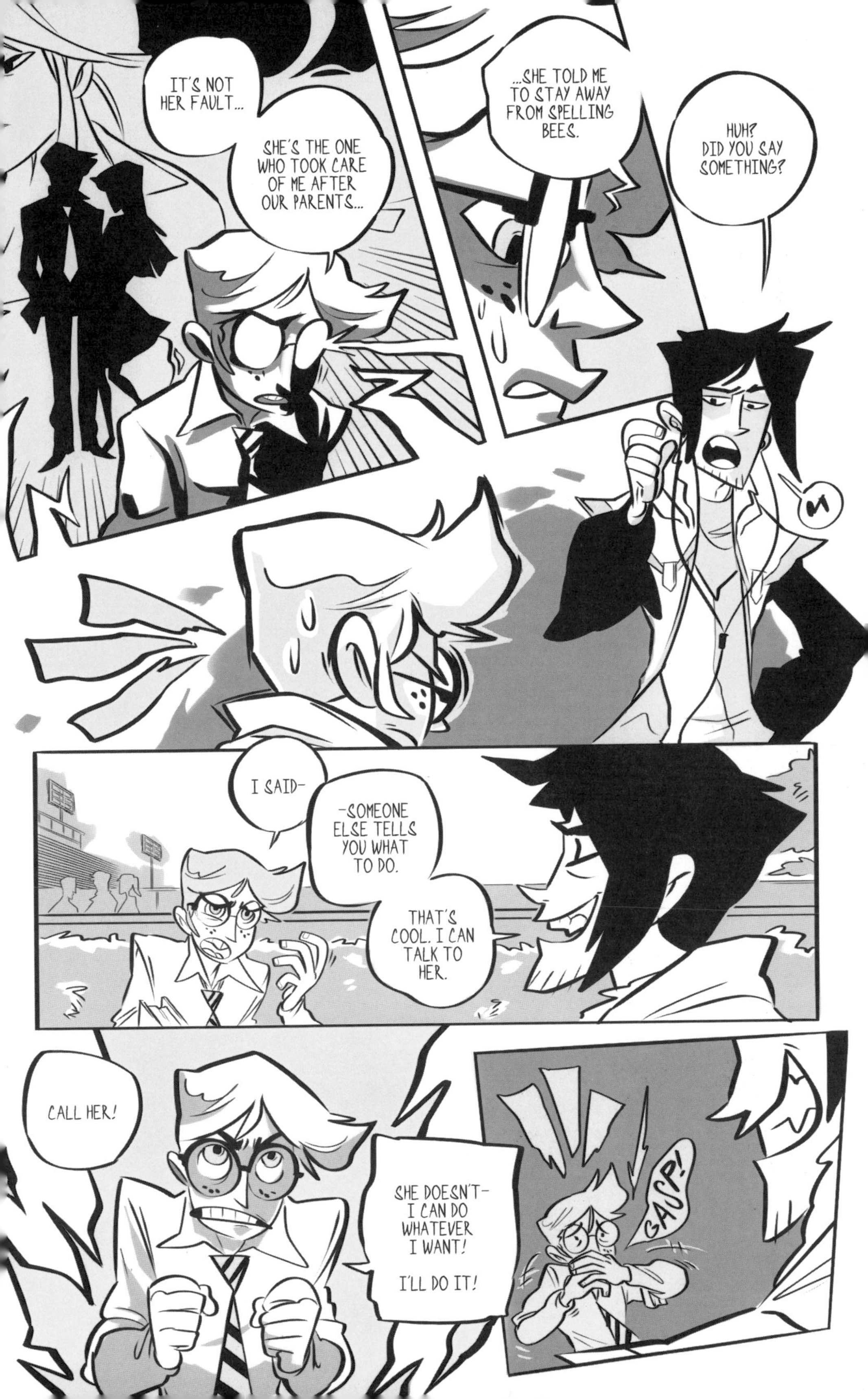
IT'S NOT HER FAULT...
SHE'S THE ONE WHO TOOK CARE OF ME AFTER OUR PARENTS...
...SHE TOLD ME TO STAY AWAY FROM SPELLING BEES.
HUH? DID YOU SAY SOMETHING?
I SAID-
-SOMEONE ELSE TELLS YOU WHAT TO DO.
THAT'S COOL. I CAN TALK TO HER.
CALL HER!
SHE DOESN'T-
I CAN DO WHATEVER I WANT!
I'LL DO IT!
GASP!

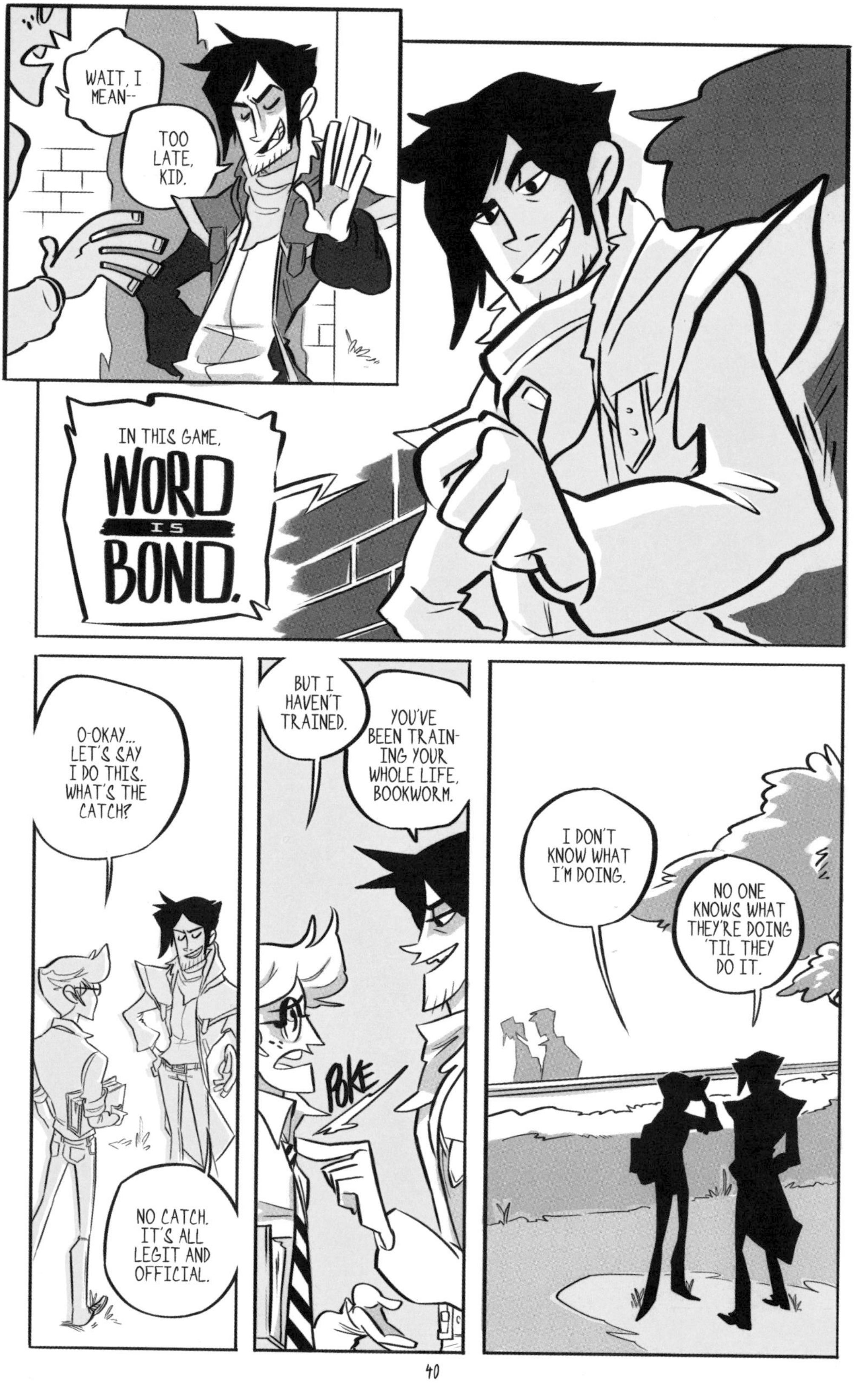
WAIT, I MEAN--
TOO LATE, KID.
IN THIS GAME, WORD IS BOND.
O-OKAY... LET'S SAY I DO THIS. WHAT'S THE CATCH?
NO CATCH. IT'S ALL LEGIT AND OFFICIAL.
BUT I HAVEN'T TRAINED.
YOU'VE BEEN TRAIN-ING YOUR WHOLE LIFE, BOOKWORM.
POKE
I DON'T KNOW WHAT I'M DOING.
NO ONE KNOWS WHAT THEY'RE DOING 'TIL THEY DO IT.

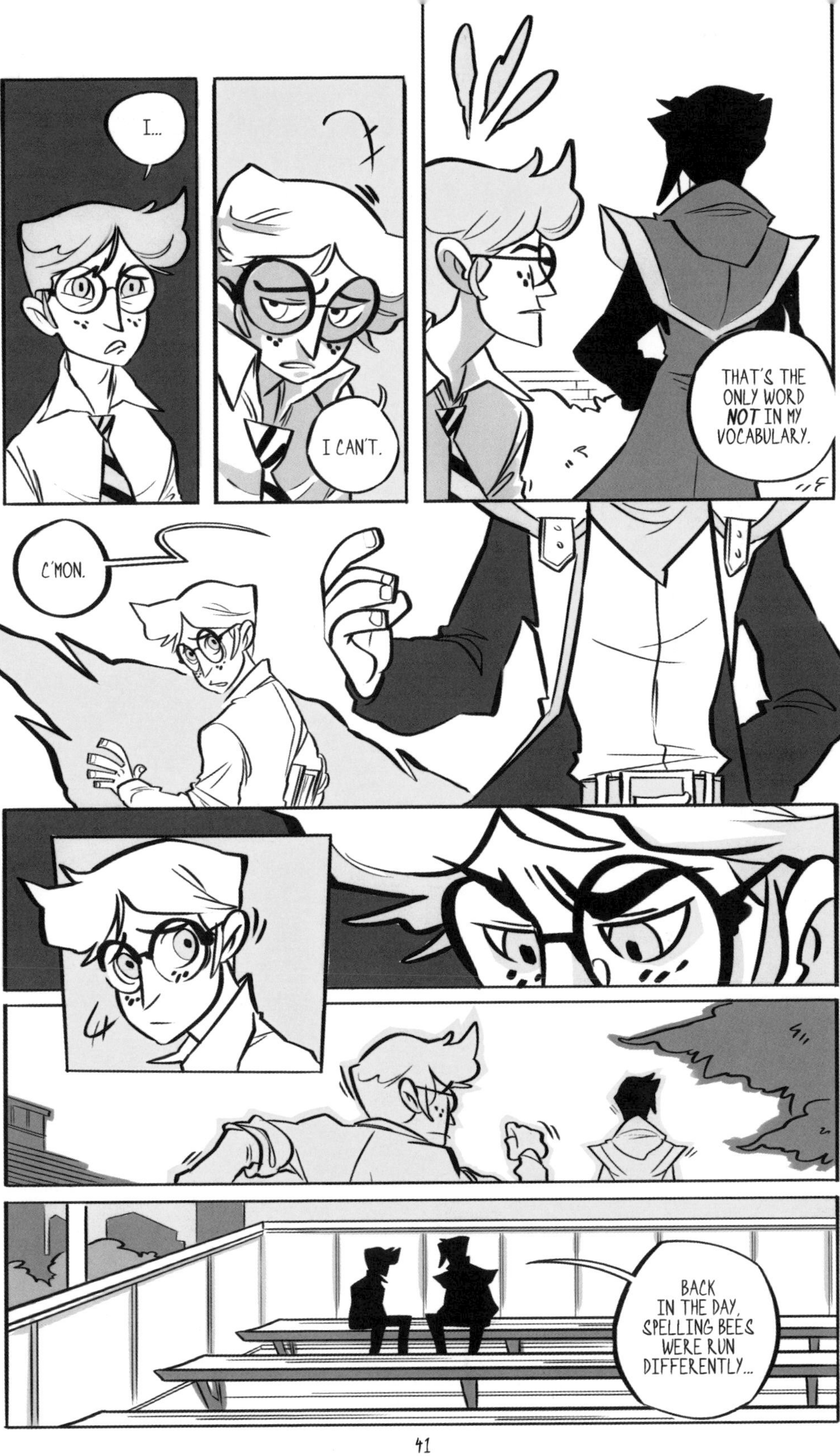
I...
I CAN'T.
THAT'S THE ONLY WORD **NOT** IN MY VOCABULARY.
C'MON.
BACK IN THE DAY, SPELLING BEES WERE RUN DIFFERENTLY...

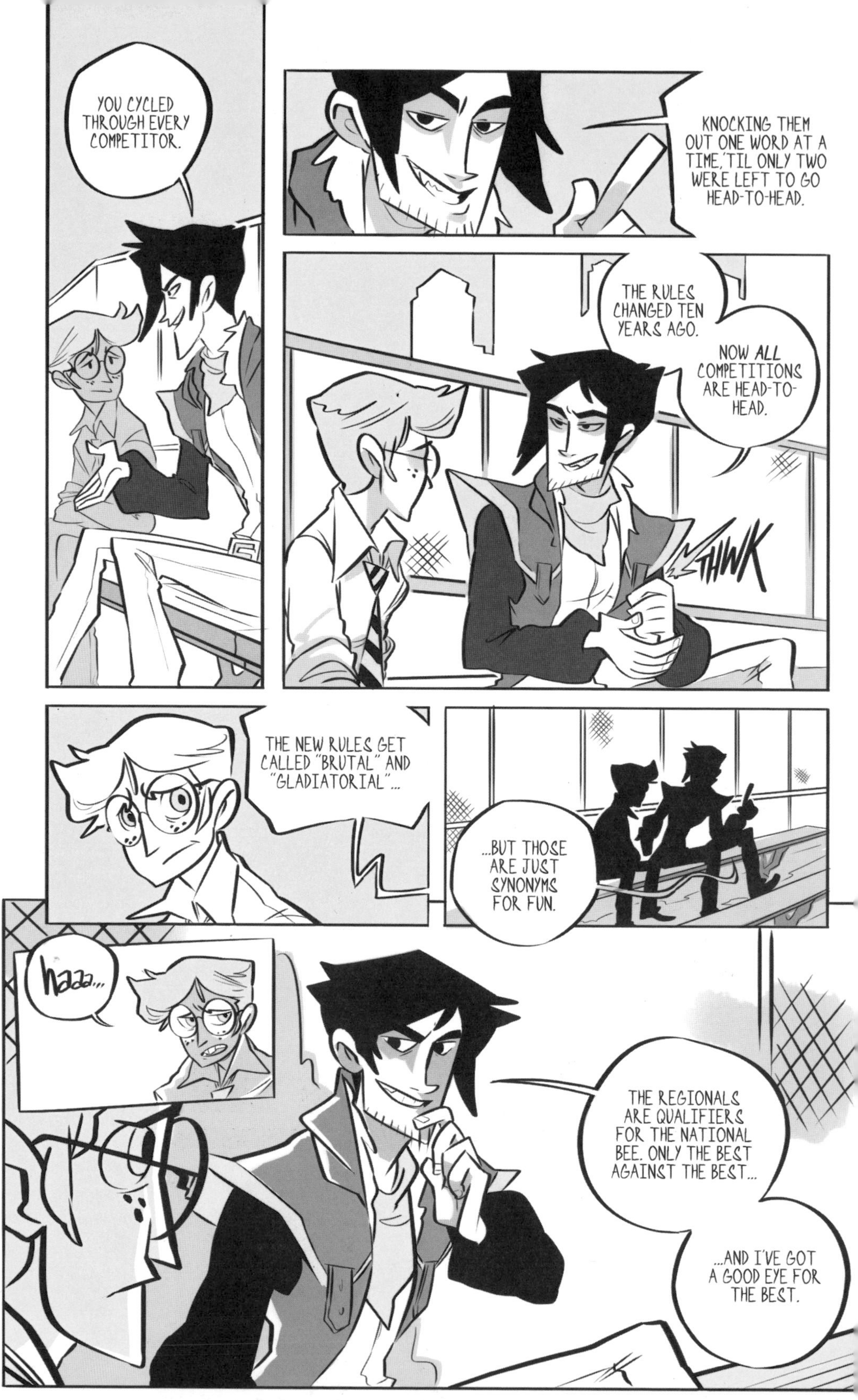
YOU CYCLED THROUGH EVERY COMPETITOR.
KNOCKING THEM OUT ONE WORD AT A TIME, 'TIL ONLY TWO WERE LEFT TO GO HEAD-TO-HEAD.
THE RULES CHANGED TEN YEARS AGO.
NOW *ALL* COMPETITIONS ARE HEAD-TO-HEAD.
THWK
THE NEW RULES GET CALLED "BRUTAL" AND "GLADIATORIAL"...
...BUT THOSE ARE JUST SYNONYMS FOR FUN.
haaa...
THE REGIONALS ARE QUALIFIERS FOR THE NATIONAL BEE. ONLY THE BEST AGAINST THE BEST...
...AND I'VE GOT A GOOD EYE FOR THE BEST.

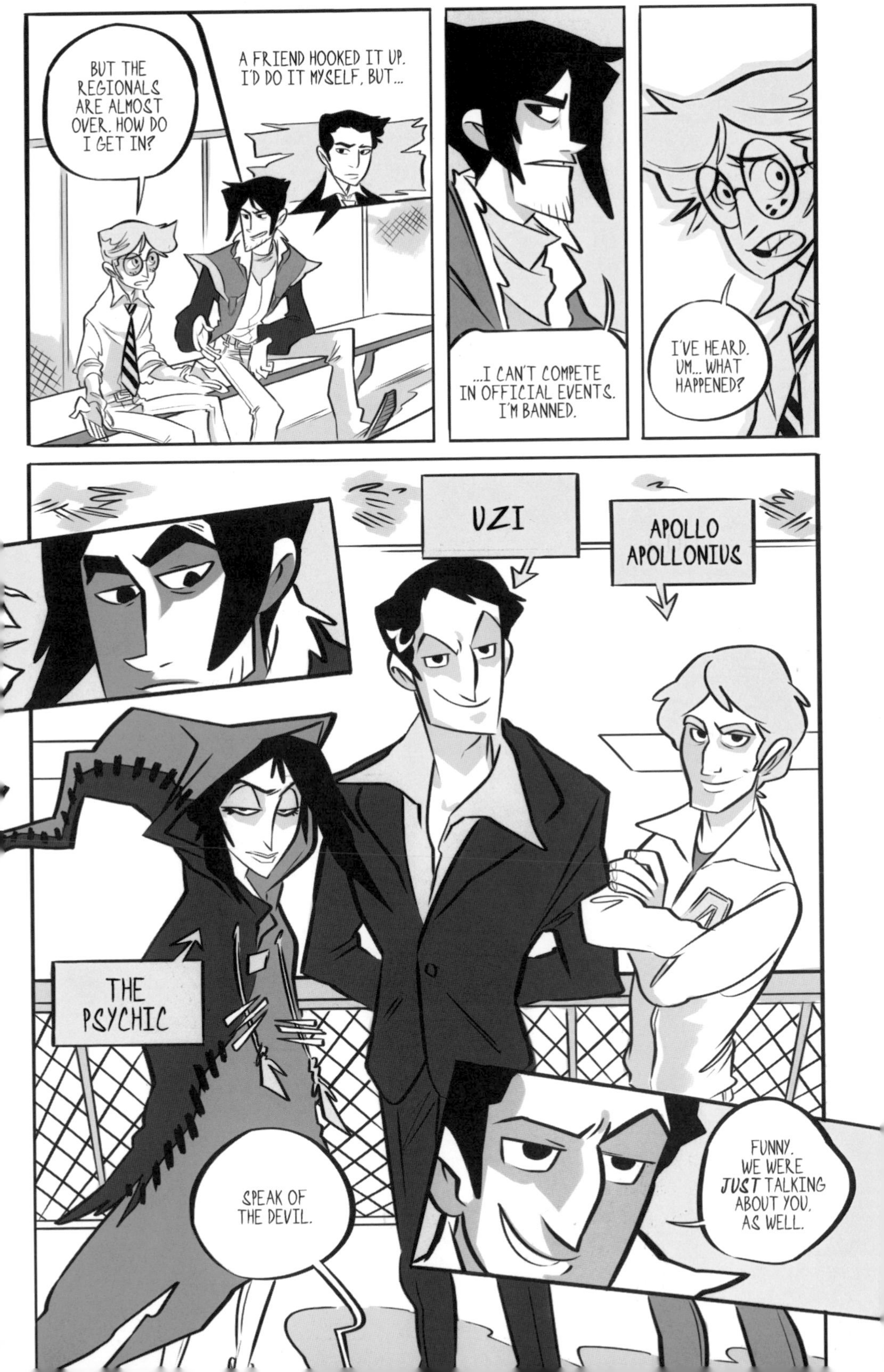
BUT THE REGIONALS ARE ALMOST OVER. HOW DO I GET IN?
A FRIEND HOOKED IT UP. I'D DO IT MYSELF, BUT...
...I CAN'T COMPETE IN OFFICIAL EVENTS. I'M BANNED.
I'VE HEARD. UM... WHAT HAPPENED?
UZI
APOLLO APOLLONIUS
THE PSYCHIC
SPEAK OF THE DEVIL.
FUNNY. WE WERE *JUST* TALKING ABOUT YOU, AS WELL.

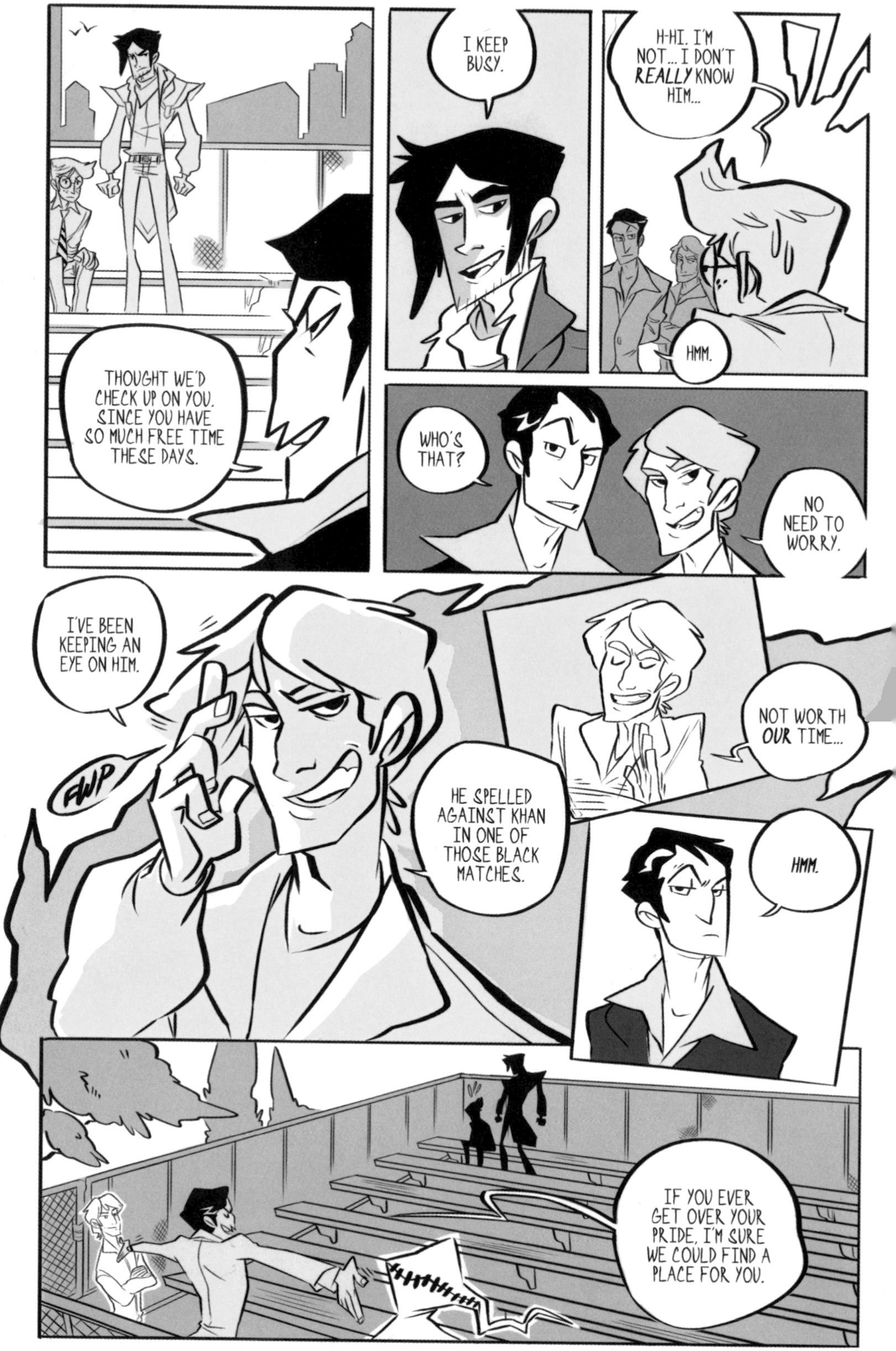
THOUGHT WE'D CHECK UP ON YOU. SINCE YOU HAVE SO MUCH FREE TIME THESE DAYS.
I KEEP BUSY.
H-HI. I'M NOT... I DON'T **REALLY** KNOW HIM...
HMM.
WHO'S THAT?
NO NEED TO WORRY.
I'VE BEEN KEEPING AN EYE ON HIM.
FWP
HE SPELLED AGAINST KHAN IN ONE OF THOSE BLACK MATCHES.
NOT WORTH **OUR** TIME...
HMM.
IF YOU EVER GET OVER YOUR PRIDE, I'M SURE WE COULD FIND A PLACE FOR YOU.

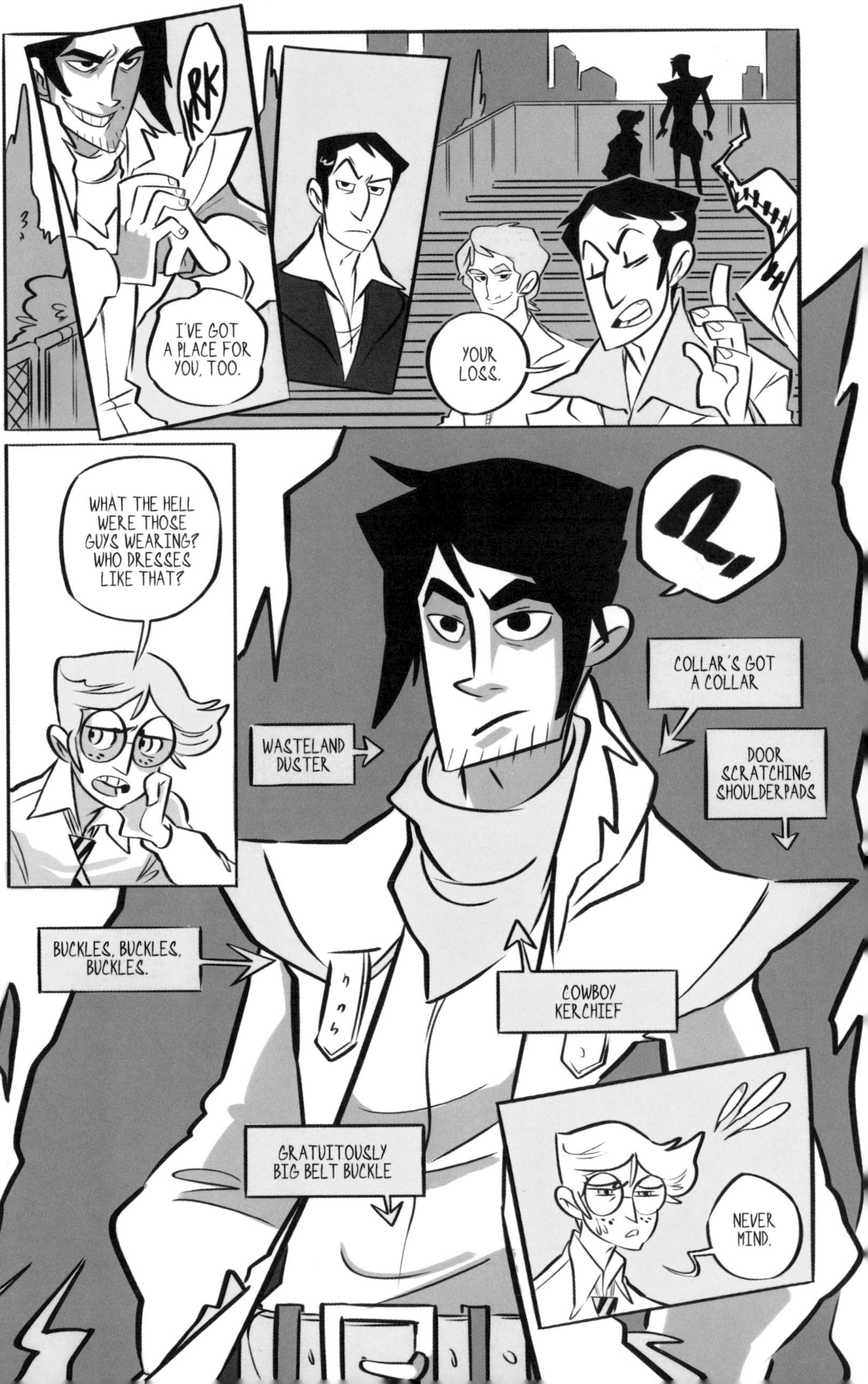
KRK
I'VE GOT A PLACE FOR YOU, TOO.
YOUR LOSS.
WHAT THE HELL WERE THOSE GUYS WEARING? WHO DRESSES LIKE THAT?
WASTELAND DUSTER
COLLAR'S GOT A COLLAR
DOOR SCRATCHING SHOULDERPADS
BUCKLES, BUCKLES, BUCKLES.
COWBOY KERCHIEF
GRATUITOUSLY BIG BELT BUCKLE
NEVER MIND.

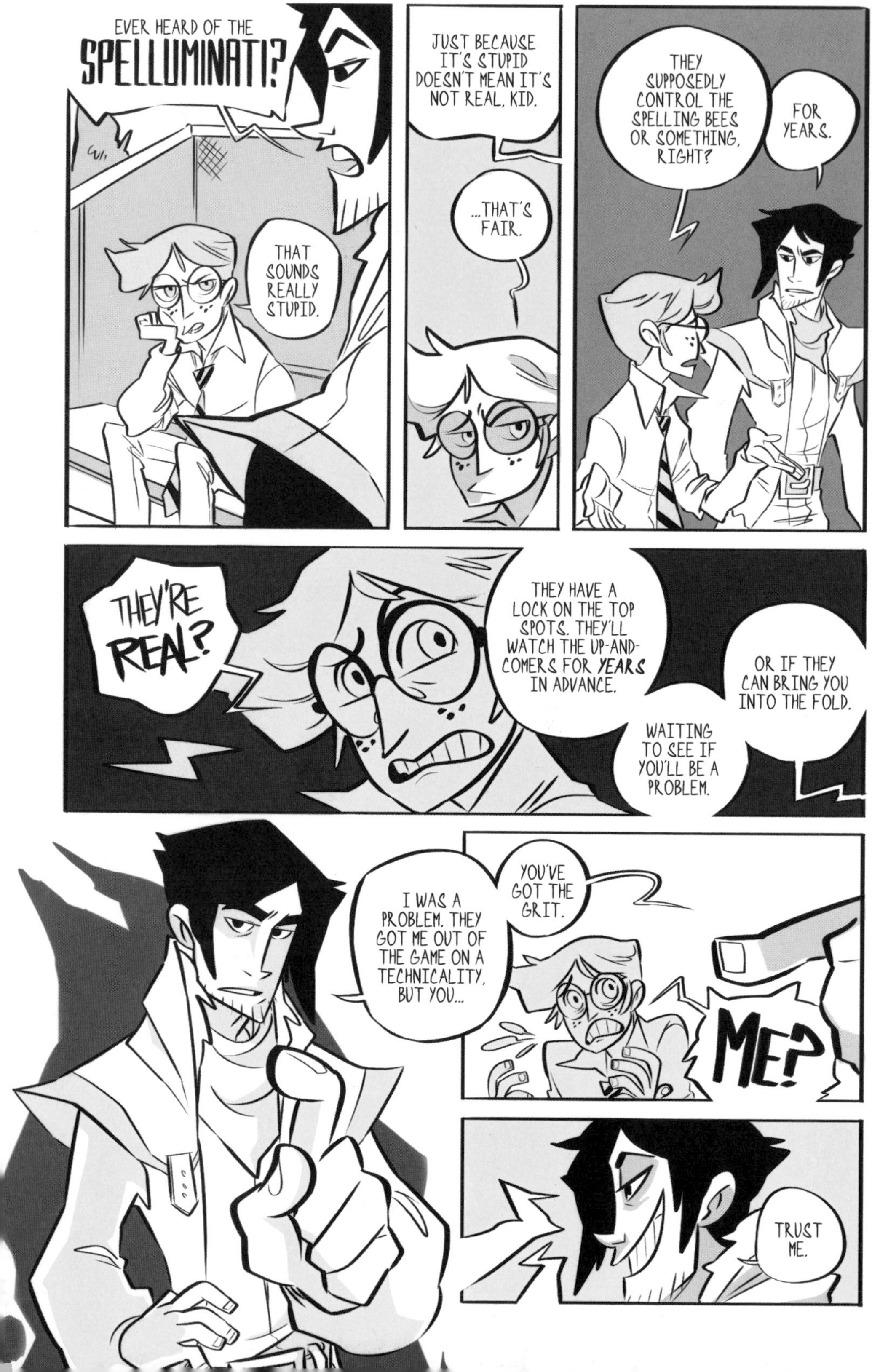
EVER HEARD OF THE SPELLUMINATI?
THAT SOUNDS REALLY STUPID.
JUST BECAUSE IT'S STUPID DOESN'T MEAN IT'S NOT REAL, KID.
...THAT'S FAIR.
THEY SUPPOSEDLY CONTROL THE SPELLING BEES OR SOMETHING, RIGHT?
FOR YEARS.
THEY'RE REAL?
THEY HAVE A LOCK ON THE TOP SPOTS. THEY'LL WATCH THE UP-AND-COMERS FOR YEARS IN ADVANCE.
WAITING TO SEE IF YOU'LL BE A PROBLEM.
OR IF THEY CAN BRING YOU INTO THE FOLD.
I WAS A PROBLEM. THEY GOT ME OUT OF THE GAME ON A TECHNICALITY, BUT YOU...
YOU'VE GOT THE GRIT.
ME?
TRUST ME.

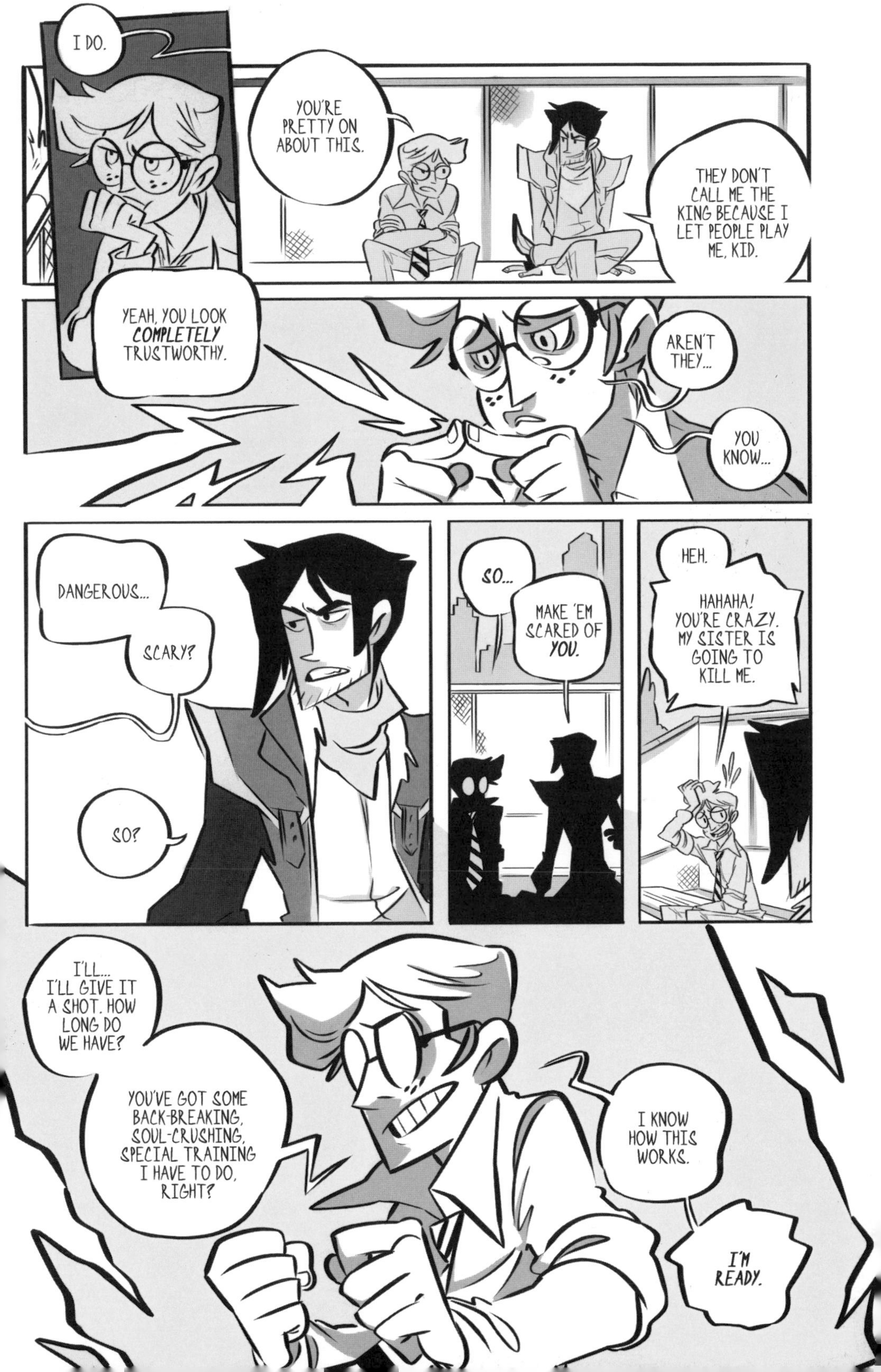
I DO.
YOU'RE PRETTY ON ABOUT THIS.
THEY DON'T CALL ME THE KING BECAUSE I LET PEOPLE PLAY ME, KID.
YEAH, YOU LOOK COMPLETELY TRUSTWORTHY.
AREN'T THEY...
YOU KNOW...
DANGEROUS...
SCARY?
SO?
SO...
MAKE 'EM SCARED OF YOU.
HEH.
HAHAHA! YOU'RE CRAZY. MY SISTER IS GOING TO KILL ME.
I'LL... I'LL GIVE IT A SHOT. HOW LONG DO WE HAVE?
YOU'VE GOT SOME BACK-BREAKING, SOUL-CRUSHING, SPECIAL TRAINING I HAVE TO DO, RIGHT?
I KNOW HOW THIS WORKS.
I'M READY.

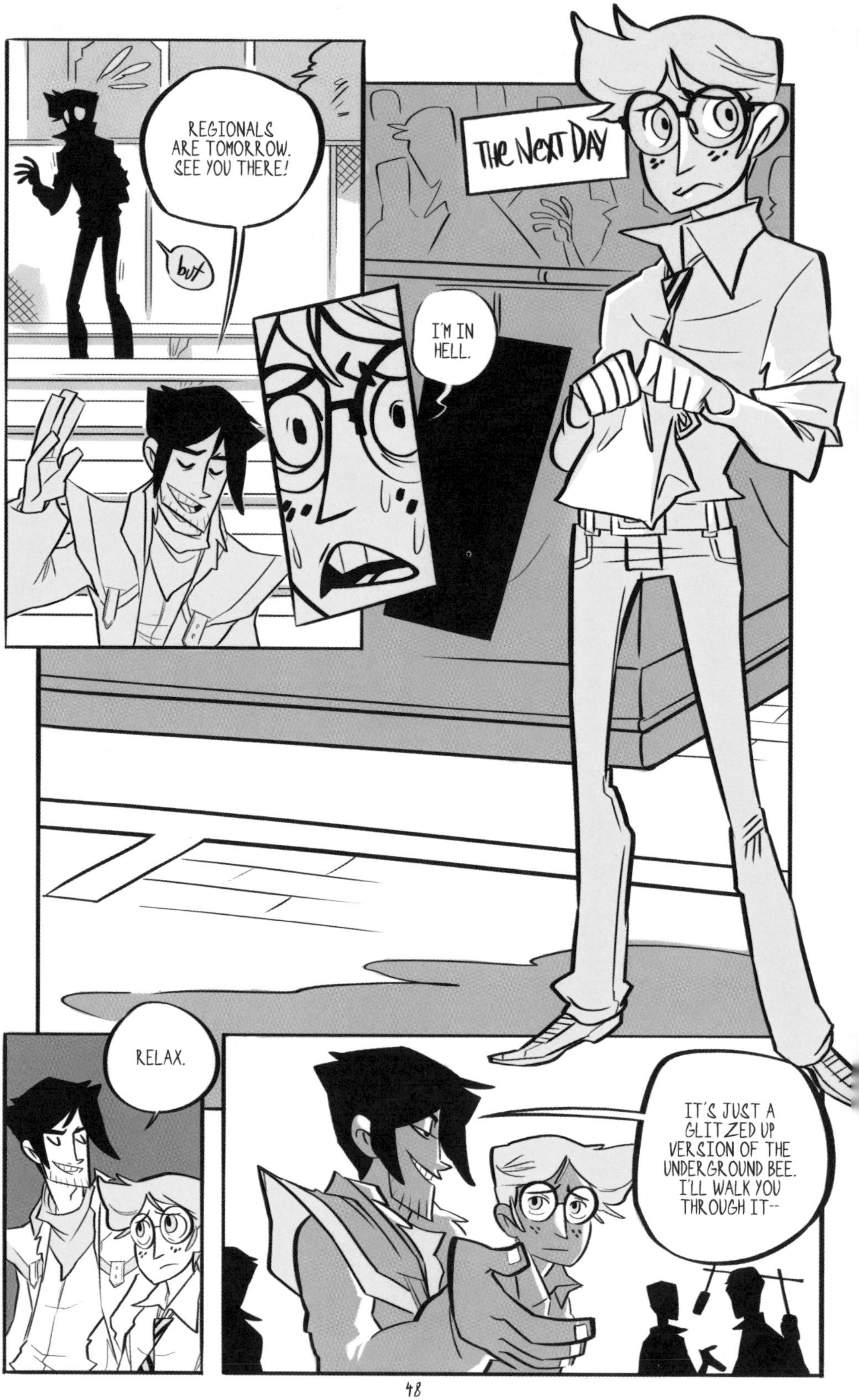
REGIONALS ARE TOMORROW. SEE YOU THERE!
but
I'M IN HELL.
The Next Day
RELAX.
IT'S JUST A GLITZED UP VERSION OF THE UNDERGROUND BEE. I'LL WALK YOU THROUGH IT--

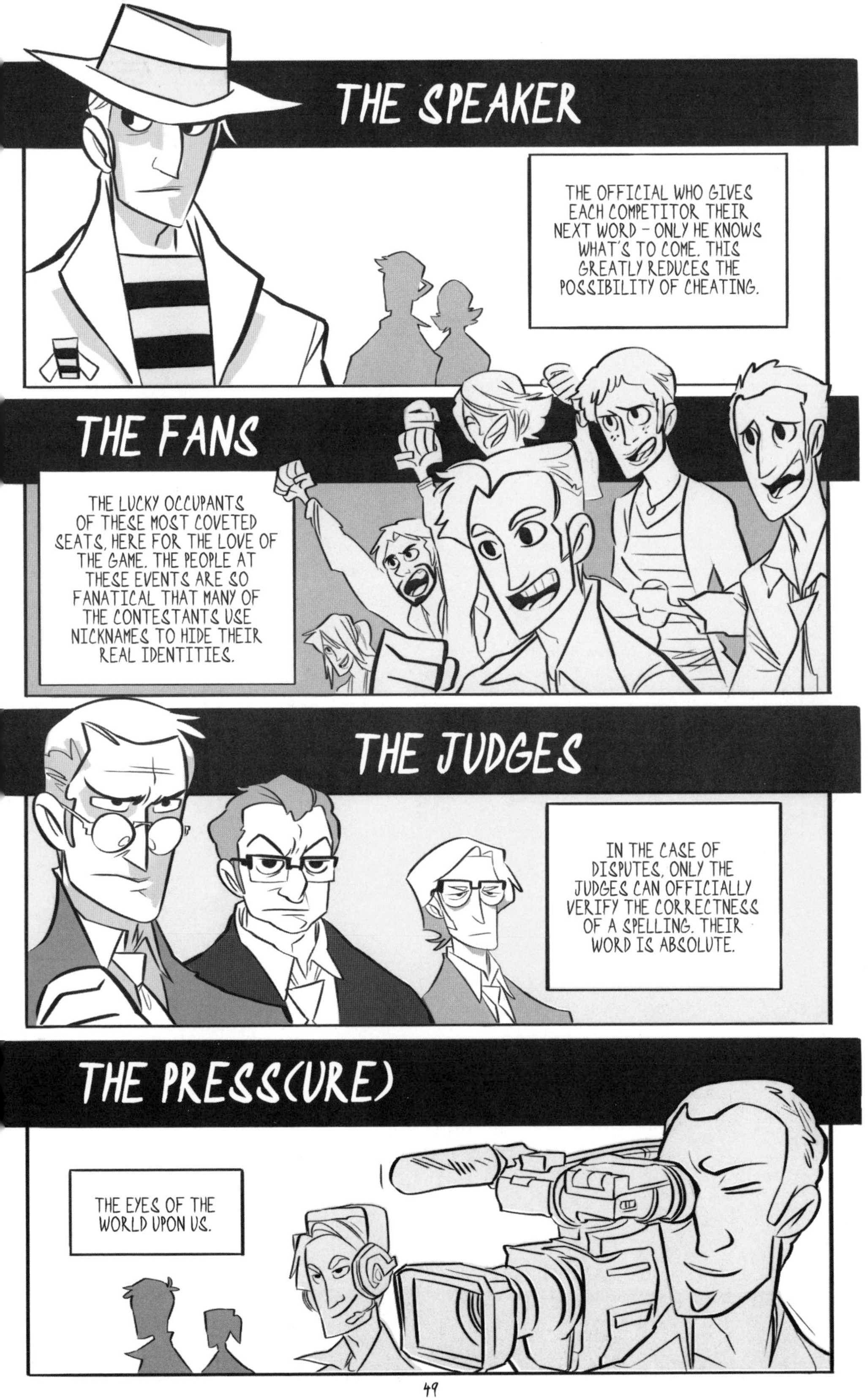
THE SPEAKER
THE OFFICIAL WHO GIVES EACH COMPETITOR THEIR NEXT WORD – ONLY HE KNOWS WHAT'S TO COME. THIS GREATLY REDUCES THE POSSIBILITY OF CHEATING.
THE FANS
THE LUCKY OCCUPANTS OF THESE MOST COVETED SEATS, HERE FOR THE LOVE OF THE GAME. THE PEOPLE AT THESE EVENTS ARE SO FANATICAL THAT MANY OF THE CONTESTANTS USE NICKNAMES TO HIDE THEIR REAL IDENTITIES.
THE JUDGES
IN THE CASE OF DISPUTES, ONLY THE JUDGES CAN OFFICIALLY VERIFY THE CORRECTNESS OF A SPELLING. THEIR WORD IS ABSOLUTE.
THE PRESS(URE)
THE EYES OF THE WORLD UPON US.

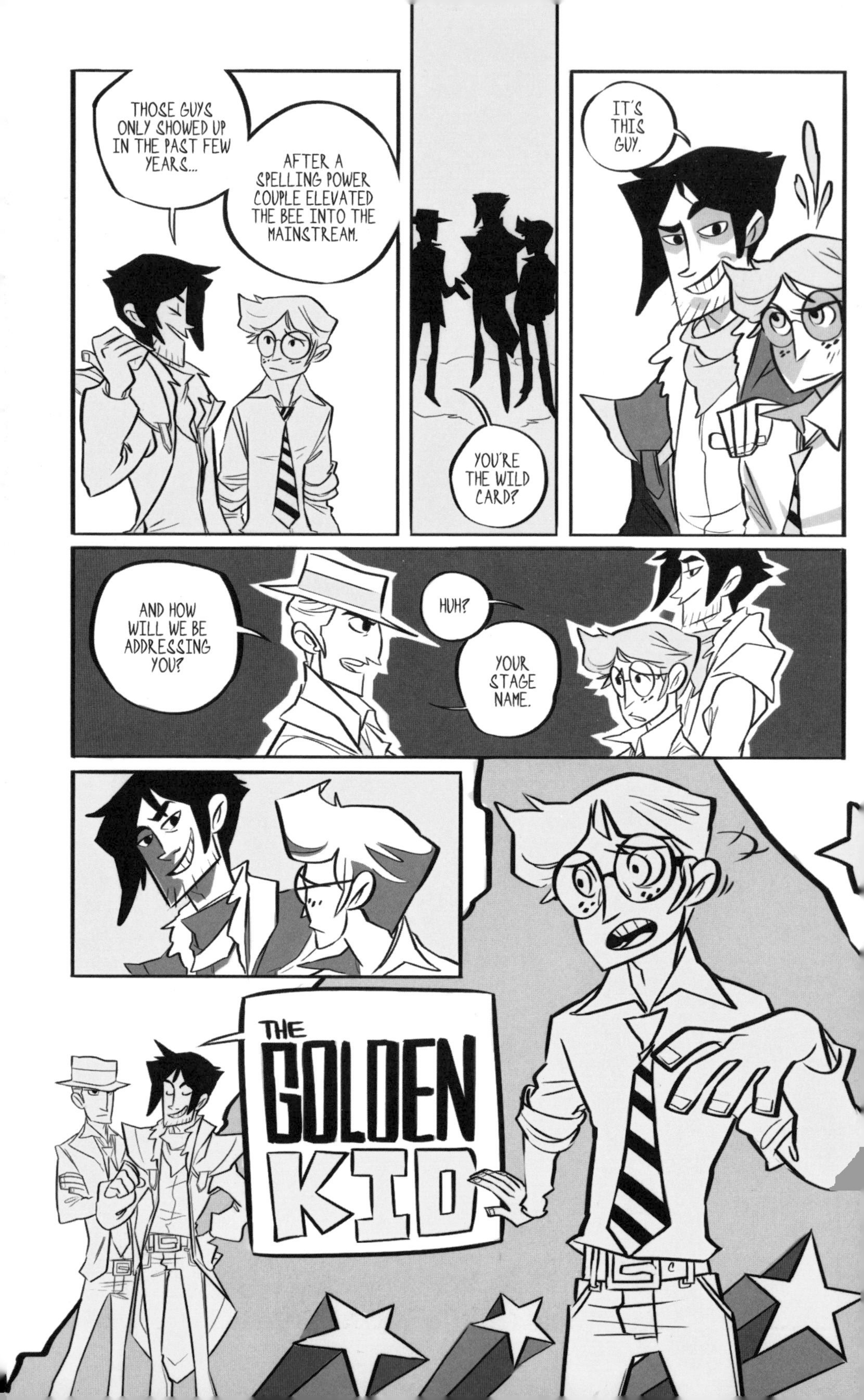
THOSE GUYS ONLY SHOWED UP IN THE PAST FEW YEARS...
AFTER A SPELLING POWER COUPLE ELEVATED THE BEE INTO THE MAINSTREAM.
YOU'RE THE WILD CARD?
IT'S THIS GUY.
AND HOW WILL WE BE ADDRESSING YOU?
HUH?
YOUR STAGE NAME.
THE GOLDEN KID

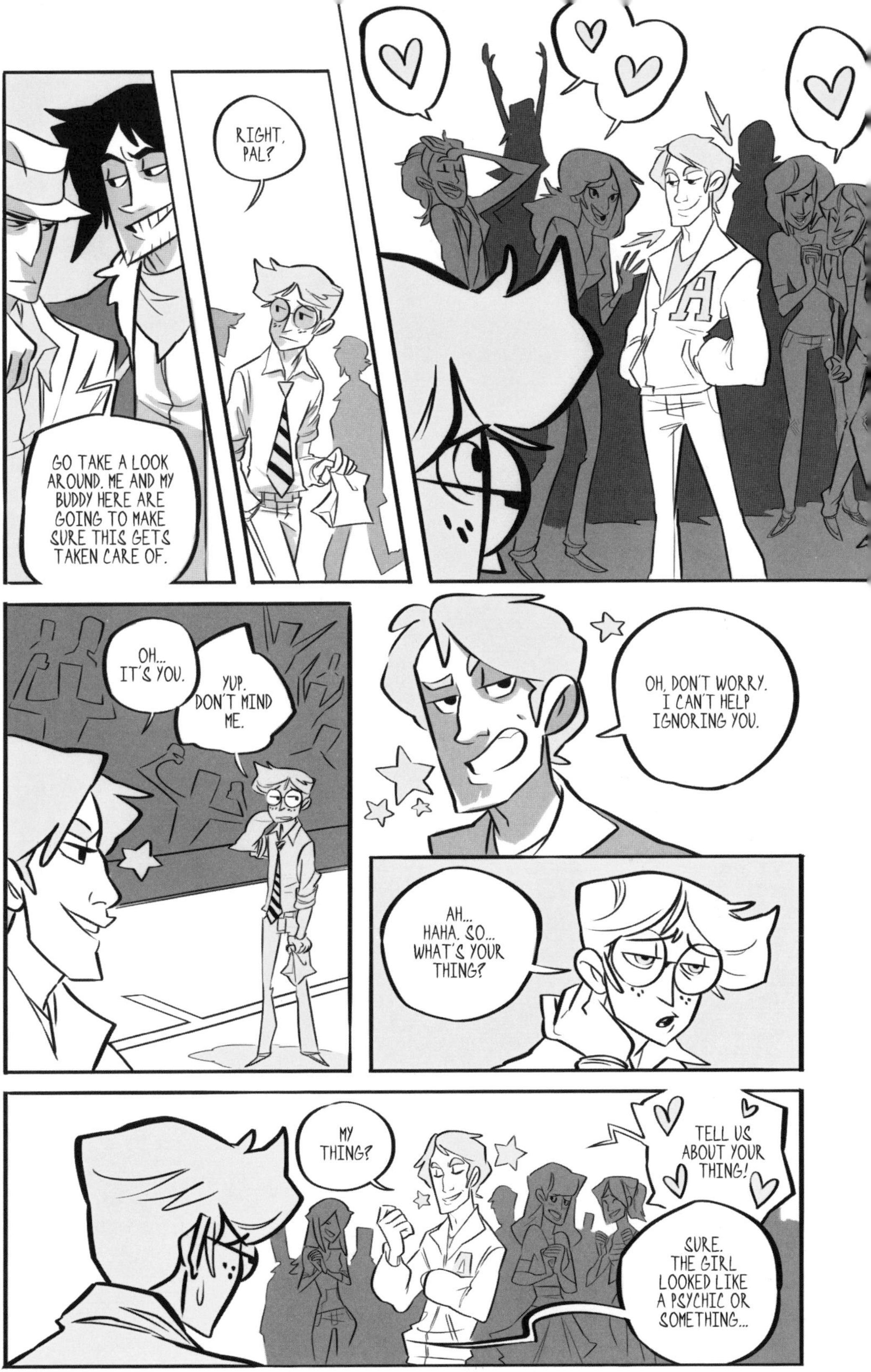
GO TAKE A LOOK AROUND. ME AND MY BUDDY HERE ARE GOING TO MAKE SURE THIS GETS TAKEN CARE OF.
RIGHT, PAL?
OH... IT'S YOU.
YUP. DON'T MIND ME.
OH, DON'T WORRY. I CAN'T HELP IGNORING YOU.
AH... HAHA. SO... WHAT'S YOUR THING?
MY THING?
TELL US ABOUT YOUR THING!
SURE. THE GIRL LOOKED LIKE A PSYCHIC OR SOMETHING...

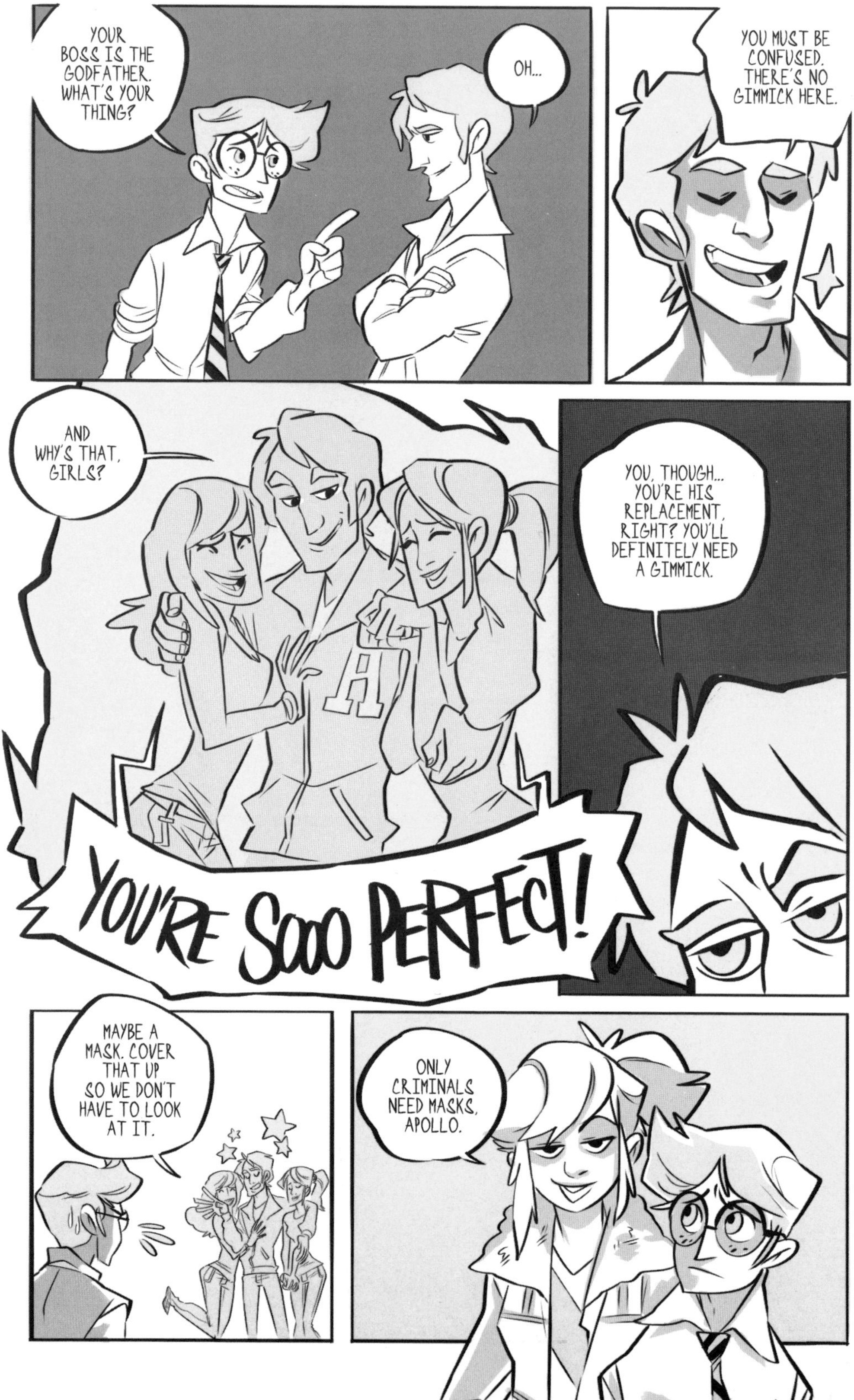
YOUR BOSS IS THE GODFATHER. WHAT'S YOUR THING?
OH...
YOU MUST BE CONFUSED. THERE'S NO GIMMICK HERE.
AND WHY'S THAT, GIRLS?
YOU'RE SOOO PERFECT!
YOU, THOUGH... YOU'RE HIS REPLACEMENT, RIGHT? YOU'LL DEFINITELY NEED A GIMMICK.
MAYBE A MASK. COVER THAT UP SO WE DON'T HAVE TO LOOK AT IT.
ONLY CRIMINALS NEED MASKS, APOLLO.

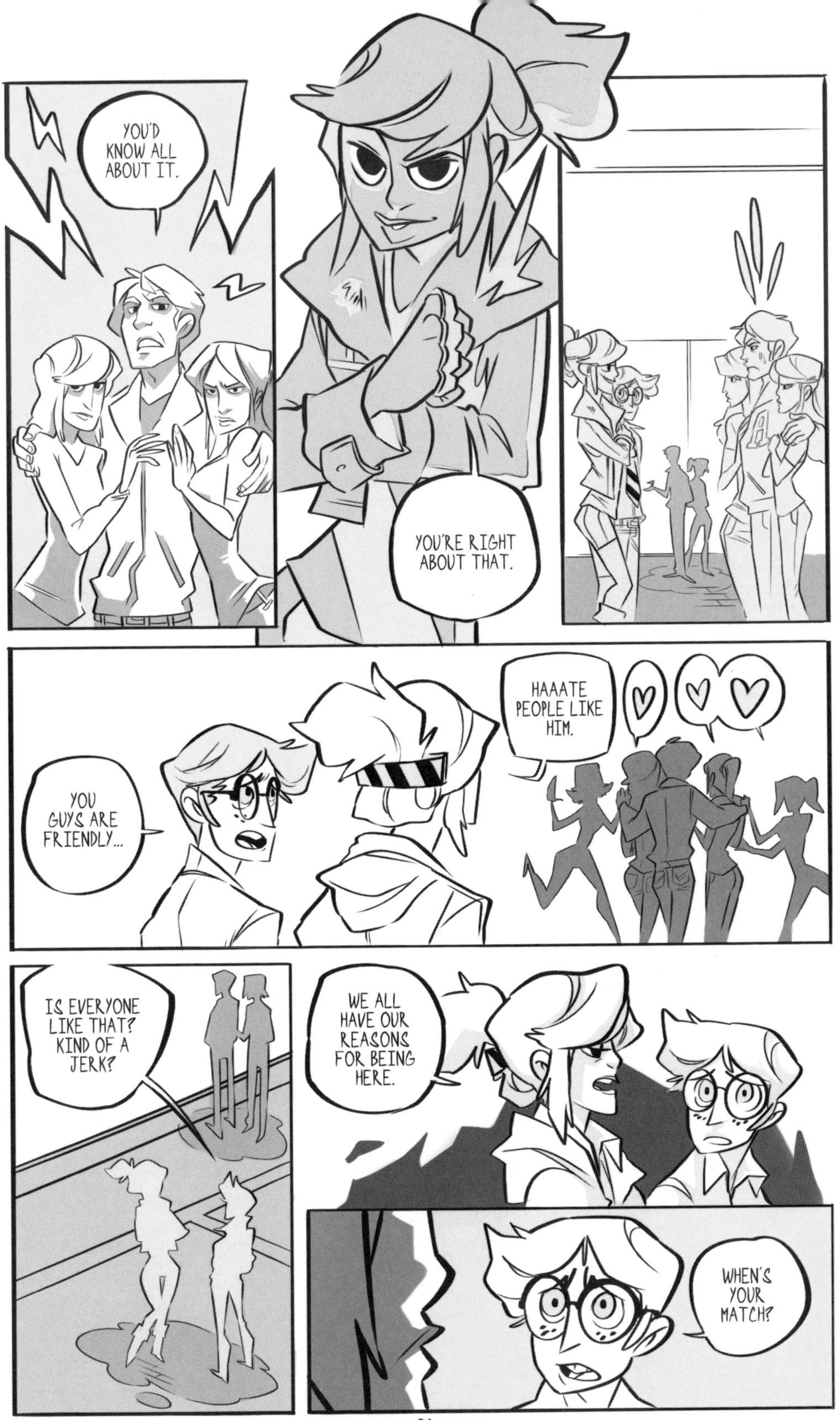
YOU'D KNOW ALL ABOUT IT.
YOU'RE RIGHT ABOUT THAT.
YOU GUYS ARE FRIENDLY...
HAAATE PEOPLE LIKE HIM.
IS EVERYONE LIKE THAT? KIND OF A JERK?
WE ALL HAVE OUR REASONS FOR BEING HERE.
WHEN'S YOUR MATCH?

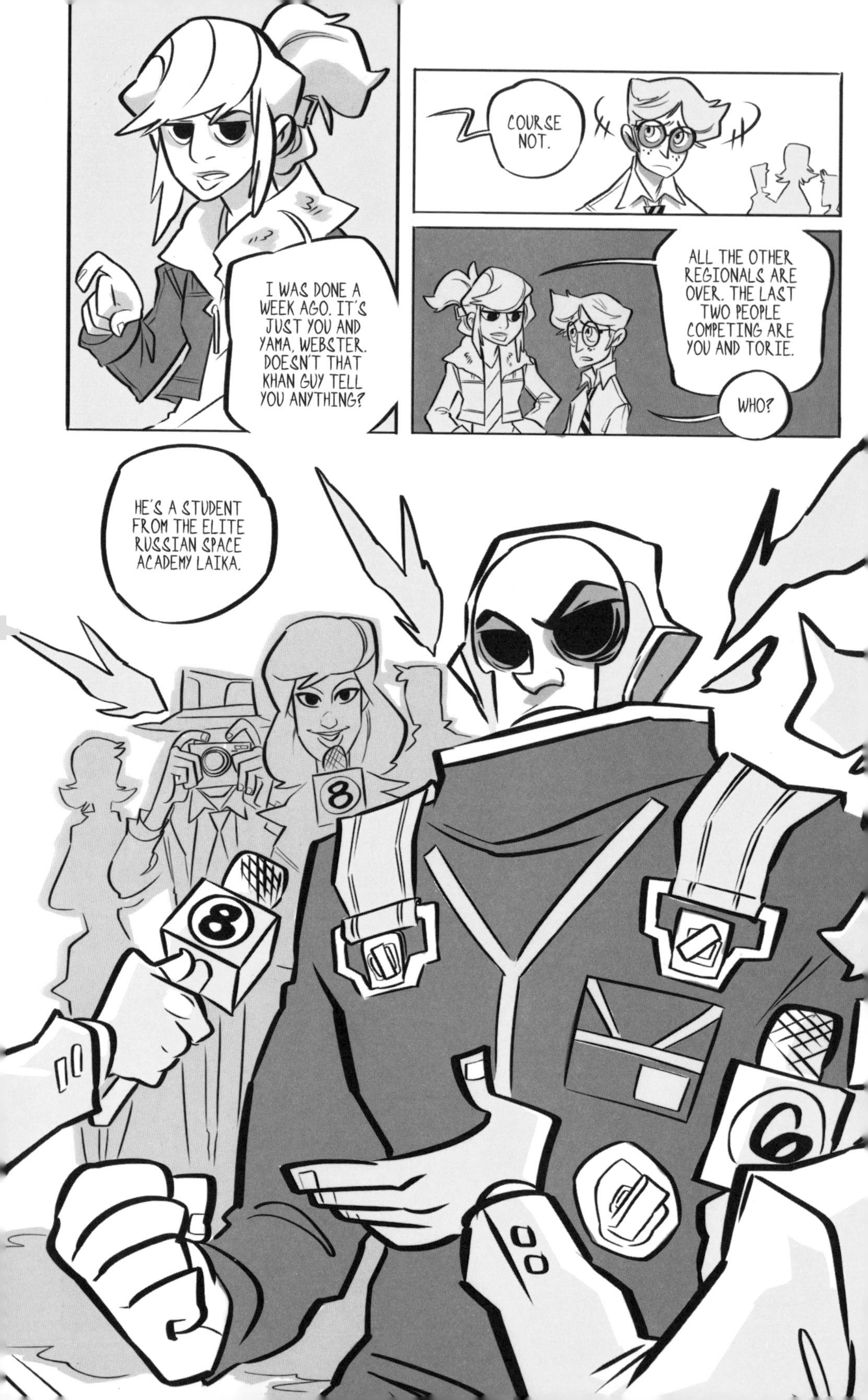
I WAS DONE A WEEK AGO. IT'S JUST YOU AND YAMA, WEBSTER. DOESN'T THAT KHAN GUY TELL YOU ANYTHING?
COURSE NOT.
ALL THE OTHER REGIONALS ARE OVER. THE LAST TWO PEOPLE COMPETING ARE YOU AND TORIE.
WHO?
HE'S A STUDENT FROM THE ELITE RUSSIAN SPACE ACADEMY LAIKA.
8
8
8
6

COSMONAUT FILE 347 : YAMA, TORIE

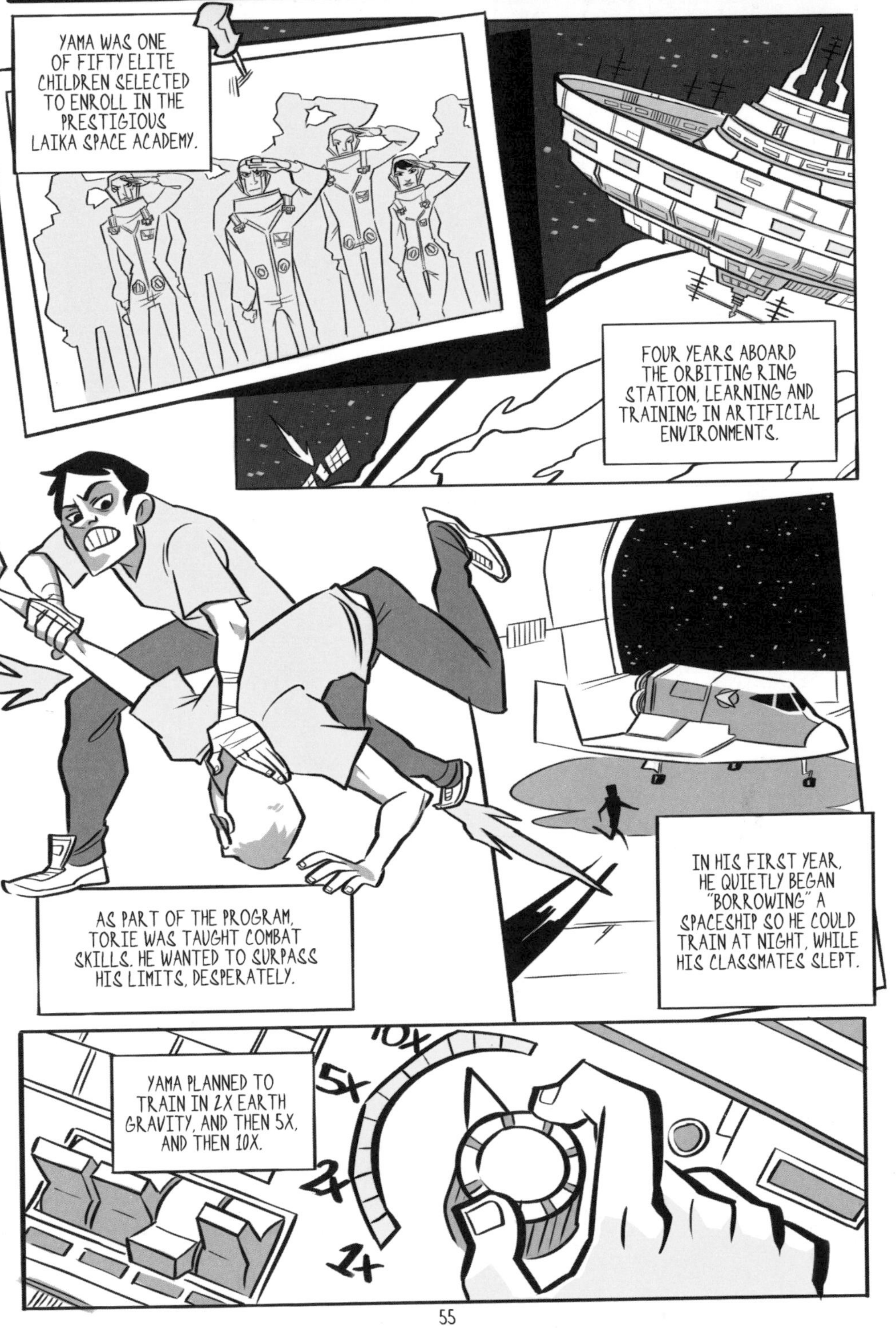
YAMA WAS ONE OF FIFTY ELITE CHILDREN SELECTED TO ENROLL IN THE PRESTIGIOUS LAIKA SPACE ACADEMY.
FOUR YEARS ABOARD THE ORBITING RING STATION, LEARNING AND TRAINING IN ARTIFICIAL ENVIRONMENTS.
AS PART OF THE PROGRAM, TORIE WAS TAUGHT COMBAT SKILLS. HE WANTED TO SURPASS HIS LIMITS, DESPERATELY.
IN HIS FIRST YEAR, HE QUIETLY BEGAN "BORROWING" A SPACESHIP SO HE COULD TRAIN AT NIGHT, WHILE HIS CLASSMATES SLEPT.
YAMA PLANNED TO TRAIN IN 2X EARTH GRAVITY, AND THEN 5X, AND THEN 10X.
10X
5X
2X
1X

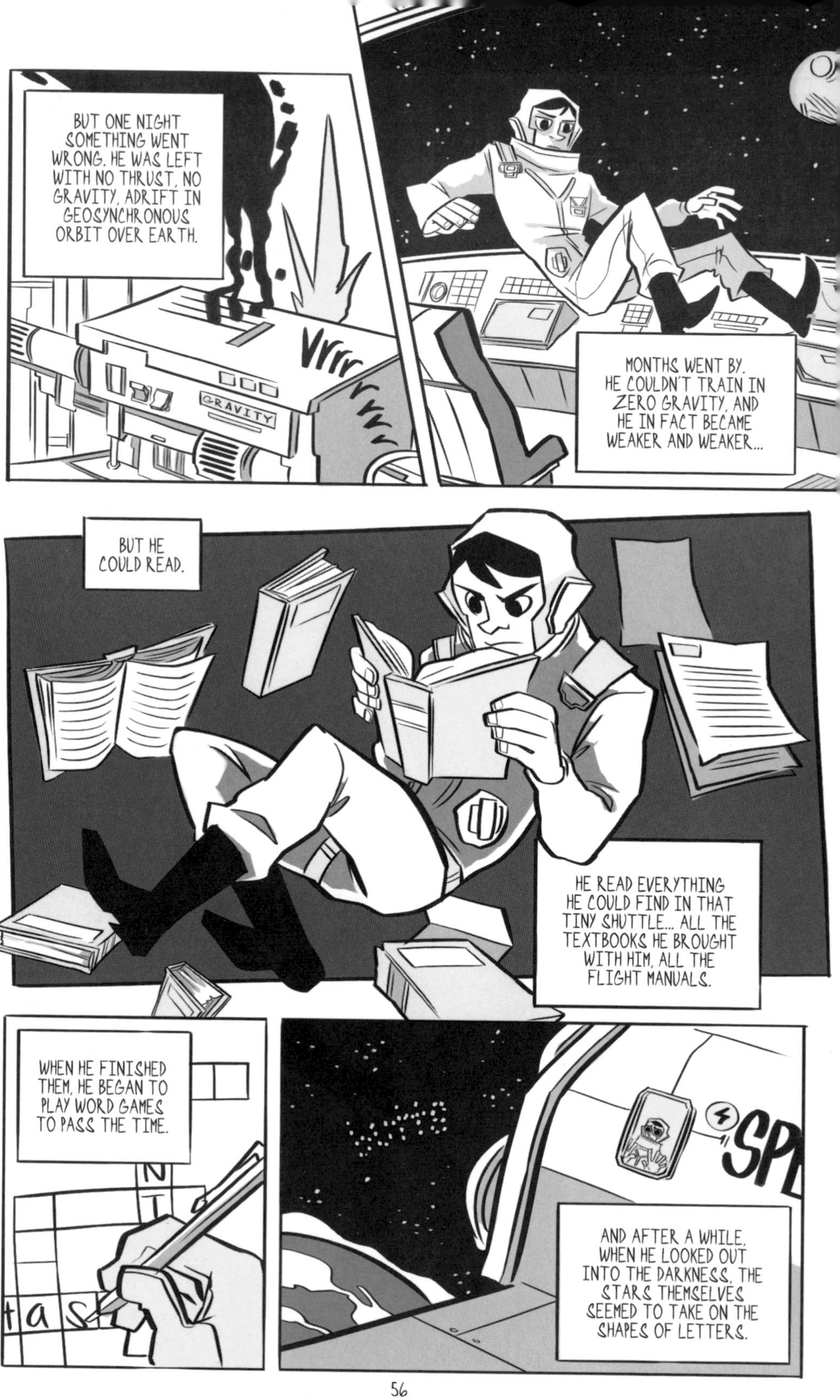
BUT ONE NIGHT SOMETHING WENT WRONG. HE WAS LEFT WITH NO THRUST, NO GRAVITY, ADRIFT IN GEOSYNCHRONOUS ORBIT OVER EARTH.
GRAVITY
Vrrr
MONTHS WENT BY. HE COULDN'T TRAIN IN ZERO GRAVITY, AND HE IN FACT BECAME WEAKER AND WEAKER...
BUT HE COULD READ.
HE READ EVERYTHING HE COULD FIND IN THAT TINY SHUTTLE... ALL THE TEXTBOOKS HE BROUGHT WITH HIM, ALL THE FLIGHT MANUALS.
WHEN HE FINISHED THEM, HE BEGAN TO PLAY WORD GAMES TO PASS THE TIME.
AND AFTER A WHILE, WHEN HE LOOKED OUT INTO THE DARKNESS, THE STARS THEMSELVES SEEMED TO TAKE ON THE SHAPES OF LETTERS.

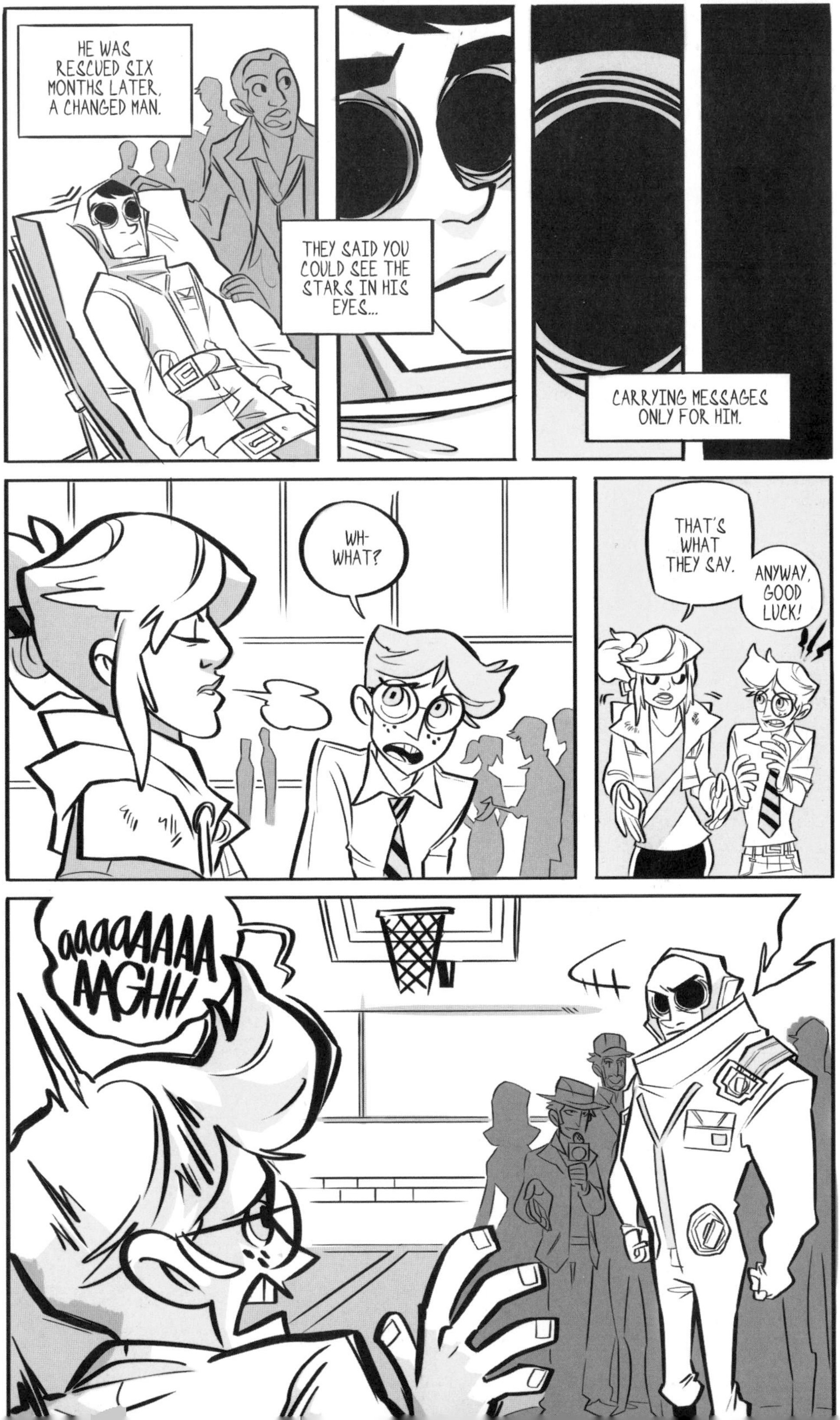
HE WAS RESCUED SIX MONTHS LATER, A CHANGED MAN.
THEY SAID YOU COULD SEE THE STARS IN HIS EYES...
CARRYING MESSAGES ONLY FOR HIM.
WH- WHAT?
THAT'S WHAT THEY SAY.
ANYWAY, GOOD LUCK!
aaaAAAA AAGHH

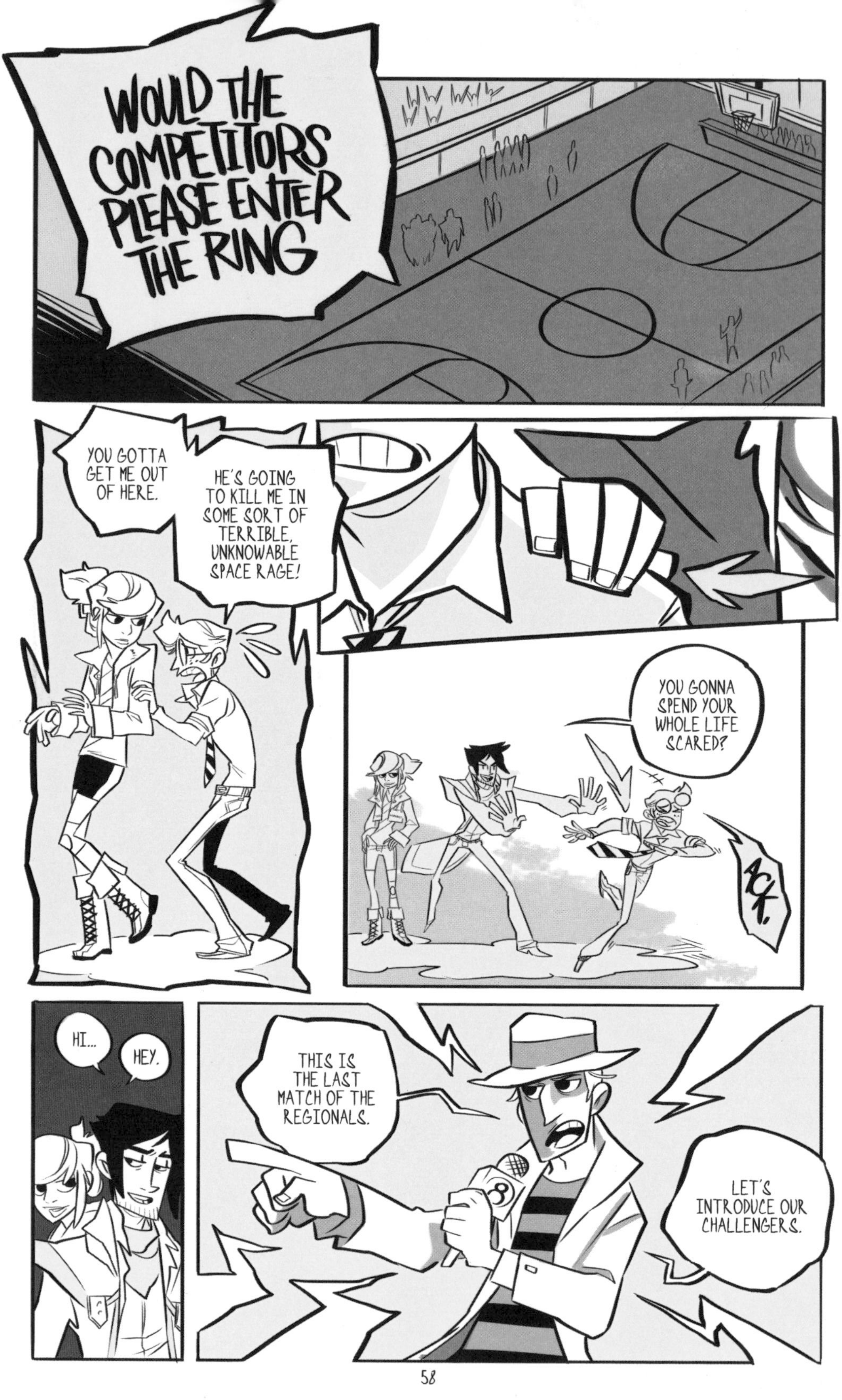
WOULD THE COMPETITORS PLEASE ENTER THE RING
YOU GOTTA GET ME OUT OF HERE.
HE'S GOING TO KILL ME IN SOME SORT OF TERRIBLE, UNKNOWABLE SPACE RAGE!
YOU GONNA SPEND YOUR WHOLE LIFE SCARED?
ACK.
HI...
HEY.
THIS IS THE LAST MATCH OF THE REGIONALS.
LET'S INTRODUCE OUR CHALLENGERS.

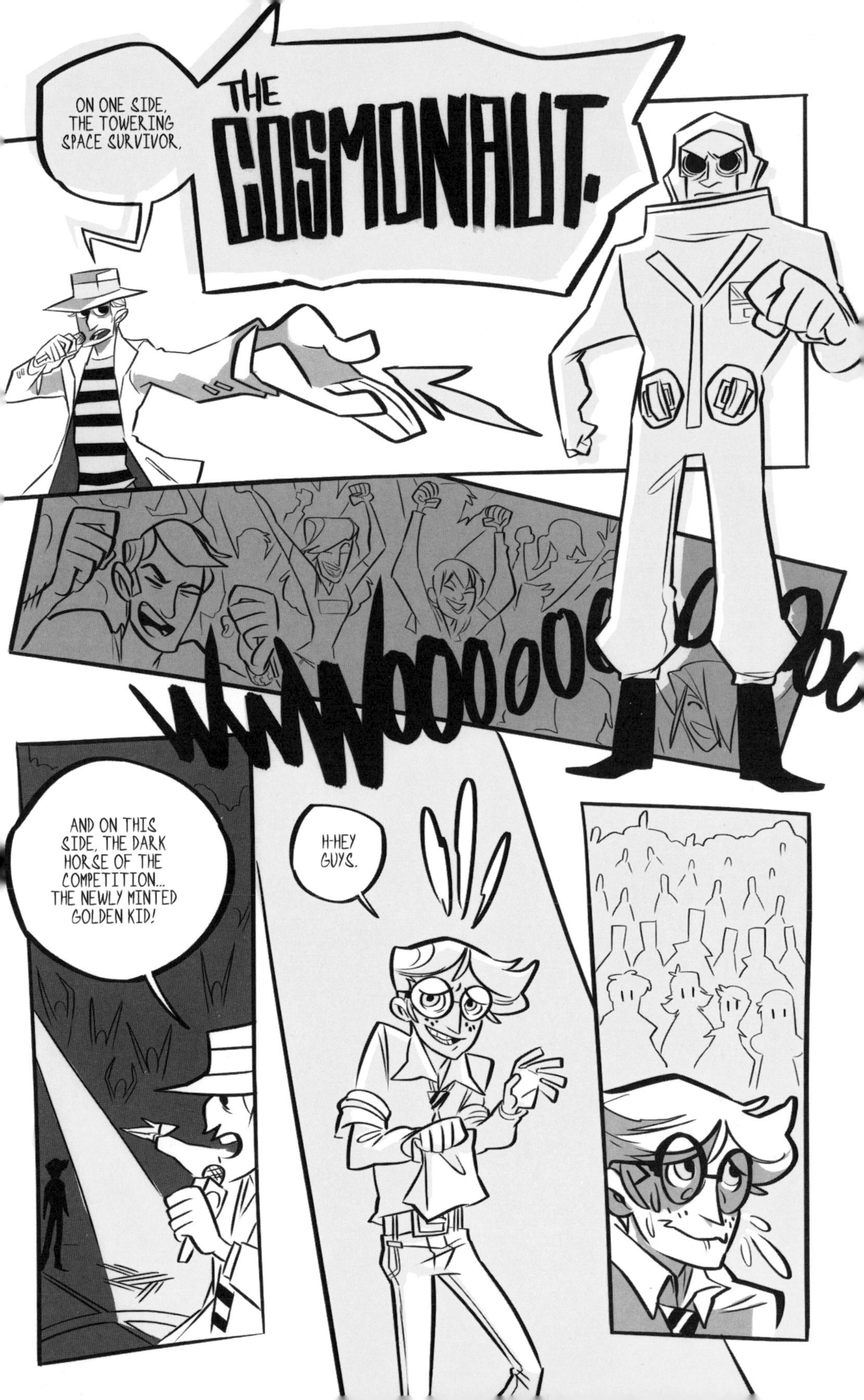

ON ONE SIDE, THE TOWERING SPACE SURVIVOR,
THE COSMONAUT.
WHHWOOOOOOOOOOO
AND ON THIS SIDE, THE DARK HORSE OF THE COMPETITION... THE NEWLY MINTED GOLDEN KID!
H-HEY GUYS.

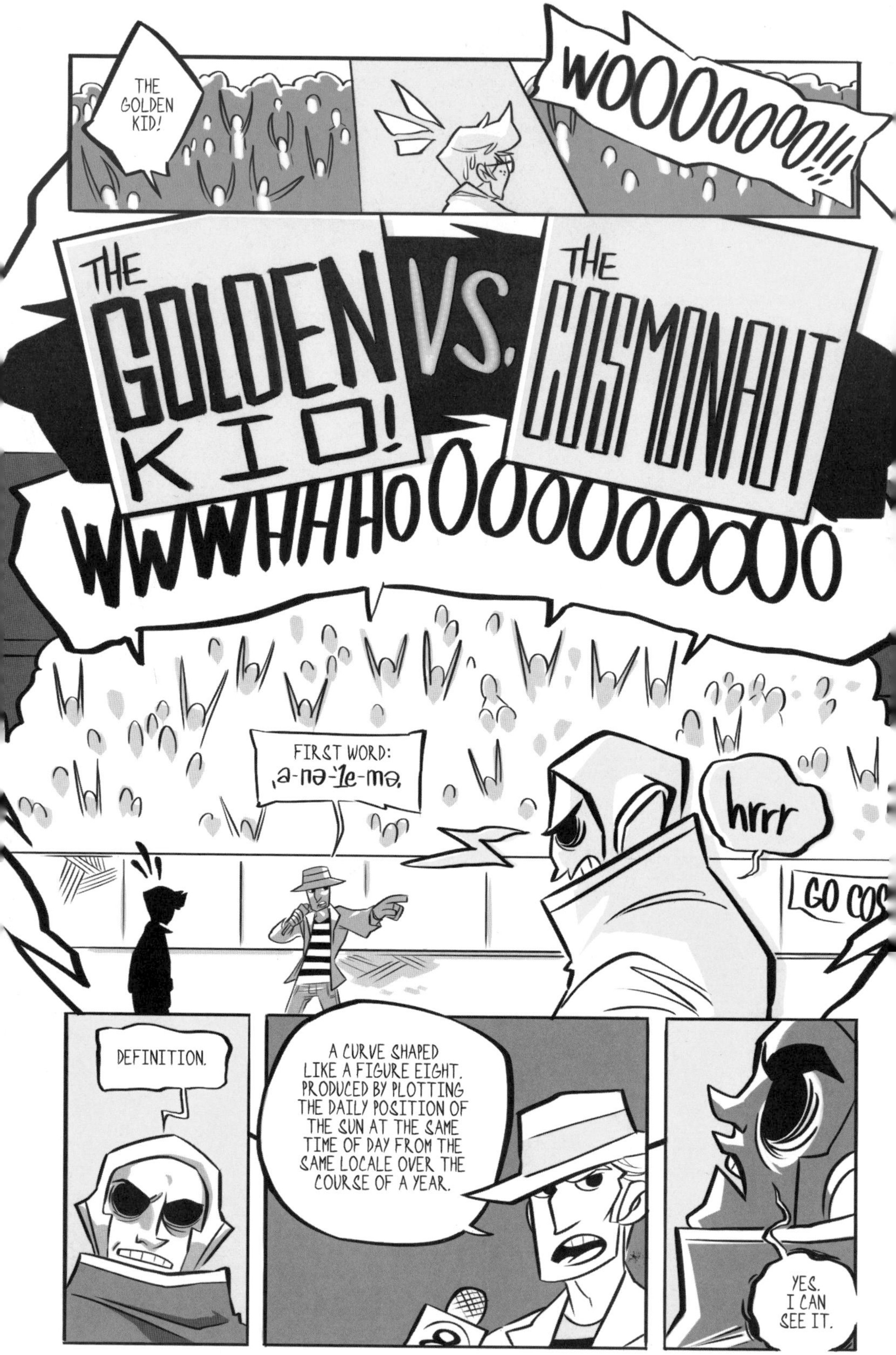
THE GOLDEN KID!
WOOOOOOOO!!!
THE GOLDEN KID!
VS.
THE COSMONAUT
WWWHHHOOOOOOOOOOO
FIRST WORD: ˌa-nə-ˈle-mə
hrrr
GO COS
DEFINITION.
A CURVE SHAPED LIKE A FIGURE EIGHT, PRODUCED BY PLOTTING THE DAILY POSITION OF THE SUN AT THE SAME TIME OF DAY FROM THE SAME LOCALE OVER THE COURSE OF A YEAR.
YES. I CAN SEE IT.

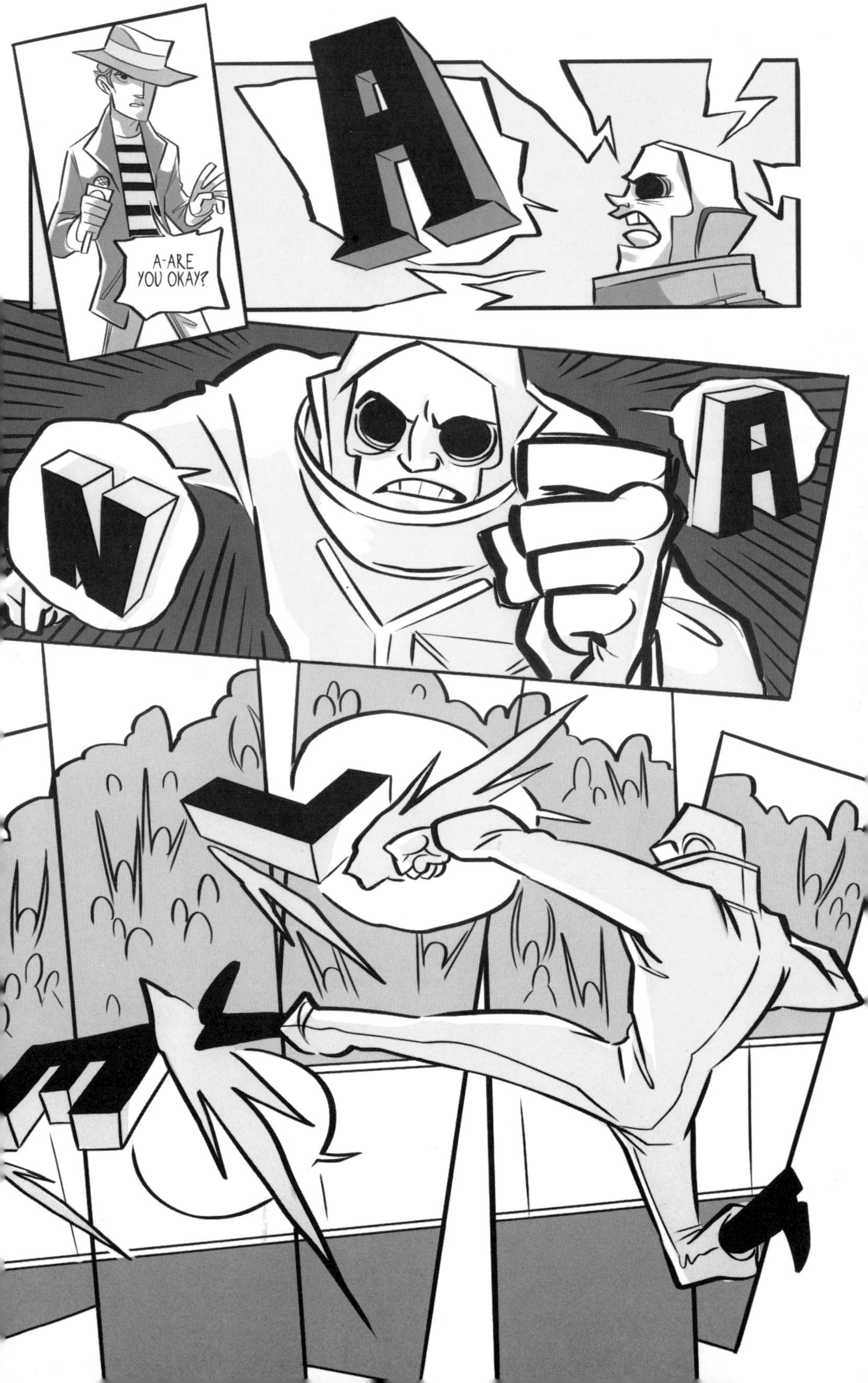
A-ARE
YOU OKAY?

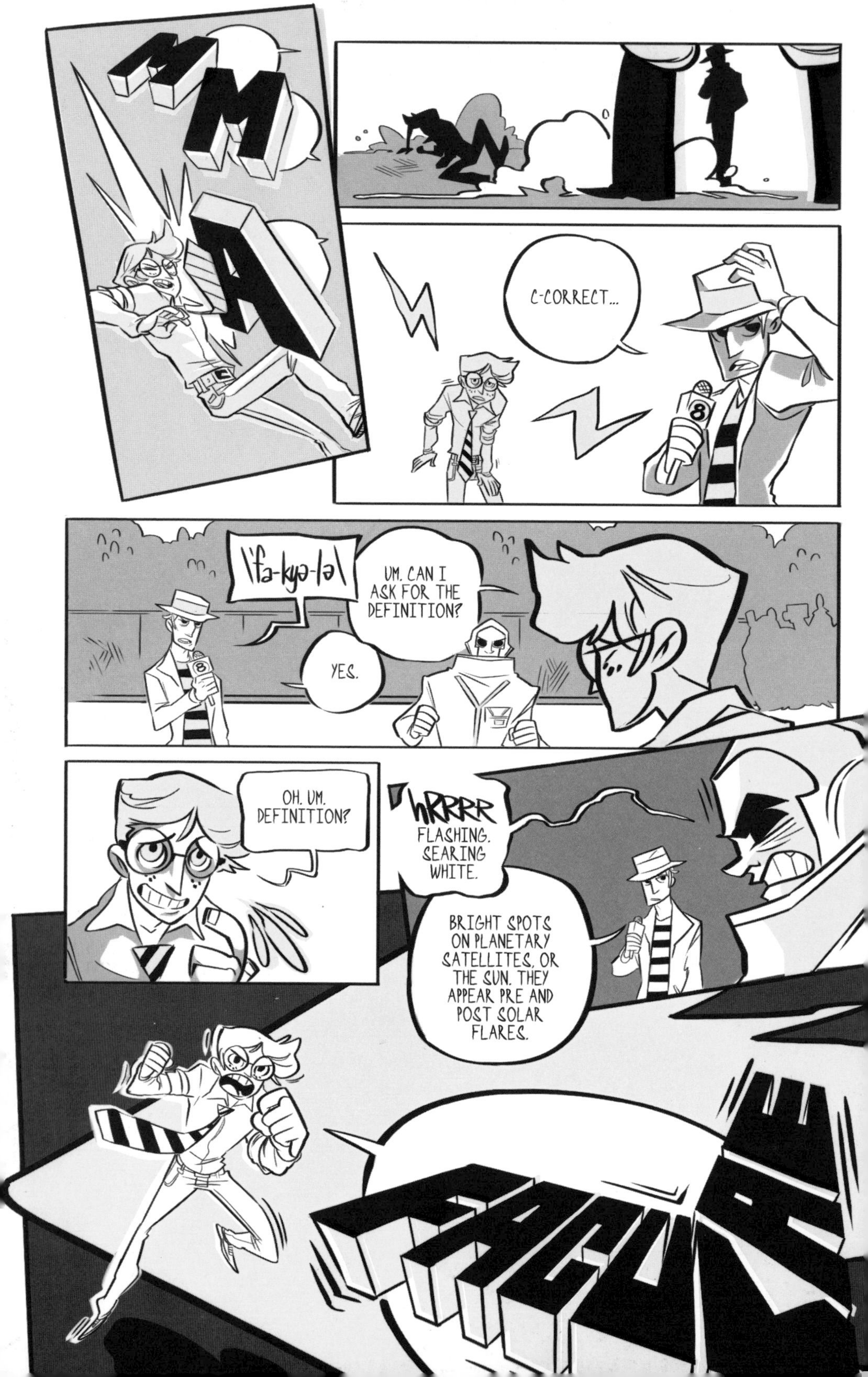
MMA
C-CORRECT...
\'fa-kyə-lə\
UM. CAN I ASK FOR THE DEFINITION?
YES.
OH. UM. DEFINITION?
hRRRR
FLASHING. SEARING WHITE.
BRIGHT SPOTS ON PLANETARY SATELLITES, OR THE SUN. THEY APPEAR PRE AND POST SOLAR FLARES.

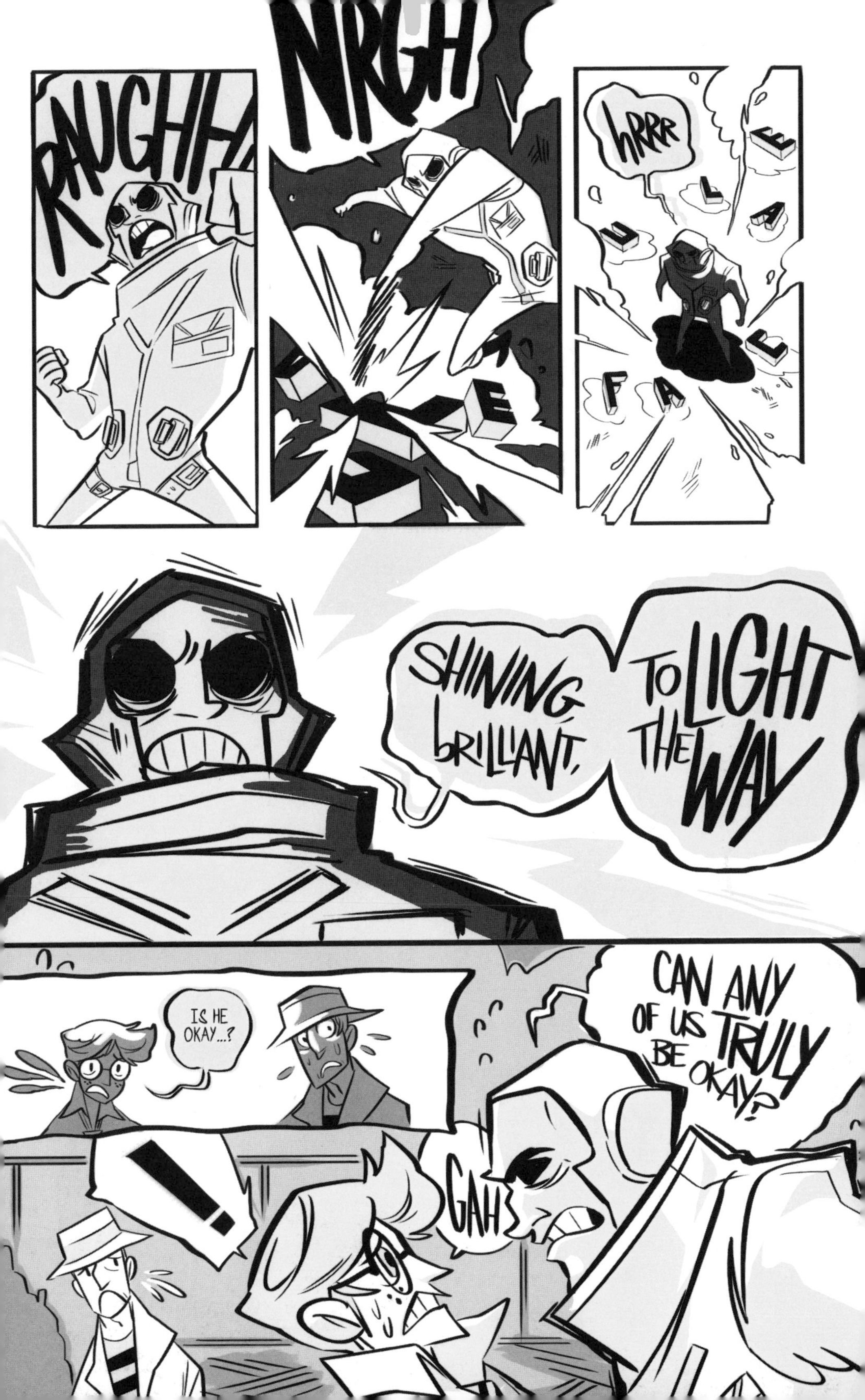
RAUGHH
NRGH
hRRR
U L A E
F A C
SHINING, brilliant,
TO LIGHT THE WAY
IS HE OKAY...?
CAN ANY OF US TRULY BE OKAY?
!
GAH

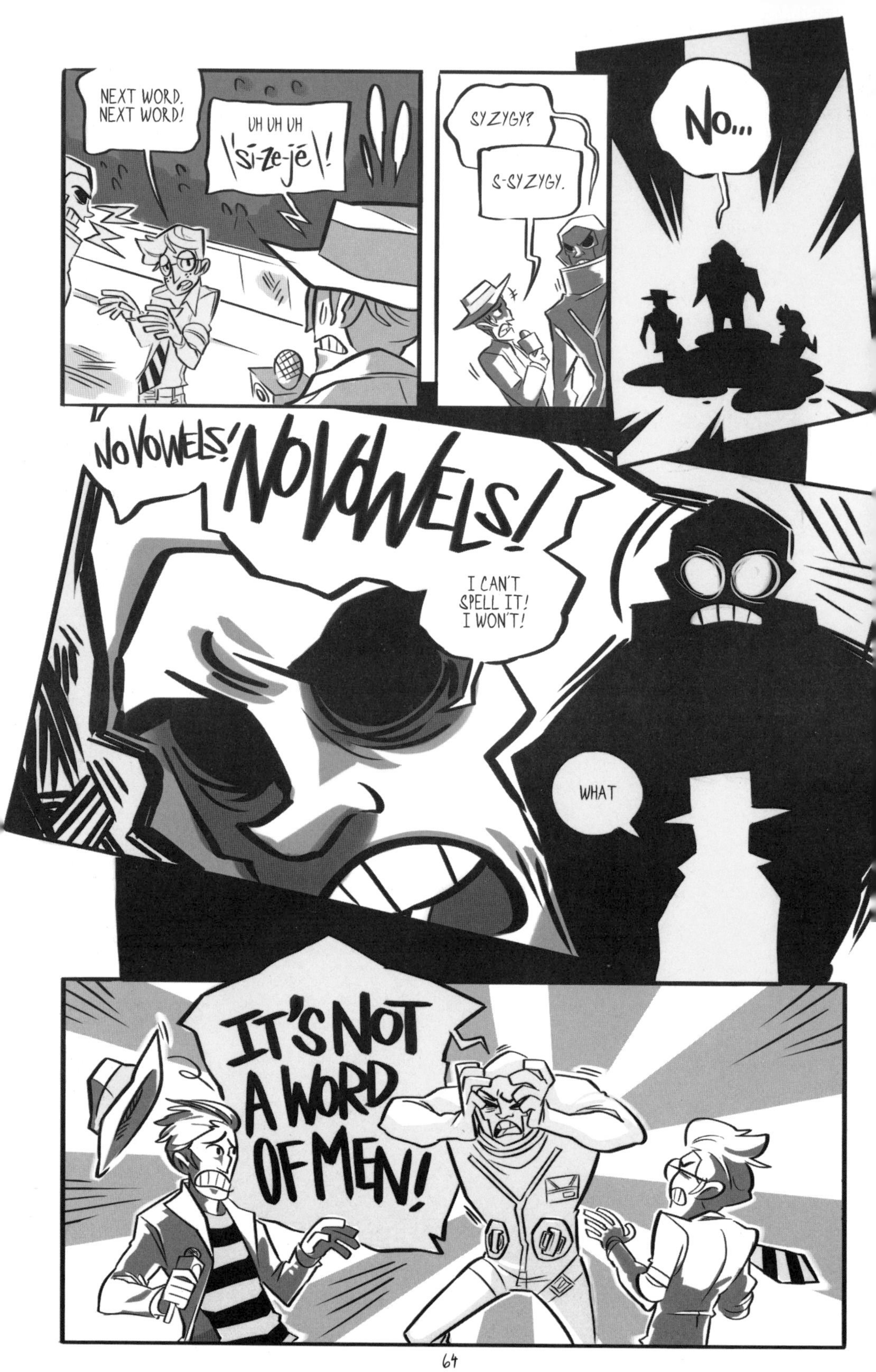
NEXT WORD. NEXT WORD!
UH UH UH \si-ze-jē\!
SYZYGY?
S-SYZYGY.
No...
NO VOWELS!
NO VOWELS!
I CAN'T SPELL IT! I WON'T!
WHAT
IT'S NOT A WORD OF MEN!

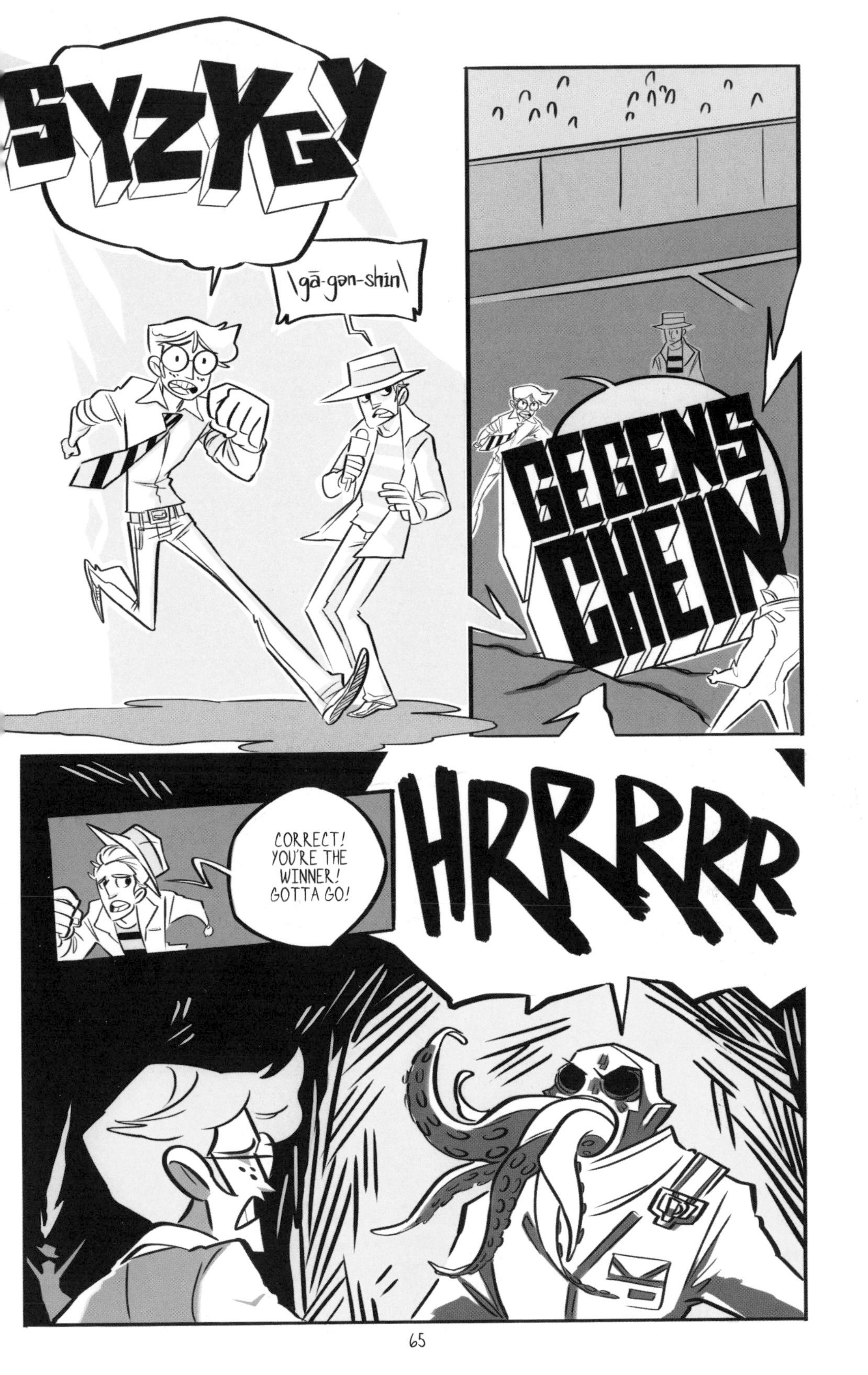
SYZYGY
\gā-gən-shīn\
GEGENSCHEIN
CORRECT! YOU'RE THE WINNER! GOTTA GO!
HRRRRR

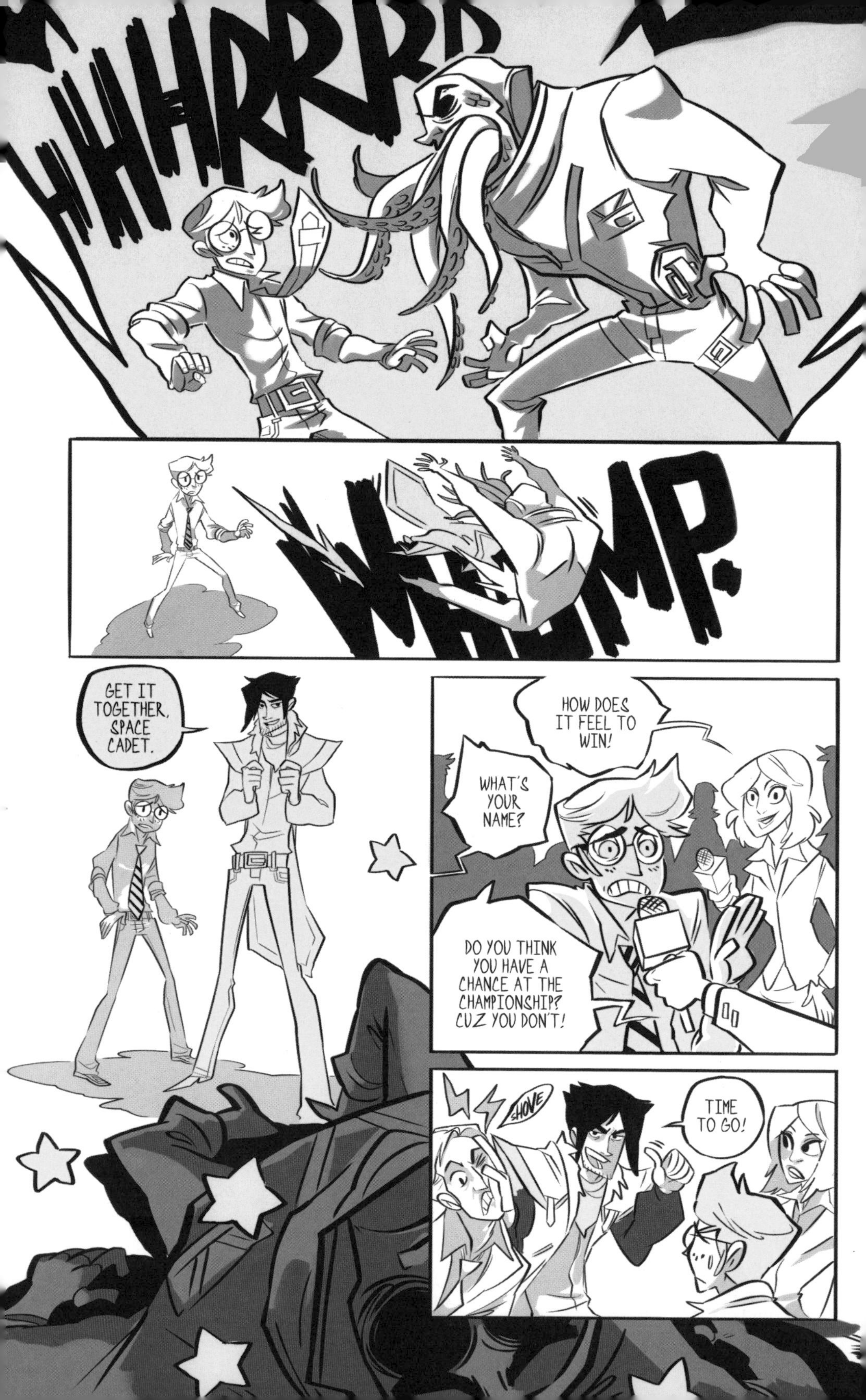
WHHHRRRR
WHUMP
GET IT TOGETHER, SPACE CADET.
HOW DOES IT FEEL TO WIN!
WHAT'S YOUR NAME?
DO YOU THINK YOU HAVE A CHANCE AT THE CHAMPIONSHIP? CUZ YOU DON'T!
SHOVE
TIME TO GO!

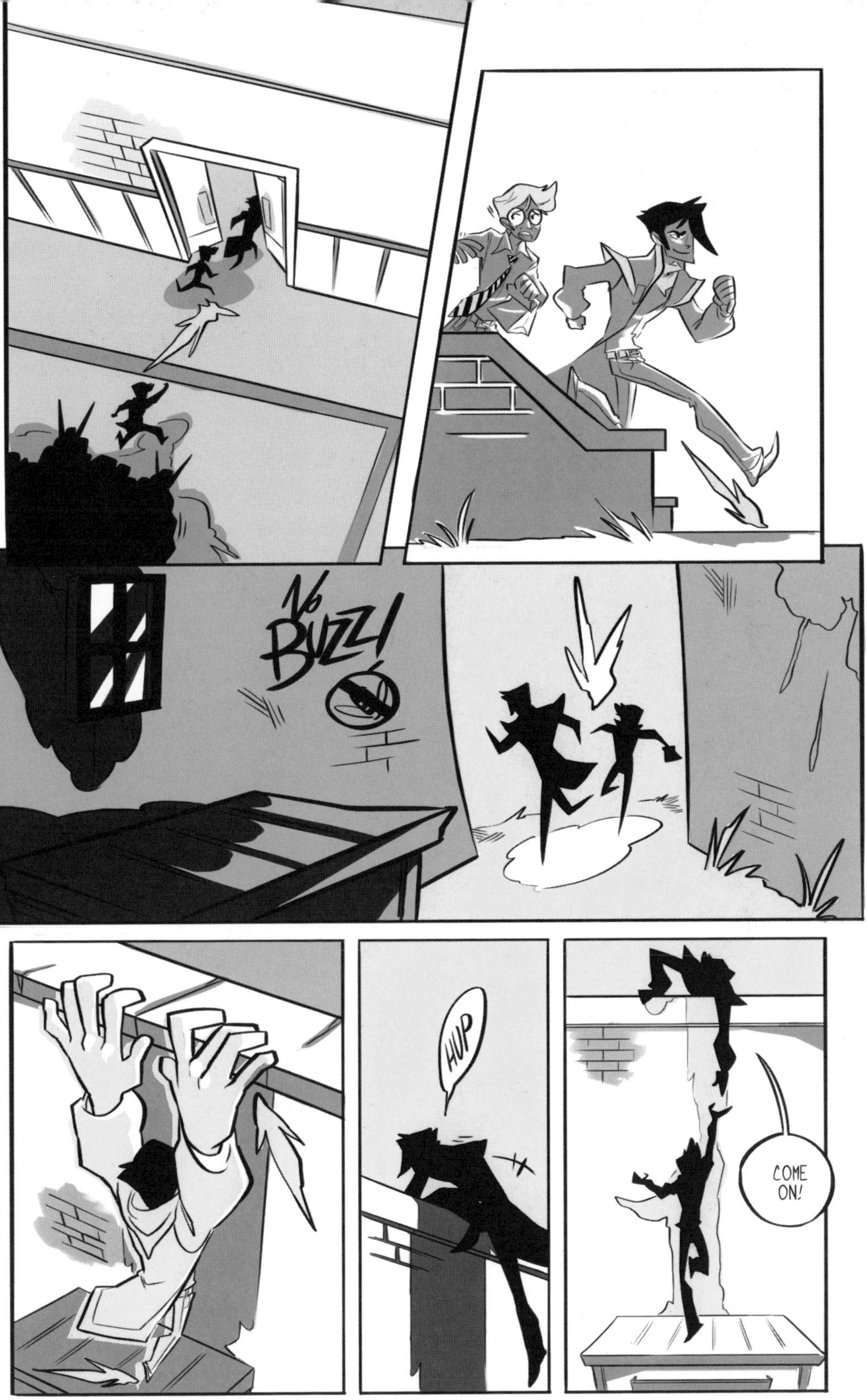
NO BUZZ!
HUP
COME ON!

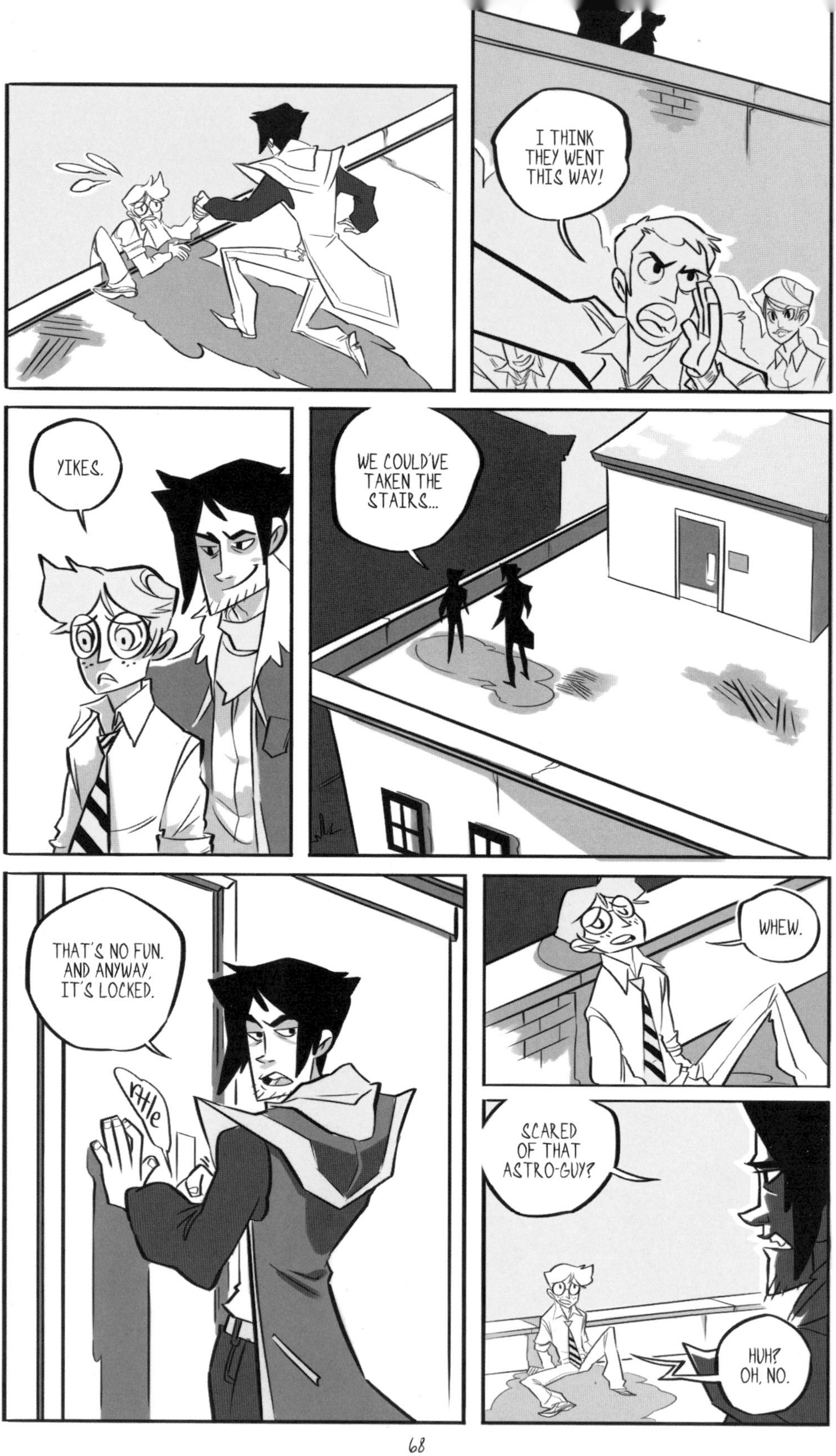
I THINK THEY WENT THIS WAY!
YIKES.
WE COULD'VE TAKEN THE STAIRS...
THAT'S NO FUN. AND ANYWAY, IT'S LOCKED.
rttle
WHEW.
SCARED OF THAT ASTRO-GUY?
HUH? OH, NO.

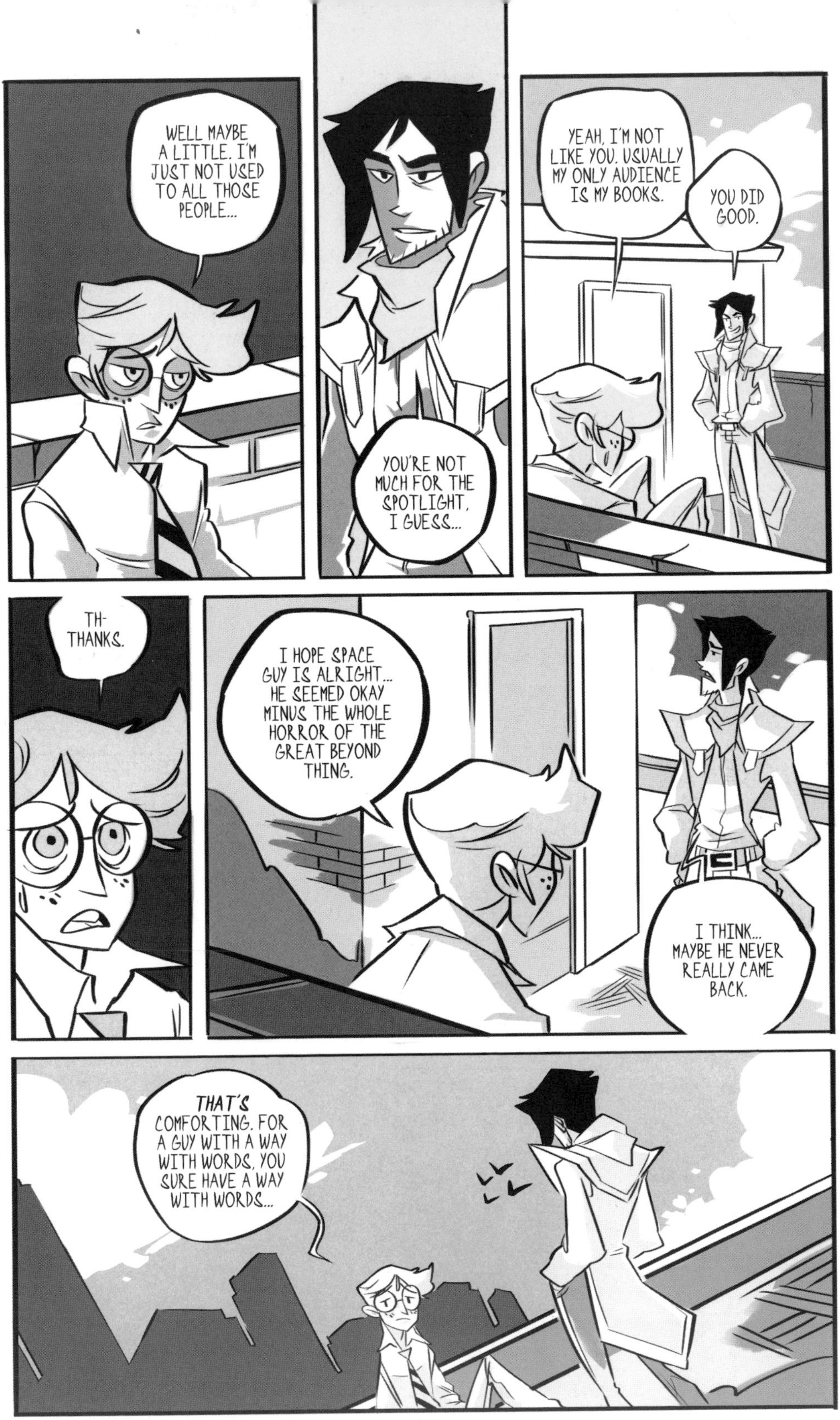
WELL MAYBE A LITTLE. I'M JUST NOT USED TO ALL THOSE PEOPLE...
YOU'RE NOT MUCH FOR THE SPOTLIGHT, I GUESS...
YEAH, I'M NOT LIKE YOU. USUALLY MY ONLY AUDIENCE IS MY BOOKS.
YOU DID GOOD.
TH- THANKS.
I HOPE SPACE GUY IS ALRIGHT... HE SEEMED OKAY MINUS THE WHOLE HORROR OF THE GREAT BEYOND THING.
I THINK... MAYBE HE NEVER REALLY CAME BACK.
THAT'S COMFORTING. FOR A GUY WITH A WAY WITH WORDS, YOU SURE HAVE A WAY WITH WORDS...

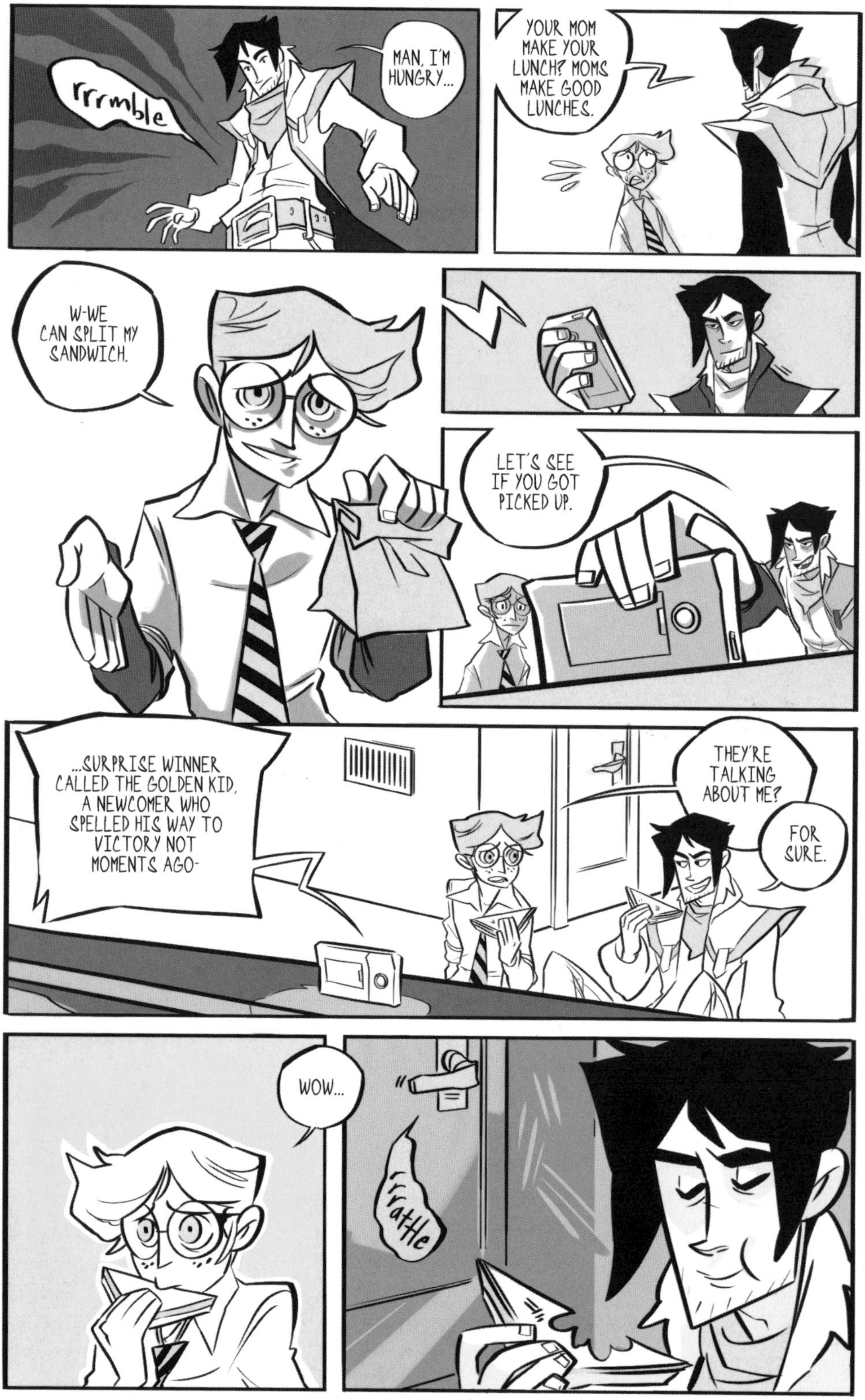
rrrmble
MAN, I'M HUNGRY...
YOUR MOM MAKE YOUR LUNCH? MOMS MAKE GOOD LUNCHES.
W-WE CAN SPLIT MY SANDWICH.
LET'S SEE IF YOU GOT PICKED UP.
...SURPRISE WINNER CALLED THE GOLDEN KID, A NEWCOMER WHO SPELLED HIS WAY TO VICTORY NOT MOMENTS AGO-
THEY'RE TALKING ABOUT ME?
FOR SURE.
WOW...
rrattle

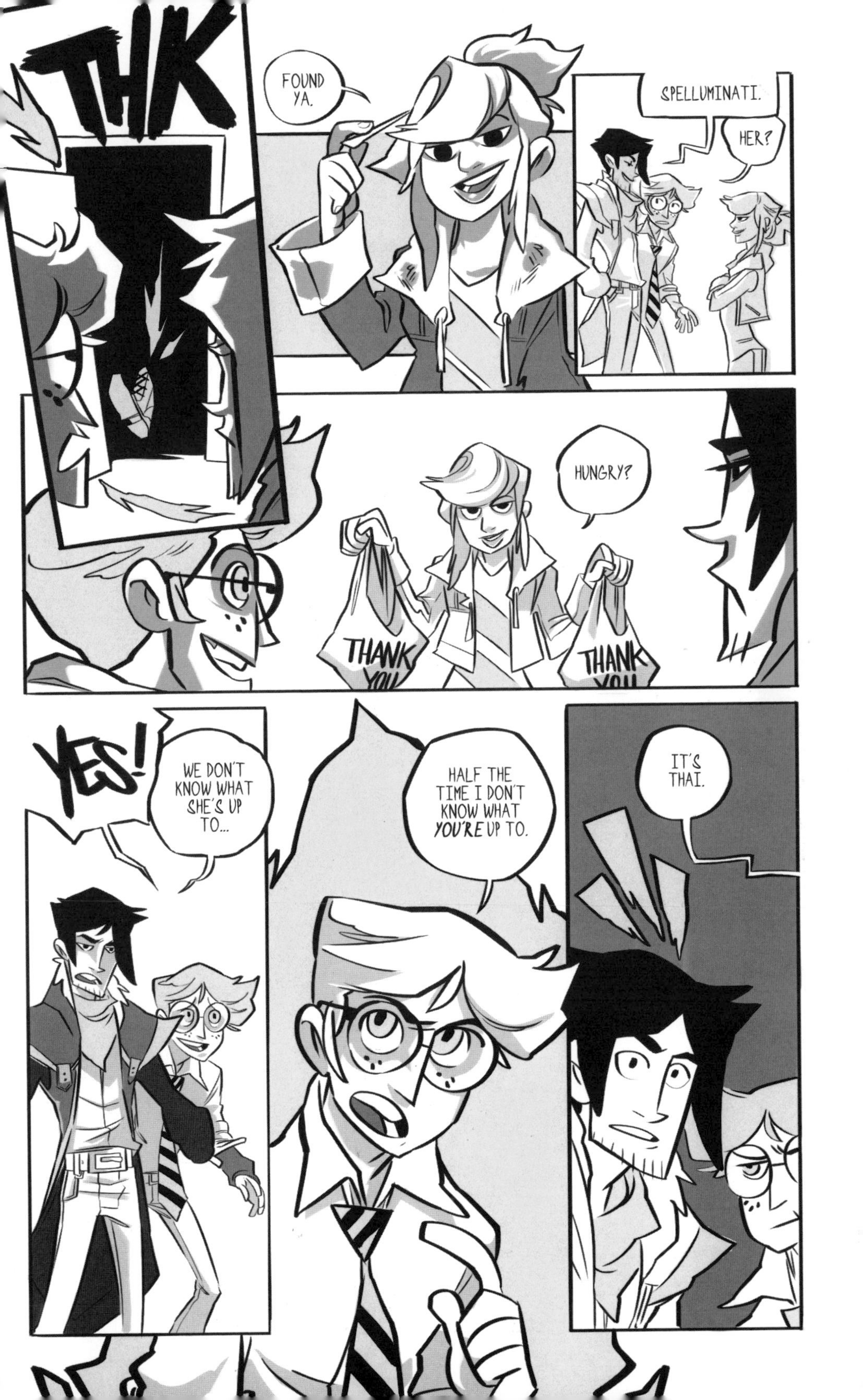
THK
FOUND YA.
SPELLUMINATI.
HER?
HUNGRY?
THANK YOU
THANK YOU
YES!
WE DON'T KNOW WHAT SHE'S UP TO...
HALF THE TIME I DON'T KNOW WHAT *YOU'RE* UP TO.
IT'S THAI.

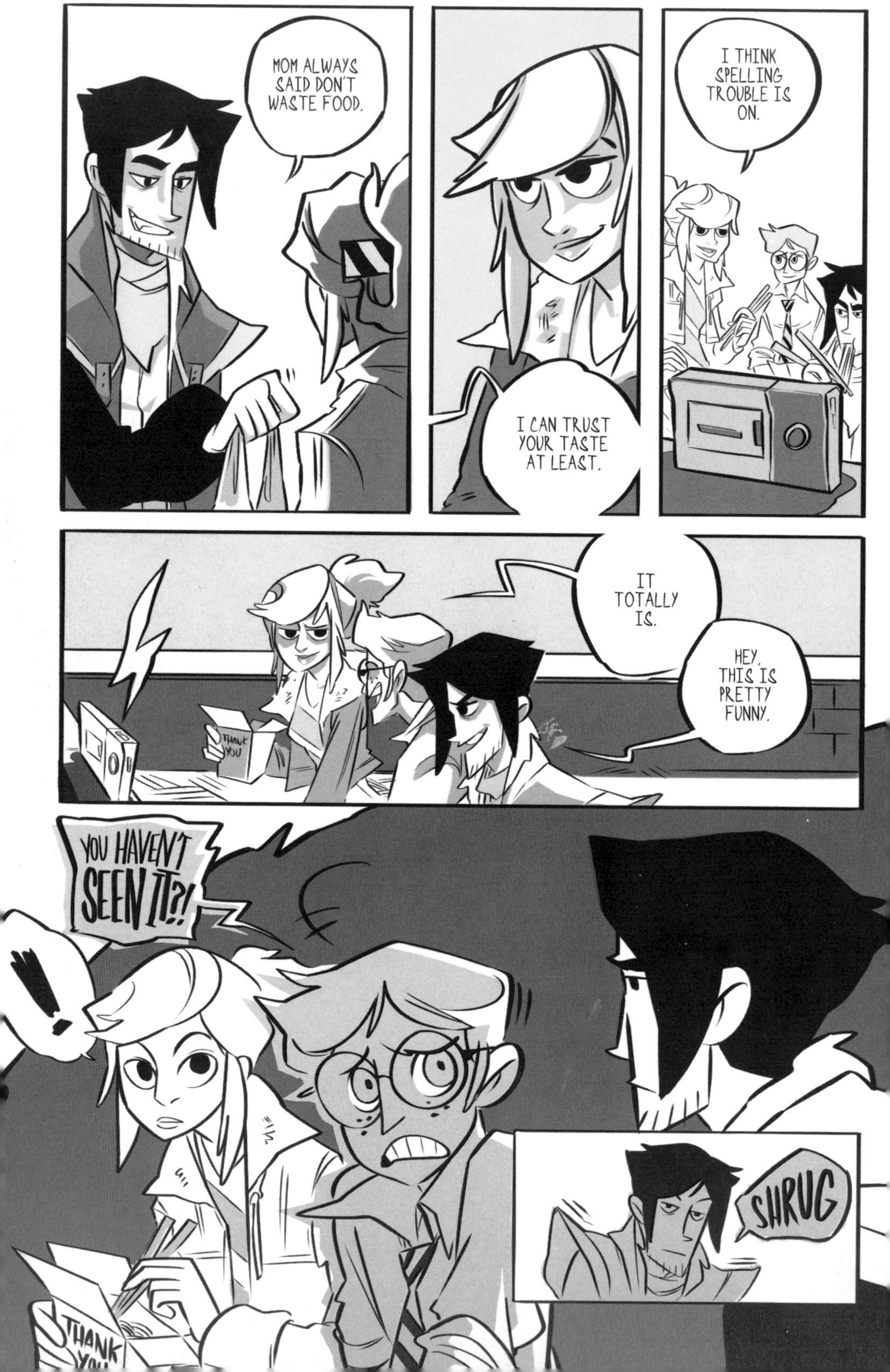
MOM ALWAYS SAID DON'T WASTE FOOD.
I CAN TRUST YOUR TASTE AT LEAST.
I THINK SPELLING TROUBLE IS ON.
IT TOTALLY IS.
HEY, THIS IS PRETTY FUNNY.
THANK YOU
YOU HAVEN'T SEEN IT?!
!
THANK YOU
SHRUG

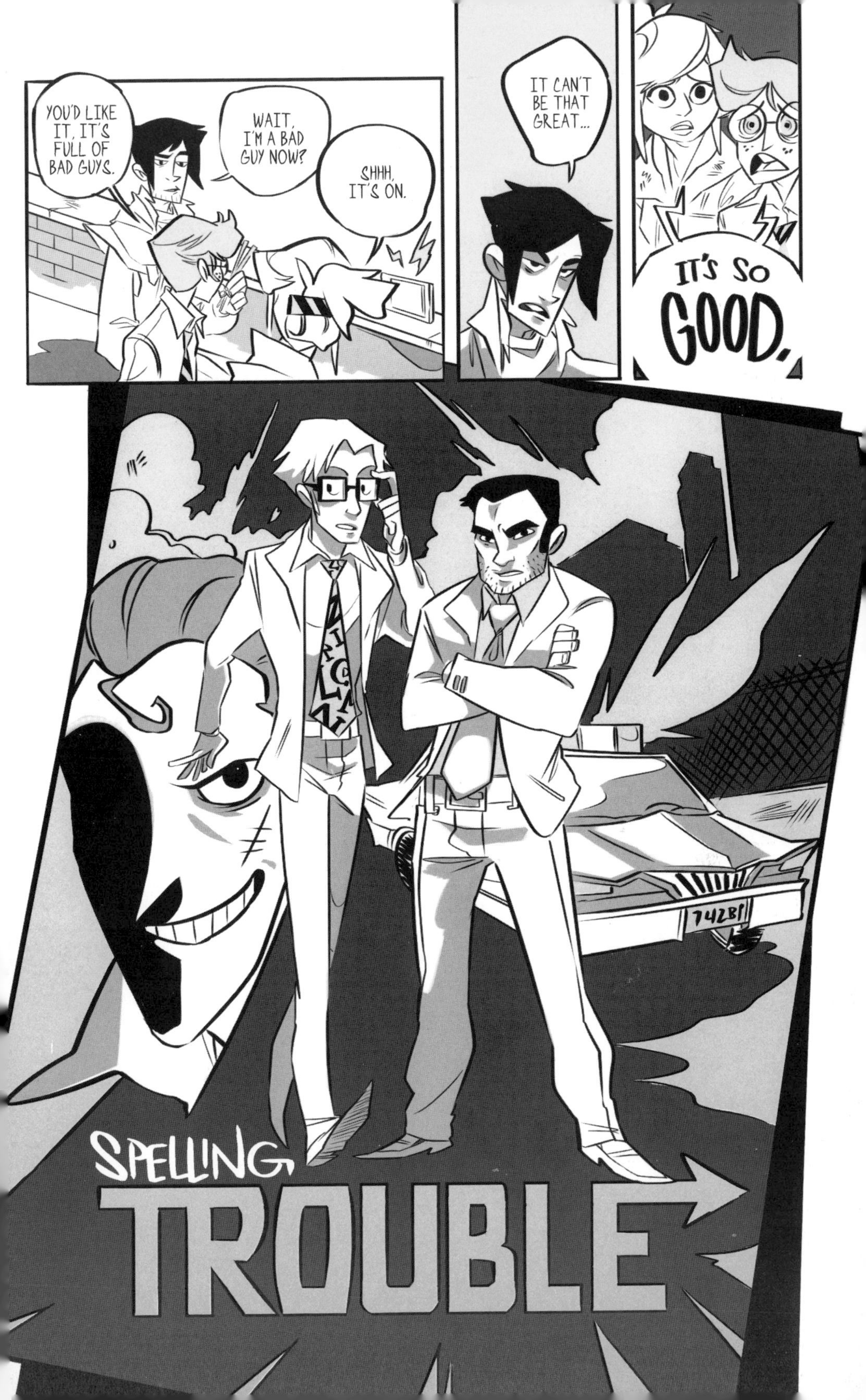
YOU'D LIKE IT, IT'S FULL OF BAD GUYS.
WAIT, I'M A BAD GUY NOW?
SHHH, IT'S ON.
IT CAN'T BE THAT GREAT...
IT'S SO GOOD.
742BI
SPELLING
TROUBLE

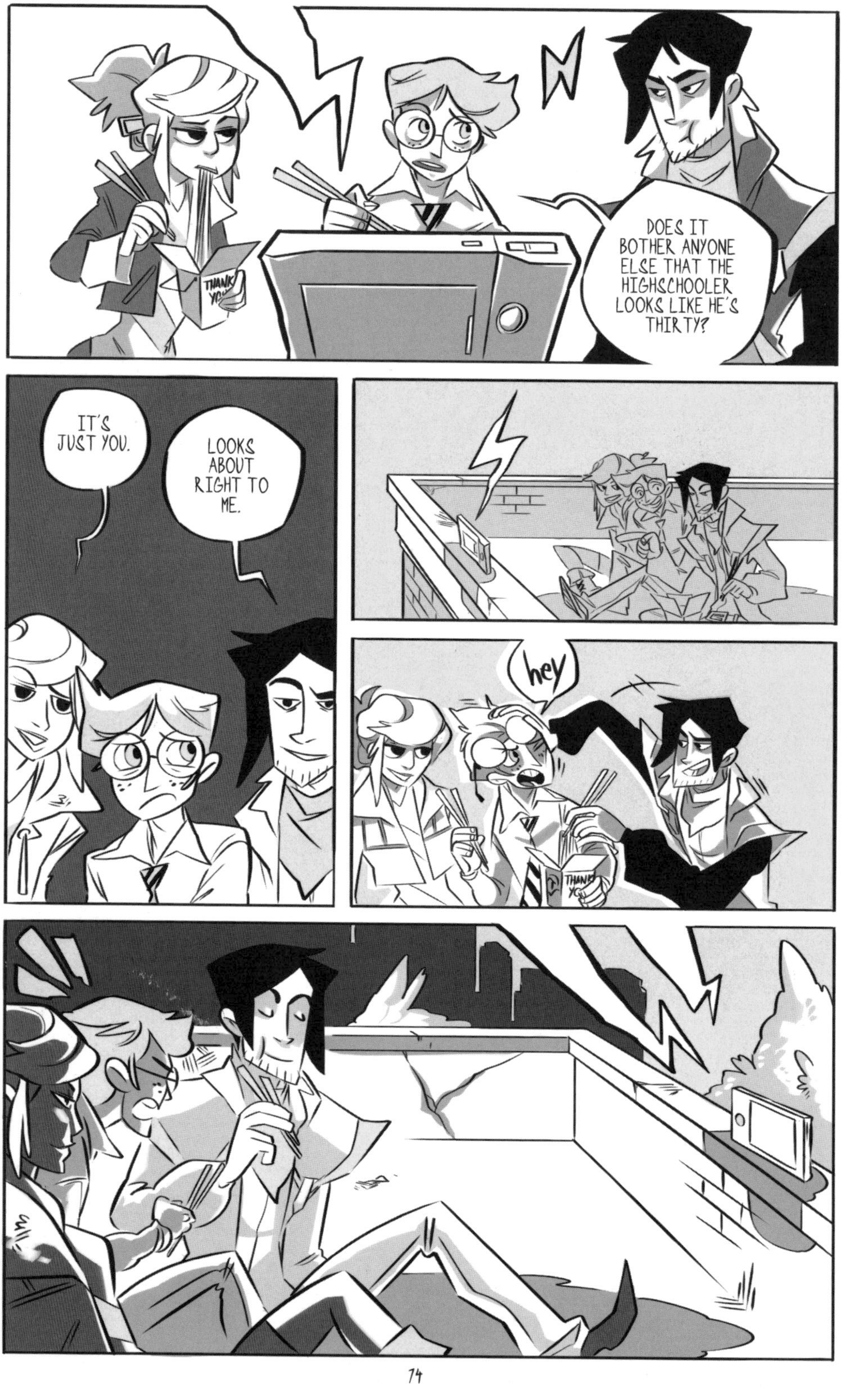
THANK YOU
DOES IT BOTHER ANYONE ELSE THAT THE HIGHSCHOOLER LOOKS LIKE HE'S THIRTY?
IT'S JUST YOU.
LOOKS ABOUT RIGHT TO ME.
hey
THANK YOU

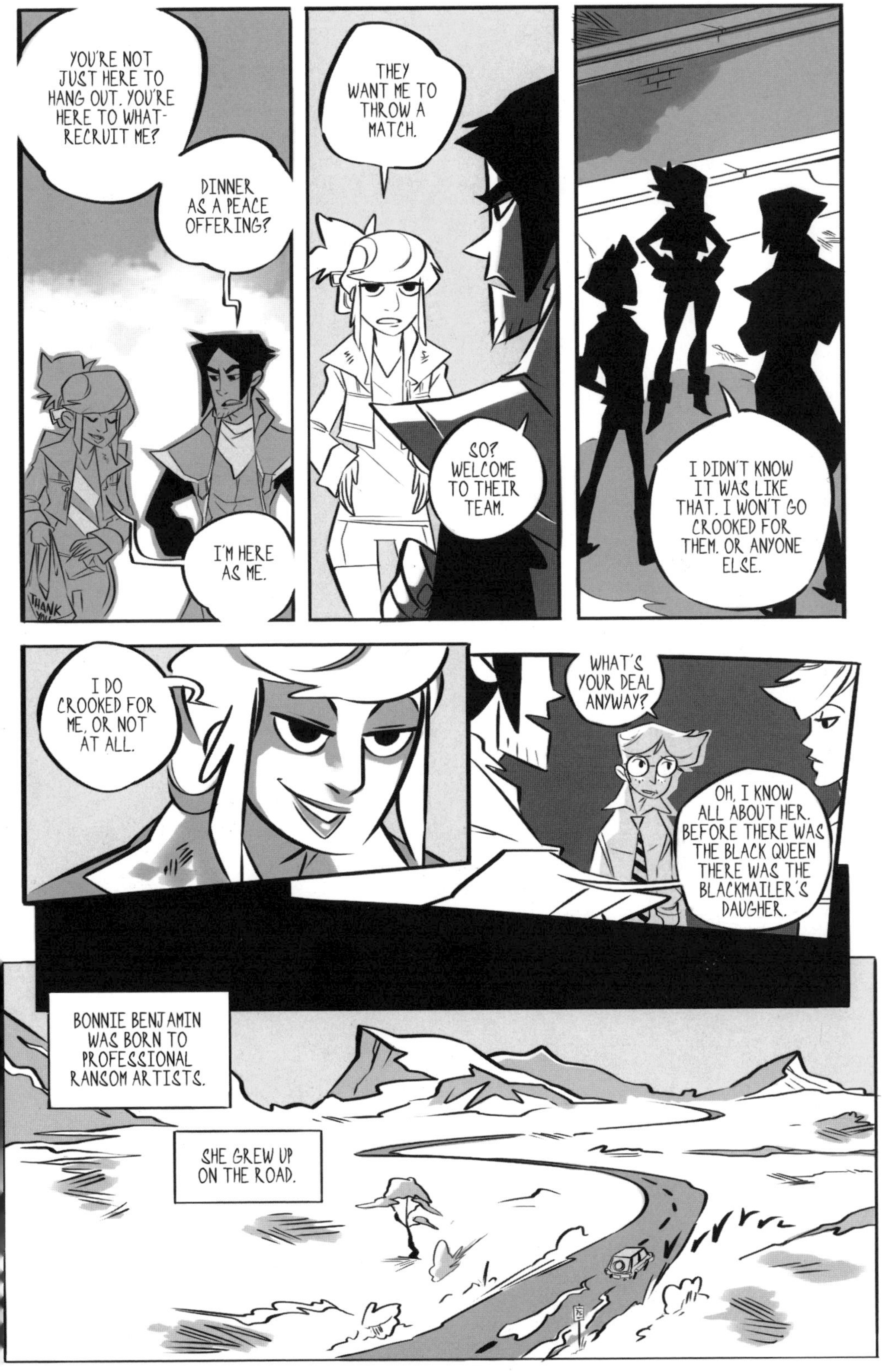
YOU'RE NOT JUST HERE TO HANG OUT. YOU'RE HERE TO WHAT- RECRUIT ME?
DINNER AS A PEACE OFFERING?
THANK YOU
I'M HERE AS ME.
THEY WANT ME TO THROW A MATCH.
SO? WELCOME TO THEIR TEAM.
I DIDN'T KNOW IT WAS LIKE THAT. I WON'T GO CROOKED FOR THEM. OR ANYONE ELSE.
I DO CROOKED FOR ME, OR NOT AT ALL.
WHAT'S YOUR DEAL ANYWAY?
OH, I KNOW ALL ABOUT HER. BEFORE THERE WAS THE BLACK QUEEN THERE WAS THE BLACKMAILER'S DAUGHER.
BONNIE BENJAMIN WAS BORN TO PROFESSIONAL RANSOM ARTISTS.
SHE GREW UP ON THE ROAD.

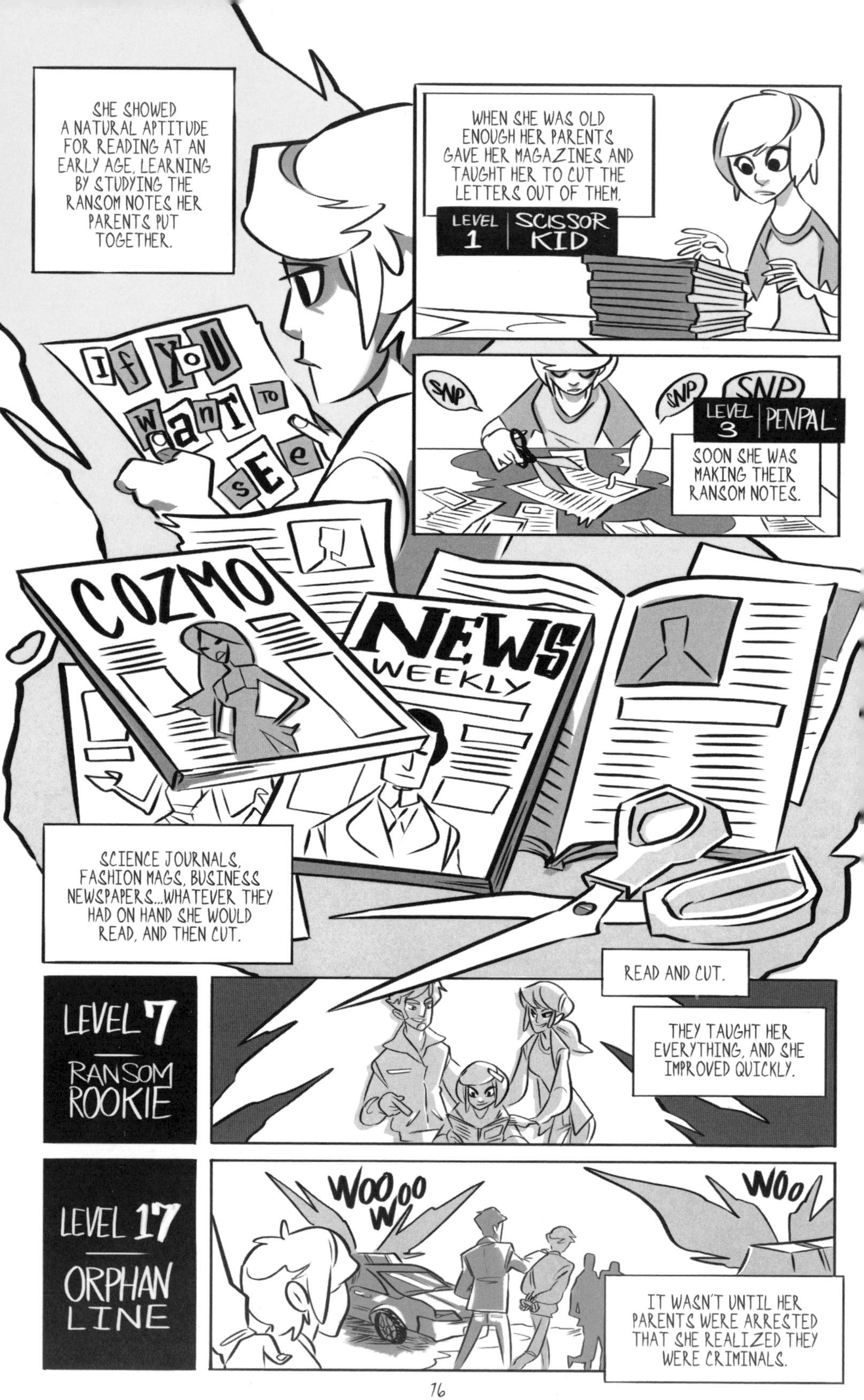

SHE SHOWED A NATURAL APTITUDE FOR READING AT AN EARLY AGE, LEARNING BY STUDYING THE RANSOM NOTES HER PARENTS PUT TOGETHER.
If YoU want TO sEe
WHEN SHE WAS OLD ENOUGH HER PARENTS GAVE HER MAGAZINES AND TAUGHT HER TO CUT THE LETTERS OUT OF THEM.
LEVEL 1 SCISSOR KID
SNP
SNP
SNP
LEVEL 3 PENPAL
SOON SHE WAS MAKING THEIR RANSOM NOTES.
COZMO
NEWS WEEKLY
SCIENCE JOURNALS, FASHION MAGS, BUSINESS NEWSPAPERS...WHATEVER THEY HAD ON HAND SHE WOULD READ, AND THEN CUT.
READ AND CUT.
LEVEL 7 RANSOM ROOKIE
THEY TAUGHT HER EVERYTHING, AND SHE IMPROVED QUICKLY.
LEVEL 17 ORPHAN LINE
WOOWOO
WOO
IT WASN'T UNTIL HER PARENTS WERE ARRESTED THAT SHE REALIZED THEY WERE CRIMINALS.

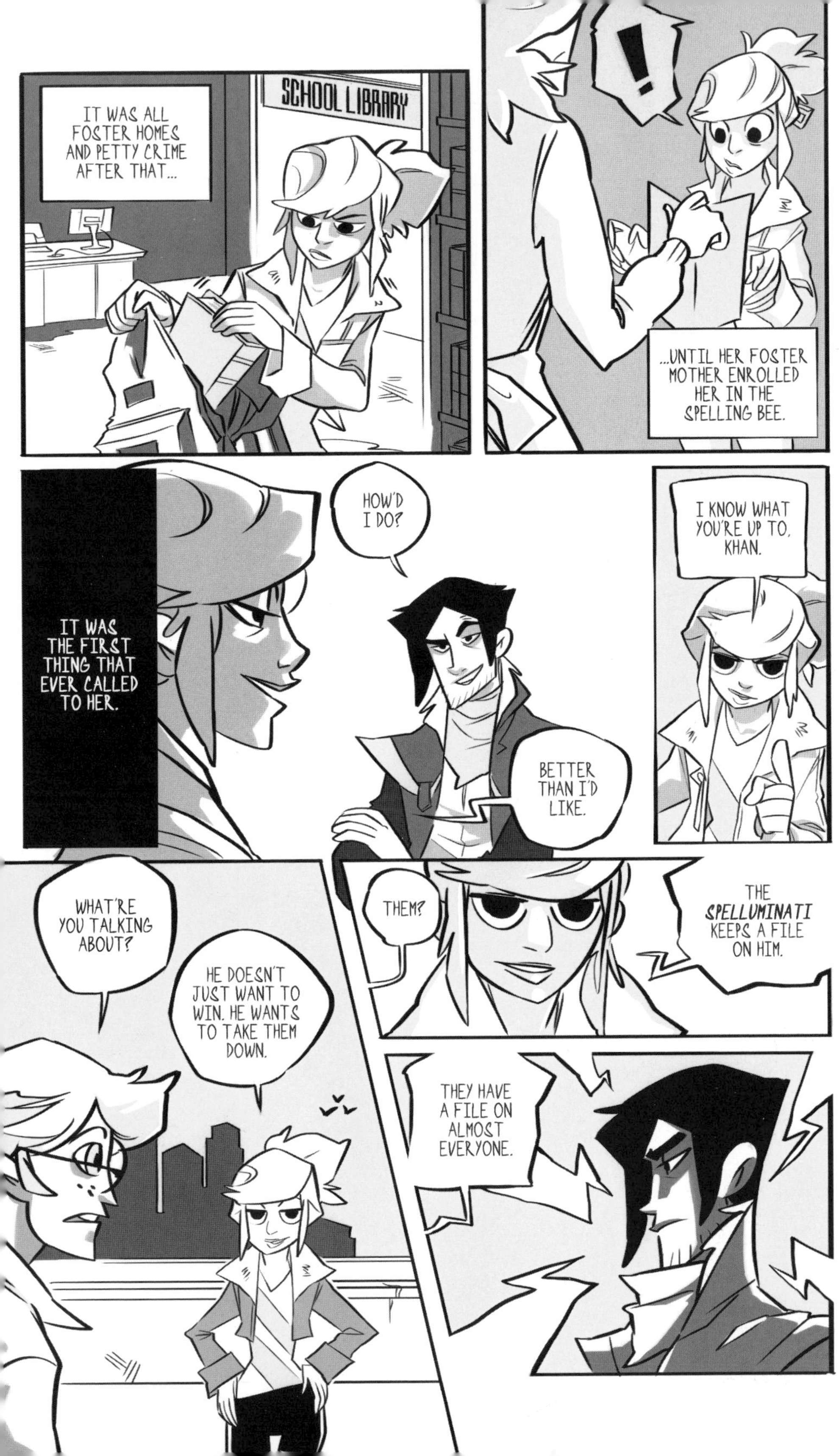
SCHOOL LIBRARY
IT WAS ALL FOSTER HOMES AND PETTY CRIME AFTER THAT...
!
...UNTIL HER FOSTER MOTHER ENROLLED HER IN THE SPELLING BEE.
IT WAS THE FIRST THING THAT EVER CALLED TO HER.
HOW'D I DO?
BETTER THAN I'D LIKE.
I KNOW WHAT YOU'RE UP TO, KHAN.
WHAT'RE YOU TALKING ABOUT?
HE DOESN'T JUST WANT TO WIN. HE WANTS TO TAKE THEM DOWN.
THEM?
THE *SPELLUMINATI* KEEPS A FILE ON HIM.
THEY HAVE A FILE ON ALMOST EVERYONE.

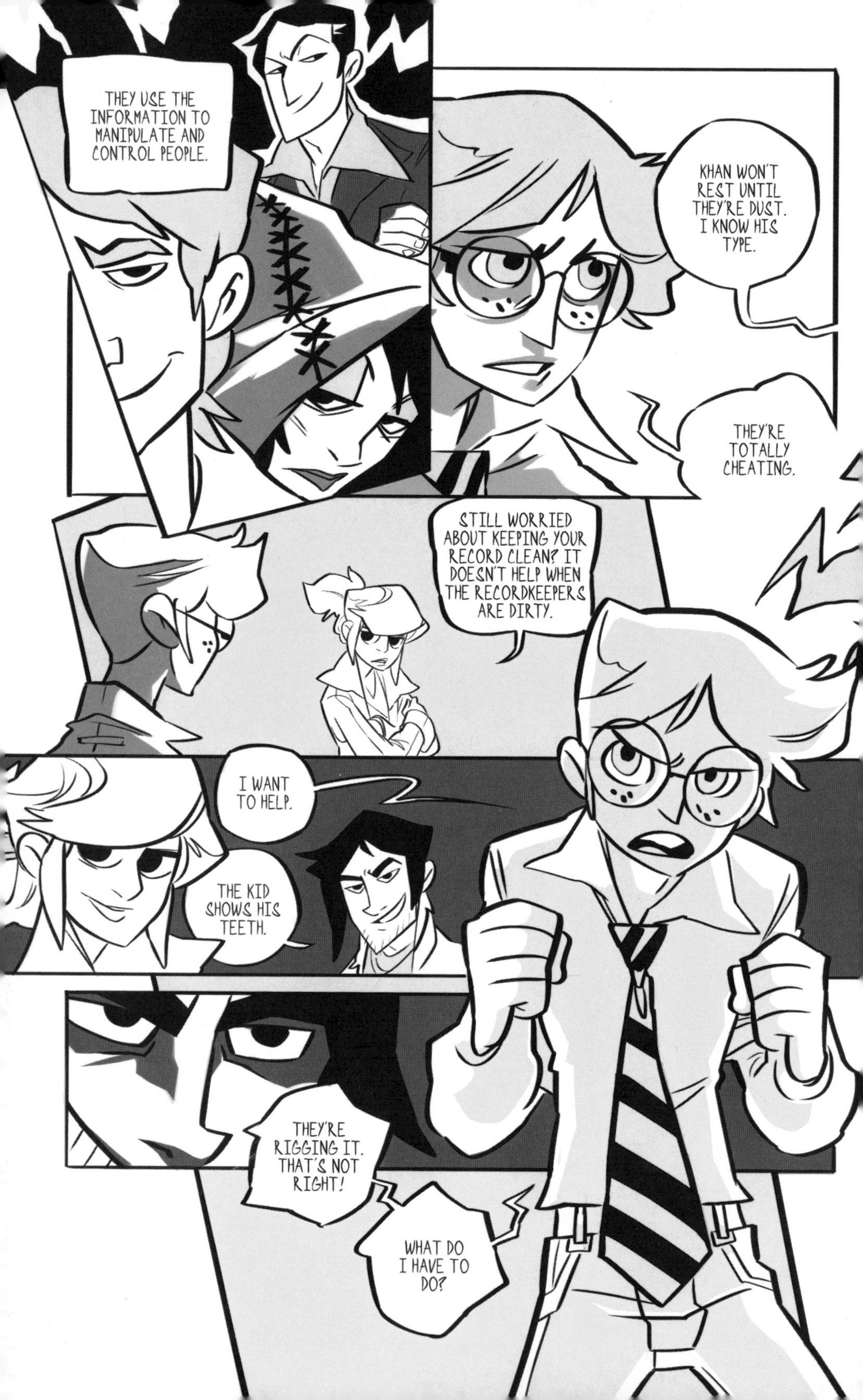
THEY USE THE INFORMATION TO MANIPULATE AND CONTROL PEOPLE.
KHAN WON'T REST UNTIL THEY'RE DUST. I KNOW HIS TYPE.
THEY'RE TOTALLY CHEATING.
STILL WORRIED ABOUT KEEPING YOUR RECORD CLEAN? IT DOESN'T HELP WHEN THE RECORDKEEPERS ARE DIRTY.
I WANT TO HELP.
THE KID SHOWS HIS TEETH.
THEY'RE RIGGING IT. THAT'S NOT RIGHT!
WHAT DO I HAVE TO DO?

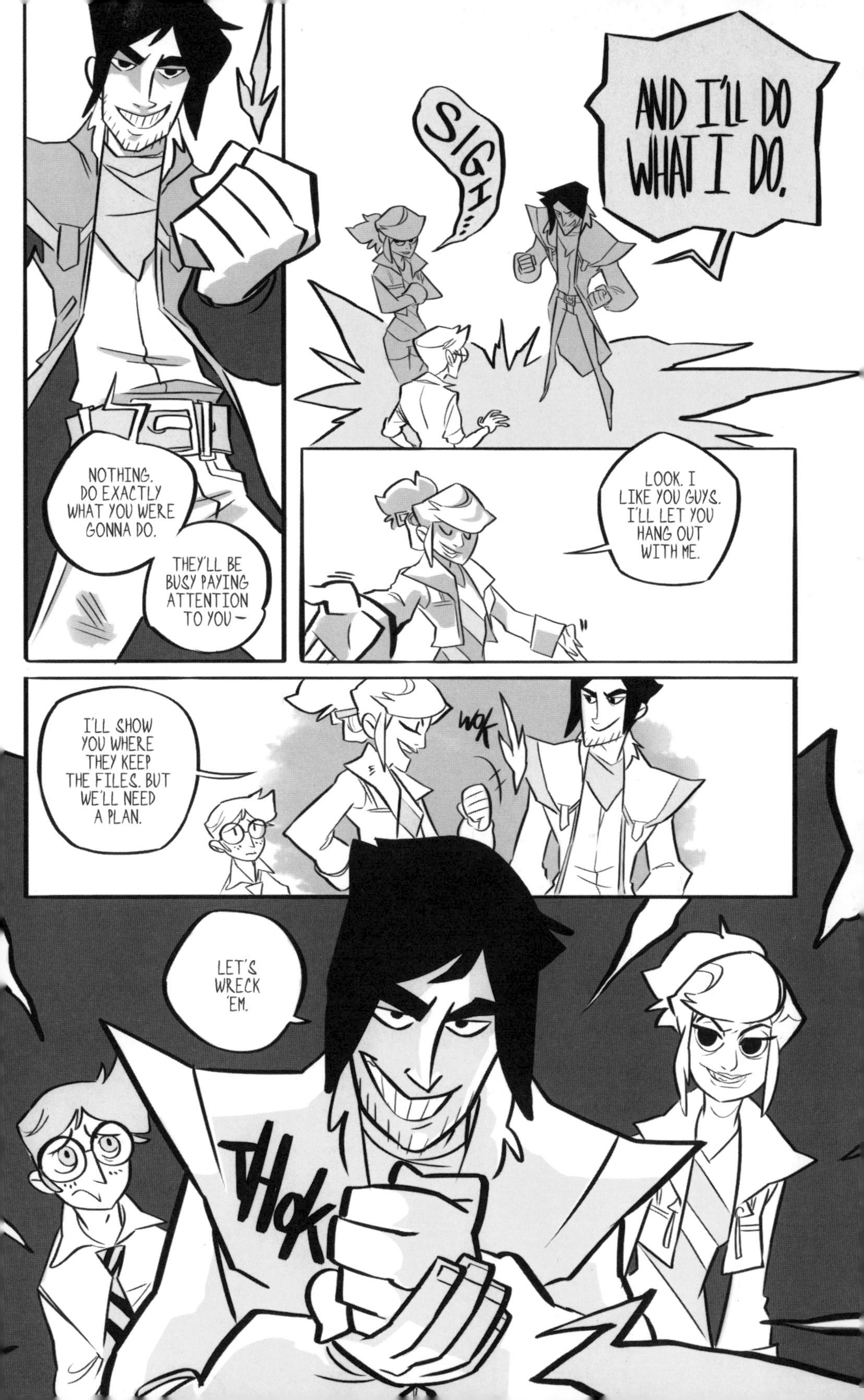
SIGI...
AND I'LL DO WHAT I DO.
NOTHING. DO EXACTLY WHAT YOU WERE GONNA DO.
THEY'LL BE BUSY PAYING ATTENTION TO YOU—
LOOK. I LIKE YOU GUYS. I'LL LET YOU HANG OUT WITH ME.
I'LL SHOW YOU WHERE THEY KEEP THE FILES. BUT WE'LL NEED A PLAN.
WOK
LET'S WRECK 'EM.
THOK

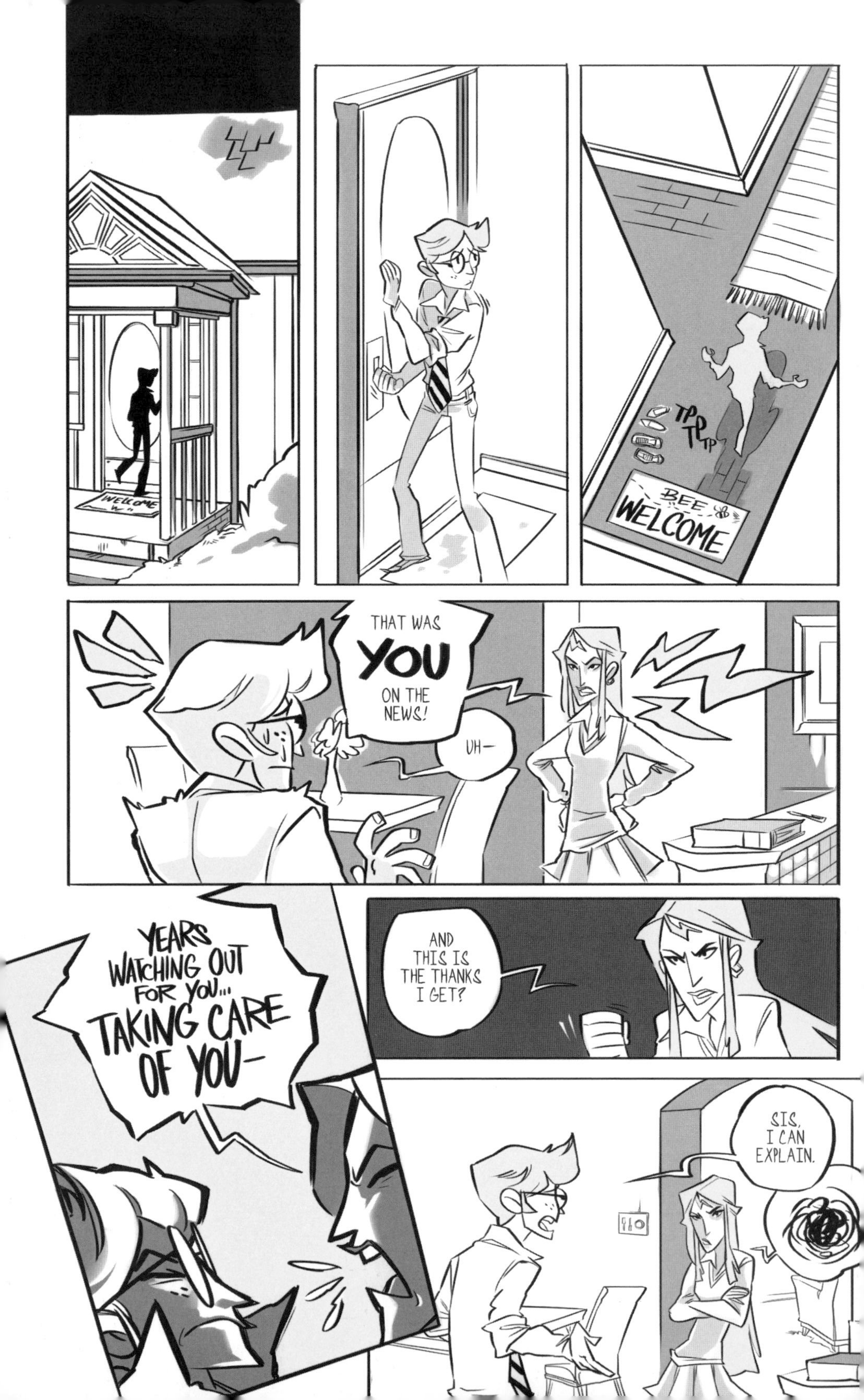
TP TP TP TP
BEE WELCOME
THAT WAS YOU ON THE NEWS!
UH–
YEARS WATCHING OUT FOR YOU... TAKING CARE OF YOU–
AND THIS IS THE THANKS I GET?
SIS, I CAN EXPLAIN.

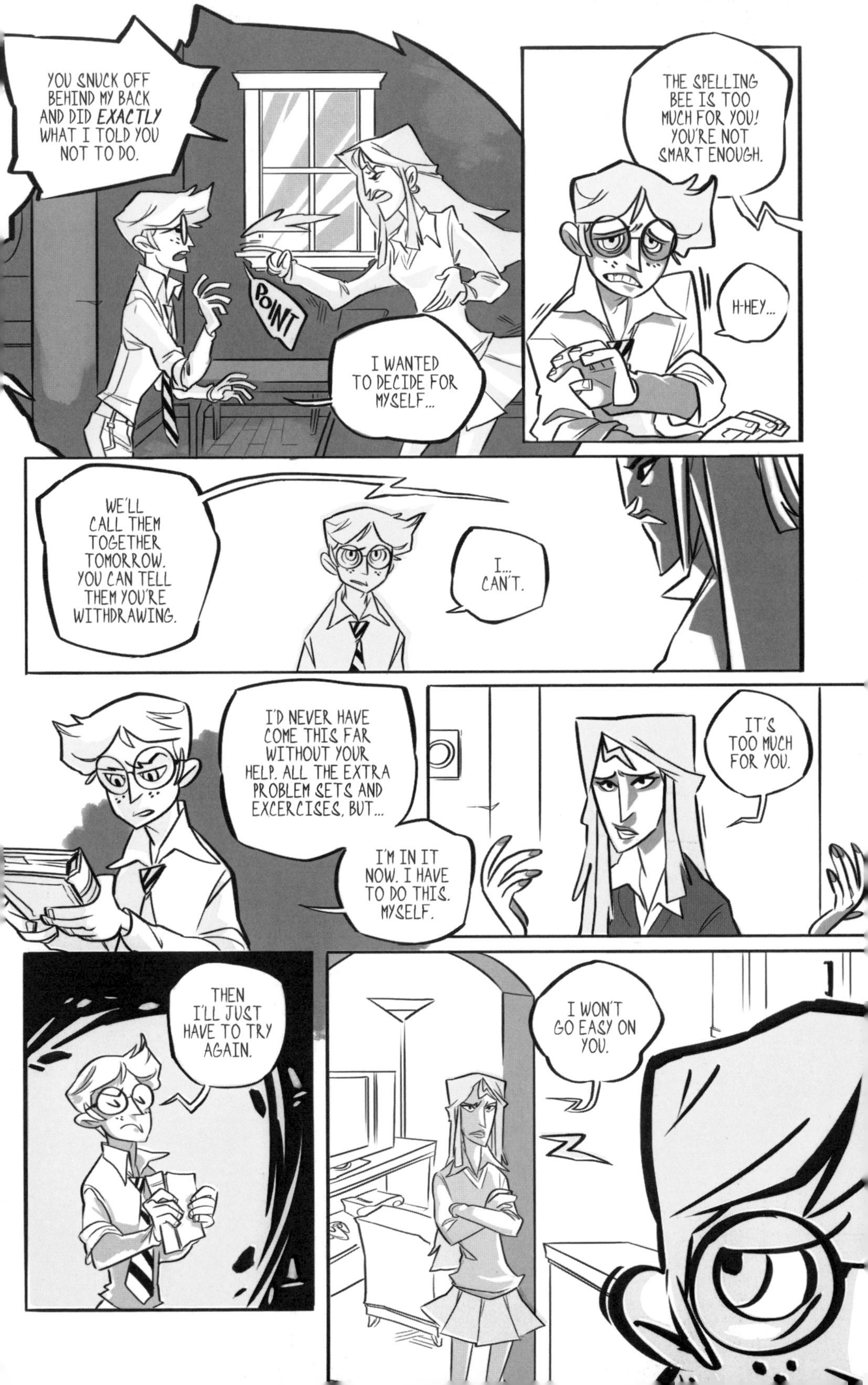
YOU SNUCK OFF BEHIND MY BACK AND DID **EXACTLY** WHAT I TOLD YOU NOT TO DO.
POINT
I WANTED TO DECIDE FOR MYSELF...
THE SPELLING BEE IS TOO MUCH FOR YOU! YOU'RE NOT SMART ENOUGH.
H-HEY...
WE'LL CALL THEM TOGETHER TOMORROW. YOU CAN TELL THEM YOU'RE WITHDRAWING.
I... CAN'T.
I'D NEVER HAVE COME THIS FAR WITHOUT YOUR HELP. ALL THE EXTRA PROBLEM SETS AND EXCERCISES, BUT...
I'M IN IT NOW. I HAVE TO DO THIS. MYSELF.
IT'S TOO MUCH FOR YOU.
THEN I'LL JUST HAVE TO TRY AGAIN.
I WON'T GO EASY ON YOU.

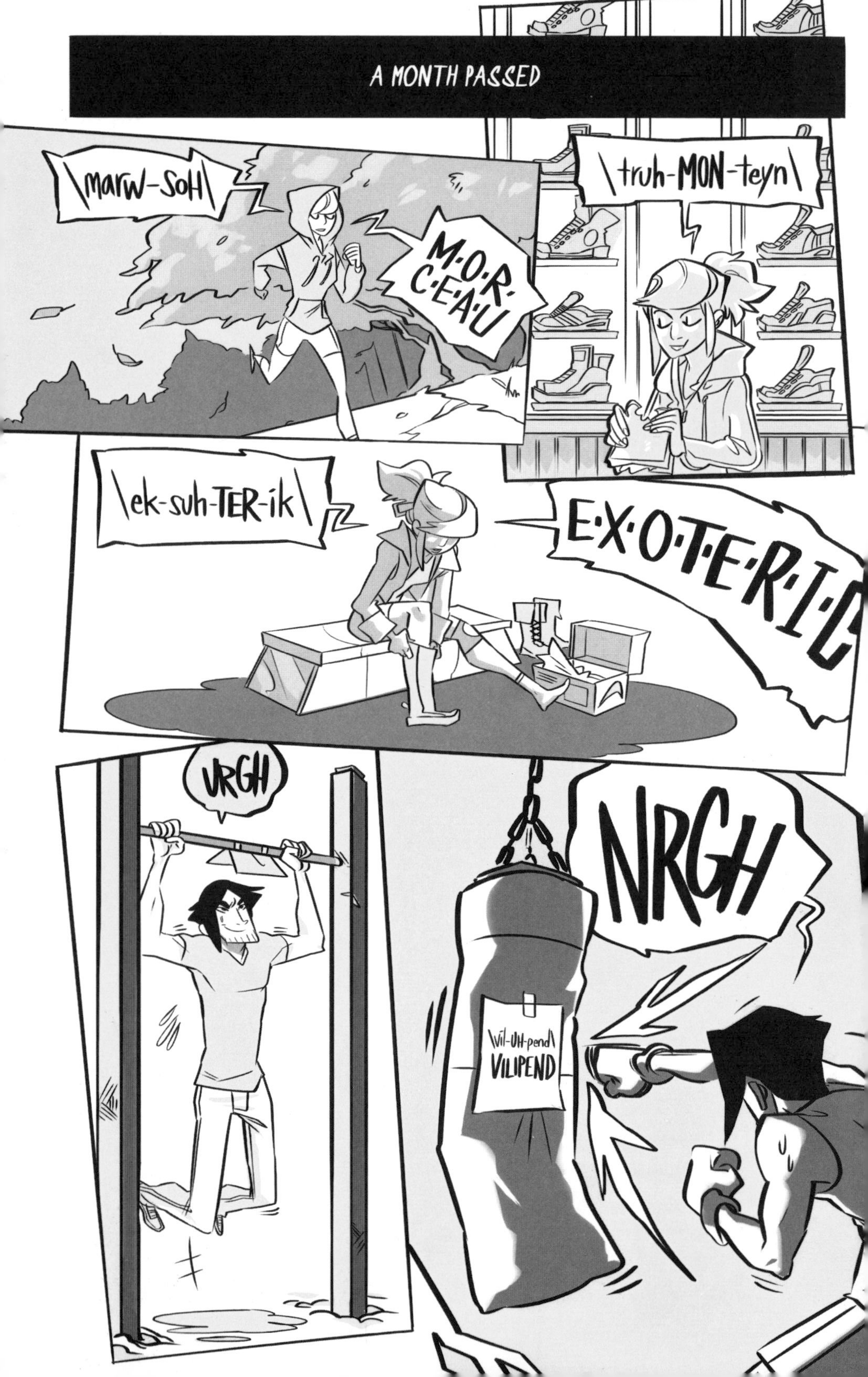
A MONTH PASSED
\marw-SOH\
M·O·R·C·E·A·U
\truh-MON-teyn\
\ek-suh-TER-ik\
E·X·O·T·E·R·I·C
URGH
NRGH
\vil-UH-pend\
VILIPEND

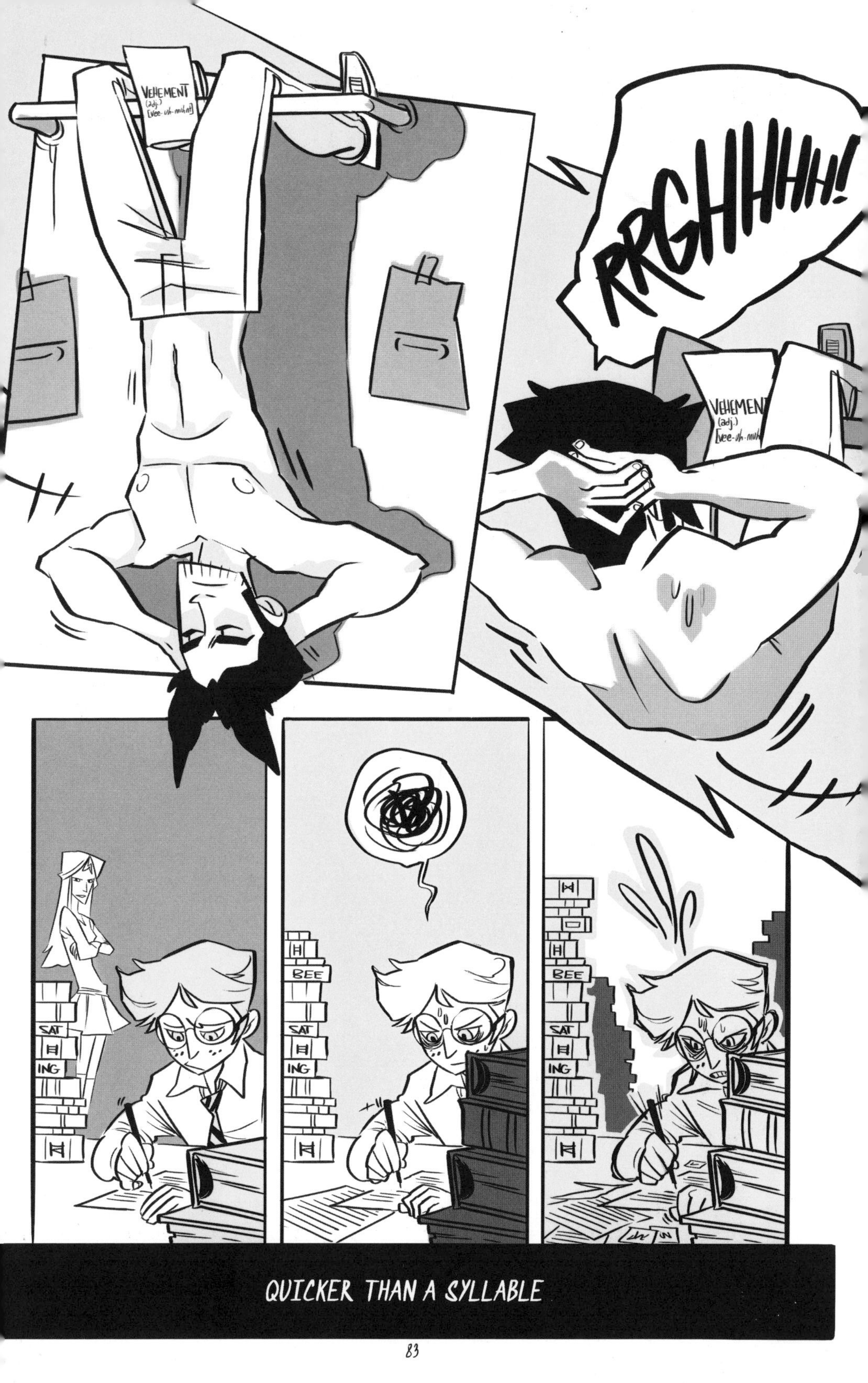

VEHEMENT
(adj.)
[vee-uh-muhnt]
RRGHHHHH!
VEHEMENT
(adj.)
BEE
SAT
ING
BEE
SAT
ING
QUICKER THAN A SYLLABLE

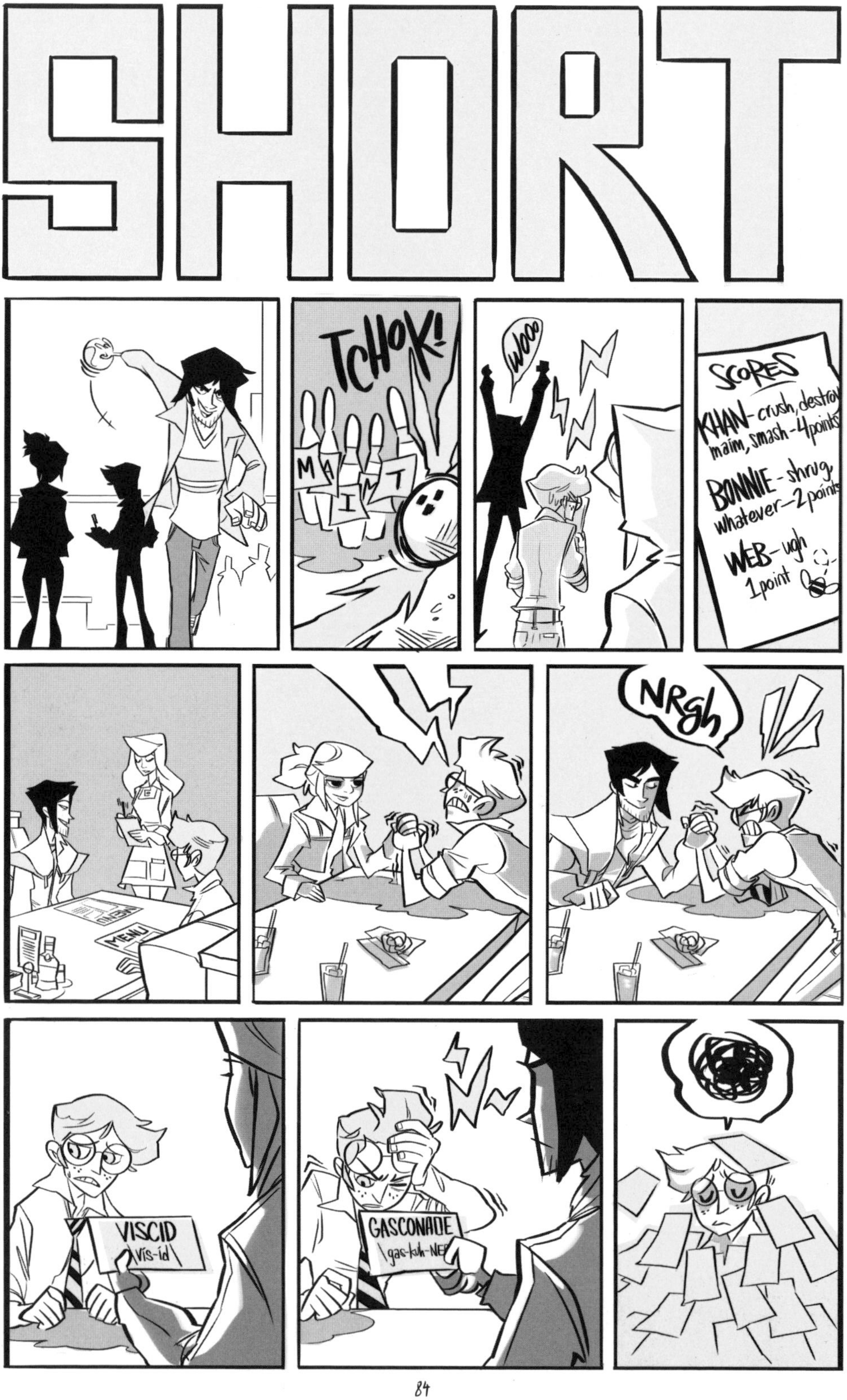
SHORT
TCHOK!
Wooo
SCORES
KHAN-crush, destro
maim, smash-4points
BONNIE-shrug,
whatever-2points
WEB-ugh
1point
MENU
NRgh
VISCID
\vís-id\
GASCONADE
\gas-kuh-NE

and SWEET

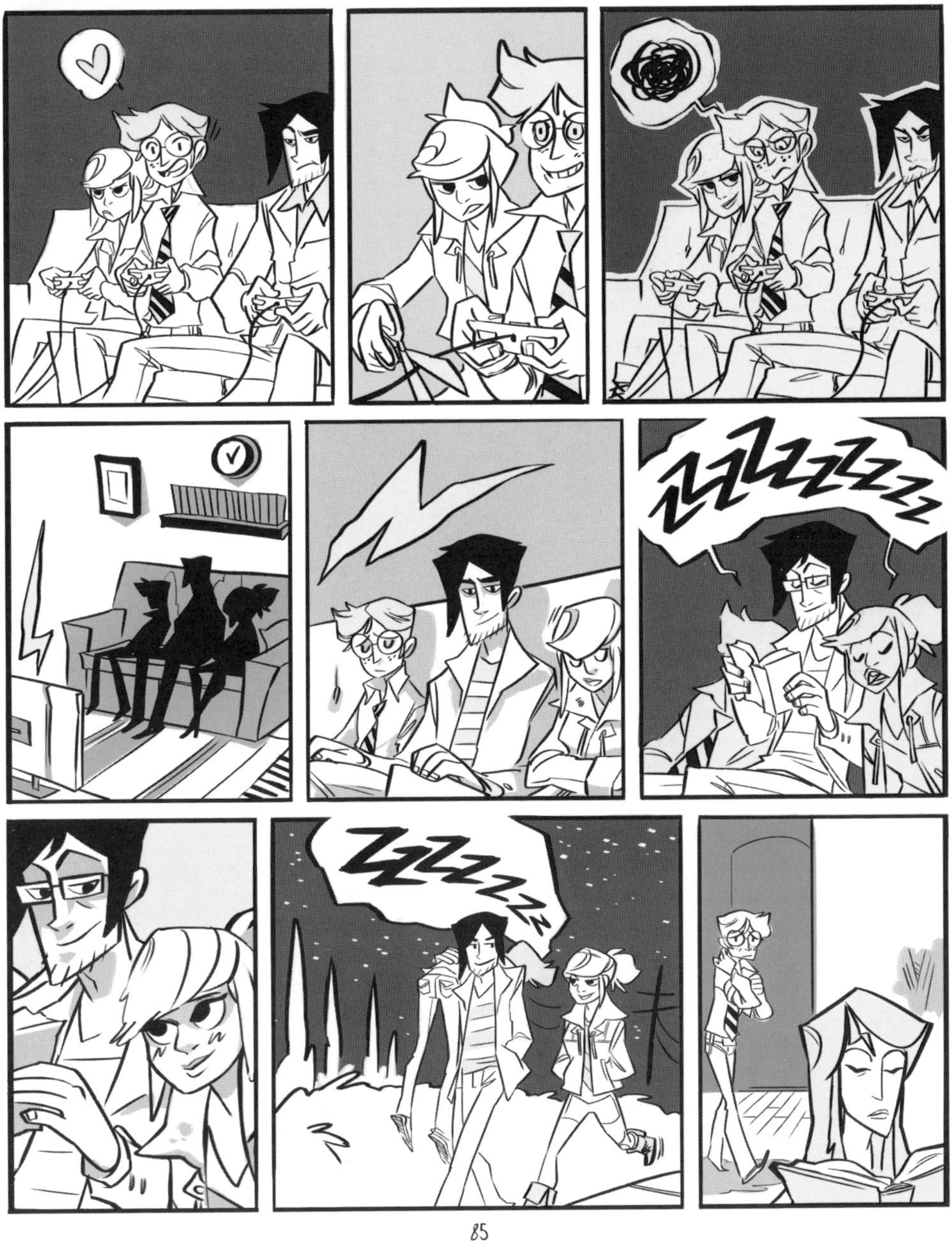
ZZZZZZZZZZ
ZZZZZZZZ

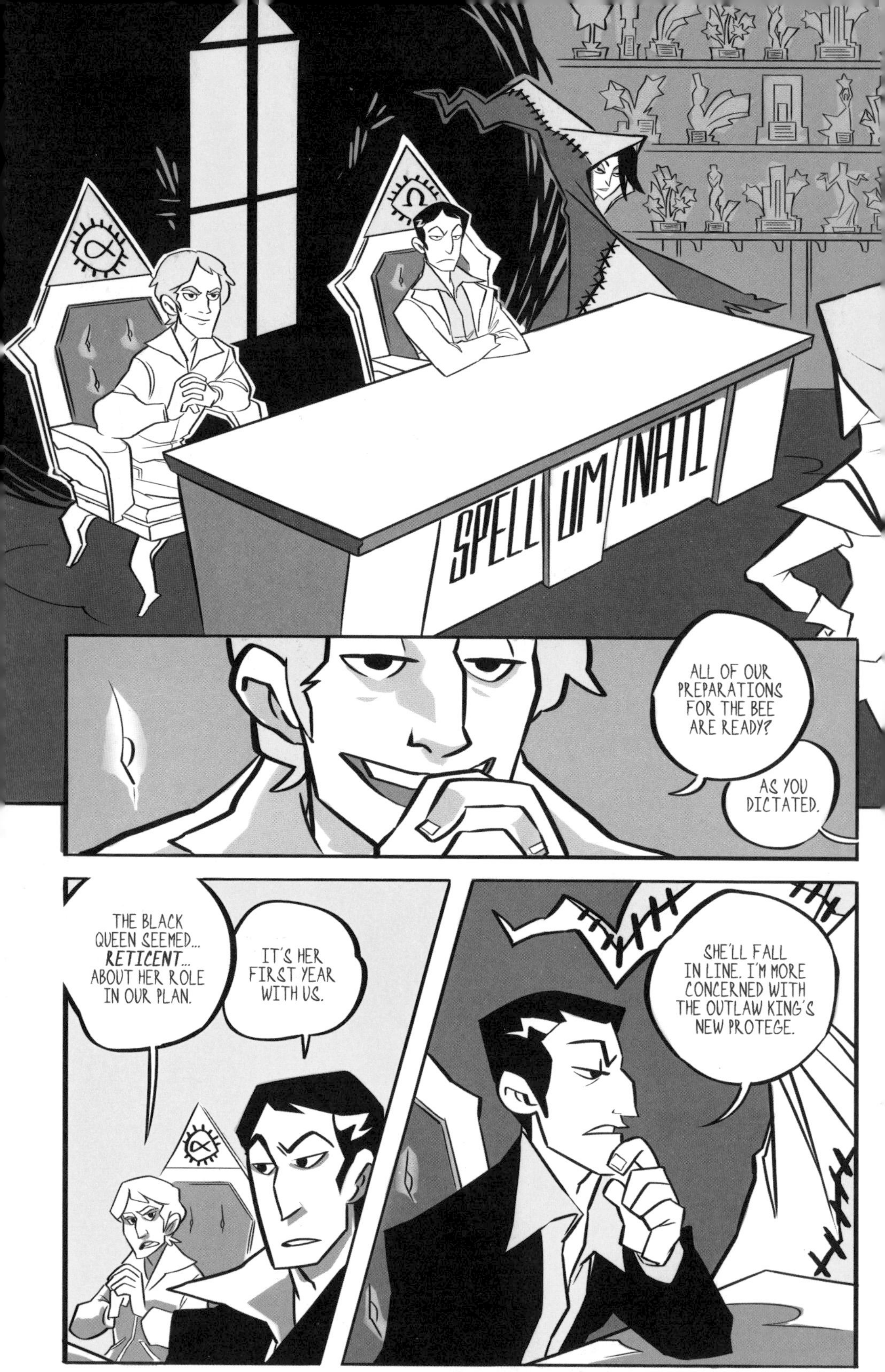

SPELL UM INATI
ALL OF OUR PREPARATIONS FOR THE BEE ARE READY?
AS YOU DICTATED.
THE BLACK QUEEN SEEMED... **RETICENT**... ABOUT HER ROLE IN OUR PLAN.
IT'S HER FIRST YEAR WITH US.
SHE'LL FALL IN LINE. I'M MORE CONCERNED WITH THE OUTLAW KING'S NEW PROTEGE.

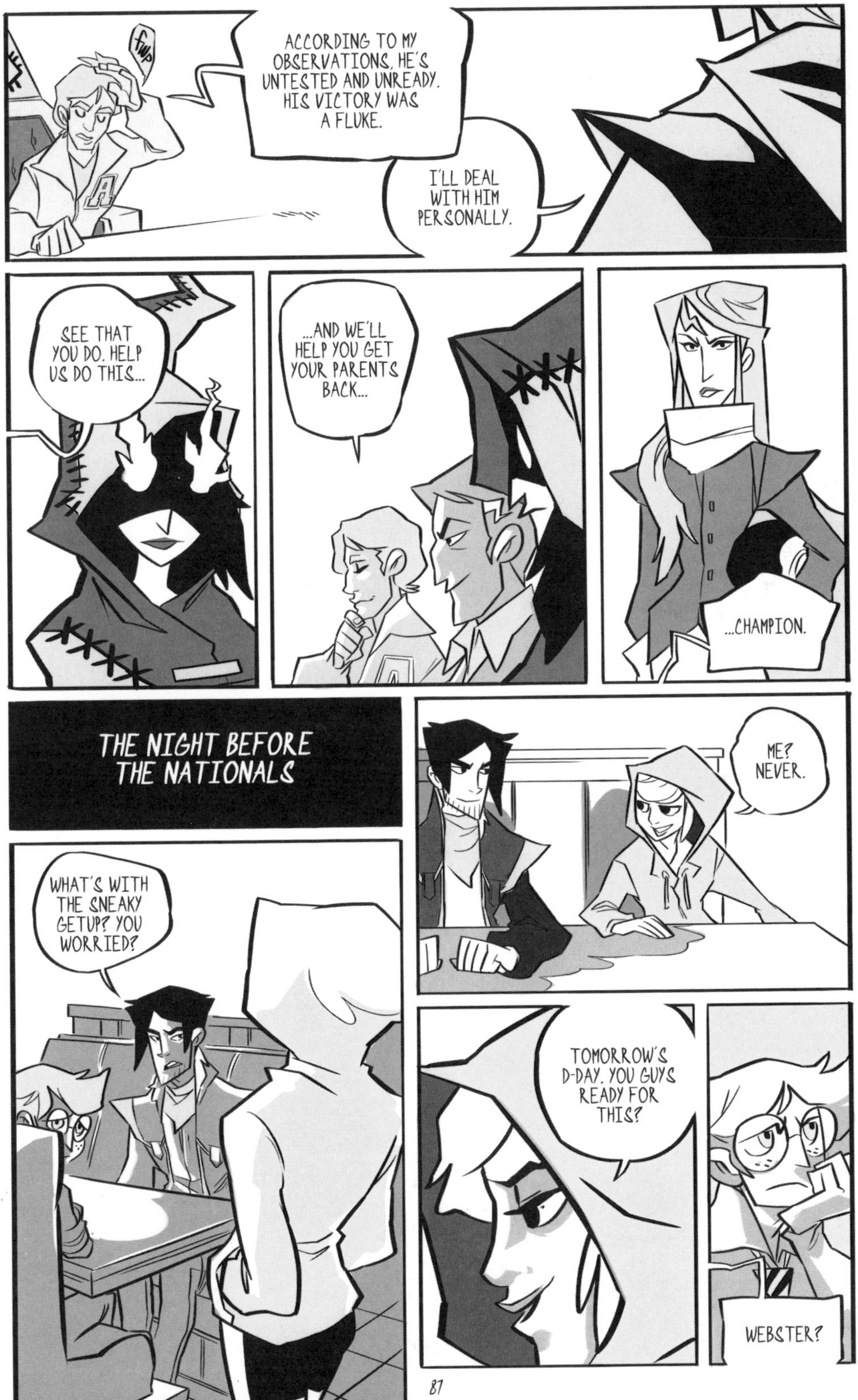
fwp
ACCORDING TO MY OBSERVATIONS, HE'S UNTESTED AND UNREADY. HIS VICTORY WAS A FLUKE.
I'LL DEAL WITH HIM PERSONALLY.
SEE THAT YOU DO. HELP US DO THIS...
...AND WE'LL HELP YOU GET YOUR PARENTS BACK...
...CHAMPION.
THE NIGHT BEFORE THE NATIONALS
ME? NEVER.
WHAT'S WITH THE SNEAKY GETUP? YOU WORRIED?
TOMORROW'S D-DAY. YOU GUYS READY FOR THIS?
WEBSTER?

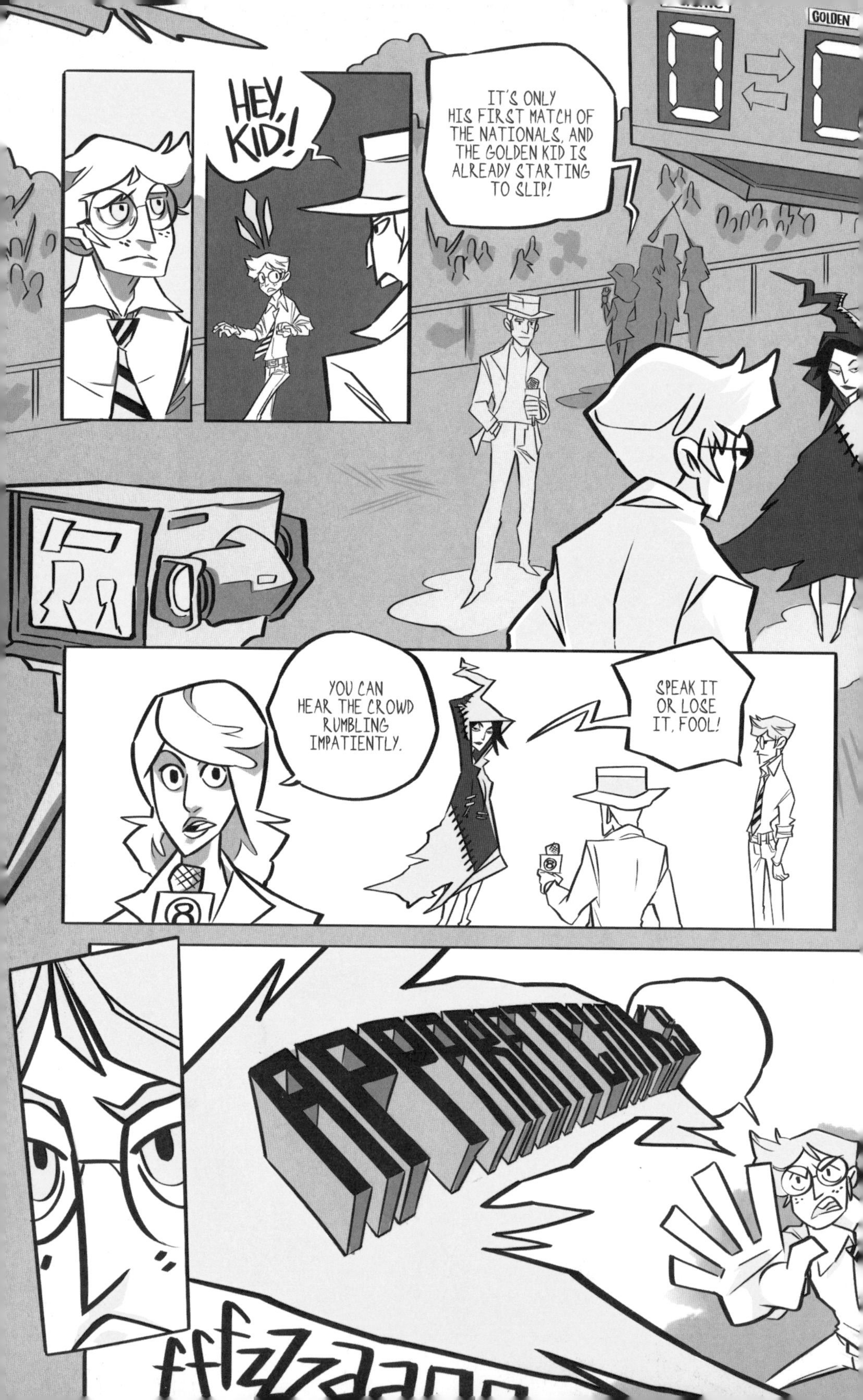
GOLDEN
HEY, KID!
IT'S ONLY HIS FIRST MATCH OF THE NATIONALS, AND THE GOLDEN KID IS ALREADY STARTING TO SLIP!
YOU CAN HEAR THE CROWD RUMBLING IMPATIENTLY.
SPEAK IT OR LOSE IT, FOOL!
APPARATCHIK!
ffzzzaann

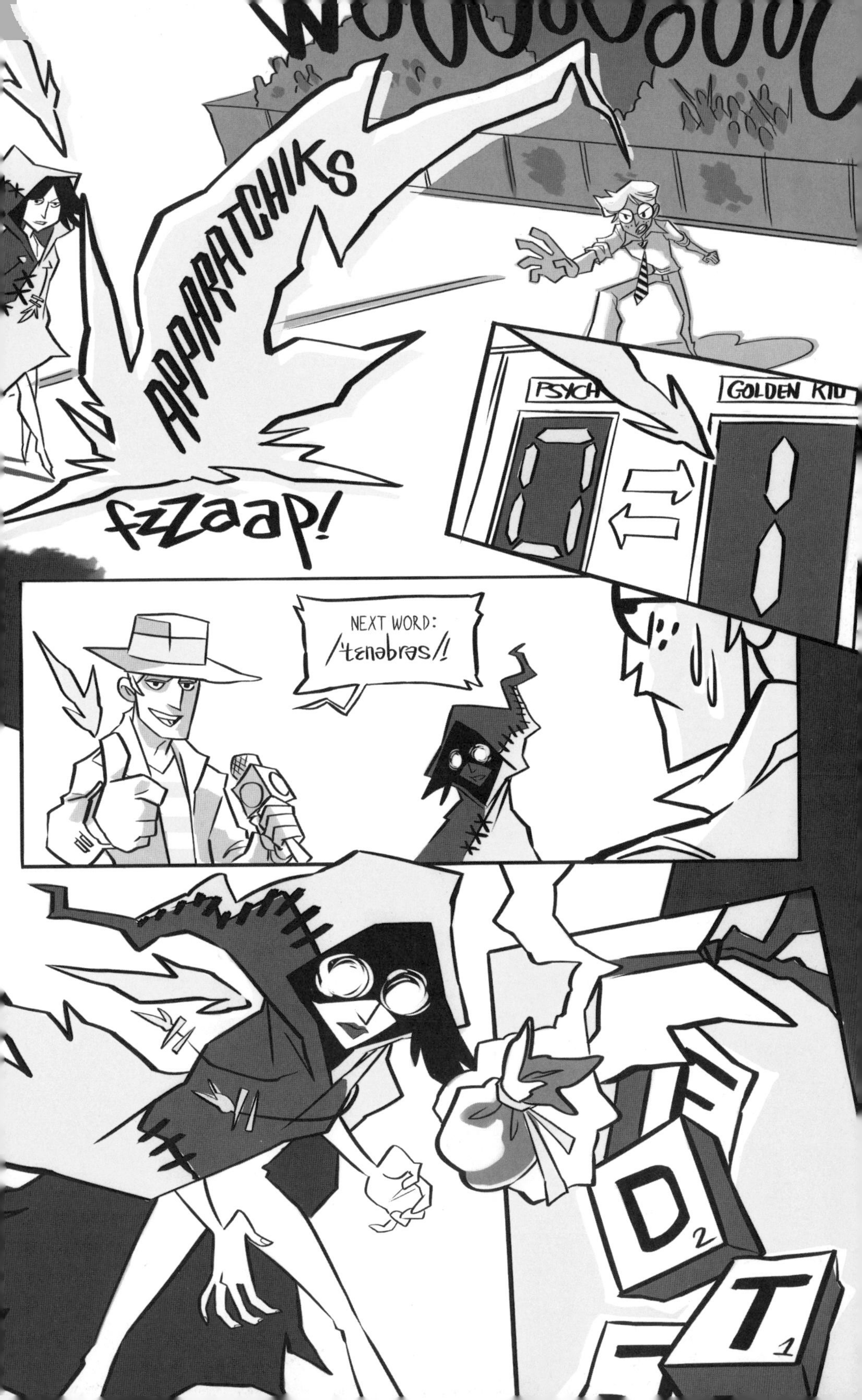

WOOOOOOOOO
APPARATCHIKS
fzzaap!
PSYCH
GOLDEN KID
NEXT WORD: /ˈtɛnəbrəs/!
D
T

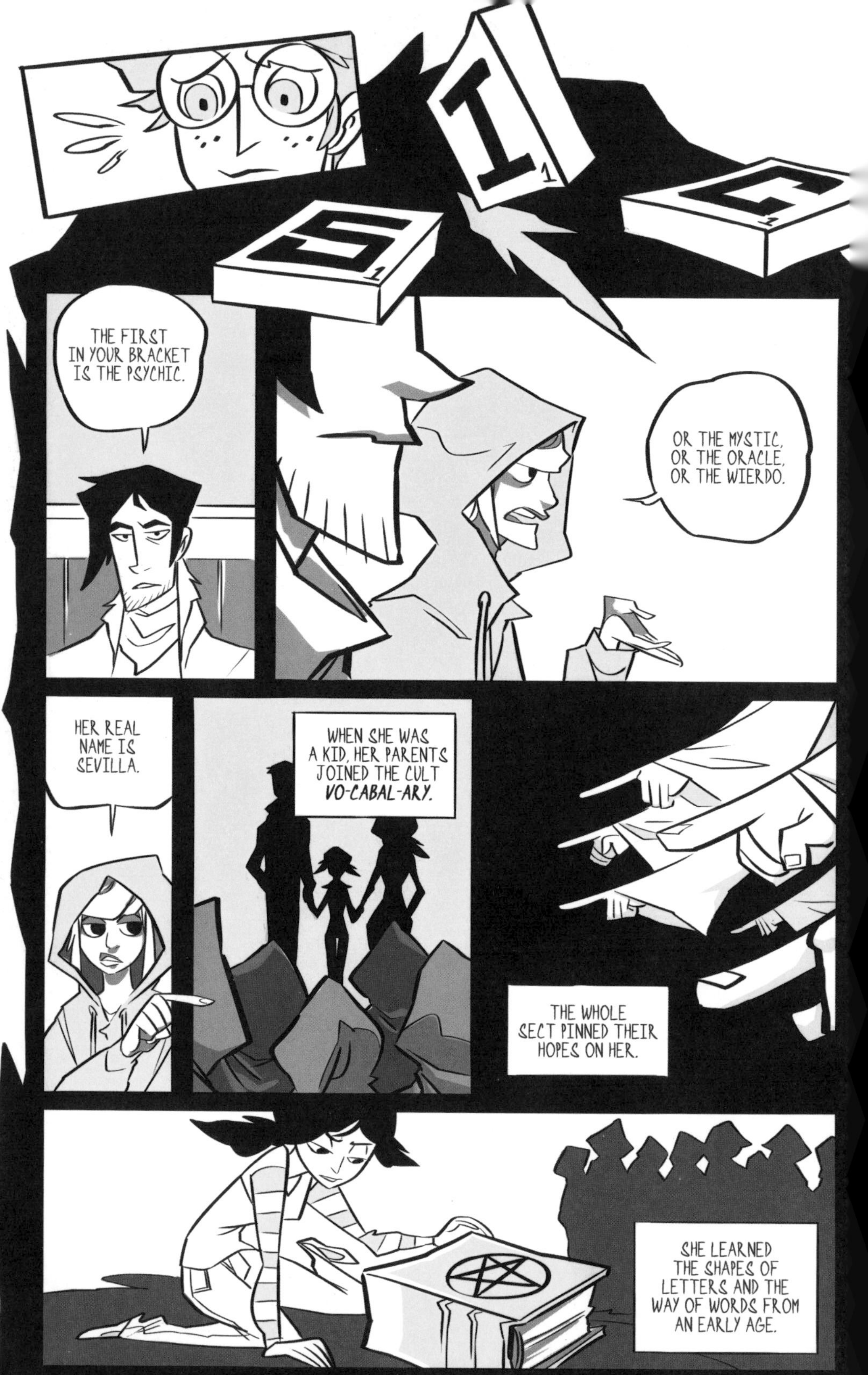

S
I
C
THE FIRST IN YOUR BRACKET IS THE PSYCHIC.
OR THE MYSTIC, OR THE ORACLE, OR THE WIERDO.
HER REAL NAME IS SEVILLA.
WHEN SHE WAS A KID, HER PARENTS JOINED THE CULT *VO-CABAL-ARY.*
THE WHOLE SECT PINNED THEIR HOPES ON HER.
SHE LEARNED THE SHAPES OF LETTERS AND THE WAY OF WORDS FROM AN EARLY AGE.

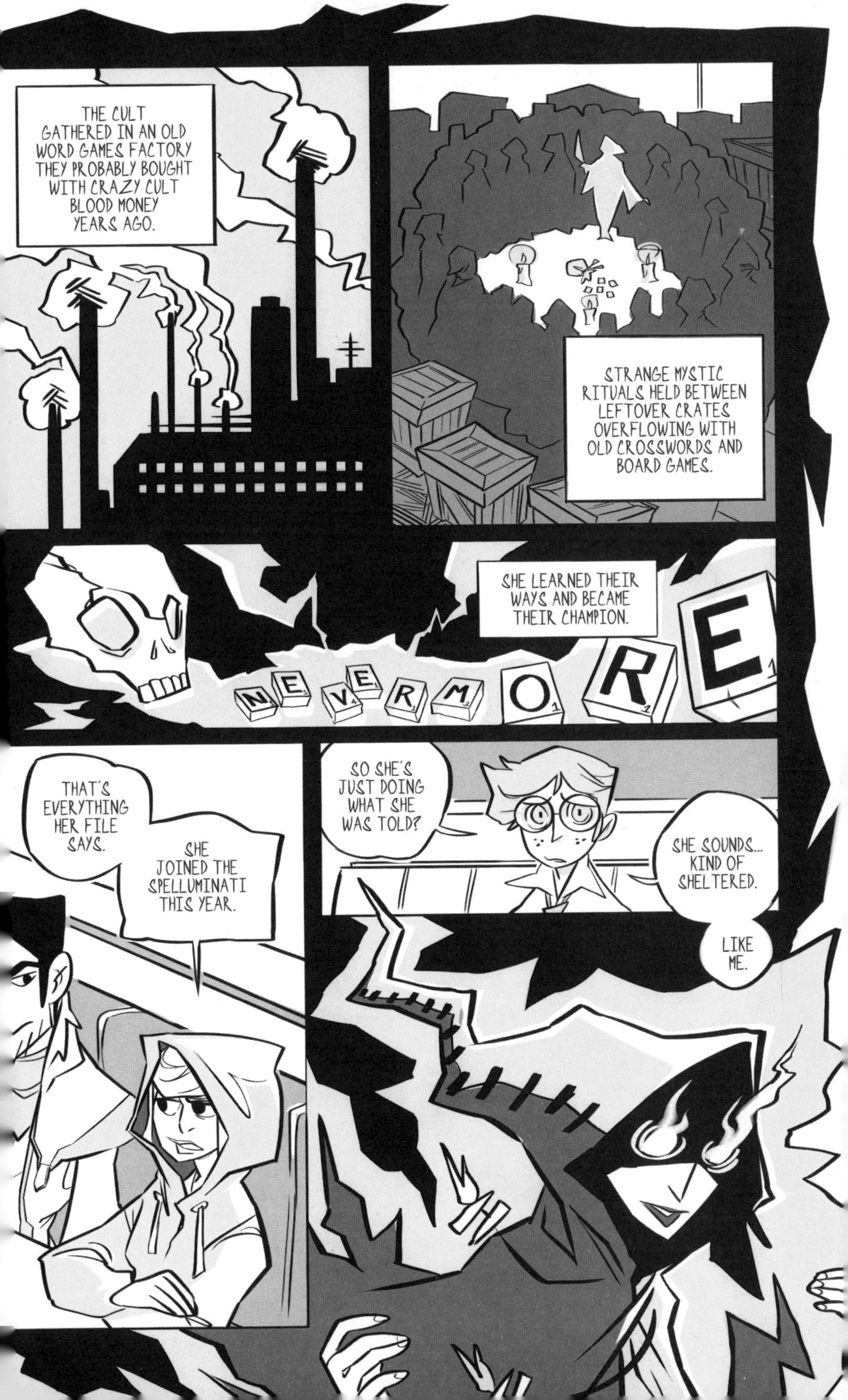
THE CULT GATHERED IN AN OLD WORD GAMES FACTORY THEY PROBABLY BOUGHT WITH CRAZY CULT BLOOD MONEY YEARS AGO.
STRANGE MYSTIC RITUALS HELD BETWEEN LEFTOVER CRATES OVERFLOWING WITH OLD CROSSWORDS AND BOARD GAMES.
SHE LEARNED THEIR WAYS AND BECAME THEIR CHAMPION.
NEVERMORE
THAT'S EVERYTHING HER FILE SAYS.
SHE JOINED THE SPELLUMINATI THIS YEAR.
SO SHE'S JUST DOING WHAT SHE WAS TOLD?
SHE SOUNDS... KIND OF SHELTERED.
LIKE ME.

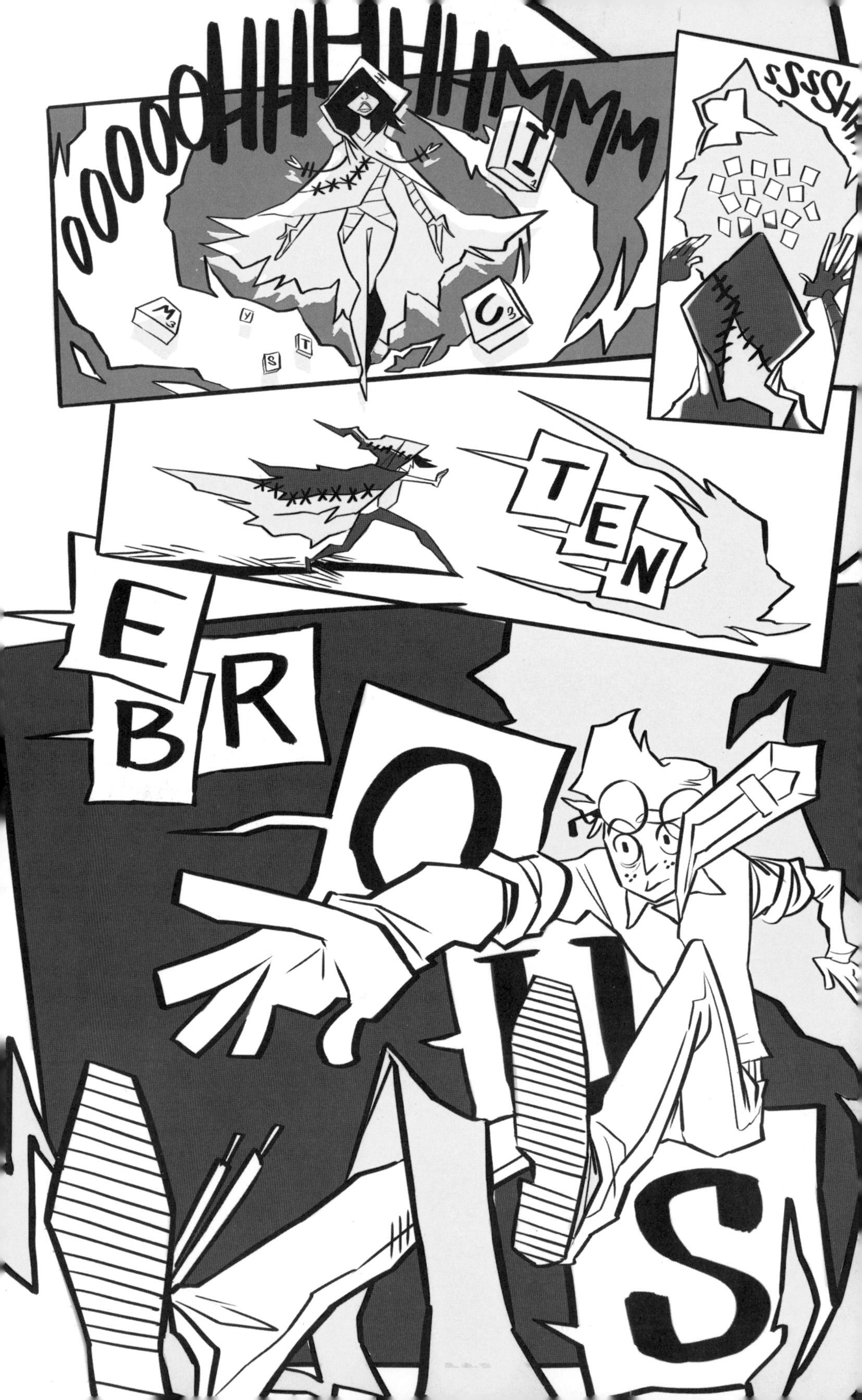

OOOOOOHHHHHHMMMM
I
M
y
s
T
C
sSSSH
TEN
E
BR
O
U
S

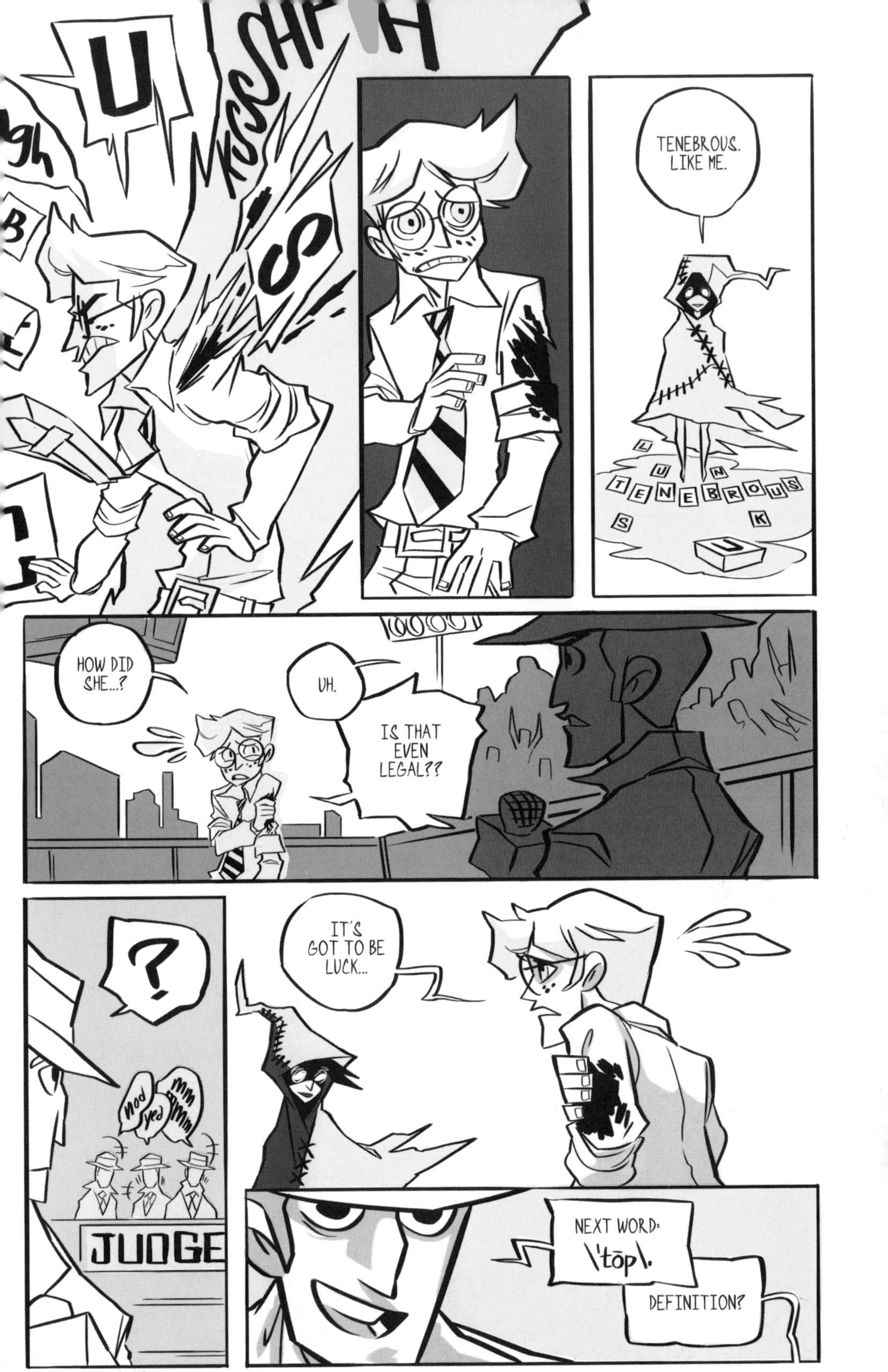
U
ugh
KSSSHPH
S
B
TENEBROUS. LIKE ME.
L
U
N
TENEBROUS
S
K
U
HOW DID SHE...?
UH.
IS THAT EVEN LEGAL??
?
nod
yea
mmmm
JUDGE
IT'S GOT TO BE LUCK...
NEXT WORD:
\'tōp\.
DEFINITION?

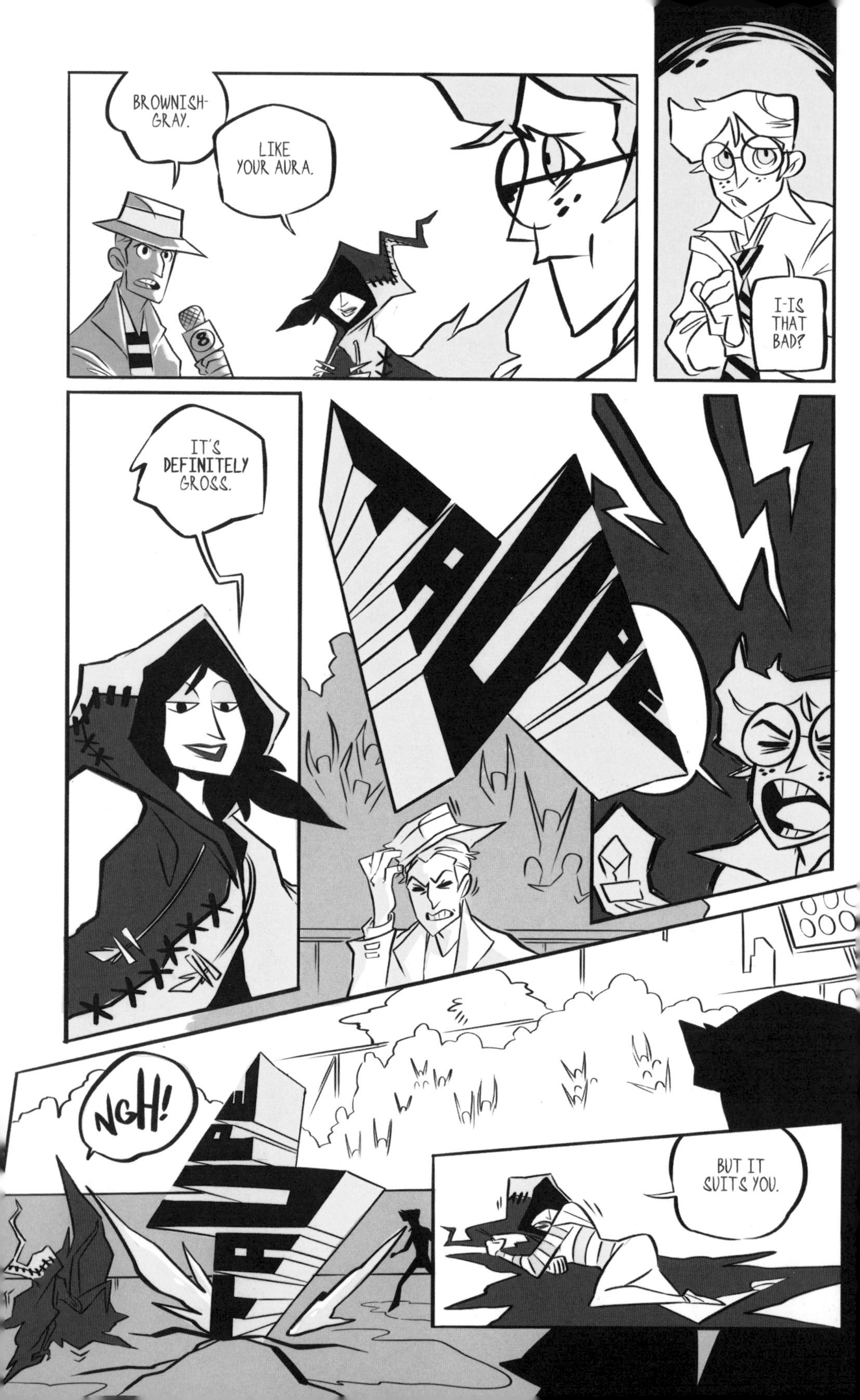
BROWNISH-GRAY.
LIKE YOUR AURA.
I-IS THAT BAD?
IT'S DEFINITELY GROSS.
NGH!
BUT IT SUITS YOU.

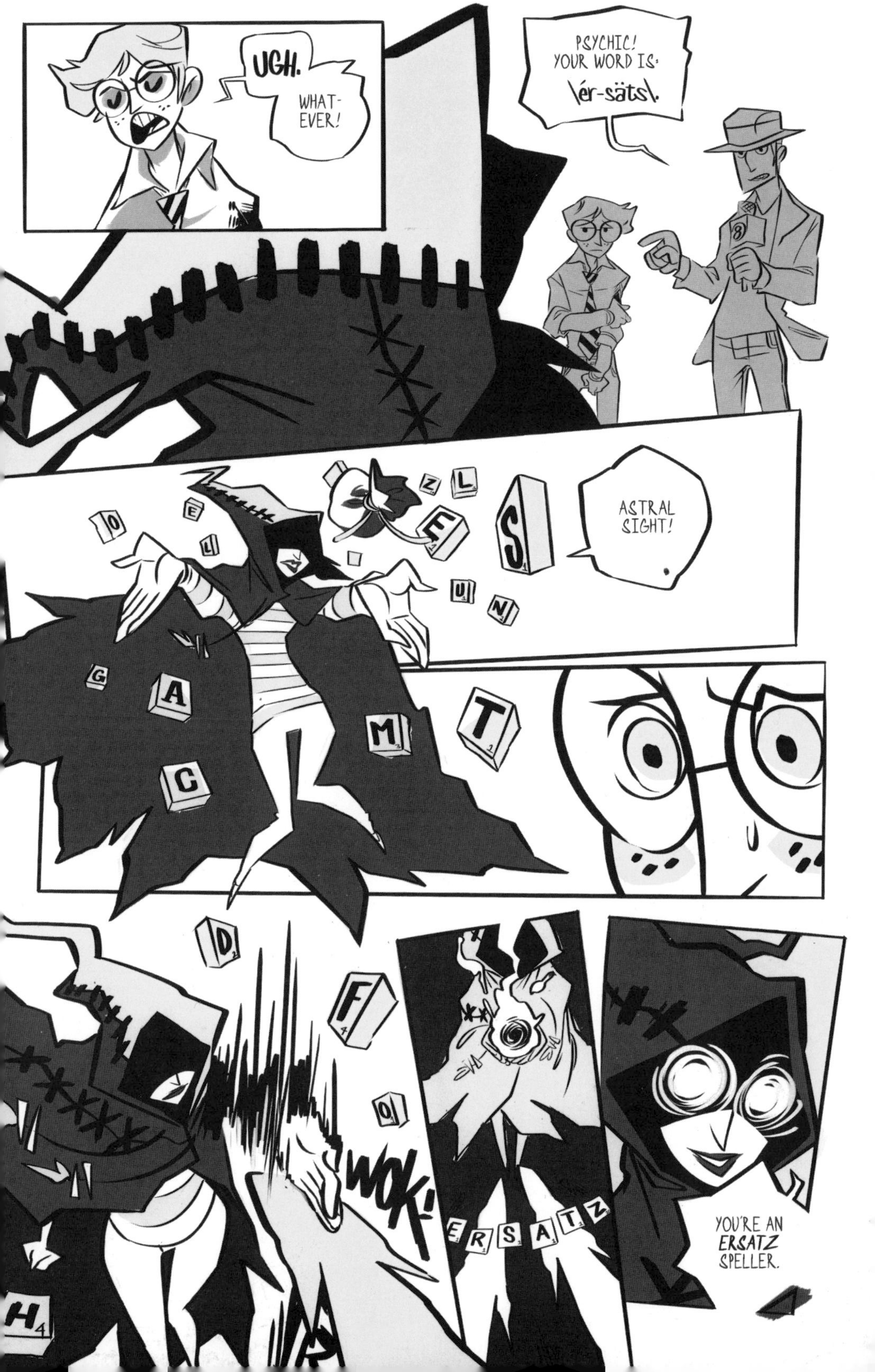
UGH.
WHAT-EVER!
PSYCHIC! YOUR WORD IS: \ér-säts\.
ASTRAL SIGHT!
WOK!
ERSATZ
YOU'RE AN ERSATZ SPELLER.

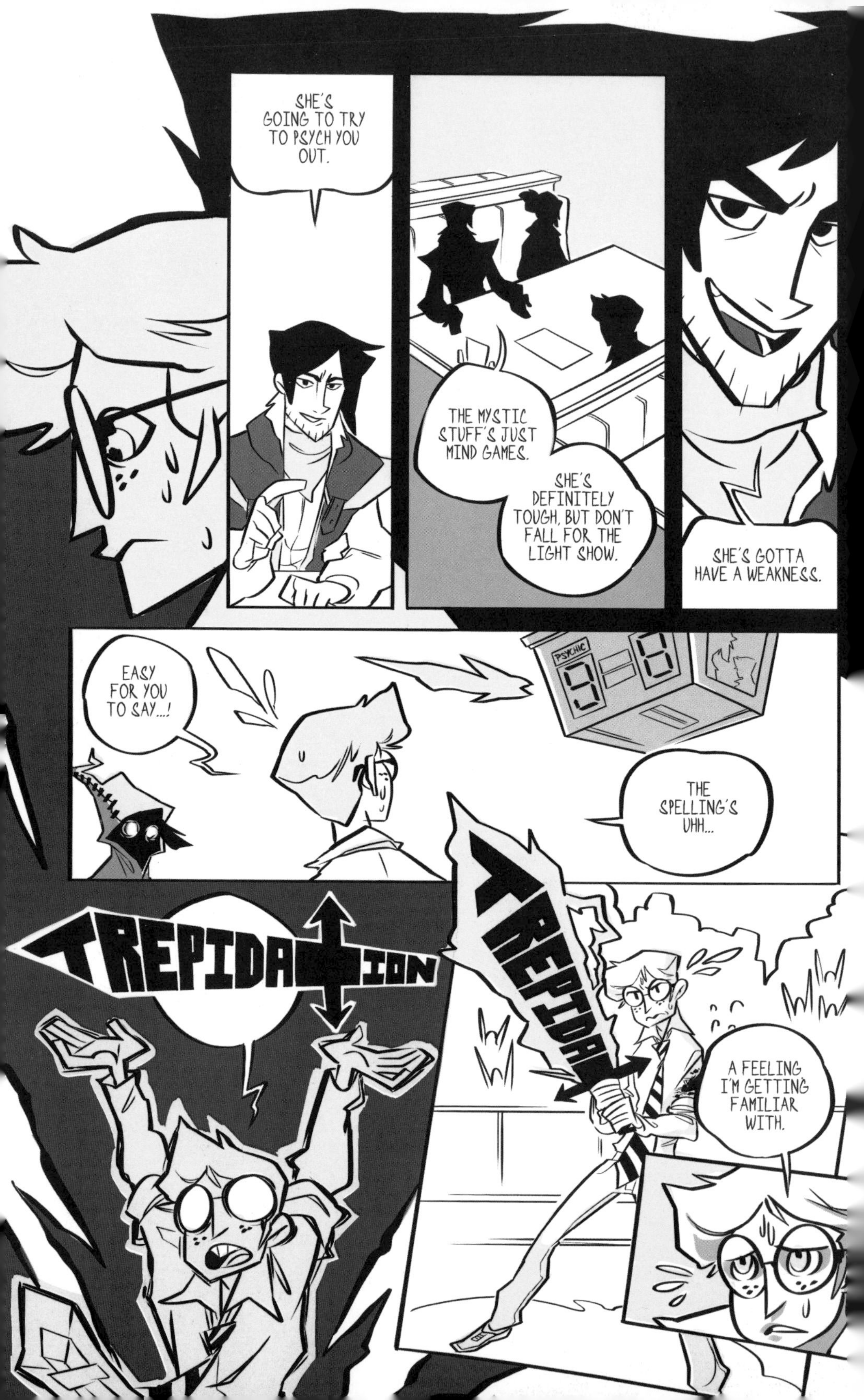
SHE'S GOING TO TRY TO PSYCH YOU OUT.
THE MYSTIC STUFF'S JUST MIND GAMES.
SHE'S DEFINITELY TOUGH, BUT DON'T FALL FOR THE LIGHT SHOW.
SHE'S GOTTA HAVE A WEAKNESS.
EASY FOR YOU TO SAY...!
PSYCHIC
THE SPELLING'S UHH...
TREPIDATION
TREPIDATI
A FEELING I'M GETTING FAMILIAR WITH.

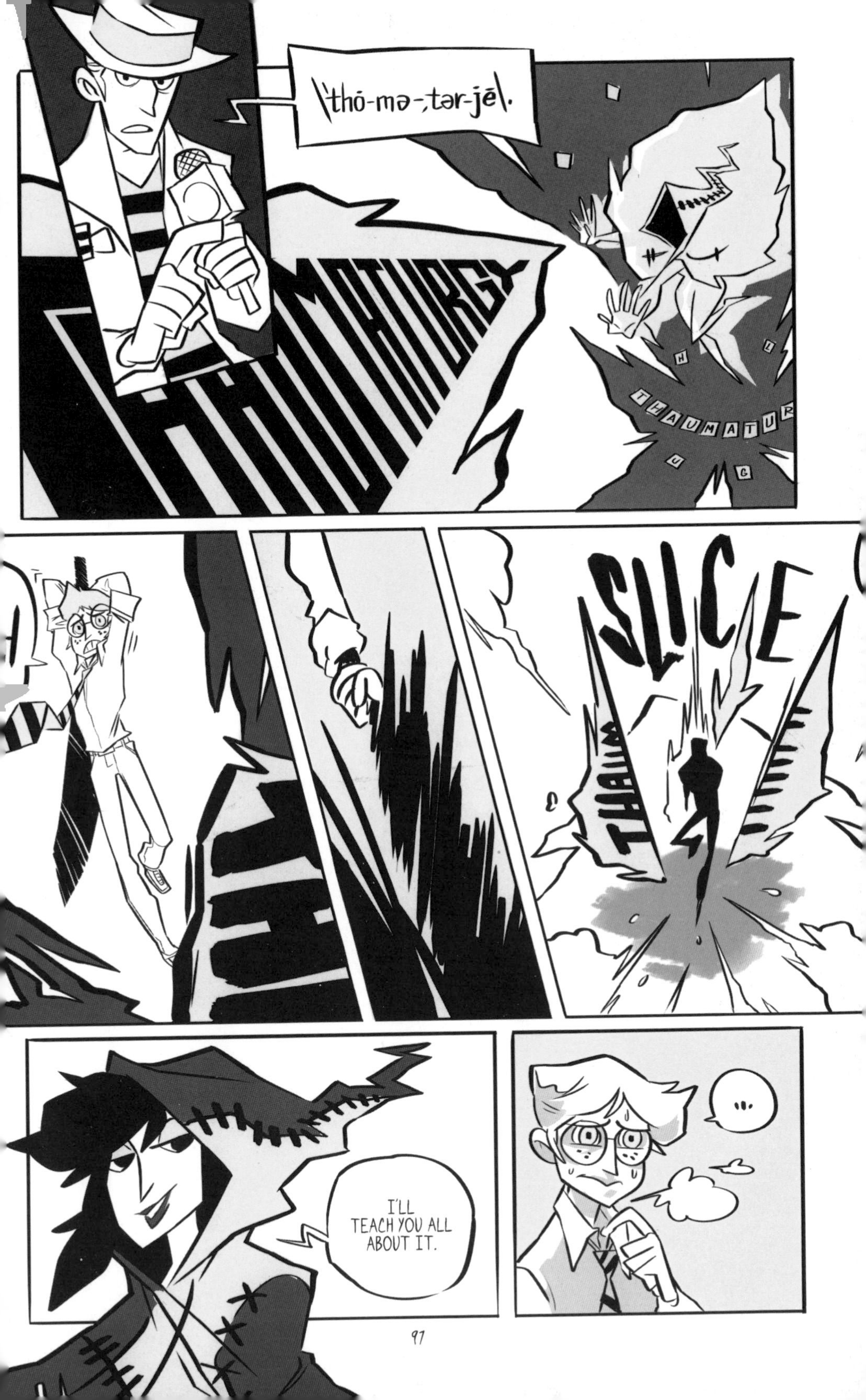
\ˈthō-mə-ˌtər-jē\.
THAUMATUR
SLICE
THAUM
I'LL TEACH YOU ALL ABOUT IT.
...

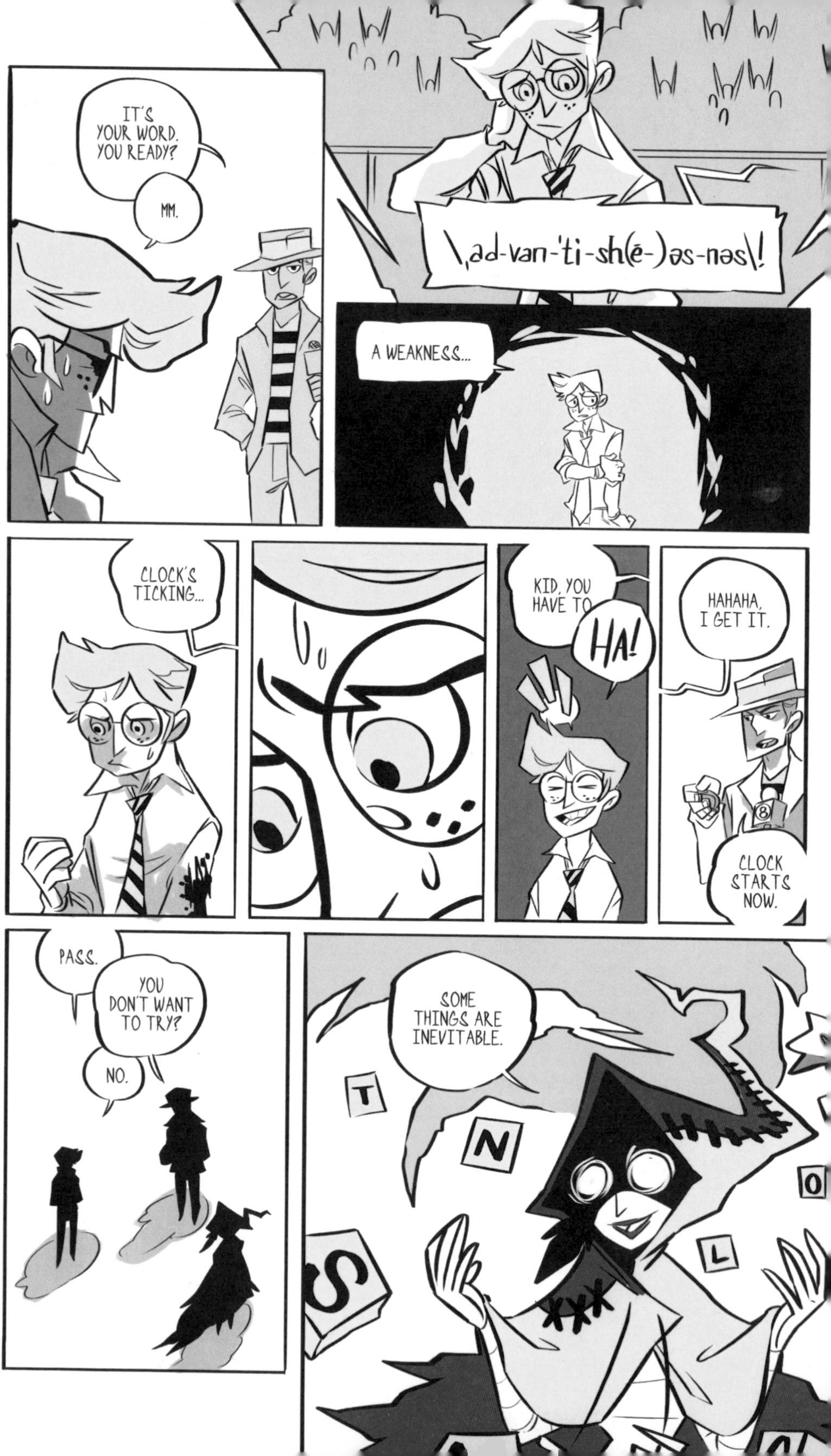
IT'S YOUR WORD. YOU READY?
MM.
\ˌad-vən-ˈti-sh(ē-)əs-nəs\!
A WEAKNESS...
CLOCK'S TICKING...
KID, YOU HAVE TO
HA!
HAHAHA, I GET IT.
CLOCK STARTS NOW.
PASS.
YOU DON'T WANT TO TRY?
NO.
SOME THINGS ARE INEVITABLE.
T
N
O
S
L

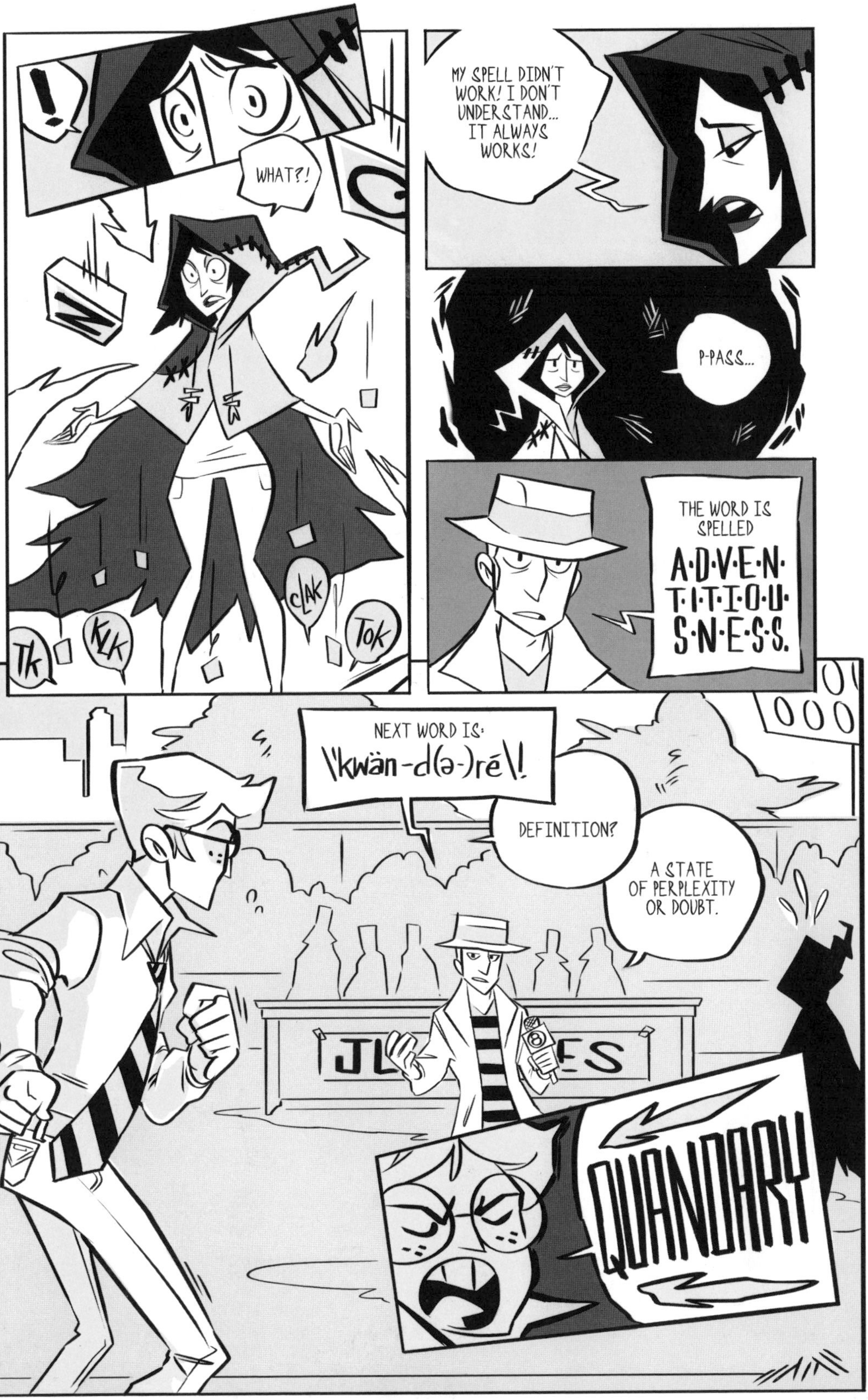
!
WHAT?!
TK
KLK
CLAK
TOK
MY SPELL DIDN'T WORK! I DON'T UNDERSTAND... IT ALWAYS WORKS!
P-PASS...
THE WORD IS SPELLED
A·D·V·E·N·T·I·T·I·O·U·S·N·E·S·S.
NEXT WORD IS:
\'kwän-d(ə-)rē\!
DEFINITION?
A STATE OF PERPLEXITY OR DOUBT.
QUANDARY

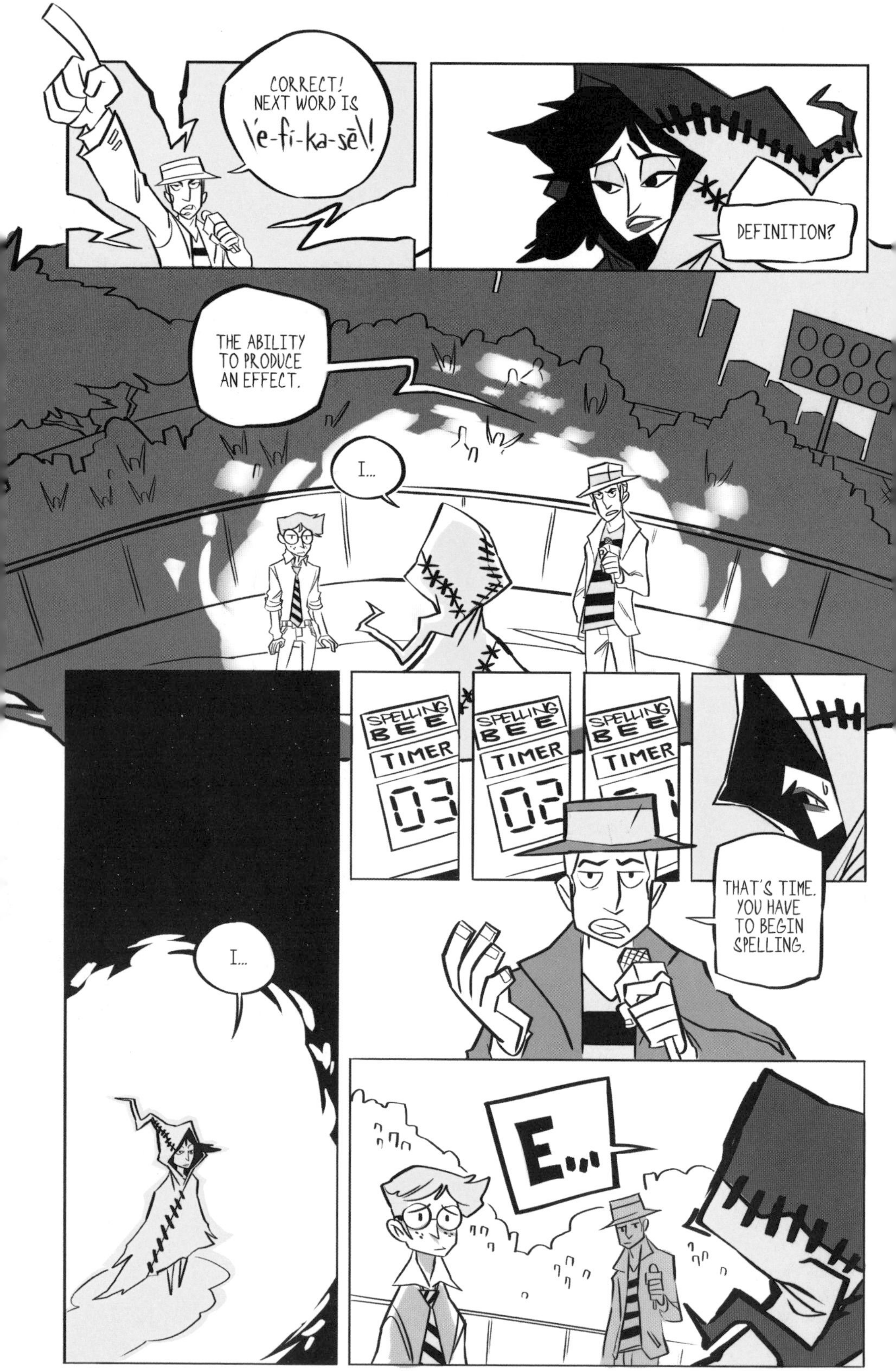
CORRECT! NEXT WORD IS \é-fi-ka-sē\!
DEFINITION?
THE ABILITY TO PRODUCE AN EFFECT.
I...
SPELLING BEE TIMER 03
SPELLING BEE TIMER 02
SPELLING BEE TIMER
I...
THAT'S TIME. YOU HAVE TO BEGIN SPELLING.
E...

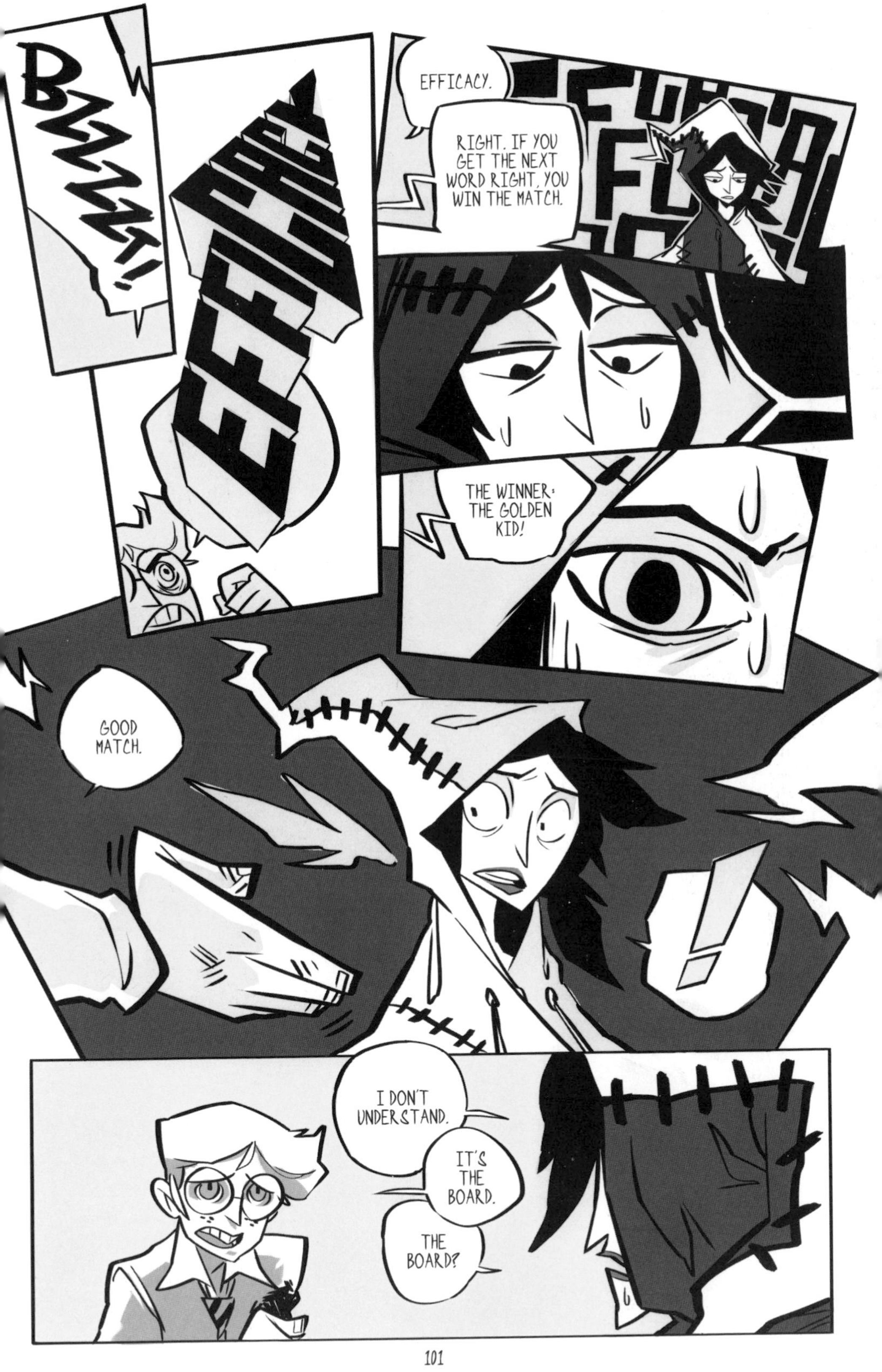
BZZZZT!
EFFICACY.
RIGHT. IF YOU GET THE NEXT WORD RIGHT, YOU WIN THE MATCH.
THE WINNER: THE GOLDEN KID!
GOOD MATCH.
!
I DON'T UNDERSTAND.
IT'S THE BOARD.
THE BOARD?

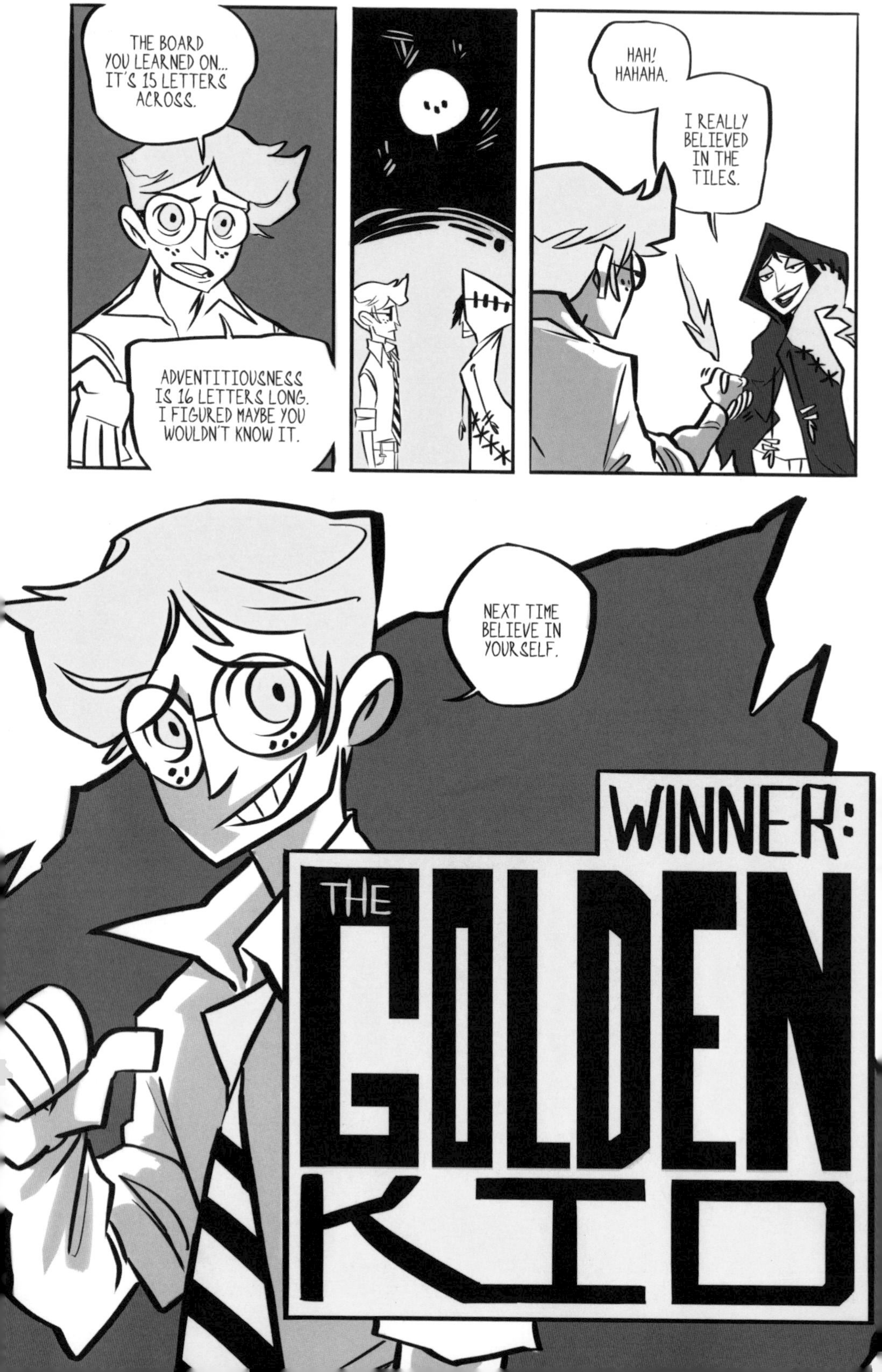
THE BOARD YOU LEARNED ON... IT'S 15 LETTERS ACROSS.
ADVENTITIOUSNESS IS 16 LETTERS LONG. I FIGURED MAYBE YOU WOULDN'T KNOW IT.
HAH! HAHAHA.
I REALLY BELIEVED IN THE TILES.
NEXT TIME BELIEVE IN YOURSELF.
WINNER:
THE GOLDEN KID

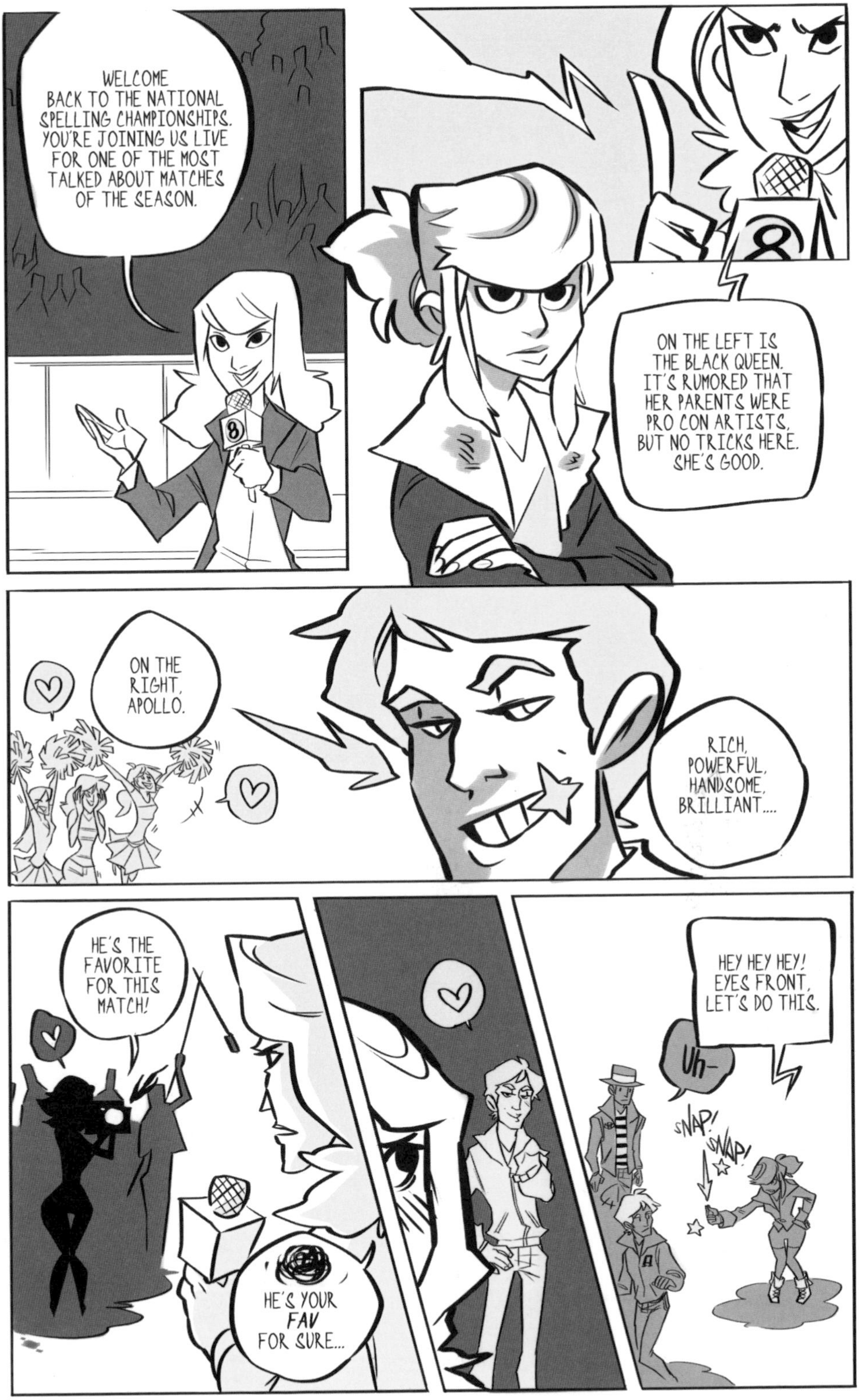
WELCOME BACK TO THE NATIONAL SPELLING CHAMPIONSHIPS. YOU'RE JOINING US LIVE FOR ONE OF THE MOST TALKED ABOUT MATCHES OF THE SEASON.
ON THE LEFT IS THE BLACK QUEEN. IT'S RUMORED THAT HER PARENTS WERE PRO CON ARTISTS, BUT NO TRICKS HERE. SHE'S GOOD.
ON THE RIGHT, APOLLO.
RICH, POWERFUL, HANDSOME, BRILLIANT....
HE'S THE FAVORITE FOR THIS MATCH!
HE'S YOUR **FAV** FOR SURE...
HEY HEY HEY! EYES FRONT, LET'S DO THIS.
Uh-
SNAP! SNAP!

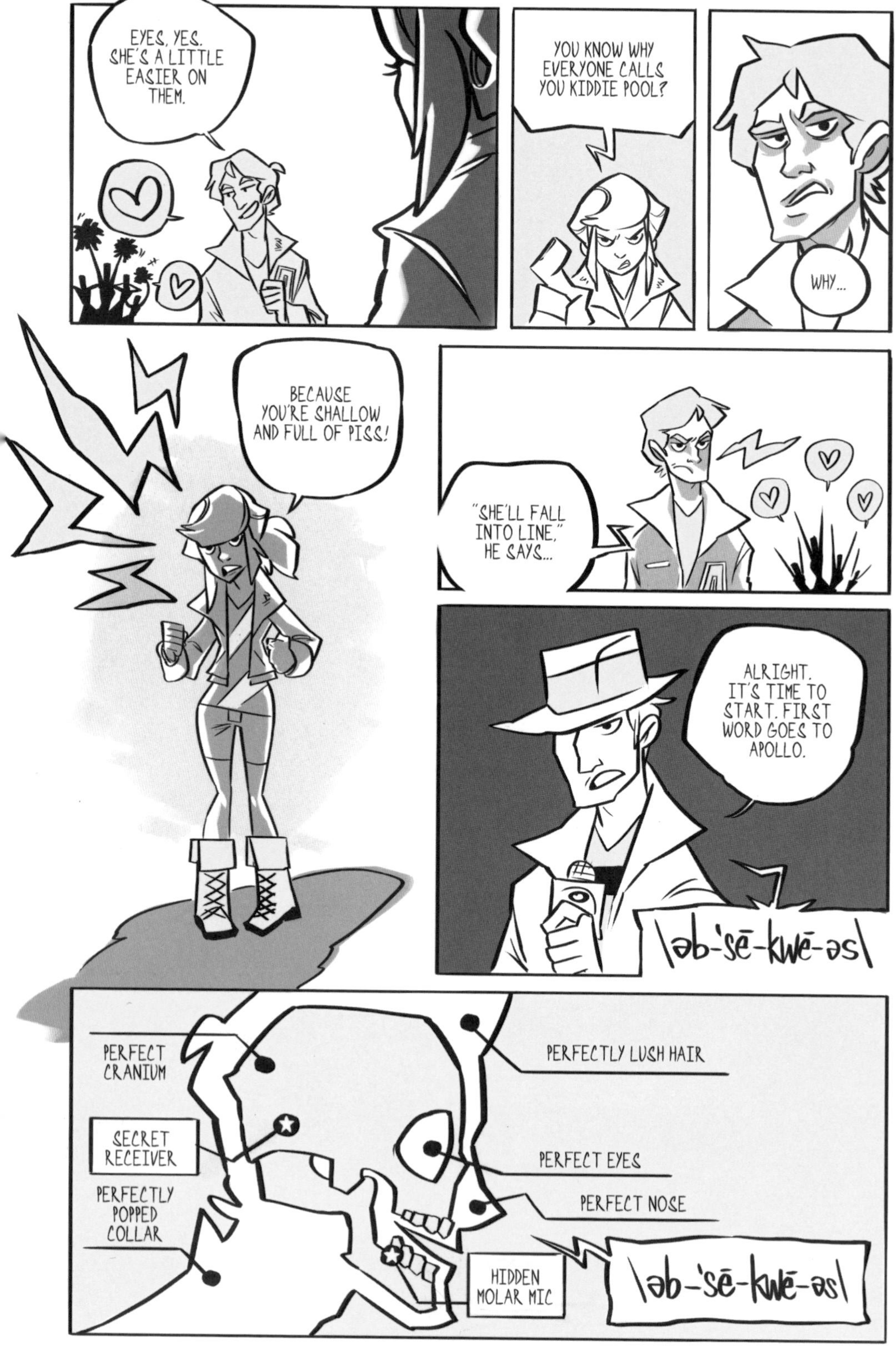
EYES, YES. SHE'S A LITTLE EASIER ON THEM.
YOU KNOW WHY EVERYONE CALLS YOU KIDDIE POOL?
WHY...
BECAUSE YOU'RE SHALLOW AND FULL OF PISS!
"SHE'LL FALL INTO LINE," HE SAYS...
ALRIGHT. IT'S TIME TO START. FIRST WORD GOES TO APOLLO.
\əb-ˈsē-kwē-əs\
PERFECT CRANIUM
PERFECTLY LUSH HAIR
SECRET RECEIVER
PERFECT EYES
PERFECTLY POPPED COLLAR
PERFECT NOSE
HIDDEN MOLAR MIC
\əb-ˈsē-kwē-əs\

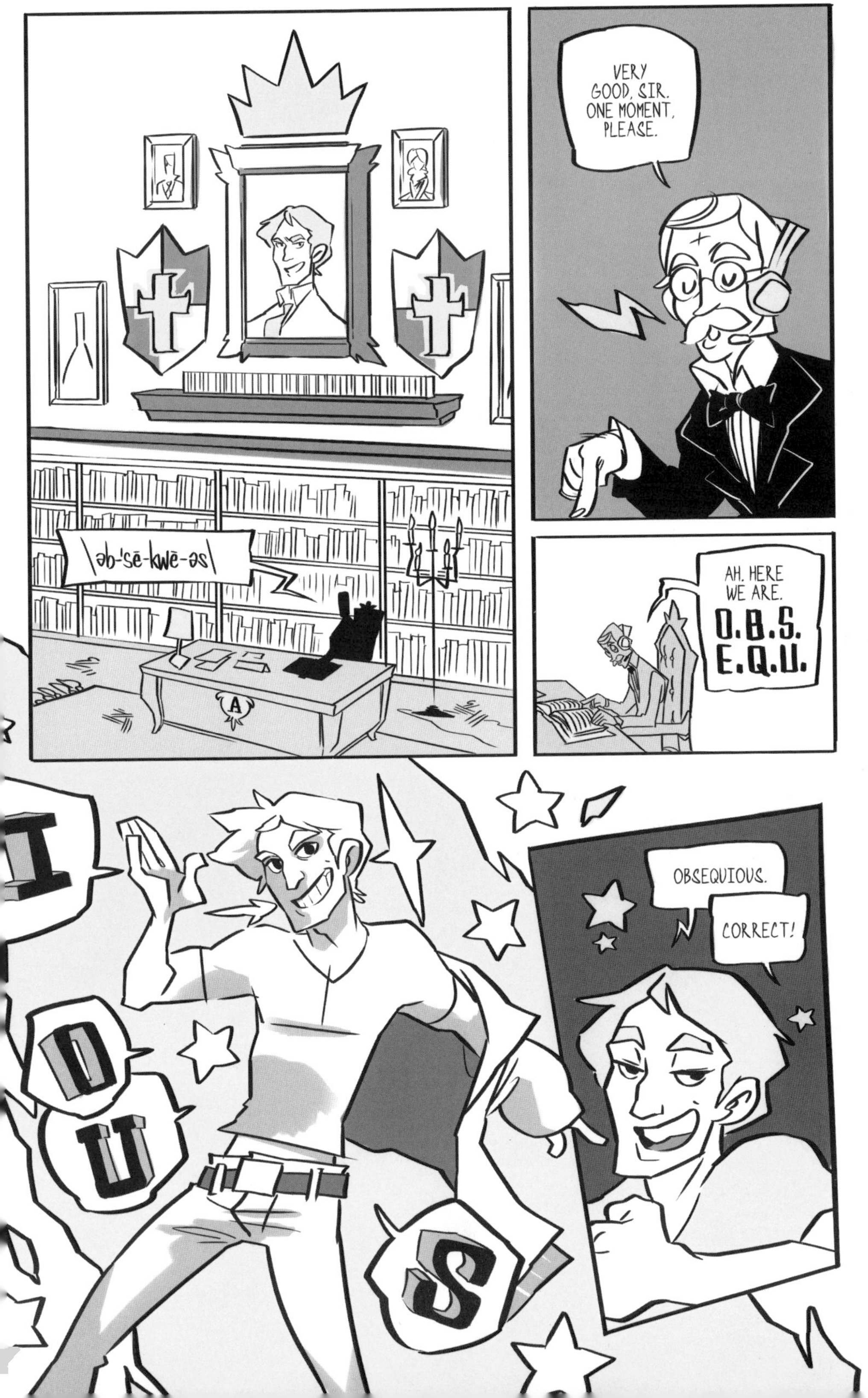
\əb-ˈsē-kwē-əs\
VERY GOOD, SIR. ONE MOMENT, PLEASE.
AH. HERE WE ARE.
O.B.S. E.Q.U.
I
O
U
S
OBSEQUIOUS.
CORRECT!

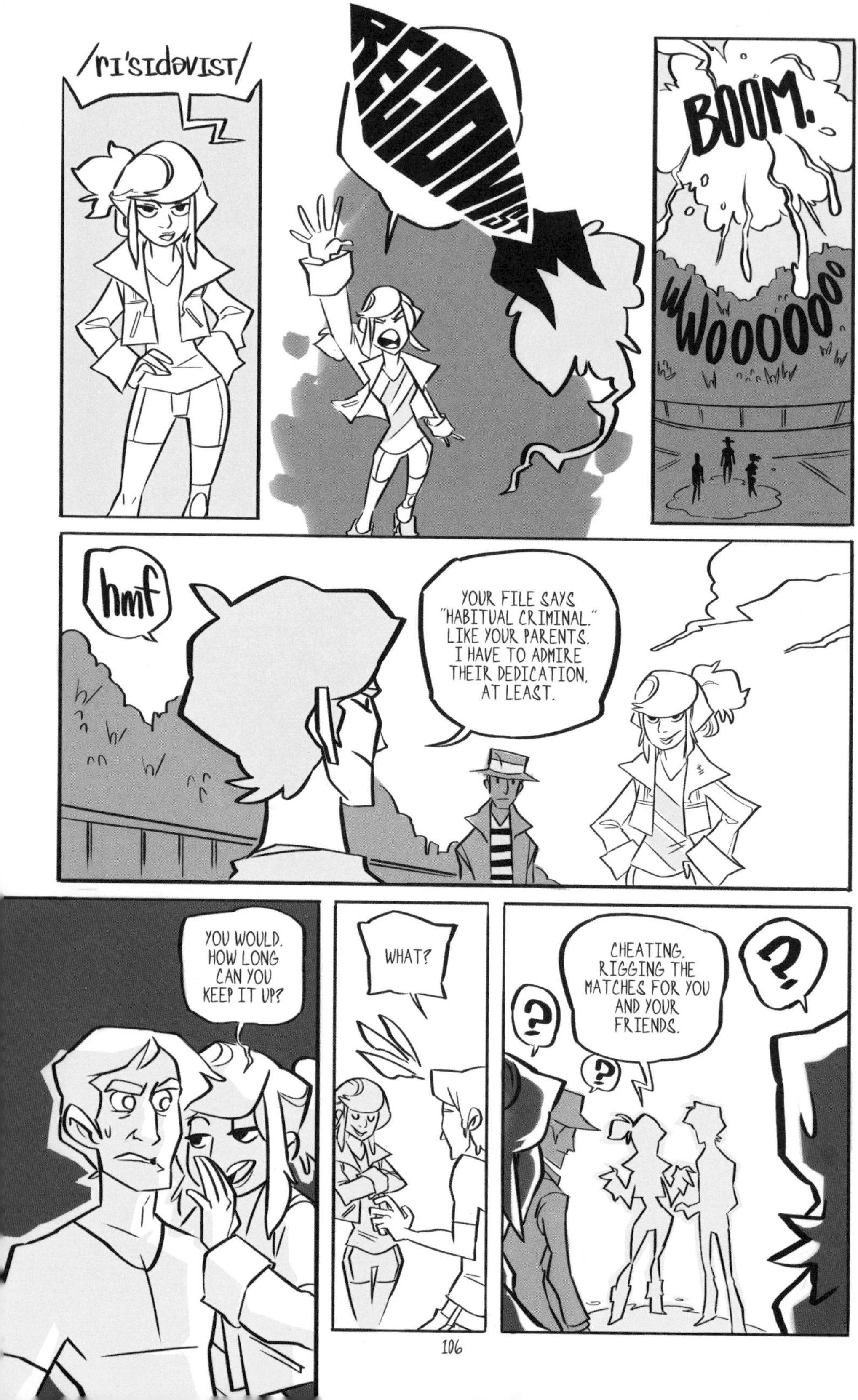
/rɪ'sɪdəvɪst/
RECIDIVIST
BOOM.
WWOOOOOOO
hmf
YOUR FILE SAYS "HABITUAL CRIMINAL." LIKE YOUR PARENTS. I HAVE TO ADMIRE THEIR DEDICATION, AT LEAST.
YOU WOULD. HOW LONG CAN YOU KEEP IT UP?
WHAT?
?
?
CHEATING. RIGGING THE MATCHES FOR YOU AND YOUR FRIENDS.
?

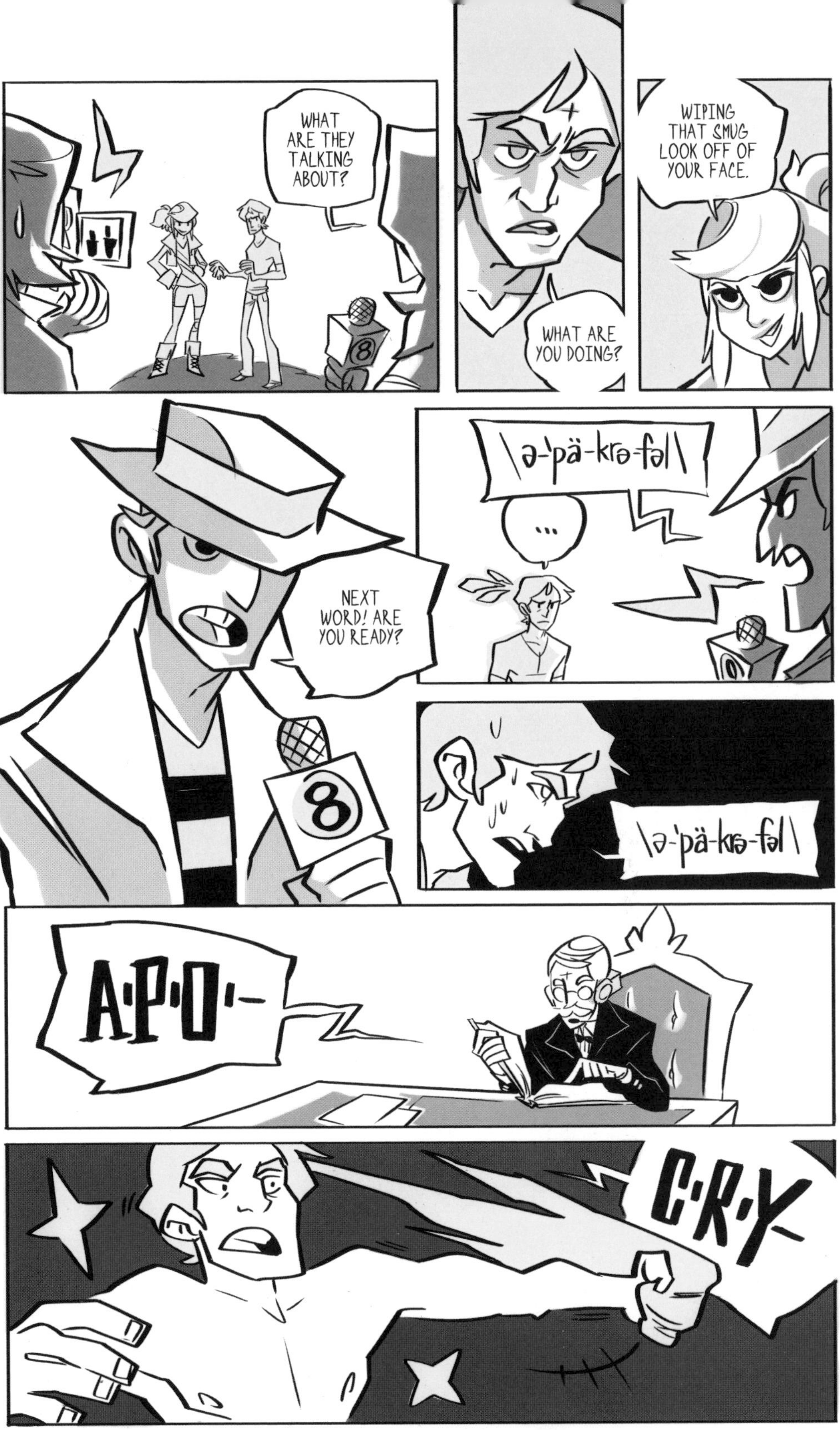
WHAT ARE THEY TALKING ABOUT?
WHAT ARE YOU DOING?
WIPING THAT SMUG LOOK OFF OF YOUR FACE.
NEXT WORD! ARE YOU READY?
\ə-ˈpä-krə-fəl\
...
\ə-ˈpä-krə-fəl\
A·P·O·-
C·R·Y·-

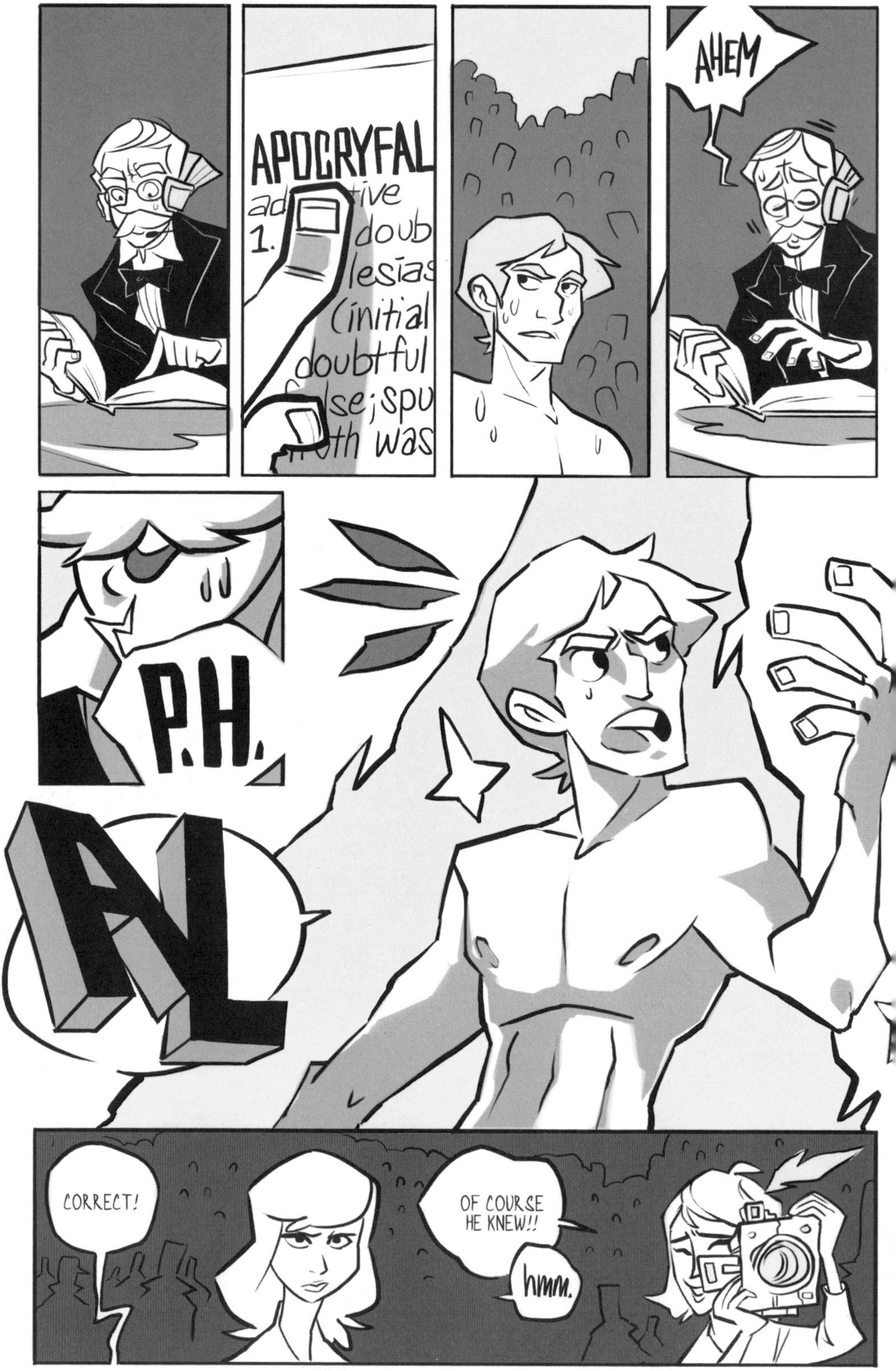
APOCRYFAL
ad tive
1. doub
lesias
(initial
doubtful
lse; spu
th was
AHEM
P.H.
AL
CORRECT!
OF COURSE HE KNEW!!
hmm.

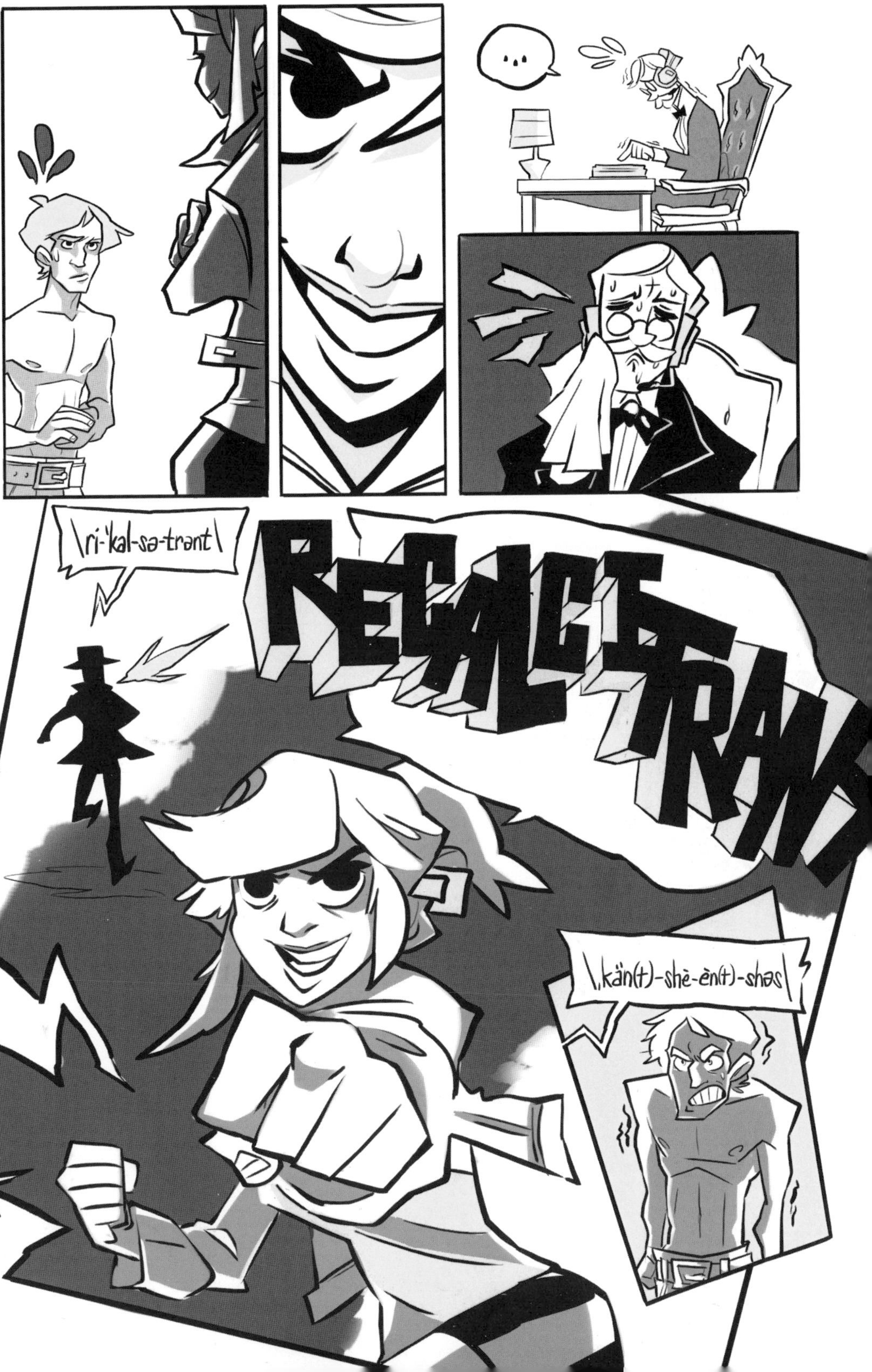
. . .
\ri-ˈkal-sə-trənt\
RECALCITRAN
\ˌkän(t)-shē-ˈen(t)-shəs\

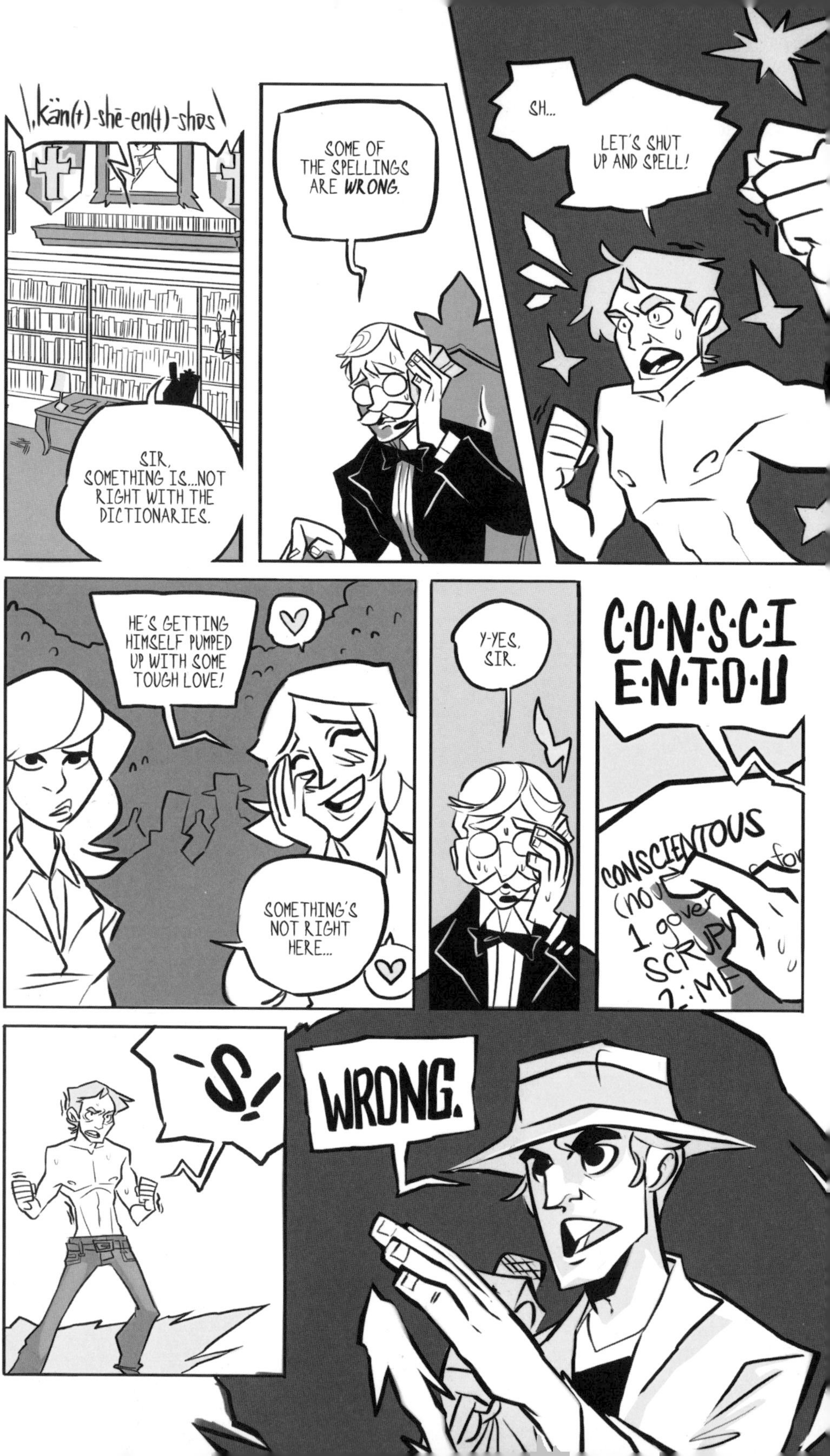
\ˌkän(t)-shē-en(t)-shəs\
SIR, SOMETHING IS...NOT RIGHT WITH THE DICTIONARIES.
SOME OF THE SPELLINGS ARE **WRONG**.
SH...
LET'S SHUT UP AND SPELL!
HE'S GETTING HIMSELF PUMPED UP WITH SOME TOUGH LOVE!
SOMETHING'S NOT RIGHT HERE...
Y-YES, SIR.
C·O·N·S·C·I E·N·T·O·U
CONSCIENTOUS
`S!
WRONG.

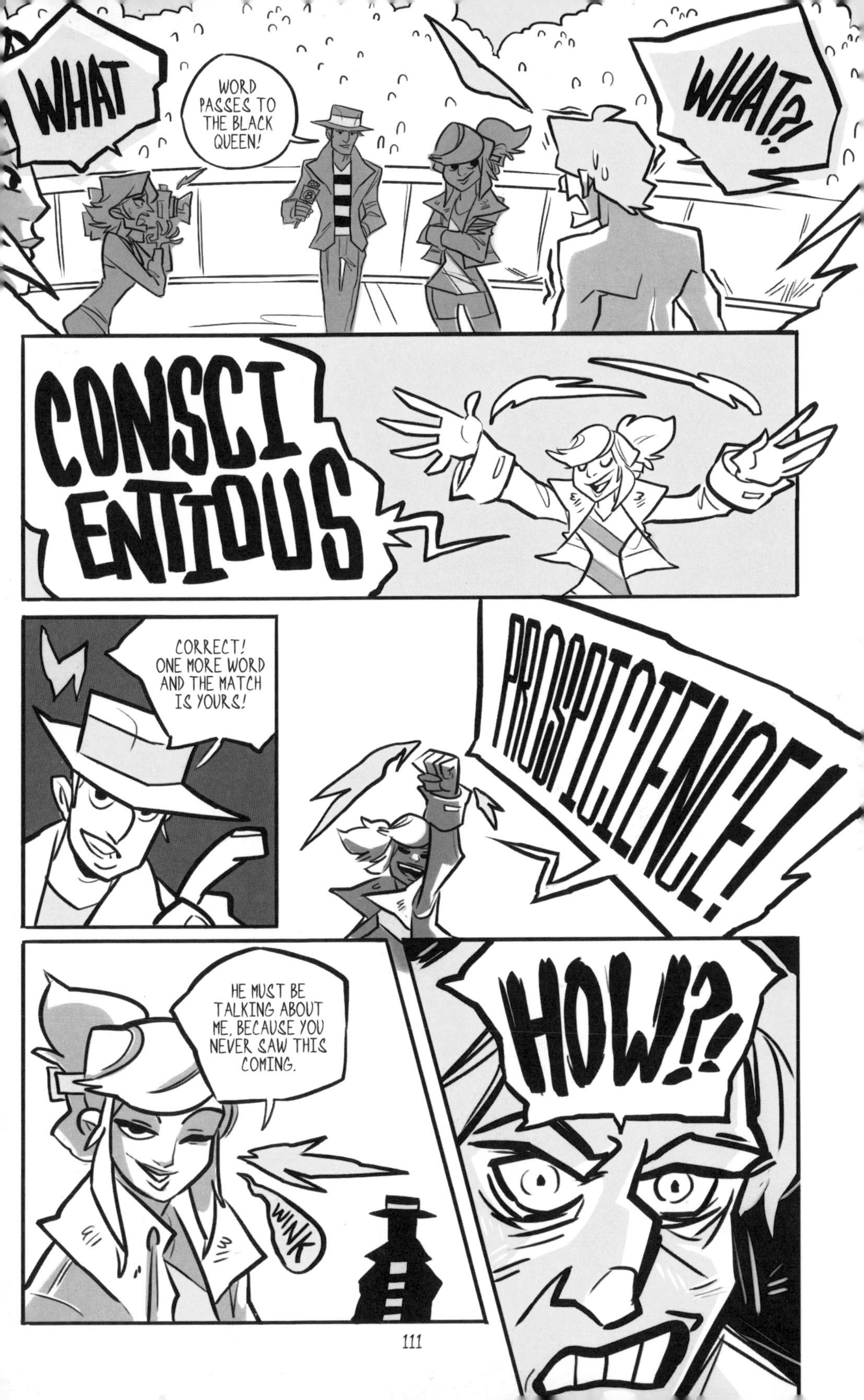
WHAT
WORD PASSES TO THE BLACK QUEEN!
WHAT!?!
CONSCIENTIOUS
CORRECT! ONE MORE WORD AND THE MATCH IS YOURS!
PROSPICIENCE!
HE MUST BE TALKING ABOUT ME, BECAUSE YOU NEVER SAW THIS COMING.
WINK
HOW!?!

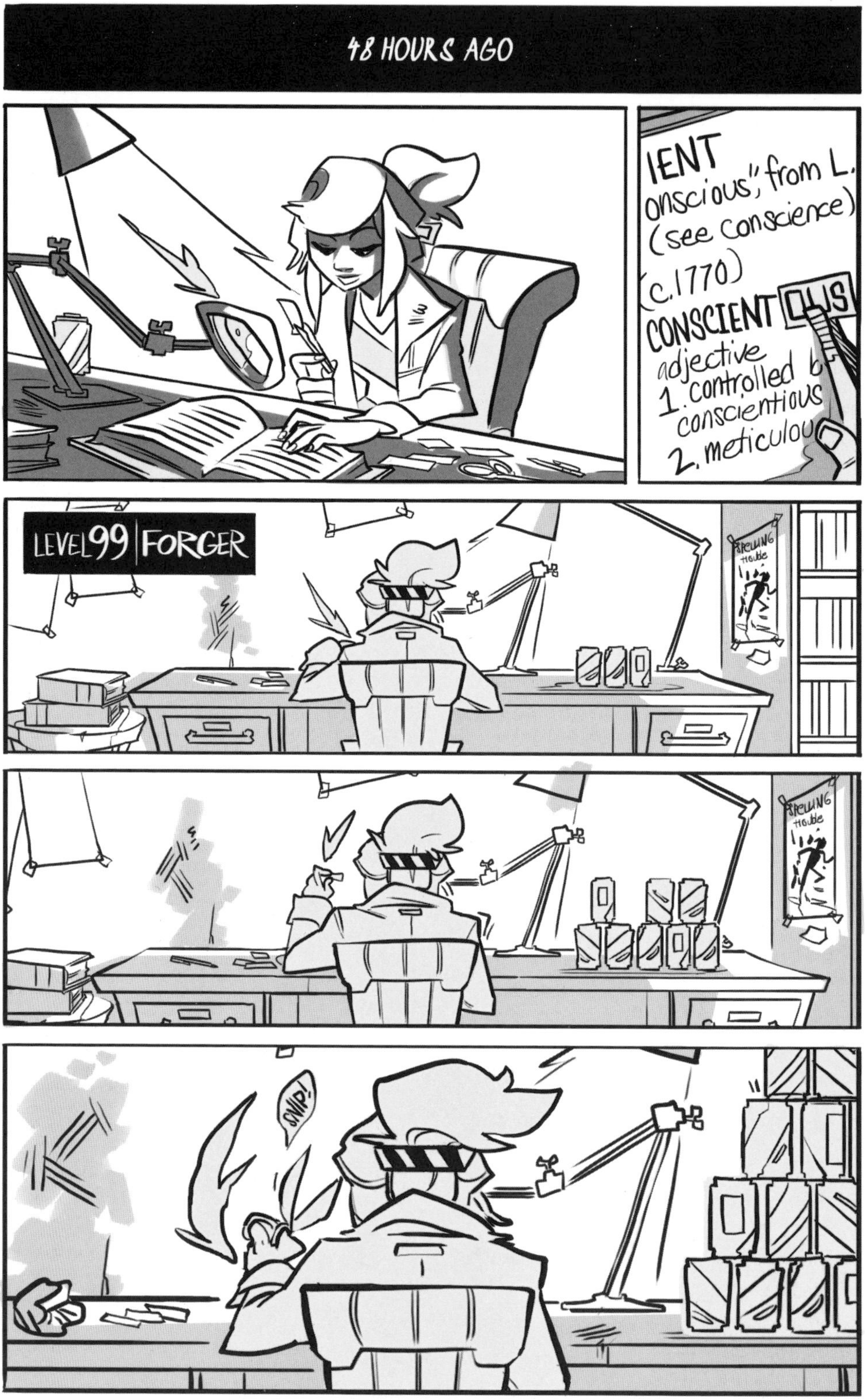
48 HOURS AGO
IENT
onscious", from L.
(see conscience)
(c.1770)
CONSCIENT OUS
adjective
1. controlled b
conscientious
2. meticulou
LEVEL 99 | FORGER
SPEWING trouble
SNIP!

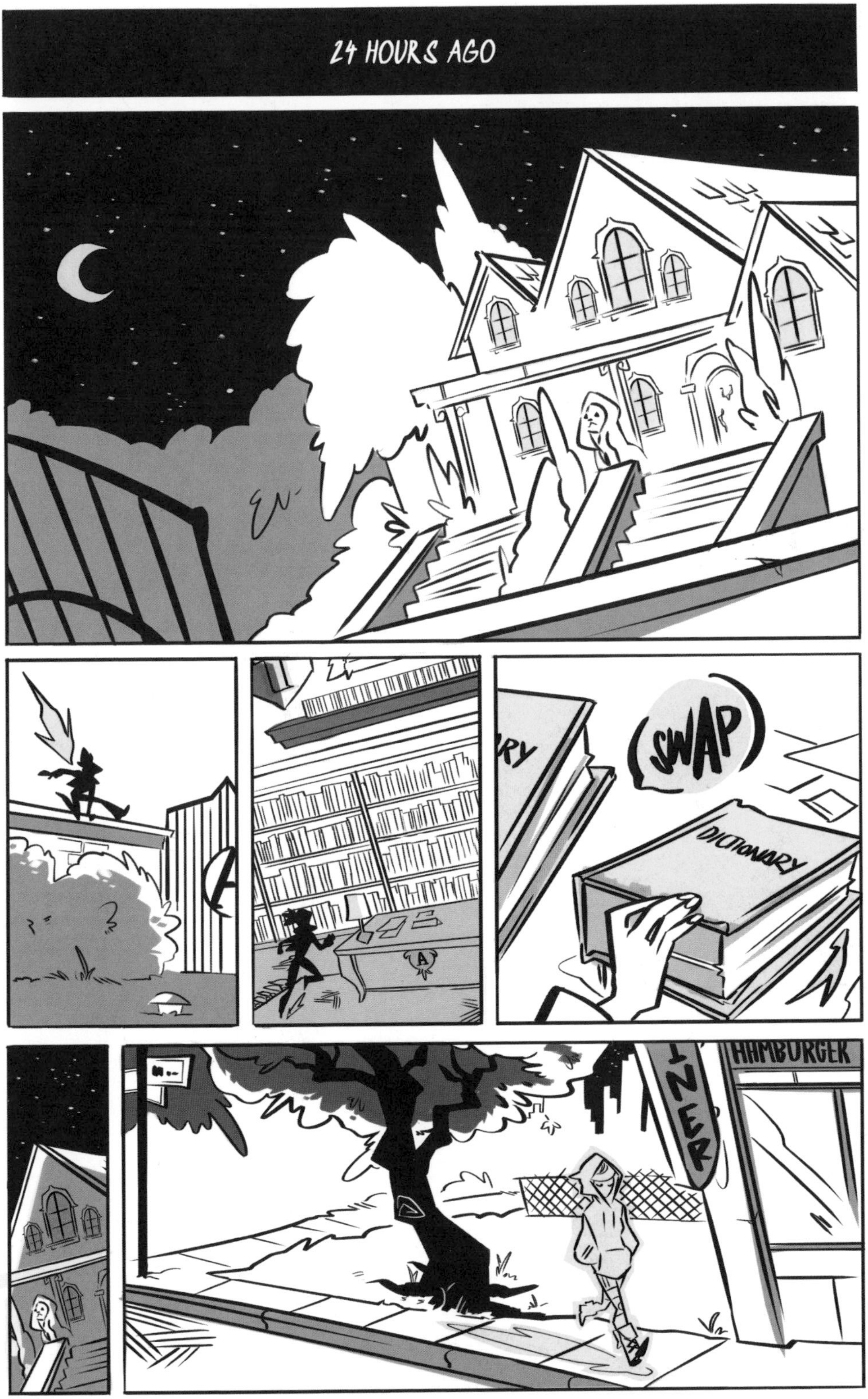
24 HOURS AGO
SWAP
DICTIONARY
HAMBURGER

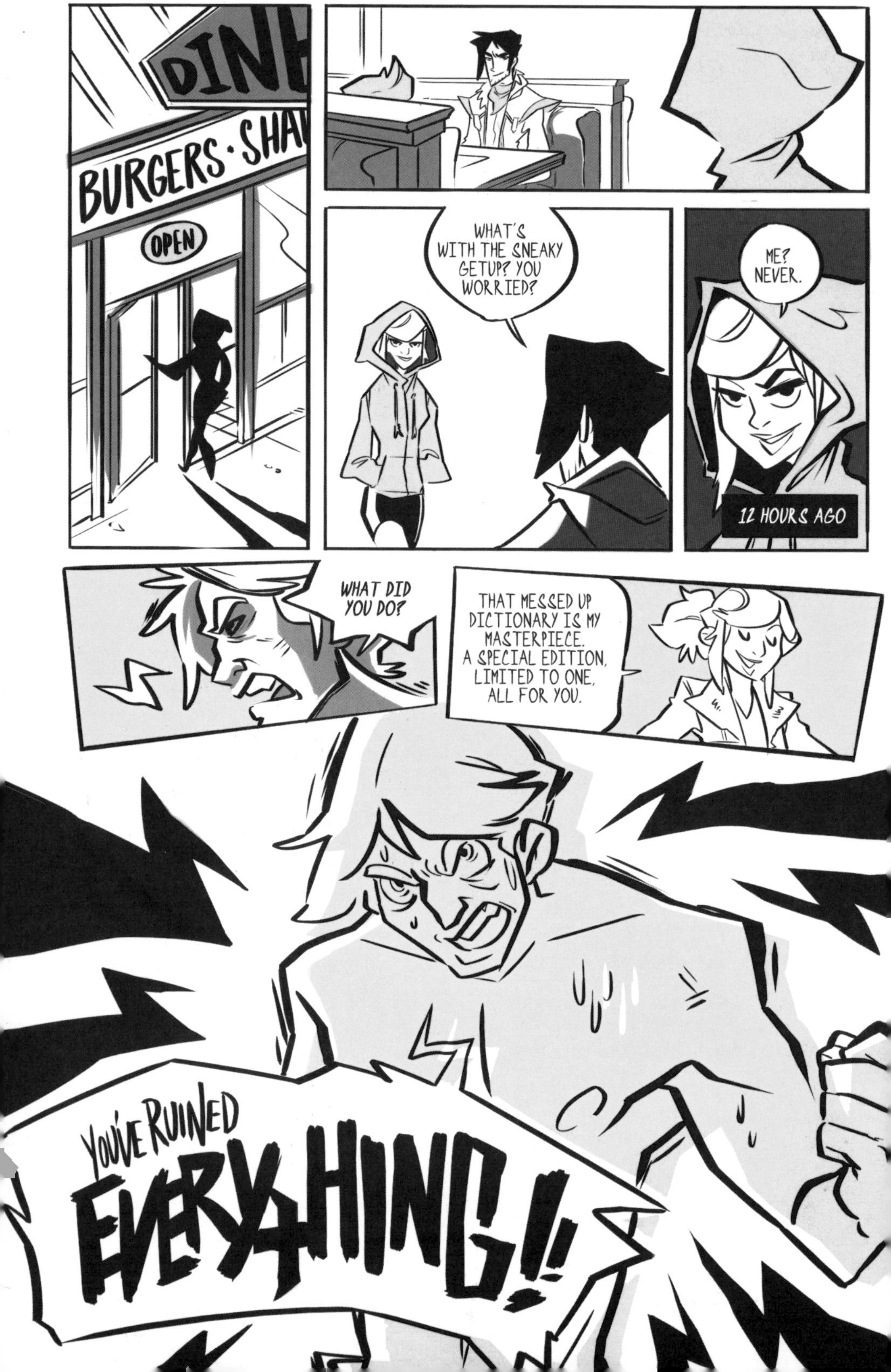
DINE
BURGERS · SHA
OPEN
WHAT'S WITH THE SNEAKY GETUP? YOU WORRIED?
ME? NEVER.
12 HOURS AGO
WHAT DID YOU DO?
THAT MESSED UP DICTIONARY IS MY MASTERPIECE. A SPECIAL EDITION, LIMITED TO ONE, ALL FOR YOU.
YOU'VE RUINED EVERYTHING!!

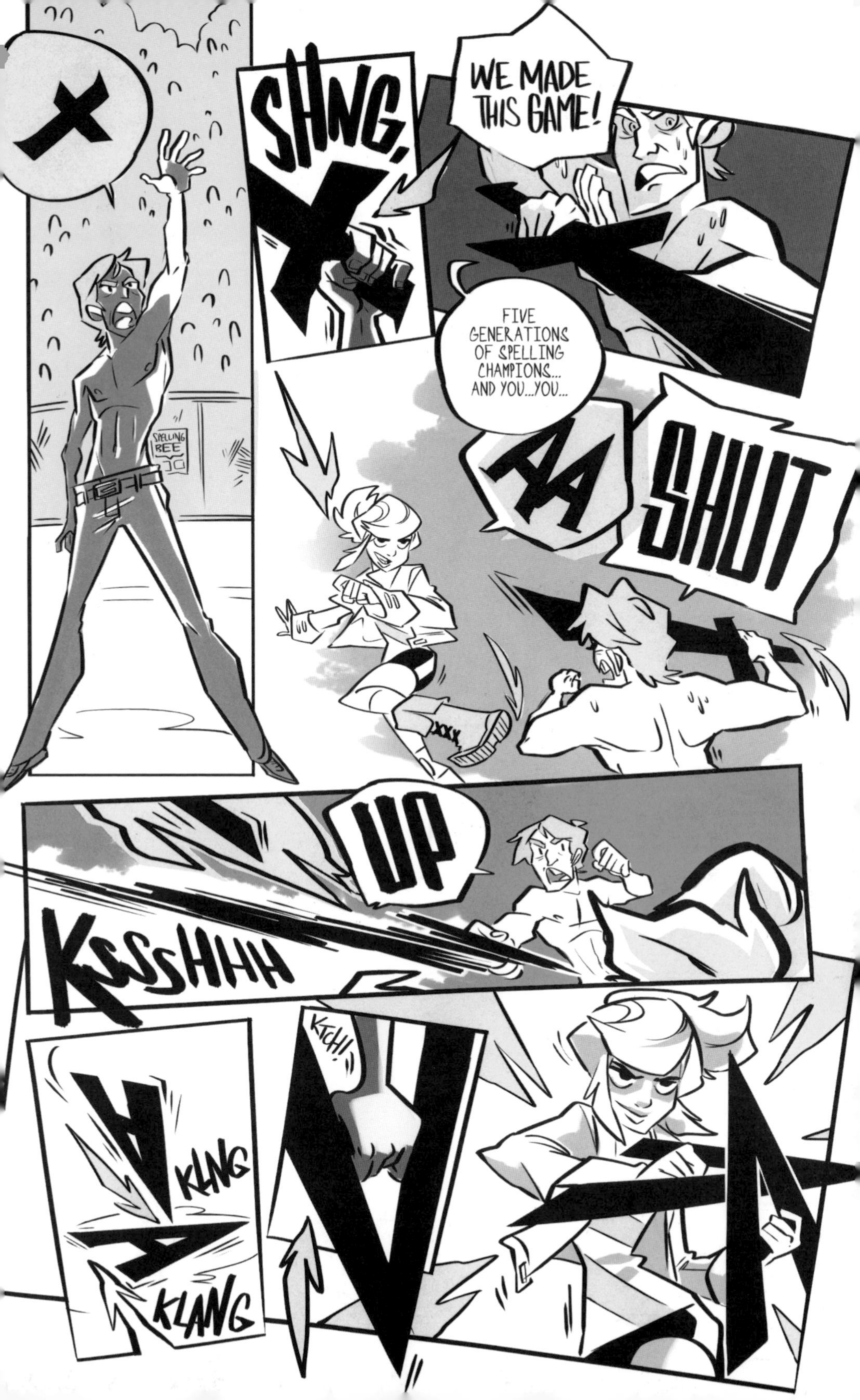
X
SHNG,
WE MADE THIS GAME!
FIVE GENERATIONS OF SPELLING CHAMPIONS... AND YOU...YOU...
SPELLING BEE
AA
SHUT
UP
KSSSHHH
KLNG
KLANG
KTCH!

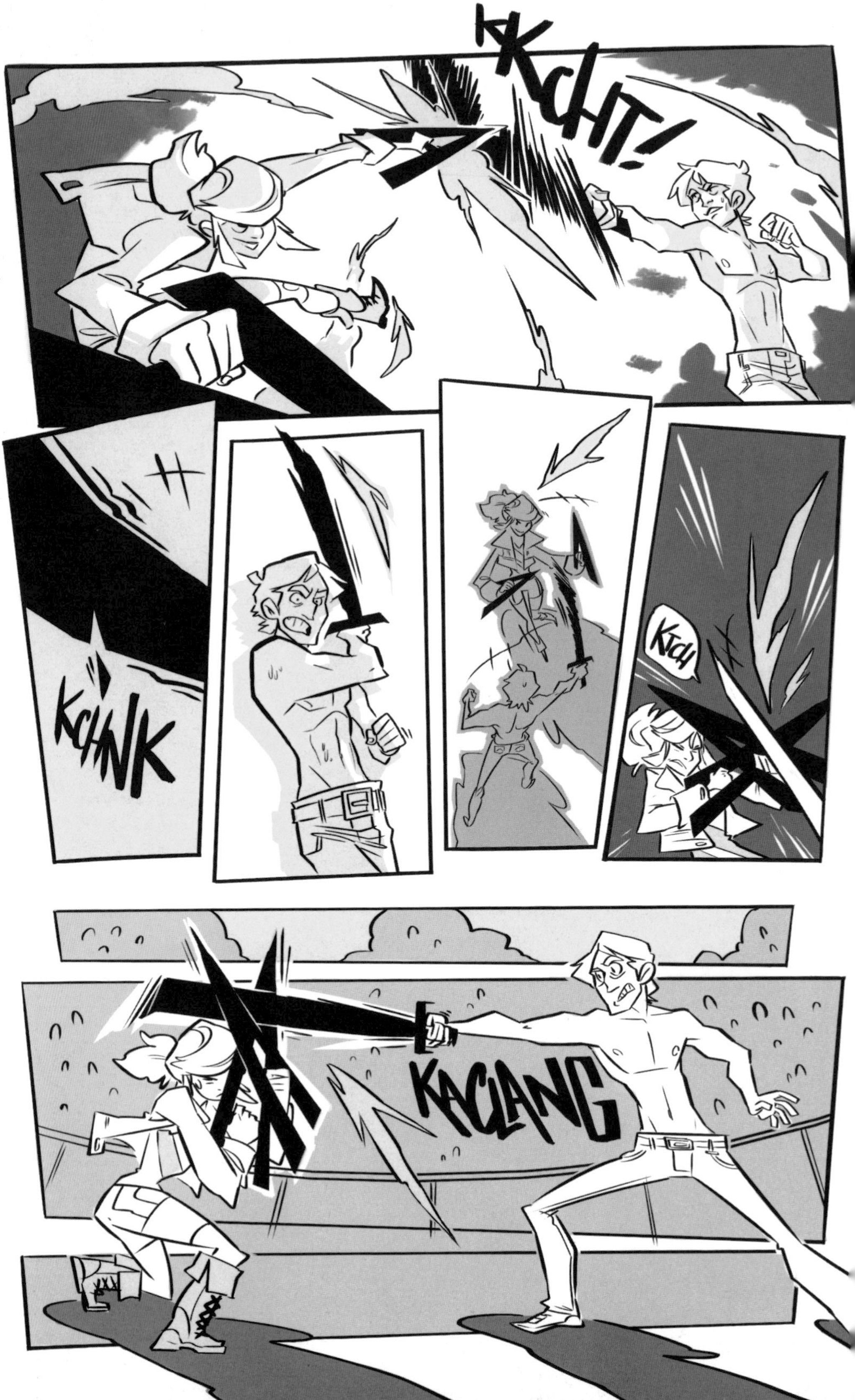
KKCHT!
KCHNK
KTCH
KACLANG

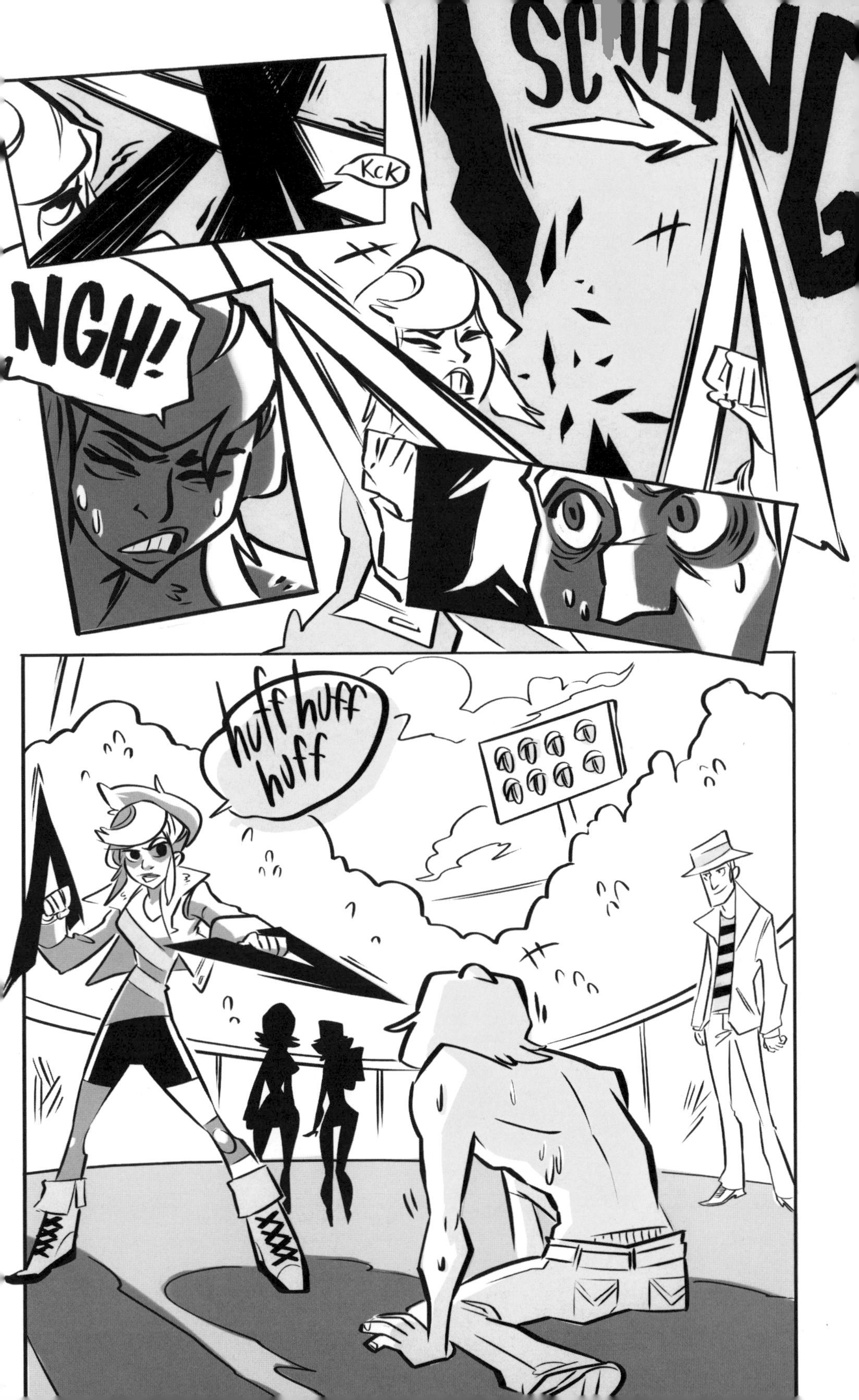
SCHHNG
KcK
NGH!
huff huff huff

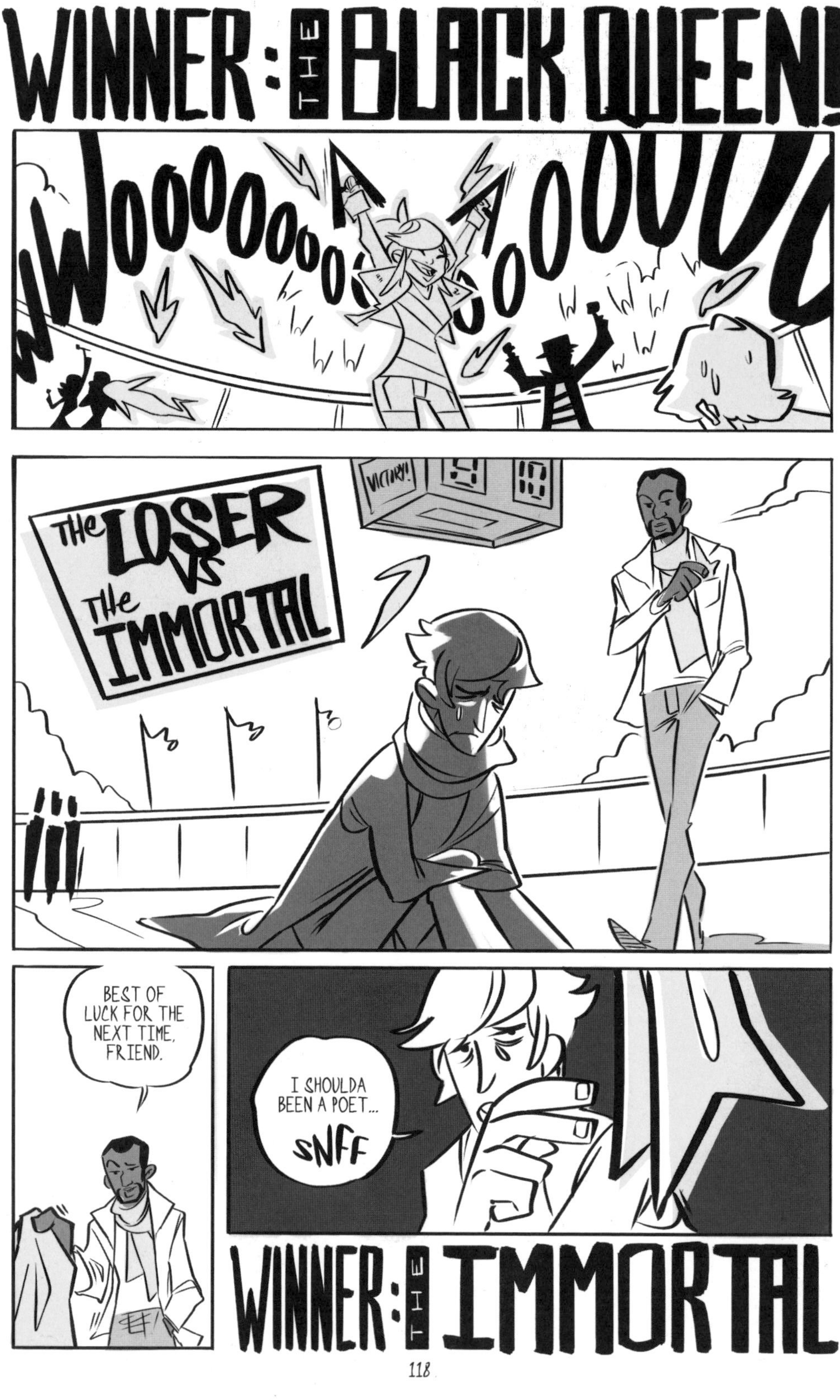
WINNER: THE BLACK QUEEN!
VICTORY!
THE LOSER VS THE IMMORTAL
BEST OF LUCK FOR THE NEXT TIME, FRIEND.
I SHOULDA BEEN A POET...
SNFF
WINNER: THE IMMORTAL

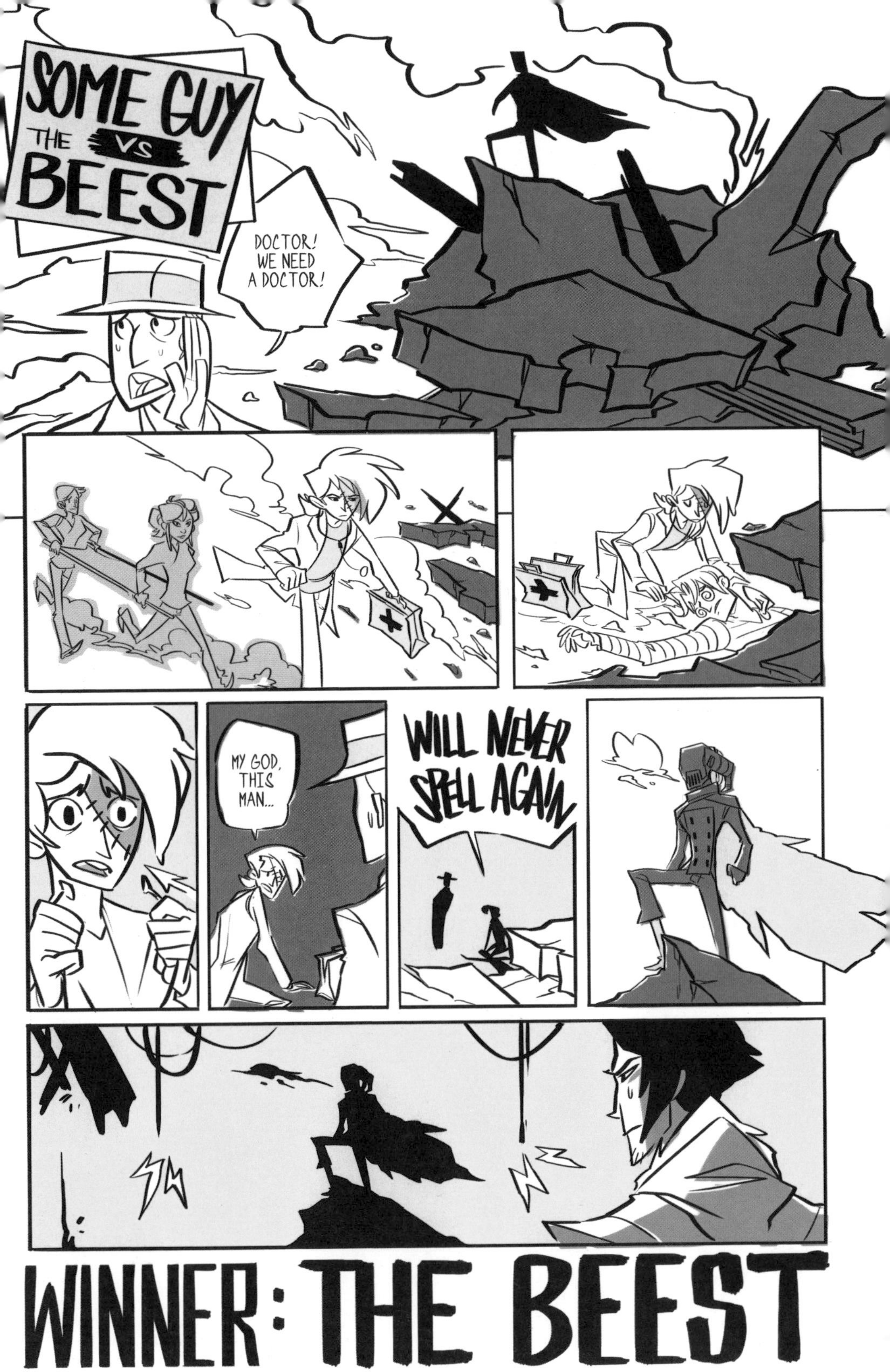
SOME GUY THE VS BEEST
DOCTOR! WE NEED A DOCTOR!
MY GOD, THIS MAN...
WILL NEVER SPELL AGAIN

WINNER: THE BEEST

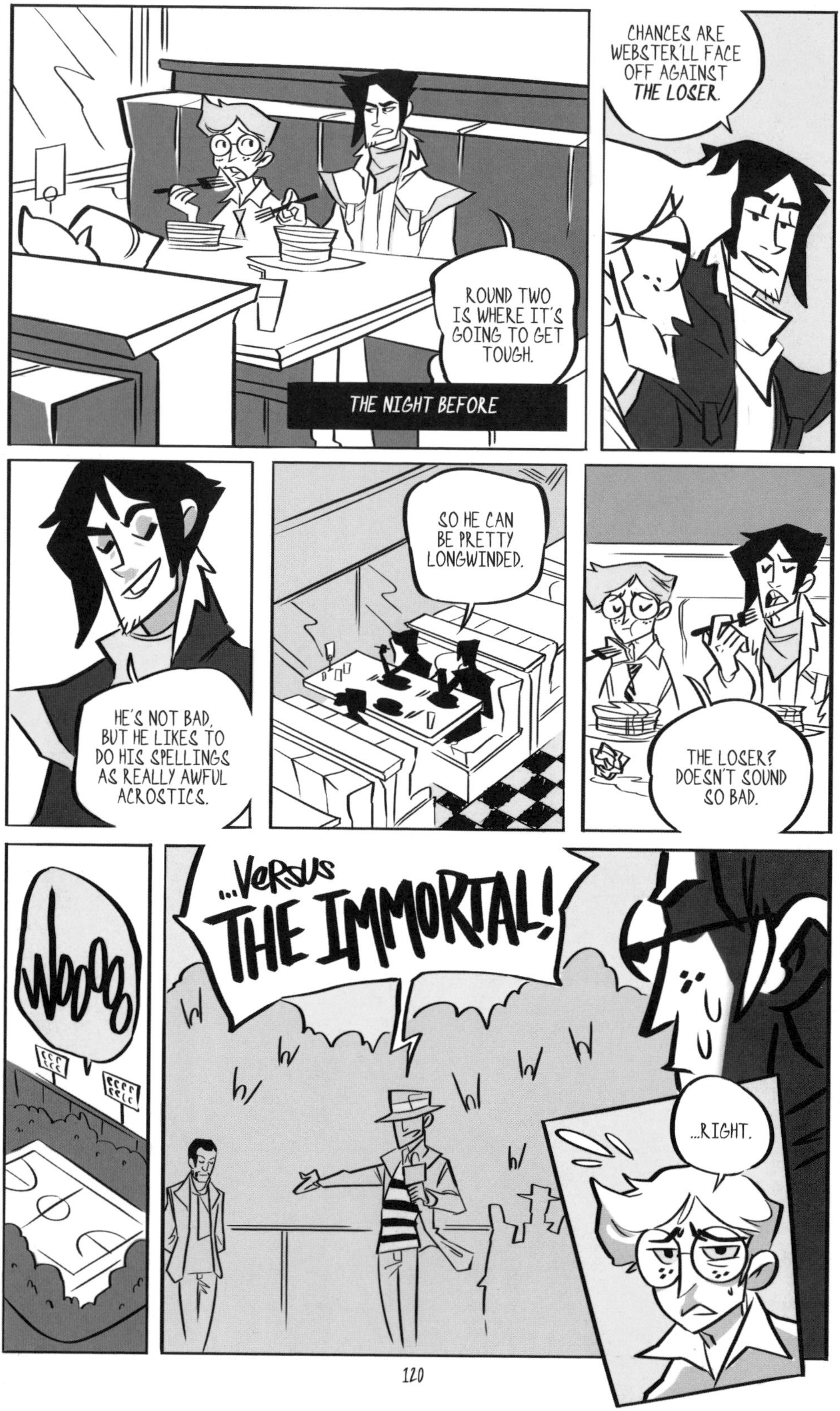
ROUND TWO IS WHERE IT'S GOING TO GET TOUGH.
THE NIGHT BEFORE
CHANCES ARE WEBSTER'LL FACE OFF AGAINST THE LOSER.
HE'S NOT BAD, BUT HE LIKES TO DO HIS SPELLINGS AS REALLY AWFUL ACROSTICS.
SO HE CAN BE PRETTY LONGWINDED.
THE LOSER? DOESN'T SOUND SO BAD.
WOOOO
...VERSUS THE IMMORTAL!
...RIGHT.

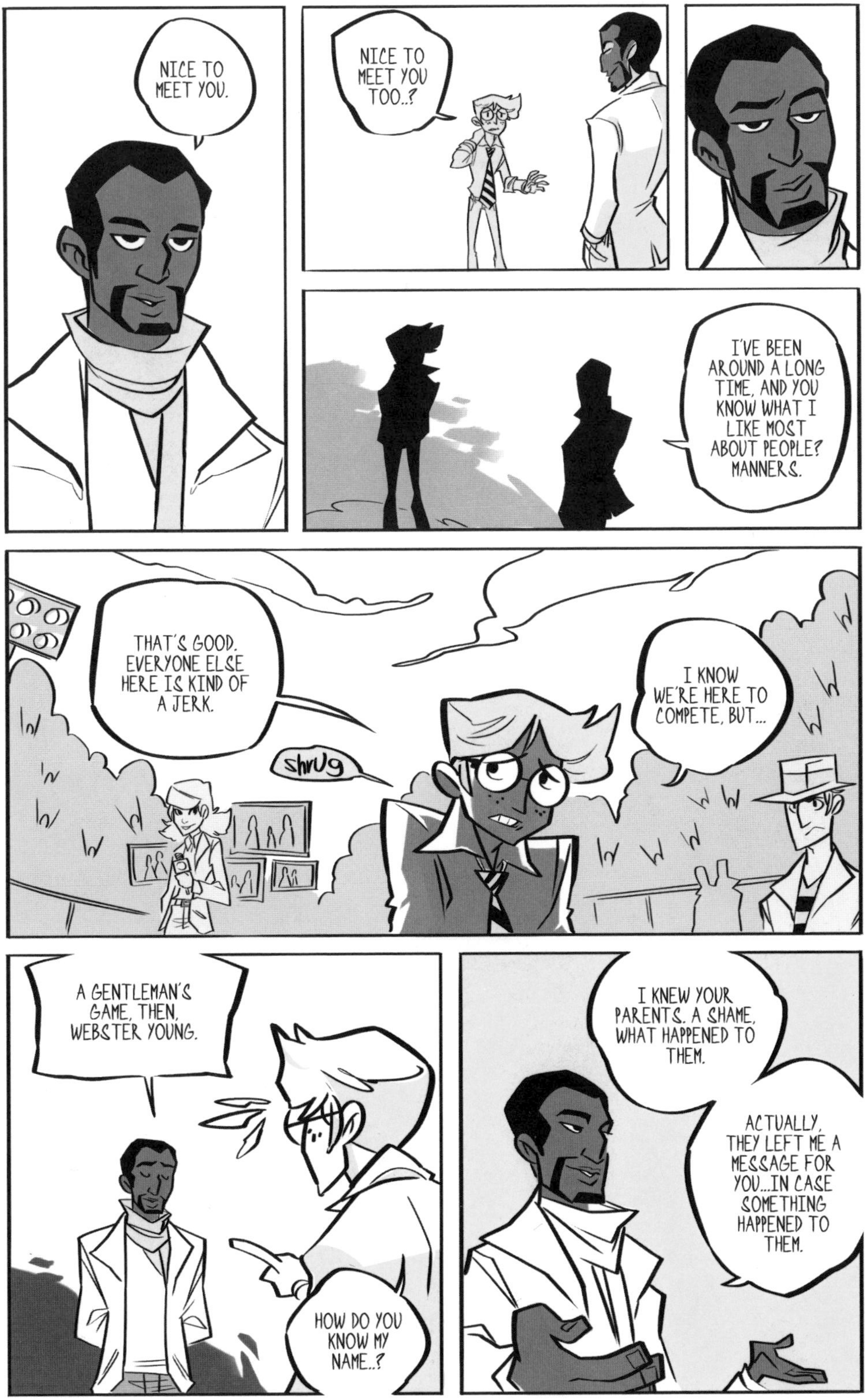
NICE TO MEET YOU.
NICE TO MEET YOU TOO..?
I'VE BEEN AROUND A LONG TIME, AND YOU KNOW WHAT I LIKE MOST ABOUT PEOPLE? MANNERS.
THAT'S GOOD. EVERYONE ELSE HERE IS KIND OF A JERK.
shrug
I KNOW WE'RE HERE TO COMPETE, BUT...
A GENTLEMAN'S GAME, THEN, WEBSTER YOUNG.
HOW DO YOU KNOW MY NAME..?
I KNEW YOUR PARENTS. A SHAME, WHAT HAPPENED TO THEM.
ACTUALLY, THEY LEFT ME A MESSAGE FOR YOU...IN CASE SOMETHING HAPPENED TO THEM.

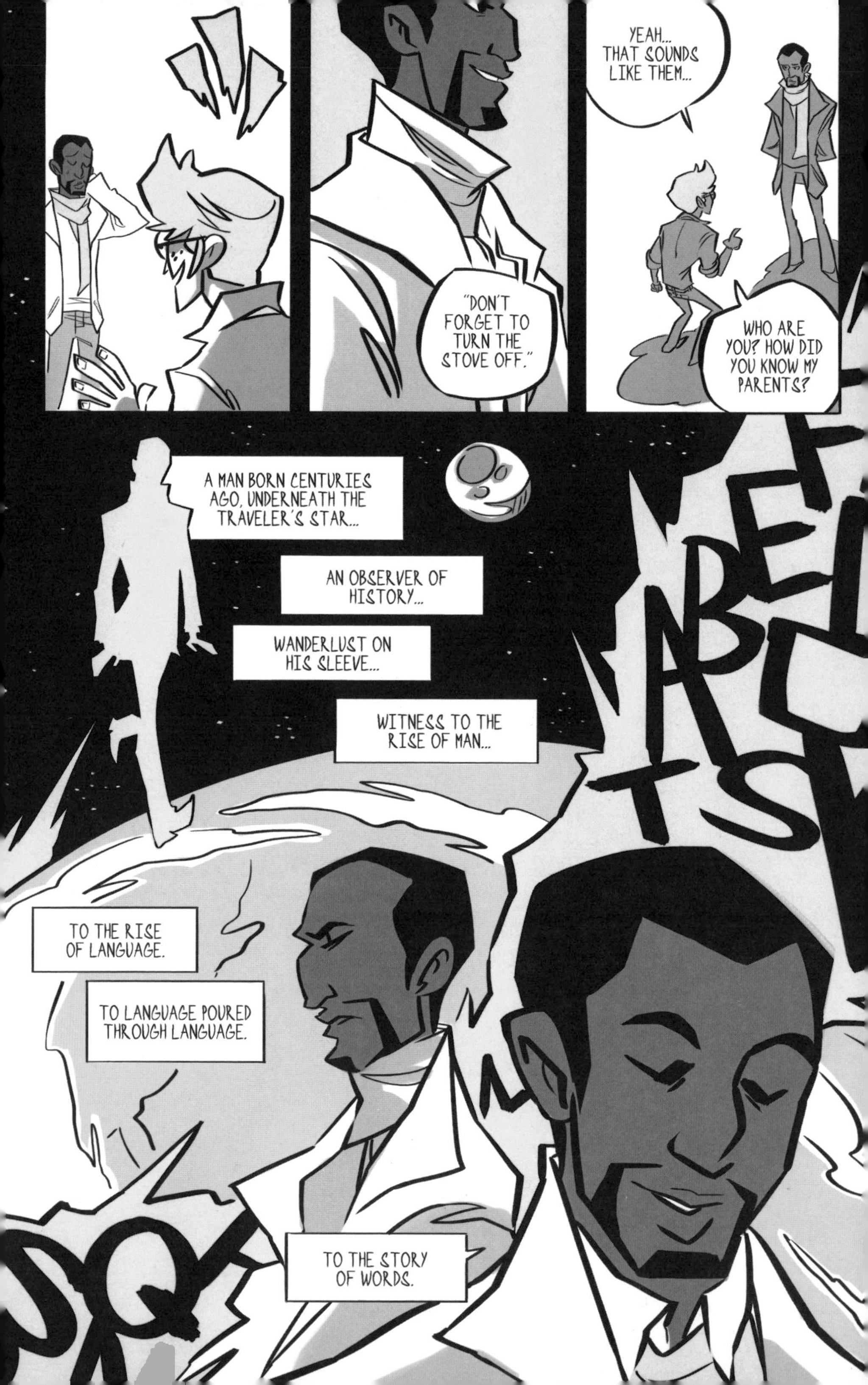
"DON'T FORGET TO TURN THE STOVE OFF."
YEAH... THAT SOUNDS LIKE THEM...
WHO ARE YOU? HOW DID YOU KNOW MY PARENTS?
A MAN BORN CENTURIES AGO, UNDERNEATH THE TRAVELER'S STAR...
AN OBSERVER OF HISTORY...
WANDERLUST ON HIS SLEEVE...
WITNESS TO THE RISE OF MAN...
TO THE RISE OF LANGUAGE.
TO LANGUAGE POURED THROUGH LANGUAGE.
TO THE STORY OF WORDS.

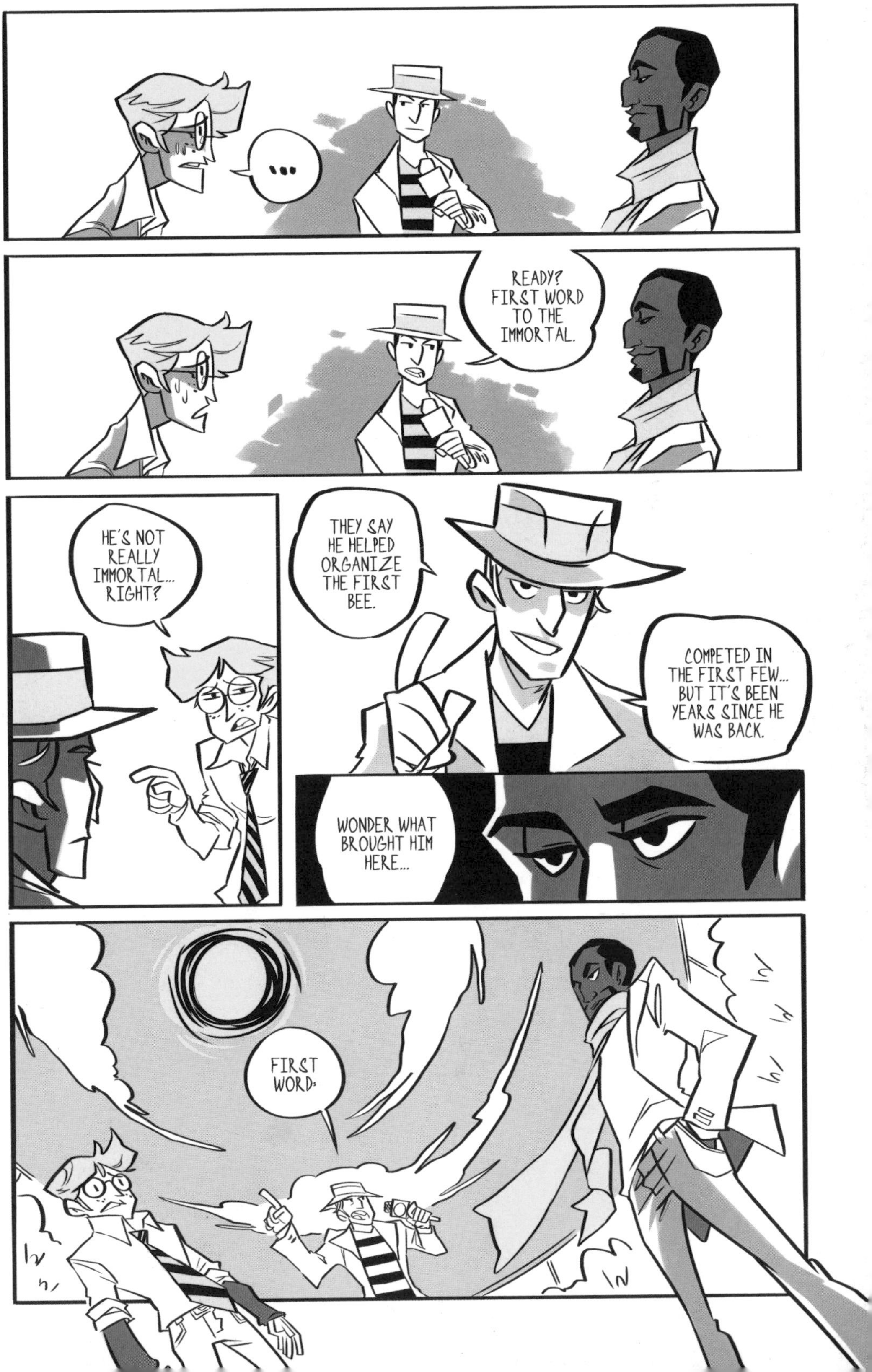
...
READY? FIRST WORD TO THE IMMORTAL.
HE'S NOT REALLY IMMORTAL... RIGHT?
THEY SAY HE HELPED ORGANIZE THE FIRST BEE.
COMPETED IN THE FIRST FEW... BUT IT'S BEEN YEARS SINCE HE WAS BACK.
WONDER WHAT BROUGHT HIM HERE...
FIRST WORD:

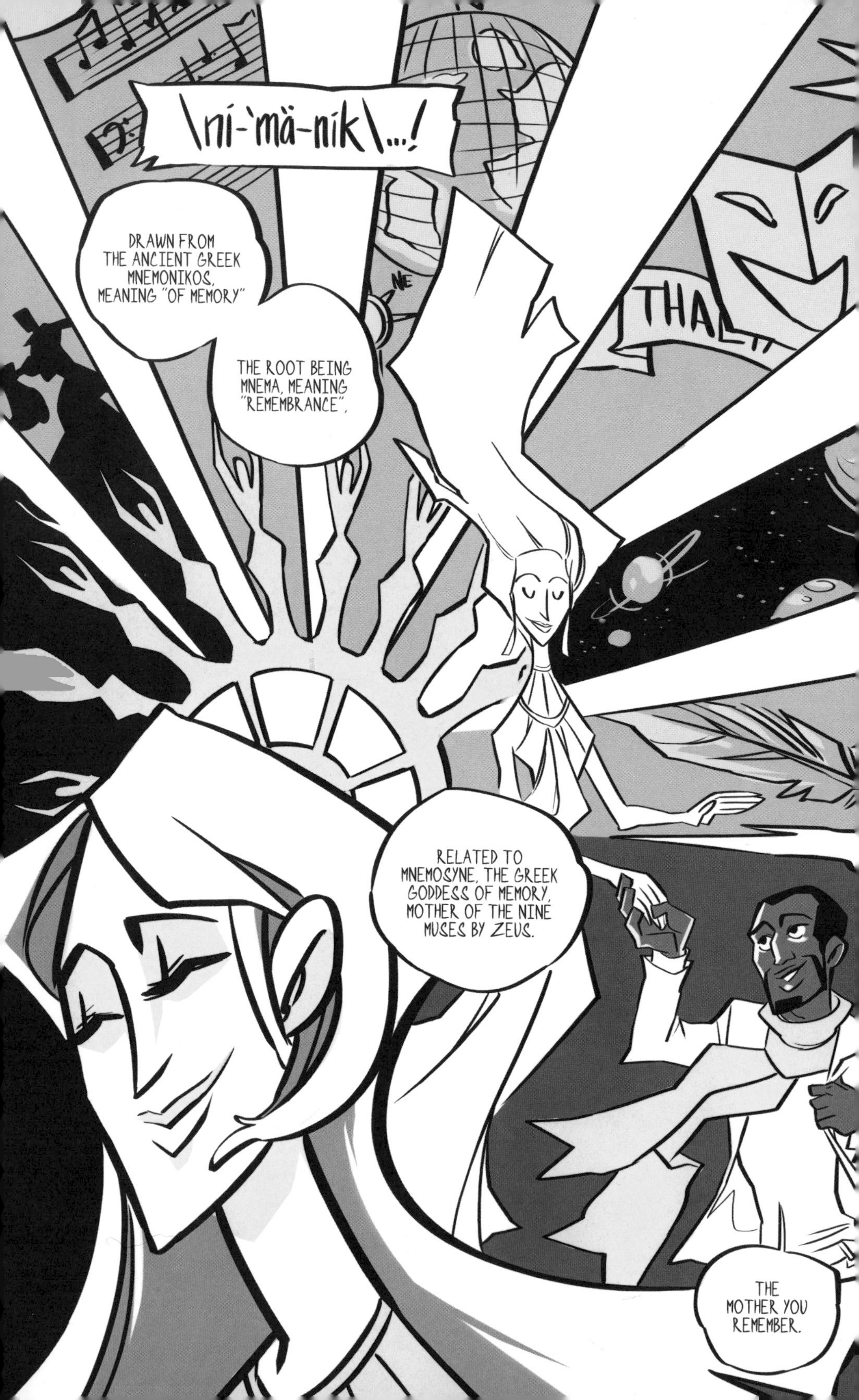
\ni-'mä-nik\...!
DRAWN FROM THE ANCIENT GREEK MNEMONIKOS, MEANING "OF MEMORY"
THE ROOT BEING MNEMA, MEANING "REMEMBRANCE",
THAL
RELATED TO MNEMOSYNE, THE GREEK GODDESS OF MEMORY, MOTHER OF THE NINE MUSES BY ZEUS.
THE MOTHER YOU REMEMBER.

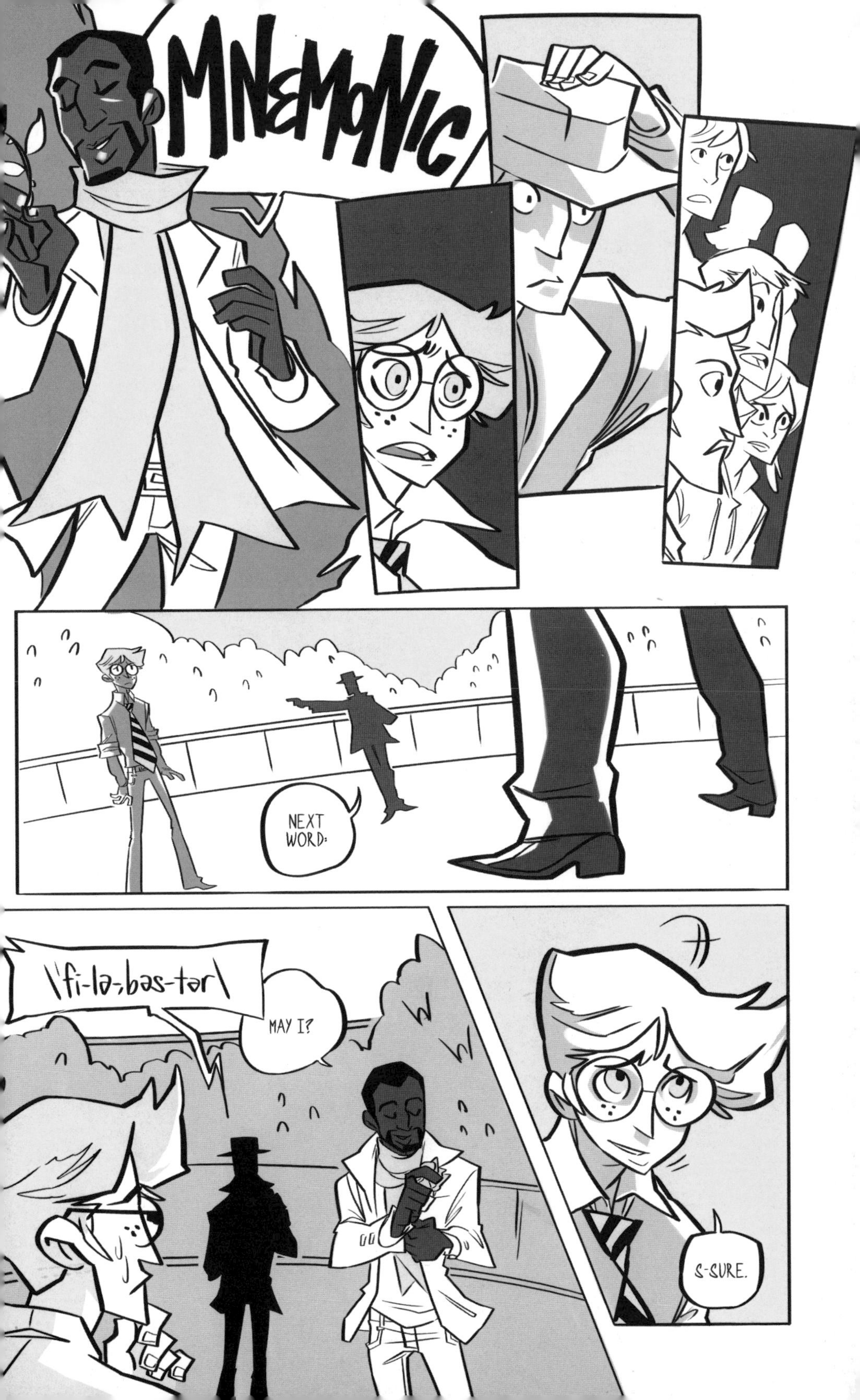
MNEMONIC
NEXT WORD:
\'fi-lə-ˌbəs-tər\
MAY I?
S-SURE.

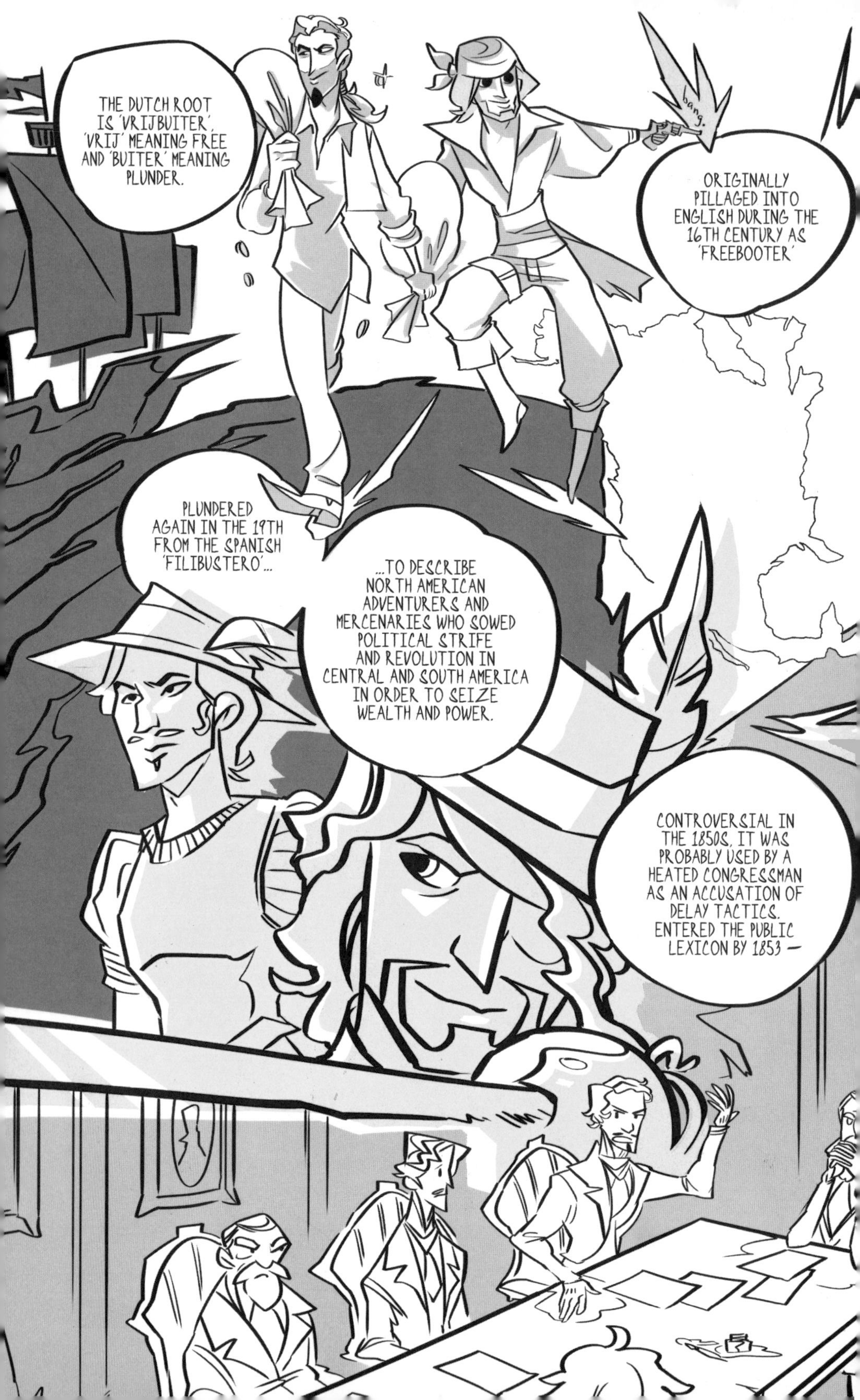
THE DUTCH ROOT IS 'VRIJBUITER', 'VRIJ' MEANING FREE AND 'BUITER' MEANING PLUNDER.
bang.
ORIGINALLY PILLAGED INTO ENGLISH DURING THE 16TH CENTURY AS 'FREEBOOTER'
PLUNDERED AGAIN IN THE 19TH FROM THE SPANISH 'FILIBUSTERO'...
...TO DESCRIBE NORTH AMERICAN ADVENTURERS AND MERCENARIES WHO SOWED POLITICAL STRIFE AND REVOLUTION IN CENTRAL AND SOUTH AMERICA IN ORDER TO SEIZE WEALTH AND POWER.
CONTROVERSIAL IN THE 1850S, IT WAS PROBABLY USED BY A HEATED CONGRESSMAN AS AN ACCUSATION OF DELAY TACTICS. ENTERED THE PUBLIC LEXICON BY 1853 —

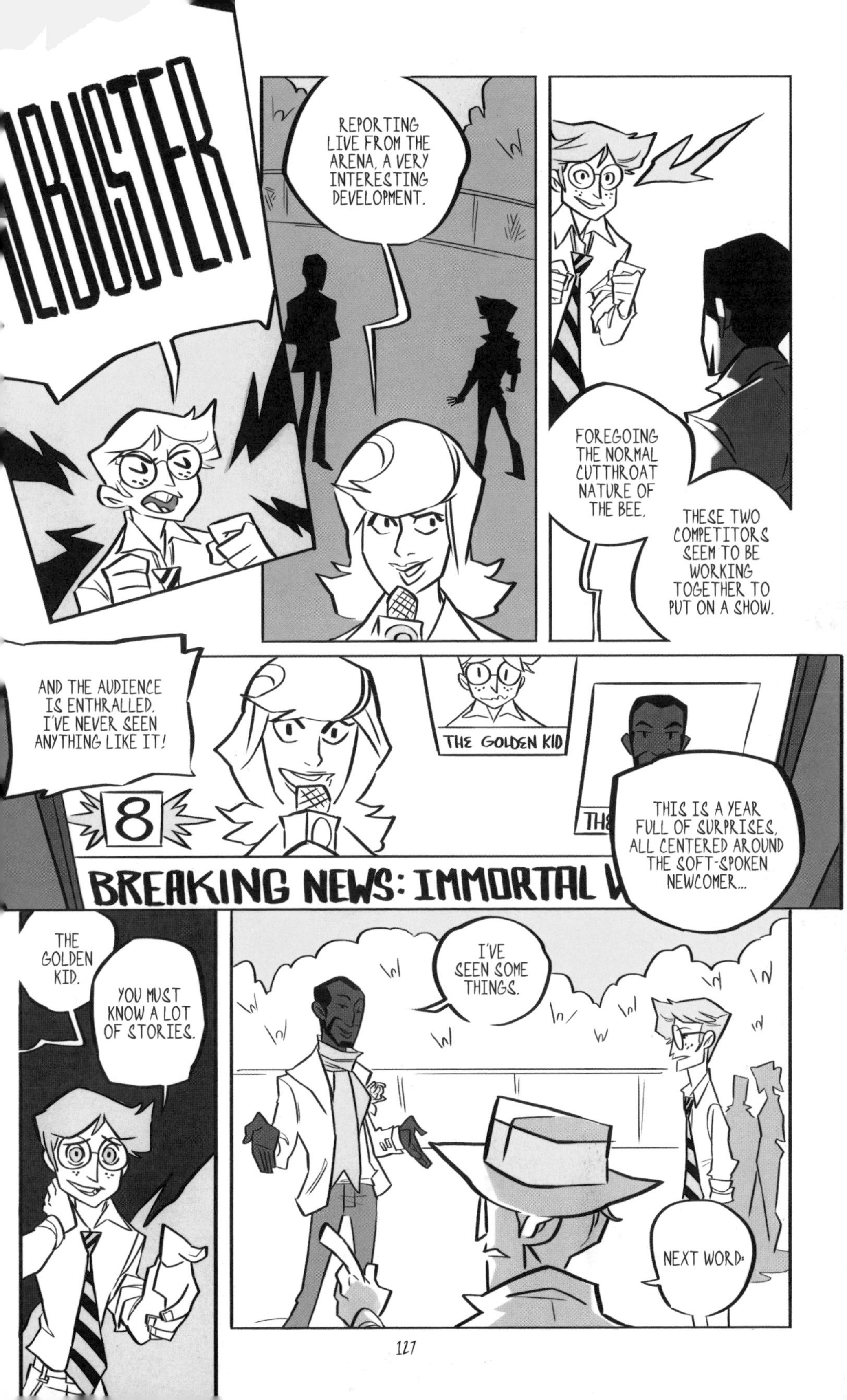
...NGBUSTER
REPORTING LIVE FROM THE ARENA, A VERY INTERESTING DEVELOPMENT.
FOREGOING THE NORMAL CUTTHROAT NATURE OF THE BEE,
THESE TWO COMPETITORS SEEM TO BE WORKING TOGETHER TO PUT ON A SHOW.
AND THE AUDIENCE IS ENTHRALLED. I'VE NEVER SEEN ANYTHING LIKE IT!
8
THE GOLDEN KID
BREAKING NEWS: IMMORTAL W
THIS IS A YEAR FULL OF SURPRISES, ALL CENTERED AROUND THE SOFT-SPOKEN NEWCOMER...
THE GOLDEN KID.
YOU MUST KNOW A LOT OF STORIES.
I'VE SEEN SOME THINGS.
NEXT WORD:

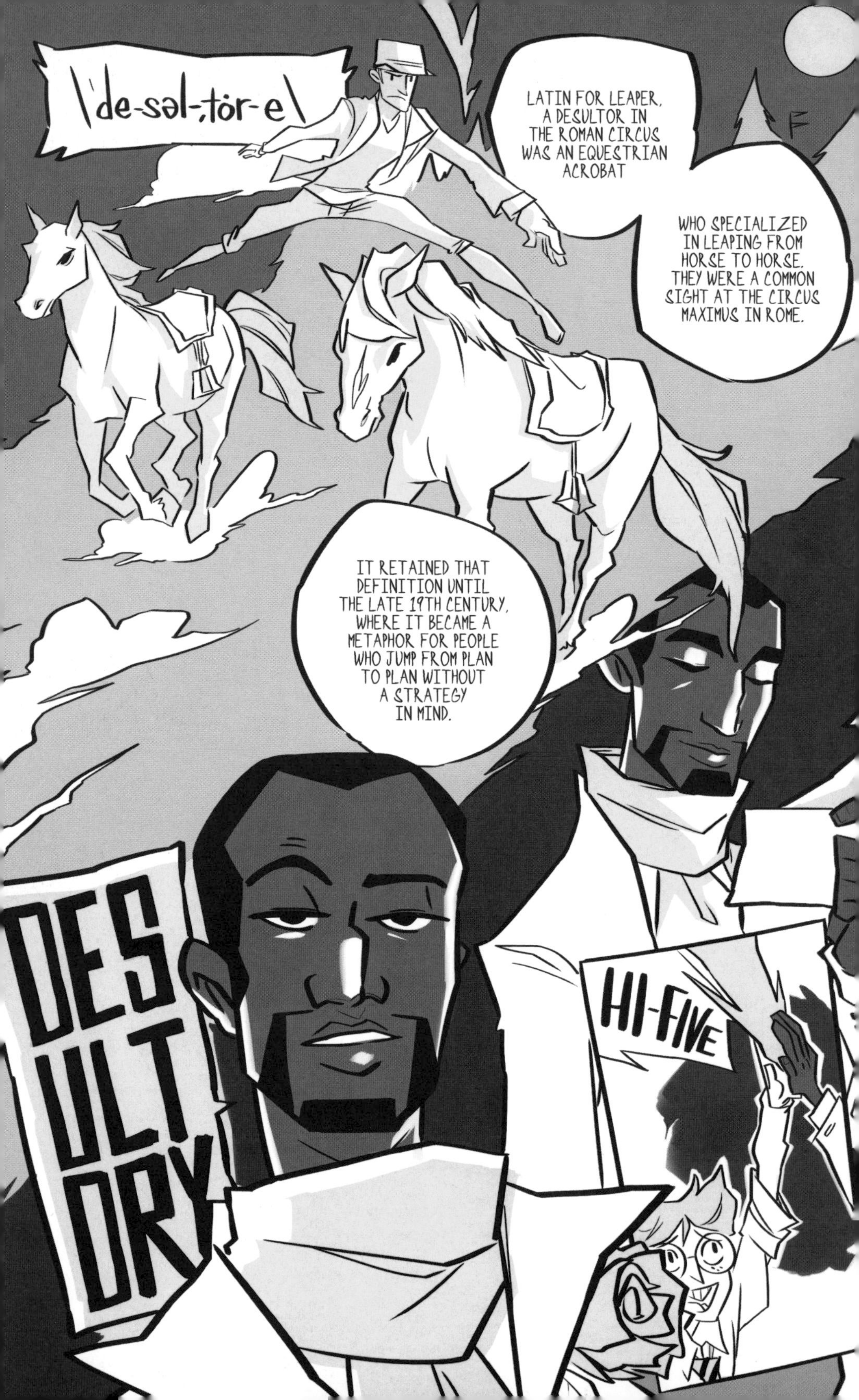

\ˈde-səl-ˌtȯr-ē\
LATIN FOR LEAPER, A DESULTOR IN THE ROMAN CIRCUS WAS AN EQUESTRIAN ACROBAT
WHO SPECIALIZED IN LEAPING FROM HORSE TO HORSE. THEY WERE A COMMON SIGHT AT THE CIRCUS MAXIMUS IN ROME.
IT RETAINED THAT DEFINITION UNTIL THE LATE 19TH CENTURY, WHERE IT BECAME A METAPHOR FOR PEOPLE WHO JUMP FROM PLAN TO PLAN WITHOUT A STRATEGY IN MIND.
DES ULT ORY
HI-FIVE

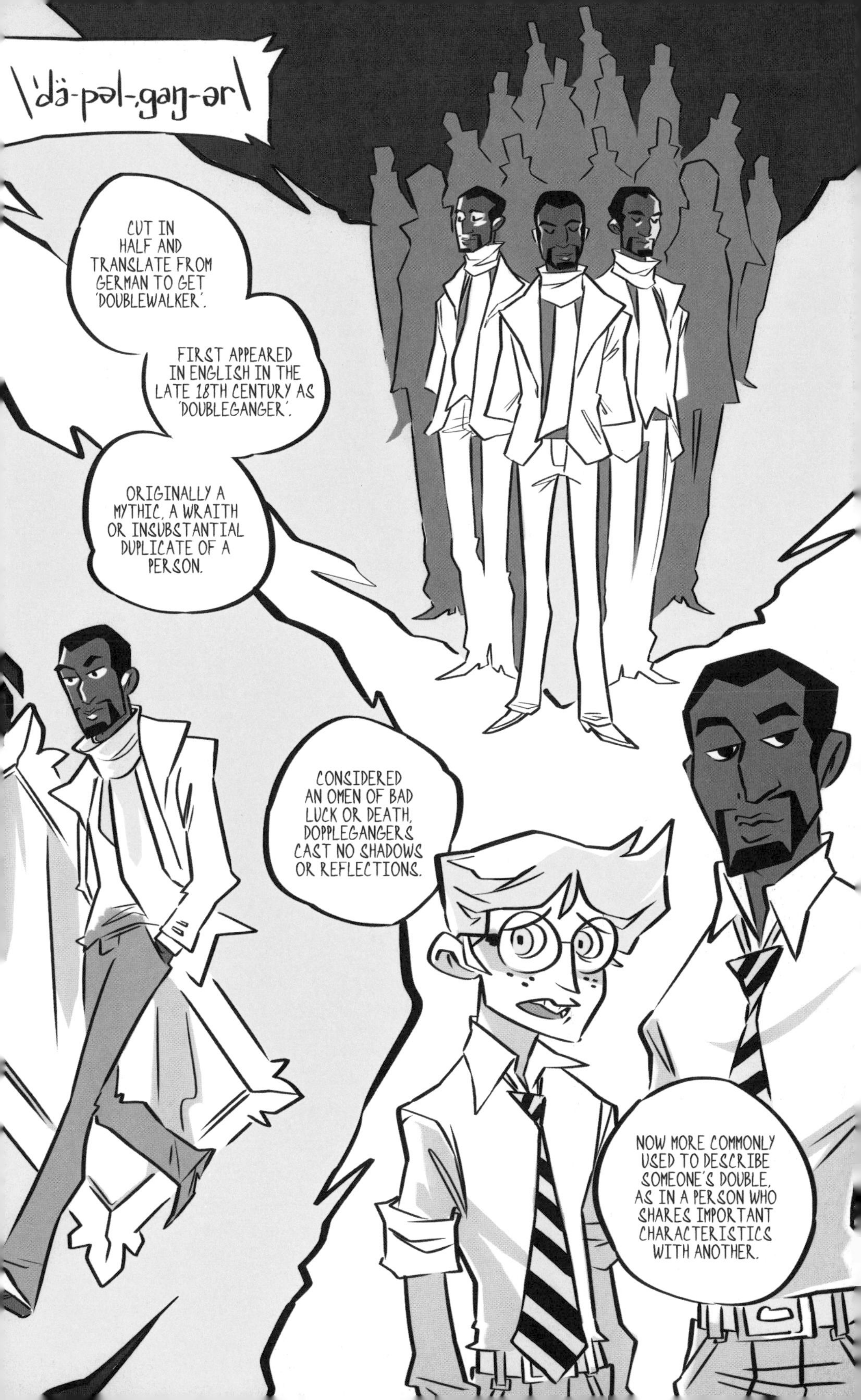
\ˈdä-pəl-ˌgaŋ-ər\
CUT IN HALF AND TRANSLATE FROM GERMAN TO GET 'DOUBLEWALKER'.
FIRST APPEARED IN ENGLISH IN THE LATE 18TH CENTURY AS 'DOUBLEGANGER'.
ORIGINALLY A MYTHIC, A WRAITH OR INSUBSTANTIAL DUPLICATE OF A PERSON.
CONSIDERED AN OMEN OF BAD LUCK OR DEATH, DOPPLEGANGERS CAST NO SHADOWS OR REFLECTIONS.
NOW MORE COMMONLY USED TO DESCRIBE SOMEONE'S DOUBLE, AS IN A PERSON WHO SHARES IMPORTANT CHARACTERISTICS WITH ANOTHER.

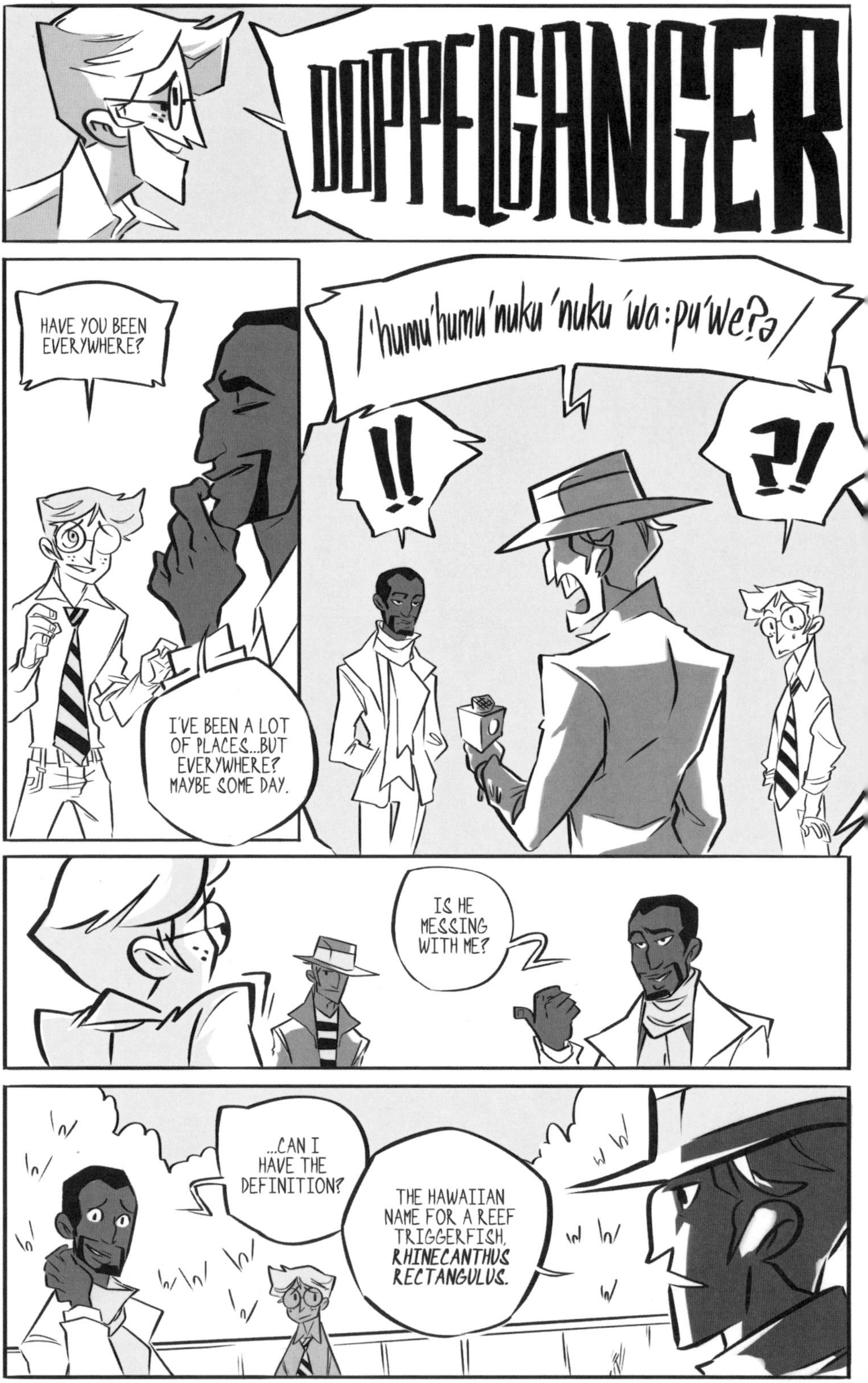
DOPPELGANGER
HAVE YOU BEEN EVERYWHERE?
I'VE BEEN A LOT OF PLACES...BUT EVERYWHERE? MAYBE SOME DAY.
/ˈhumuˈhumuˈnukuˈnukuˈwa:puˈweʔə/
!!
?!
IS HE MESSING WITH ME?
...CAN I HAVE THE DEFINITION?
THE HAWAIIAN NAME FOR A REEF TRIGGERFISH, ***RHINECANTHUS RECTANGULUS.***

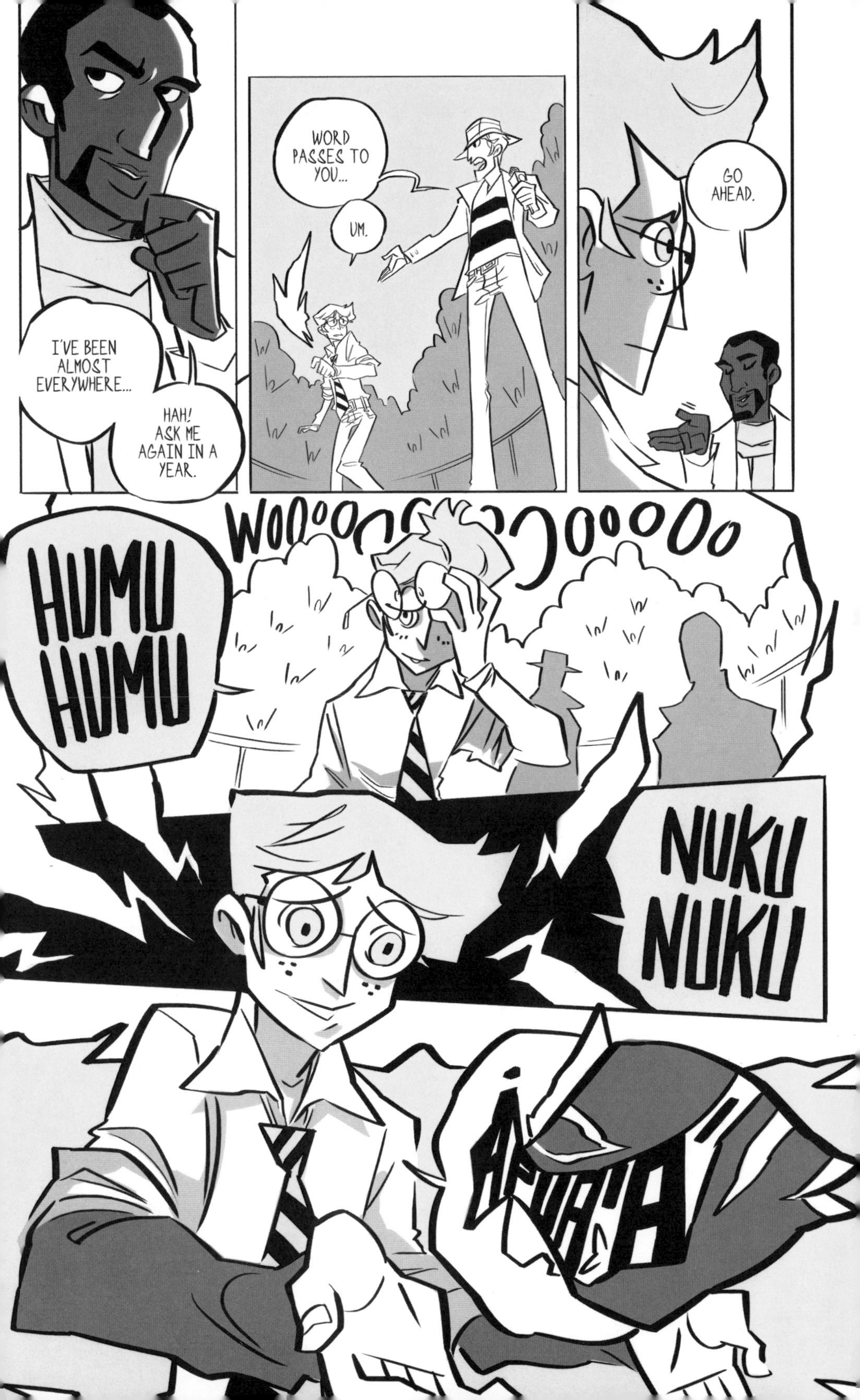
I'VE BEEN ALMOST EVERYWHERE...
HAH! ASK ME AGAIN IN A YEAR.
WORD PASSES TO YOU...
UM.
GO AHEAD.
HUMU HUMU
WOOOOOOOOOOOOO
NUKU NUKU
APUA'A

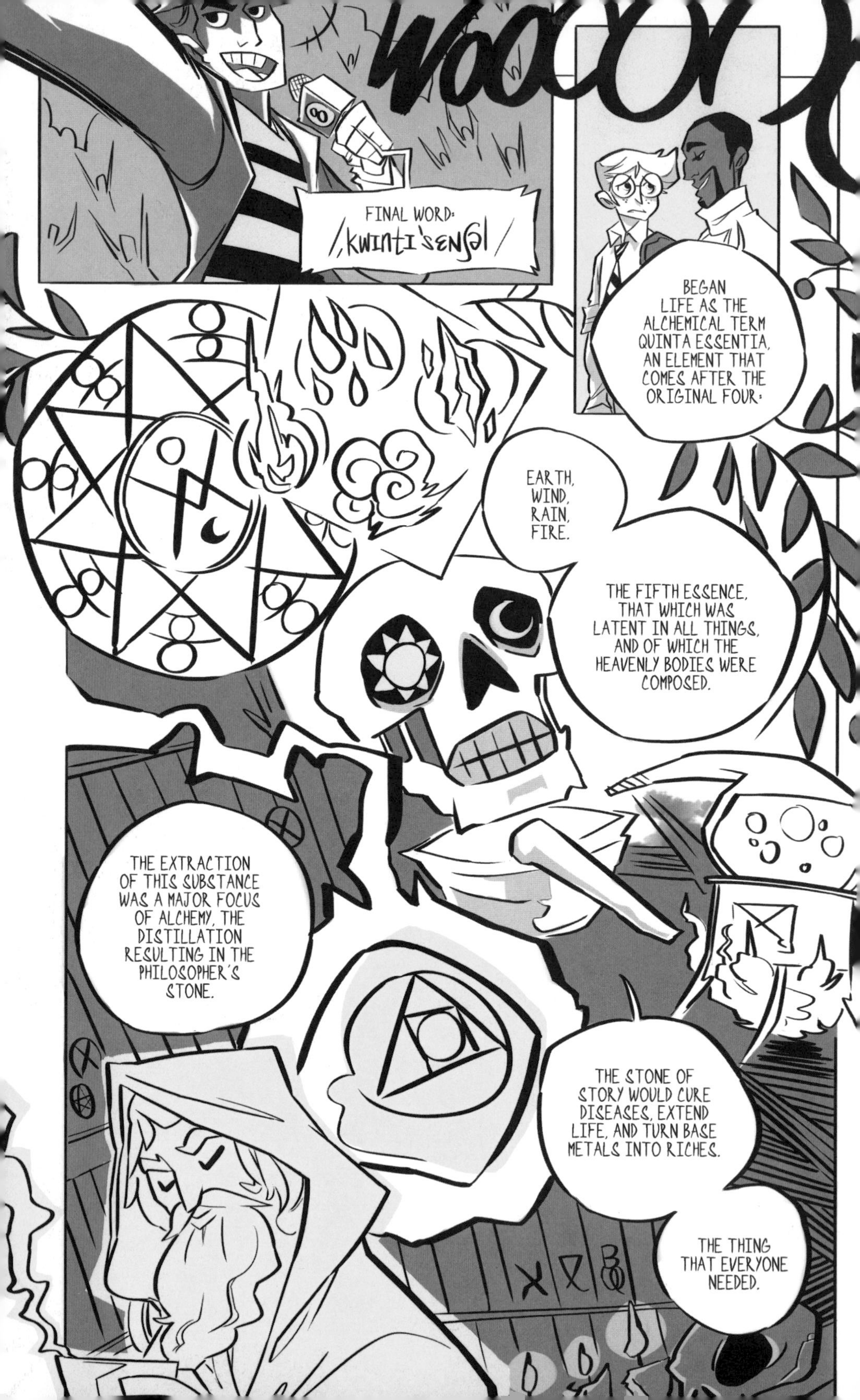

WOOOO
FINAL WORD:
/ˌkwɪntɪˈsɛnʃəl/
BEGAN LIFE AS THE ALCHEMICAL TERM QUINTA ESSENTIA, AN ELEMENT THAT COMES AFTER THE ORIGINAL FOUR:
EARTH, WIND, RAIN, FIRE.
THE FIFTH ESSENCE, THAT WHICH WAS LATENT IN ALL THINGS, AND OF WHICH THE HEAVENLY BODIES WERE COMPOSED.
THE EXTRACTION OF THIS SUBSTANCE WAS A MAJOR FOCUS OF ALCHEMY, THE DISTILLATION RESULTING IN THE PHILOSOPHER'S STONE.
THE STONE OF STORY WOULD CURE DISEASES, EXTEND LIFE, AND TURN BASE METALS INTO RICHES.
THE THING THAT EVERYONE NEEDED.

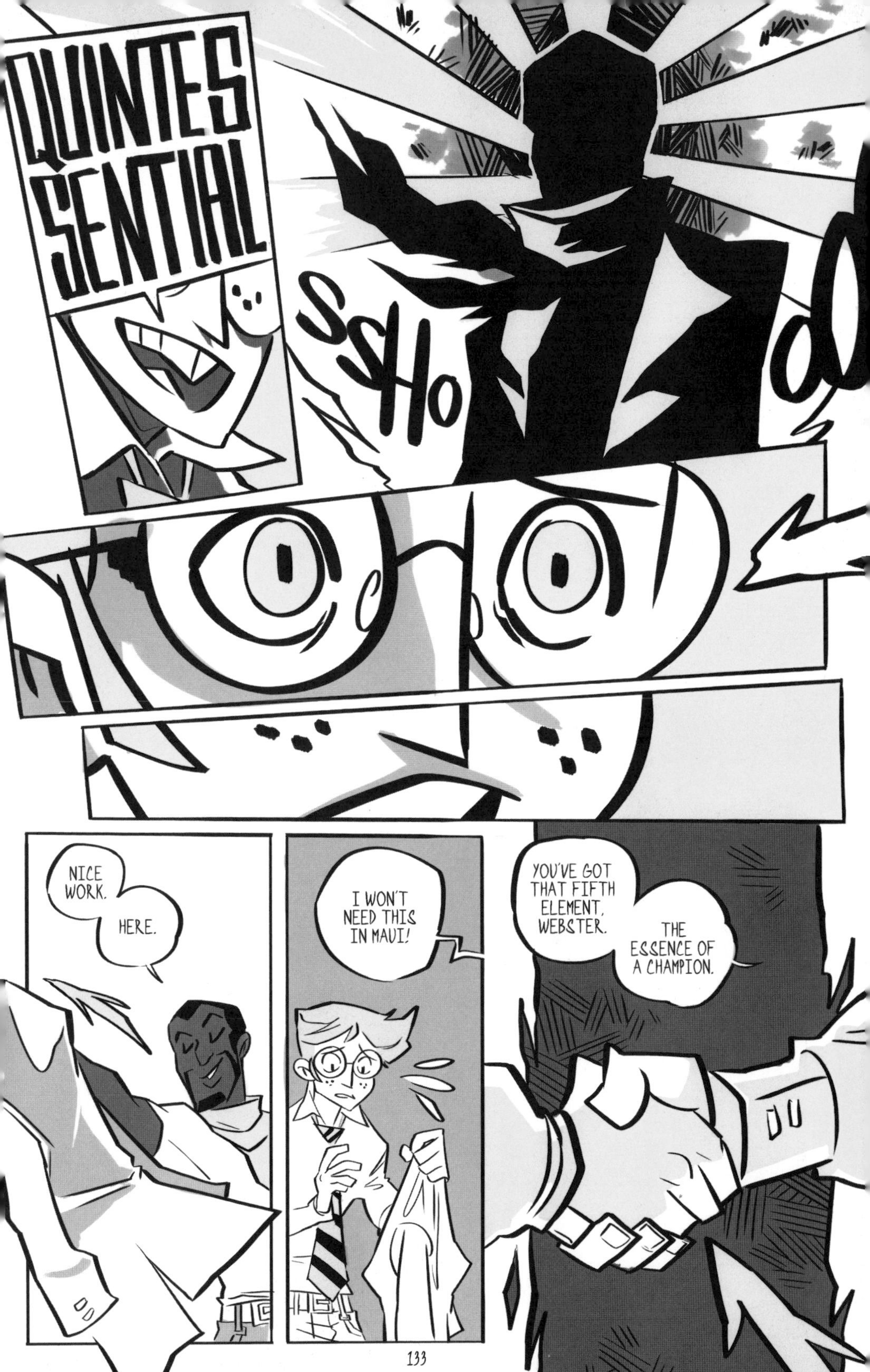
QUINTESSENTIAL
SSHOO
NICE WORK.
HERE.
I WON'T NEED THIS IN MAUI!
YOU'VE GOT THAT FIFTH ELEMENT, WEBSTER.
THE ESSENCE OF A CHAMPION.

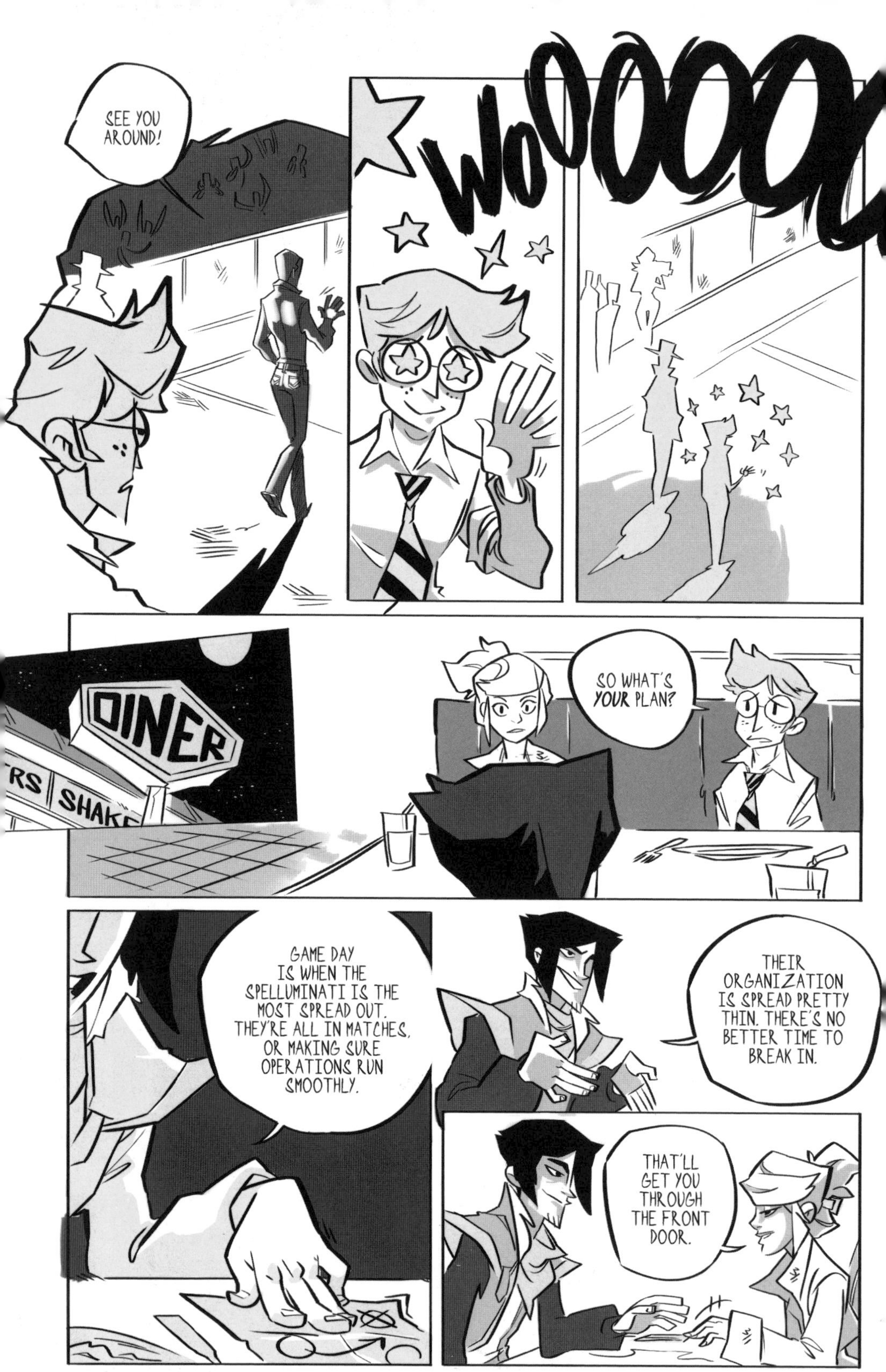
SEE YOU AROUND!
WOOOOO
DINER
SHAKE
SO WHAT'S YOUR PLAN?
GAME DAY IS WHEN THE SPELLUMINATI IS THE MOST SPREAD OUT. THEY'RE ALL IN MATCHES, OR MAKING SURE OPERATIONS RUN SMOOTHLY.
THEIR ORGANIZATION IS SPREAD PRETTY THIN. THERE'S NO BETTER TIME TO BREAK IN.
THAT'LL GET YOU THROUGH THE FRONT DOOR.

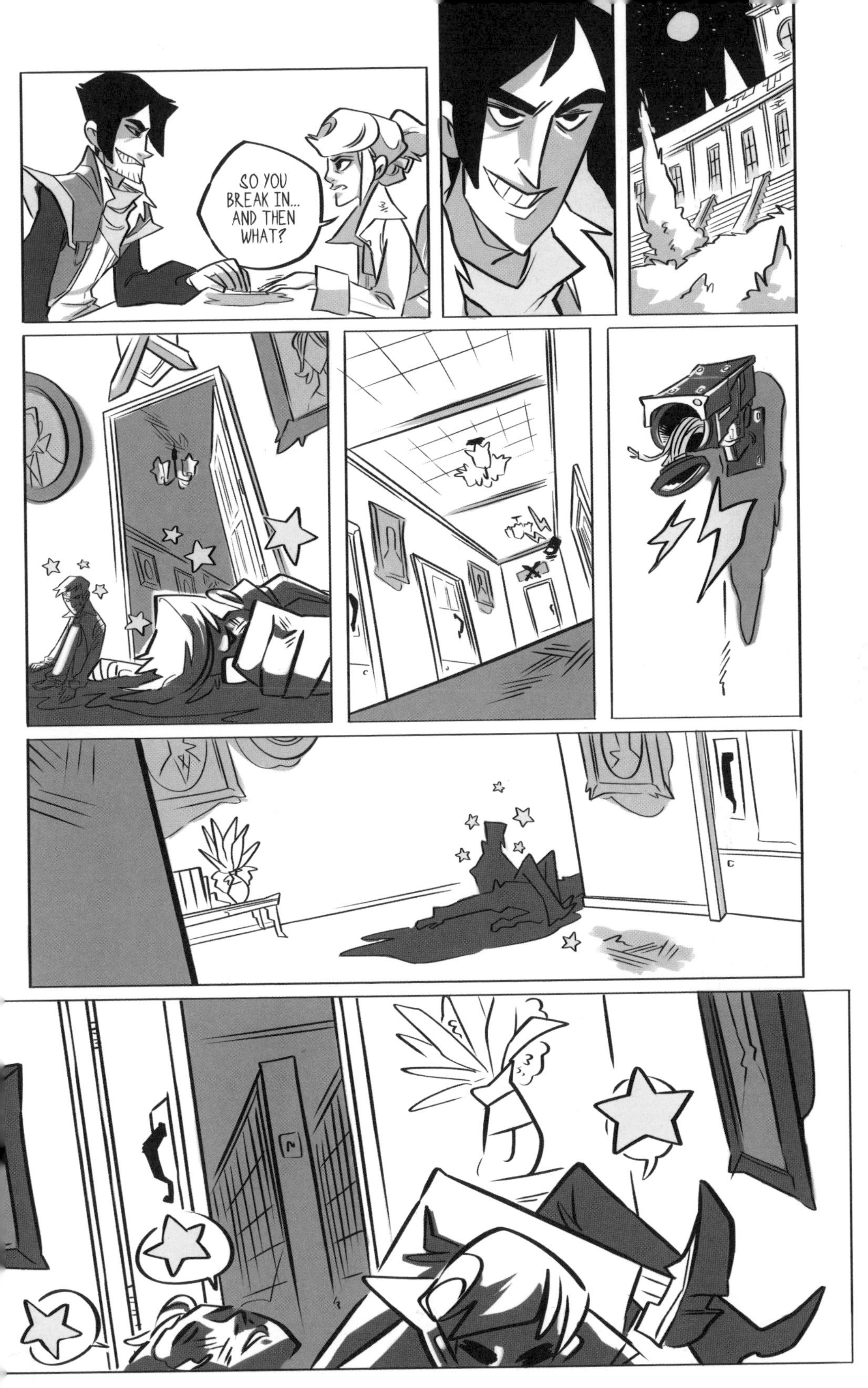
SO YOU BREAK IN... AND THEN WHAT?

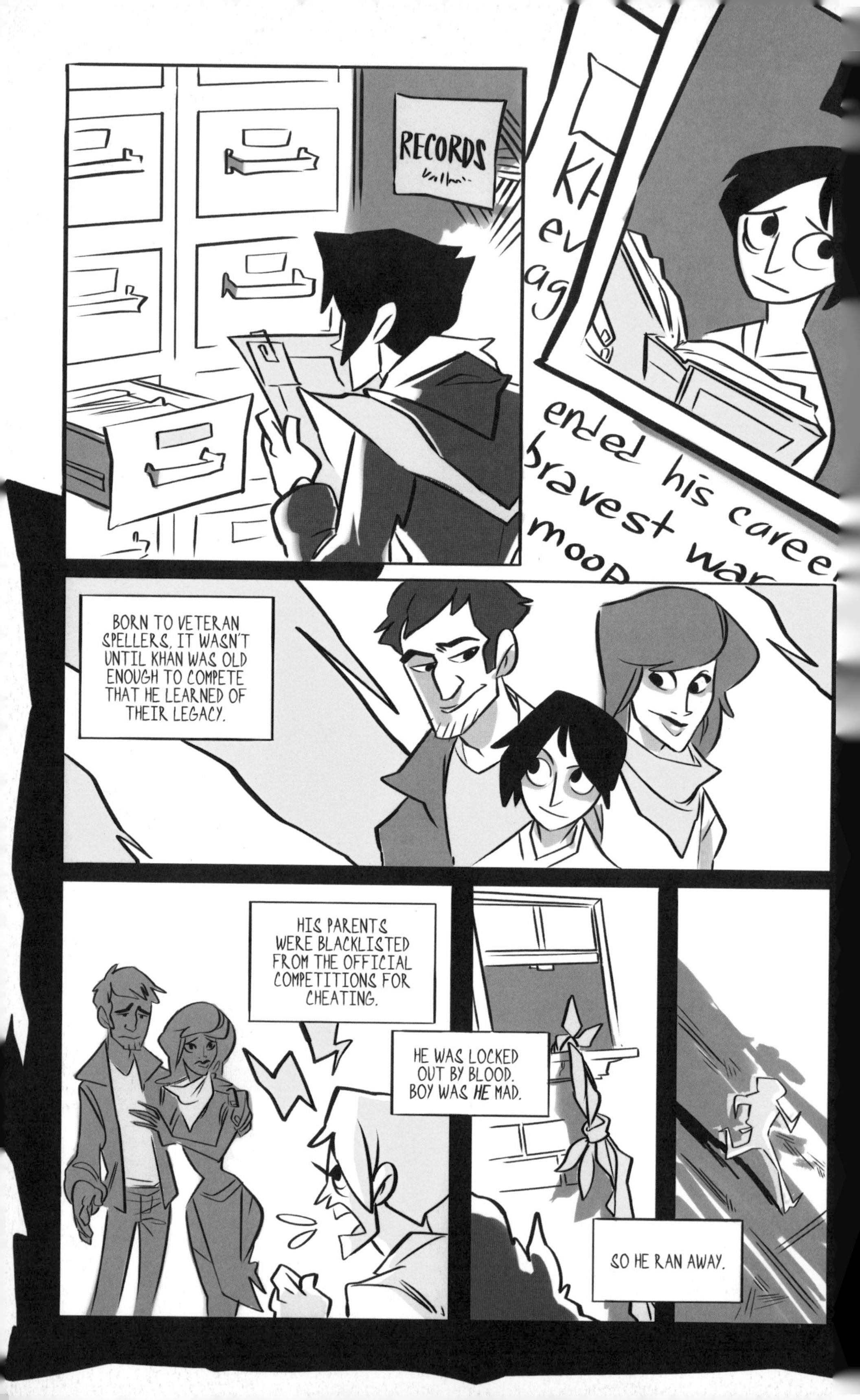
RECORDS
ended his caree
bravest wa
BORN TO VETERAN SPELLERS, IT WASN'T UNTIL KHAN WAS OLD ENOUGH TO COMPETE THAT HE LEARNED OF THEIR LEGACY.
HIS PARENTS WERE BLACKLISTED FROM THE OFFICIAL COMPETITIONS FOR CHEATING.
HE WAS LOCKED OUT BY BLOOD. BOY WAS *HE* MAD.
SO HE RAN AWAY.

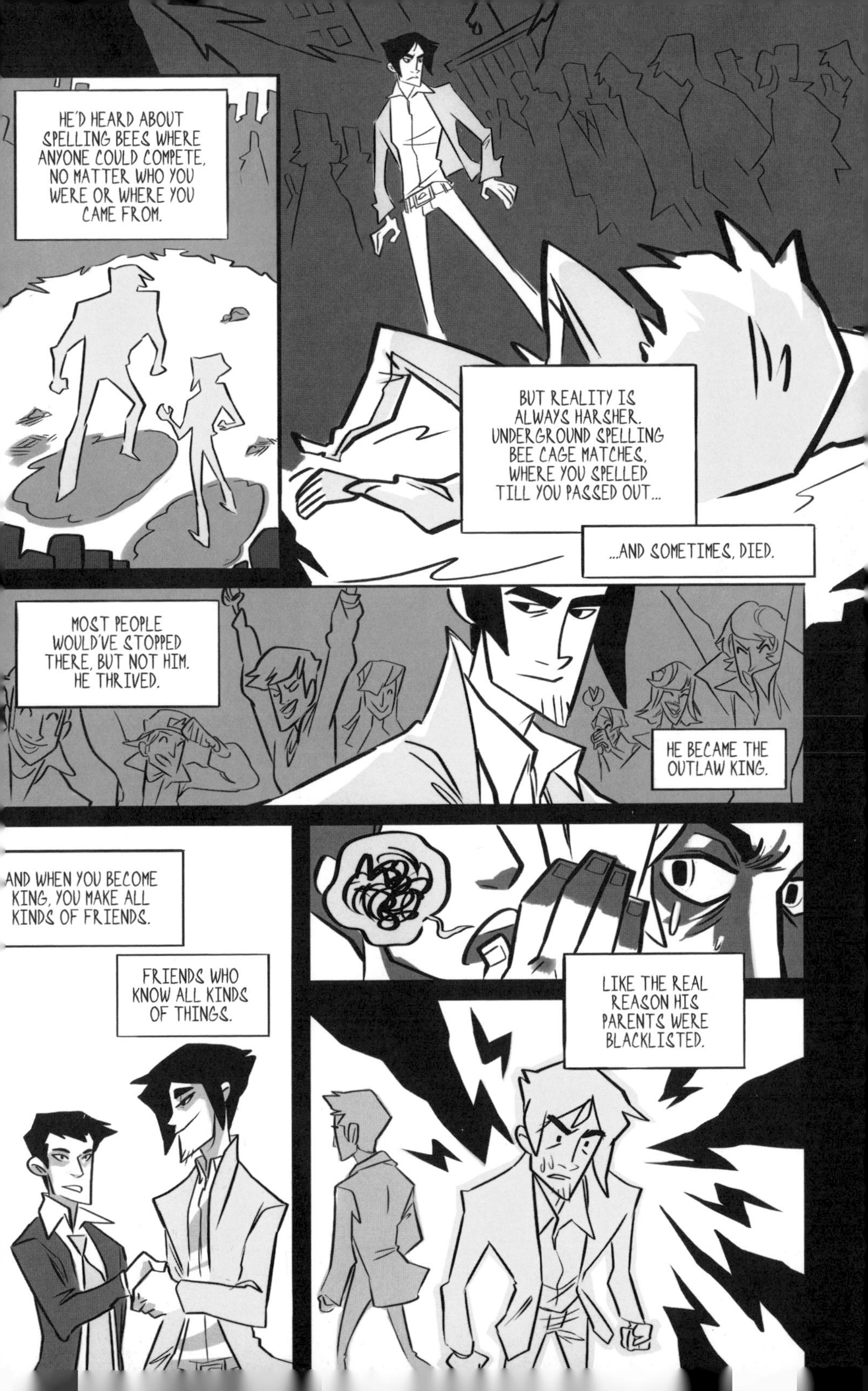
HE'D HEARD ABOUT SPELLING BEES WHERE ANYONE COULD COMPETE, NO MATTER WHO YOU WERE OR WHERE YOU CAME FROM.
BUT REALITY IS ALWAYS HARSHER. UNDERGROUND SPELLING BEE CAGE MATCHES, WHERE YOU SPELLED TILL YOU PASSED OUT...
...AND SOMETIMES, DIED.
MOST PEOPLE WOULD'VE STOPPED THERE, BUT NOT HIM. HE THRIVED.
HE BECAME THE OUTLAW KING.
AND WHEN YOU BECOME KING, YOU MAKE ALL KINDS OF FRIENDS.
FRIENDS WHO KNOW ALL KINDS OF THINGS.
LIKE THE REAL REASON HIS PARENTS WERE BLACKLISTED.

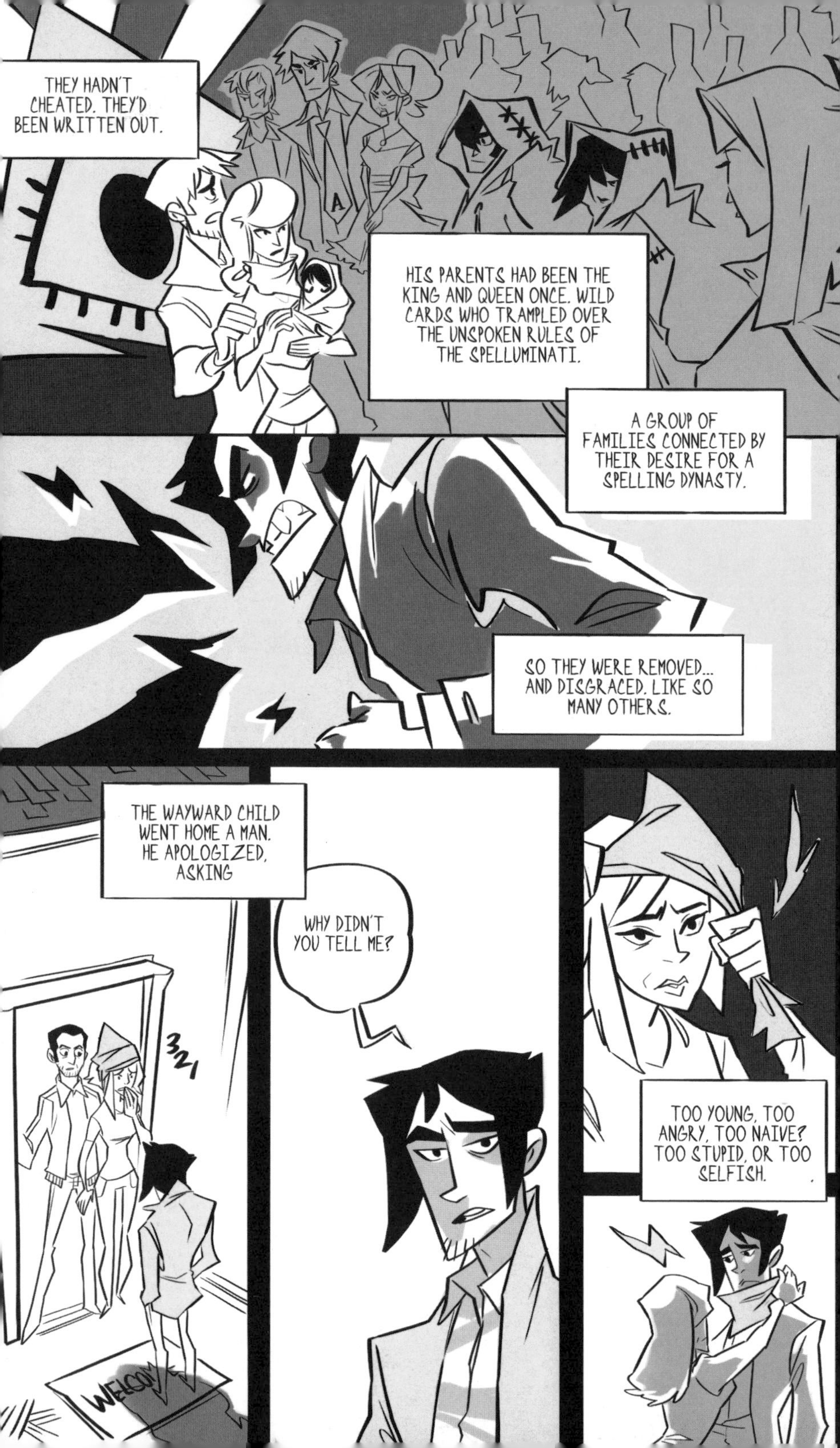
THEY HADN'T CHEATED. THEY'D BEEN WRITTEN OUT.
HIS PARENTS HAD BEEN THE KING AND QUEEN ONCE. WILD CARDS WHO TRAMPLED OVER THE UNSPOKEN RULES OF THE SPELLUMINATI.
A GROUP OF FAMILIES CONNECTED BY THEIR DESIRE FOR A SPELLING DYNASTY.
SO THEY WERE REMOVED... AND DISGRACED. LIKE SO MANY OTHERS.
THE WAYWARD CHILD WENT HOME A MAN. HE APOLOGIZED, ASKING
WELCOME
WHY DIDN'T YOU TELL ME?
TOO YOUNG, TOO ANGRY, TOO NAIVE? TOO STUPID, OR TOO SELFISH.

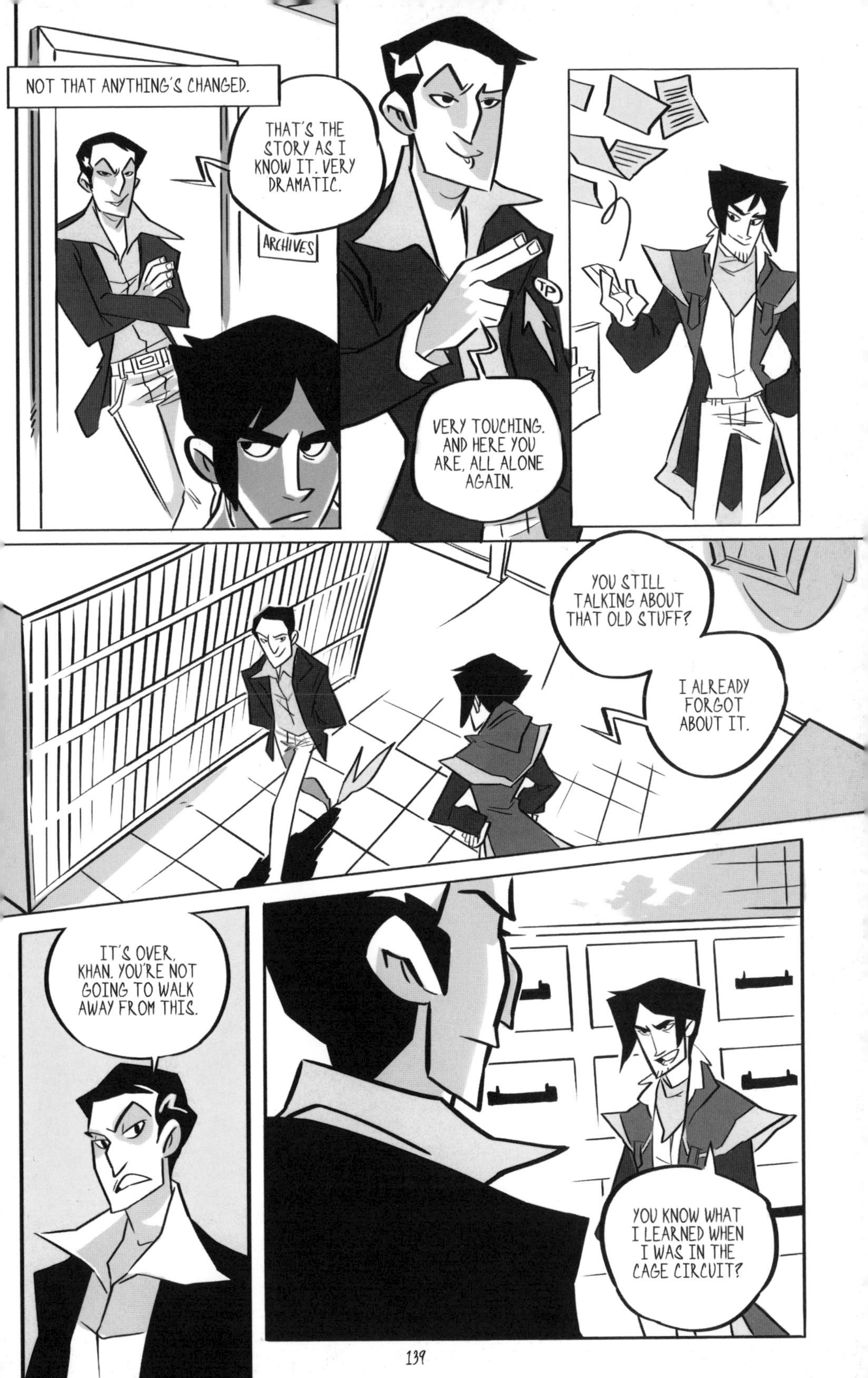
NOT THAT ANYTHING'S CHANGED.
ARCHIVES
THAT'S THE STORY AS I KNOW IT. VERY DRAMATIC.
VERY TOUCHING. AND HERE YOU ARE, ALL ALONE AGAIN.
YOU STILL TALKING ABOUT THAT OLD STUFF?
I ALREADY FORGOT ABOUT IT.
IT'S OVER, KHAN. YOU'RE NOT GOING TO WALK AWAY FROM THIS.
YOU KNOW WHAT I LEARNED WHEN I WAS IN THE CAGE CIRCUIT?

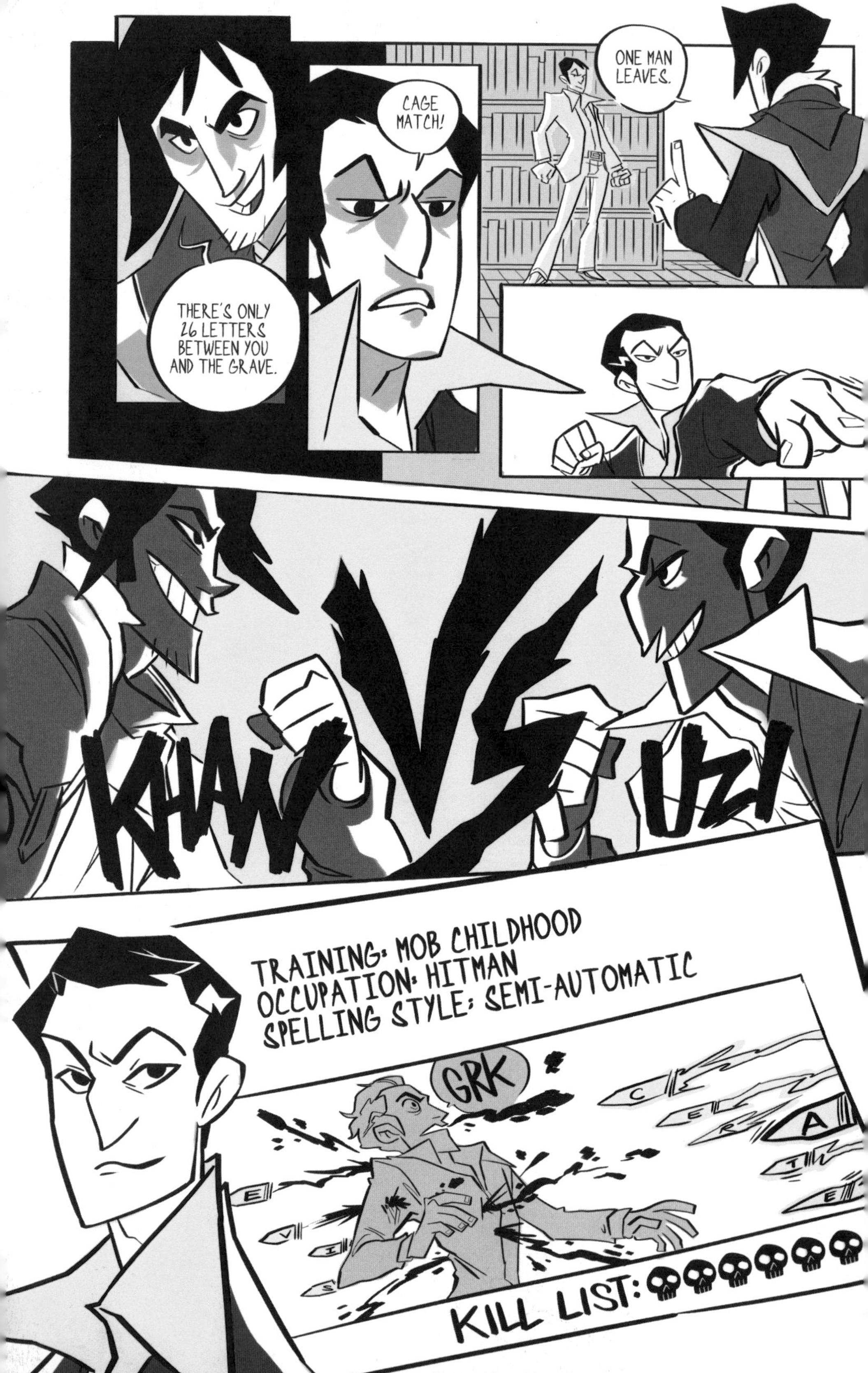
CAGE MATCH!
THERE'S ONLY 26 LETTERS BETWEEN YOU AND THE GRAVE.
ONE MAN LEAVES.
KHAW VS UZI
TRAINING: MOB CHILDHOOD
OCCUPATION: HITMAN
SPELLING STYLE: SEMI-AUTOMATIC
GRK
KILL LIST:

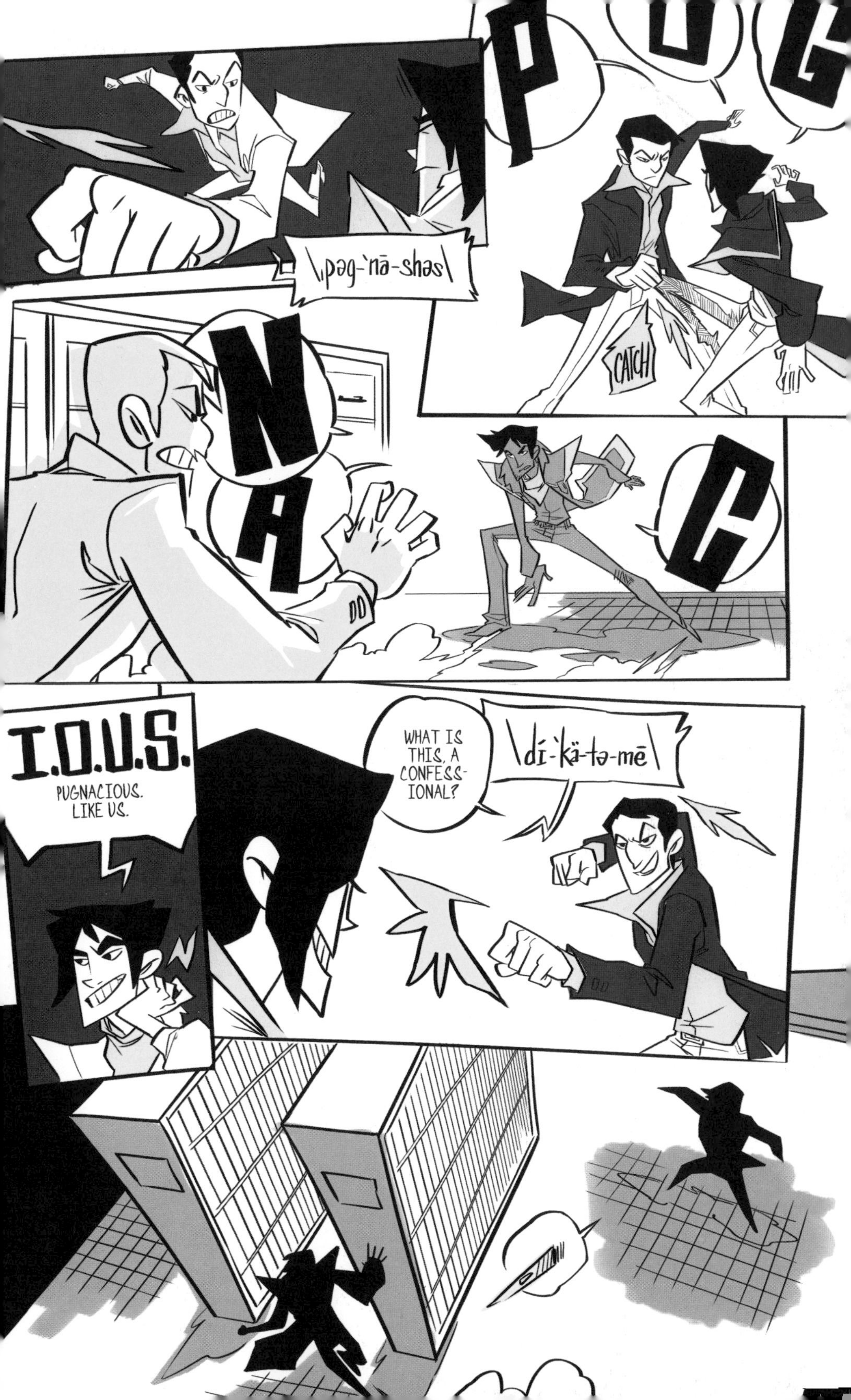
\ˌpəg-ˋnā-shəs\
P
U
G
CATCH
N
A
C
I.O.U.S.
PUGNACIOUS. LIKE US.
WHAT IS THIS, A CONFESS-IONAL?
\dí-ˋkä-tə-mē\

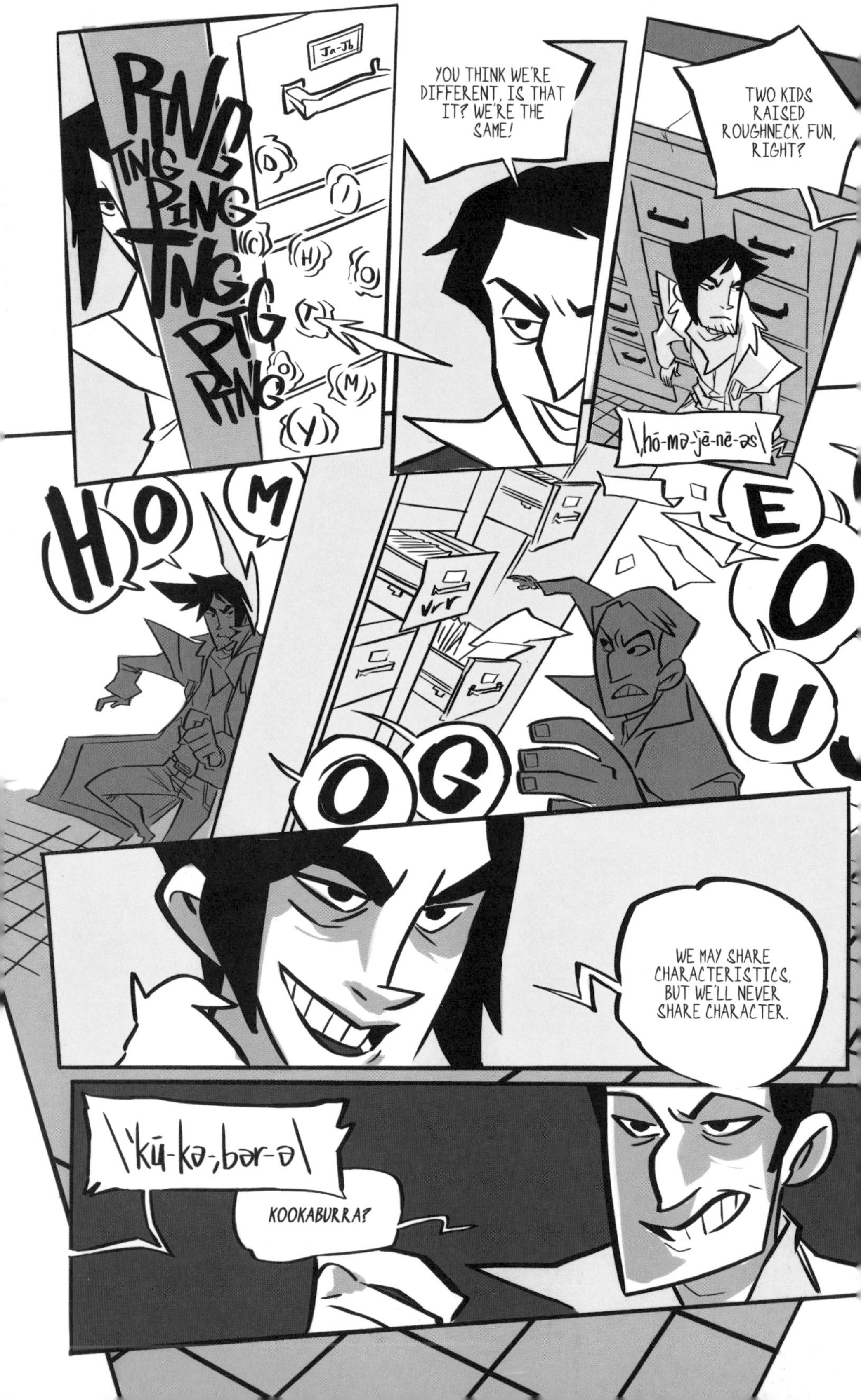
RING TING PING TING PTG RING
YOU THINK WE'RE DIFFERENT, IS THAT IT? WE'RE THE SAME!
TWO KIDS RAISED ROUGHNECK. FUN, RIGHT?
\ˌhō-mə-ˈjē-nē-əs\
H O M
O G
E O U S
WE MAY SHARE CHARACTERISTICS, BUT WE'LL NEVER SHARE CHARACTER.
\ˈku̇-kə-ˌbər-ə\
KOOKABURRA?

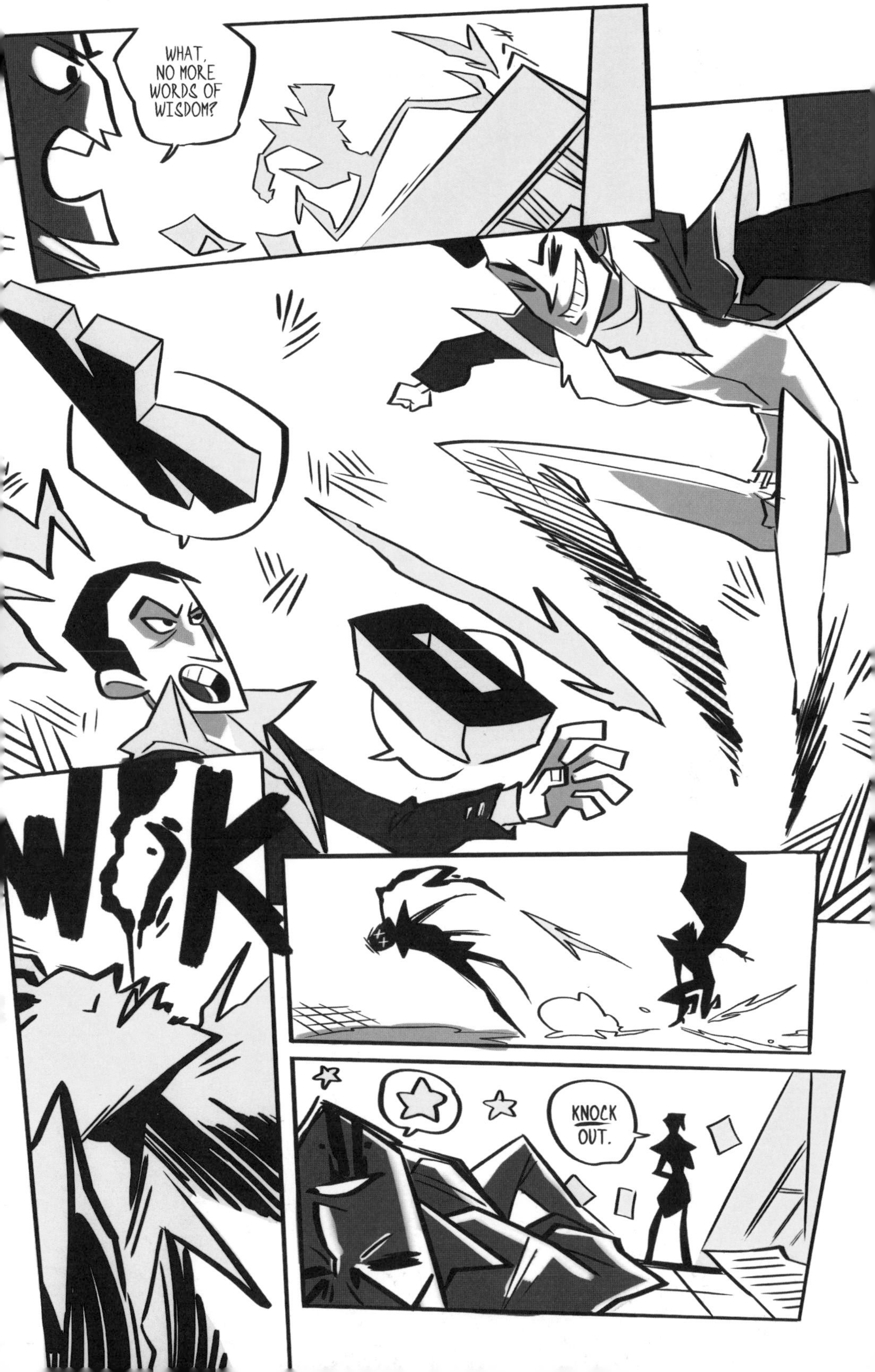
WHAT, NO MORE WORDS OF WISDOM?
KO
WOK
KNOCK OUT.

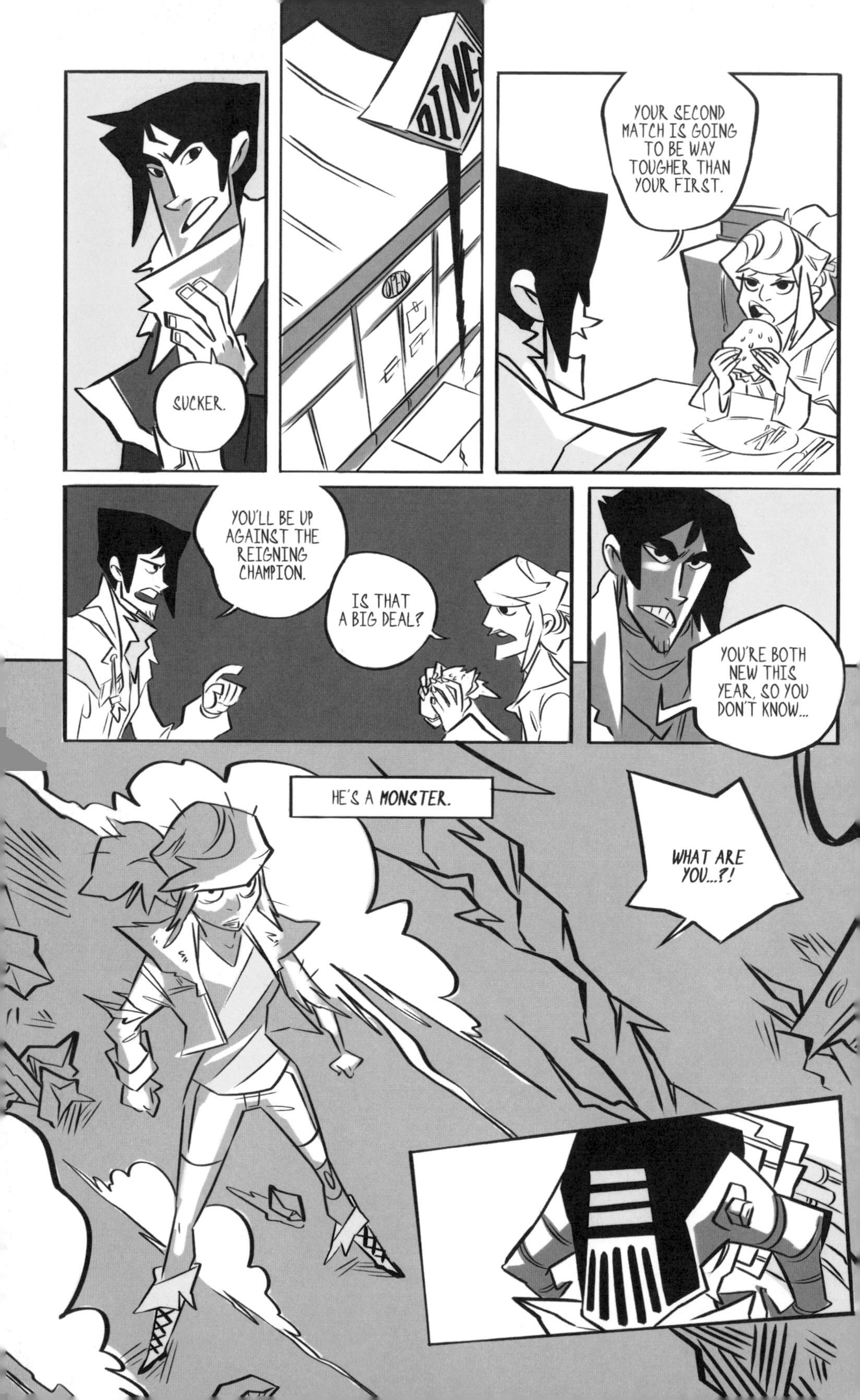
SUCKER.
DINER
OPEN
YOUR SECOND MATCH IS GOING TO BE WAY TOUGHER THAN YOUR FIRST.
YOU'LL BE UP AGAINST THE REIGNING CHAMPION.
IS THAT A BIG DEAL?
YOU'RE BOTH NEW THIS YEAR, SO YOU DON'T KNOW...
HE'S A **MONSTER.**
WHAT ARE YOU...?!

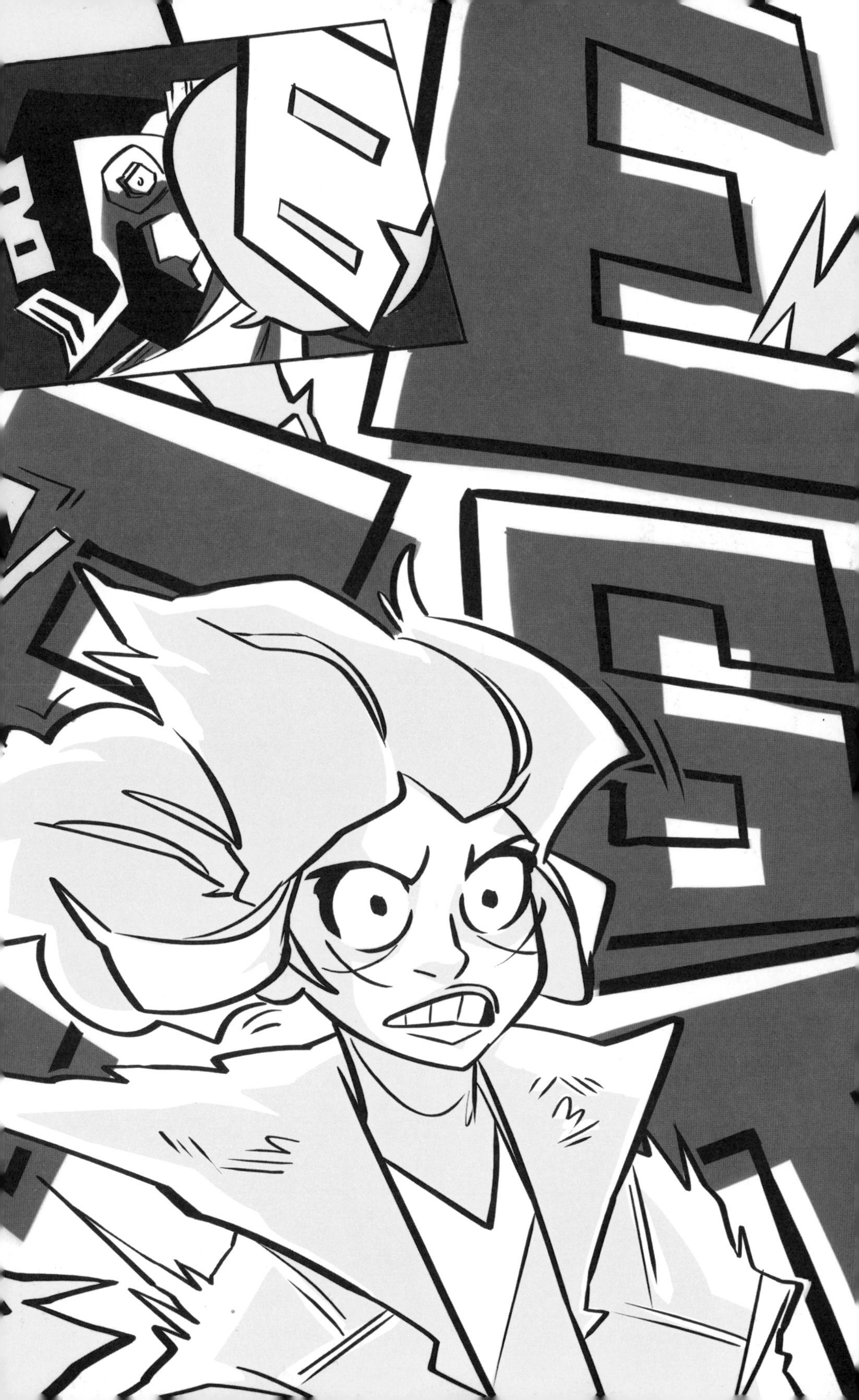

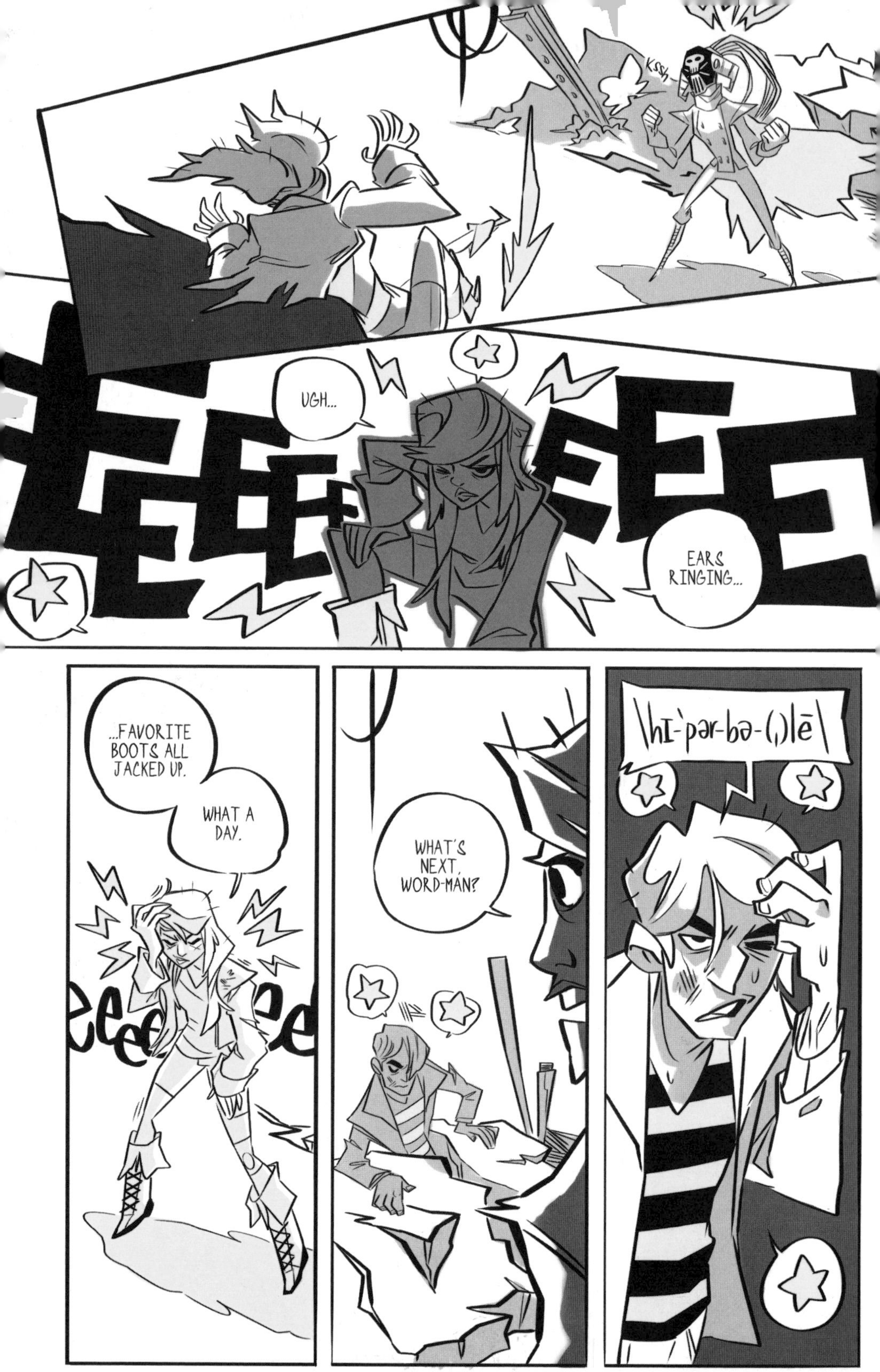
Kssh
UGH...
EARS RINGING...
...FAVORITE BOOTS ALL JACKED UP.
WHAT A DAY.
WHAT'S NEXT, WORD-MAN?
\hī-ˈpər-bə-(ˌ)lē\

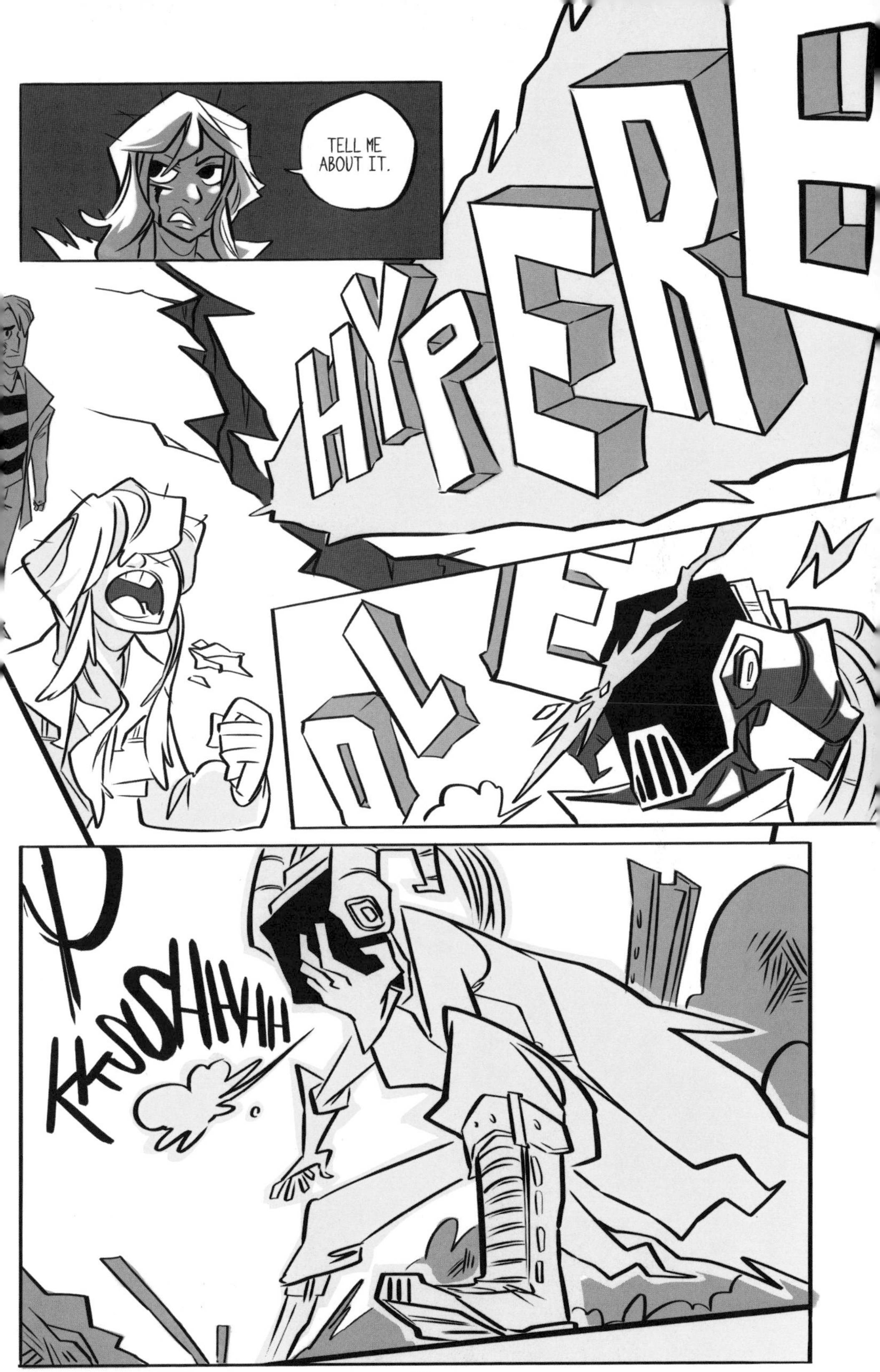
TELL ME ABOUT IT.
HYPER:
OLE
KFOOSHHHHH

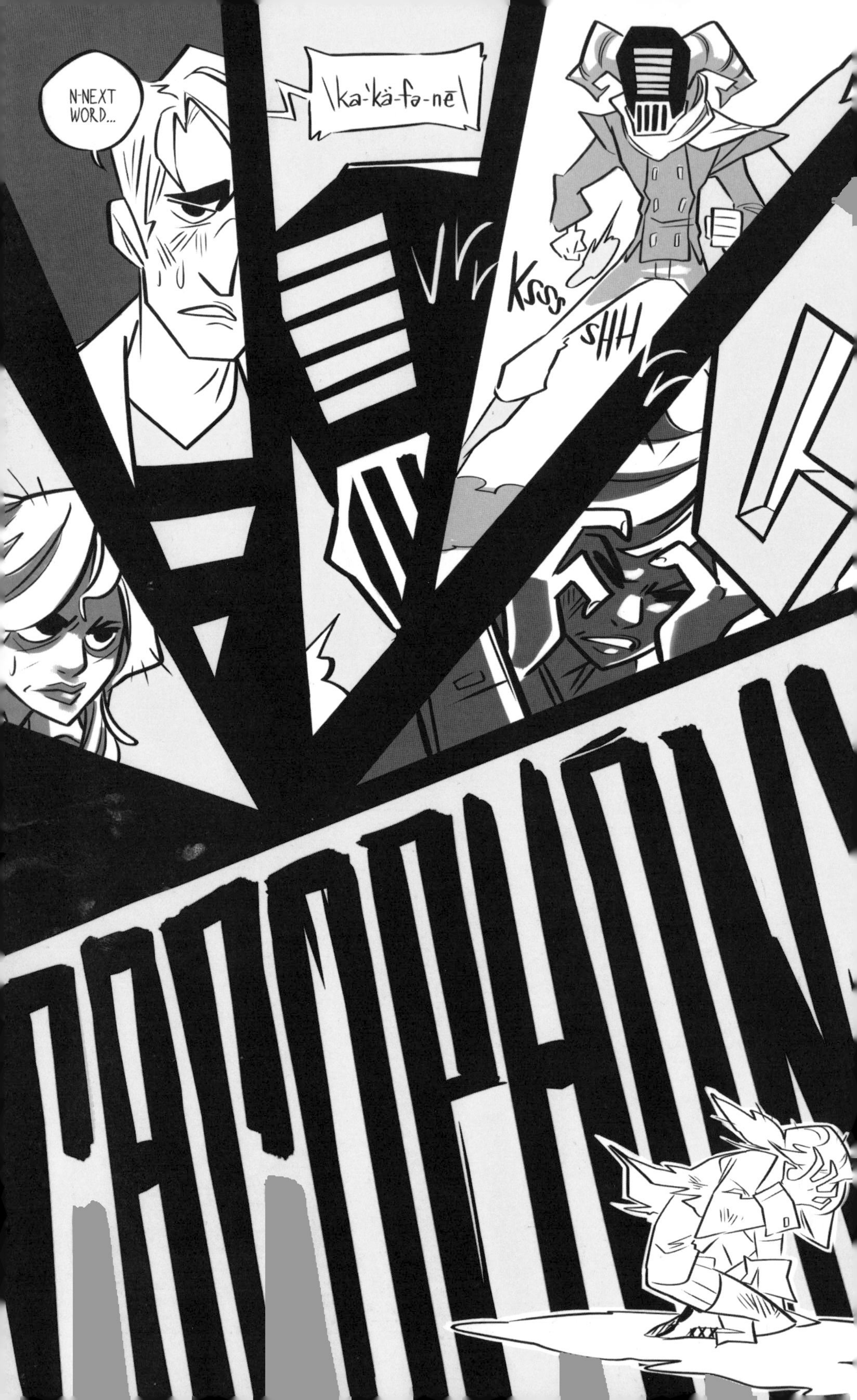
N-NEXT WORD...
\ka-'kä-fə-nē\
KSSS
SHH

eeeeEe

WHAT'RE YOU EVEN SAYING..?

eeeeeeee

eeeeeeeeeee

JUDGES RULE MATCH OVER ON ACCOUNT OF INJURY. WINNER BY DEFAULT...

eeeeee

THE BEEST!

eeeee

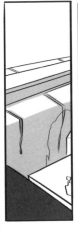

I'VE GOT THE CHECK.

BIIIIG SPENDER.

149

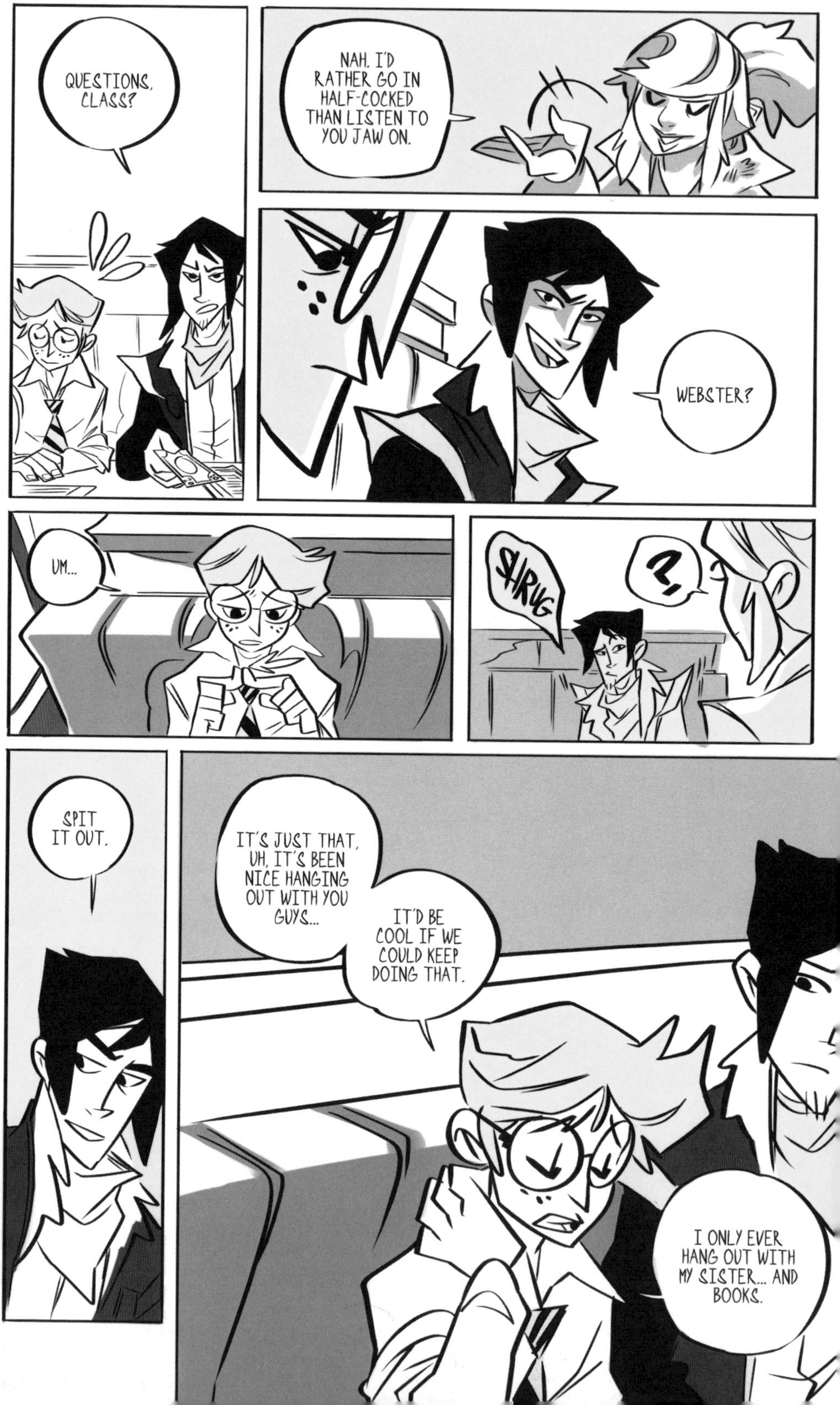
QUESTIONS, CLASS?
NAH. I'D RATHER GO IN HALF-COCKED THAN LISTEN TO YOU JAW ON.
WEBSTER?
UM...
SHRUG
?
SPIT IT OUT.
IT'S JUST THAT, UH, IT'S BEEN NICE HANGING OUT WITH YOU GUYS...
IT'D BE COOL IF WE COULD KEEP DOING THAT.
I ONLY EVER HANG OUT WITH MY SISTER... AND BOOKS.

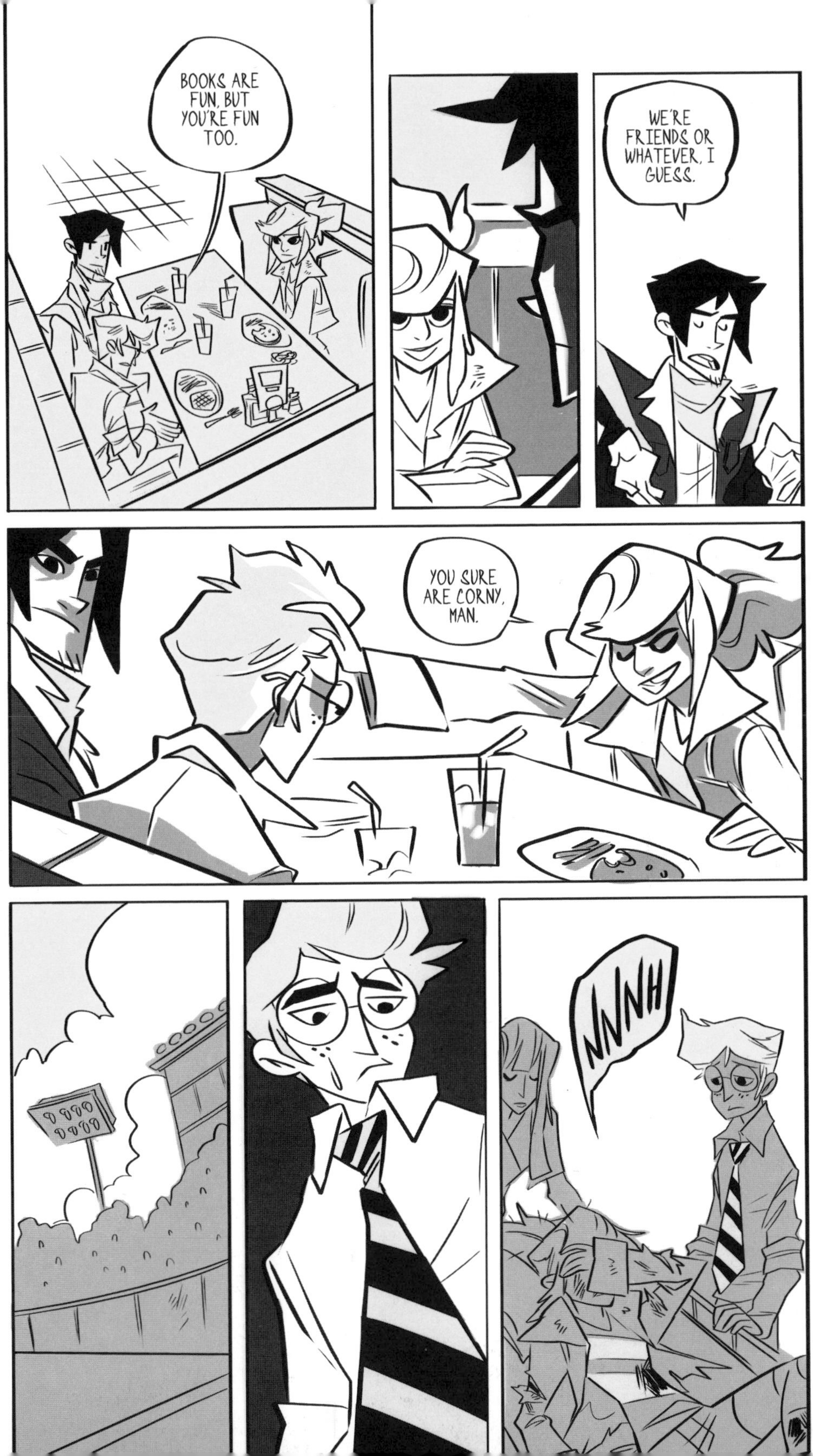
BOOKS ARE FUN, BUT YOU'RE FUN TOO.
WE'RE FRIENDS OR WHATEVER, I GUESS.
YOU SURE ARE CORNY, MAN.
NNNH

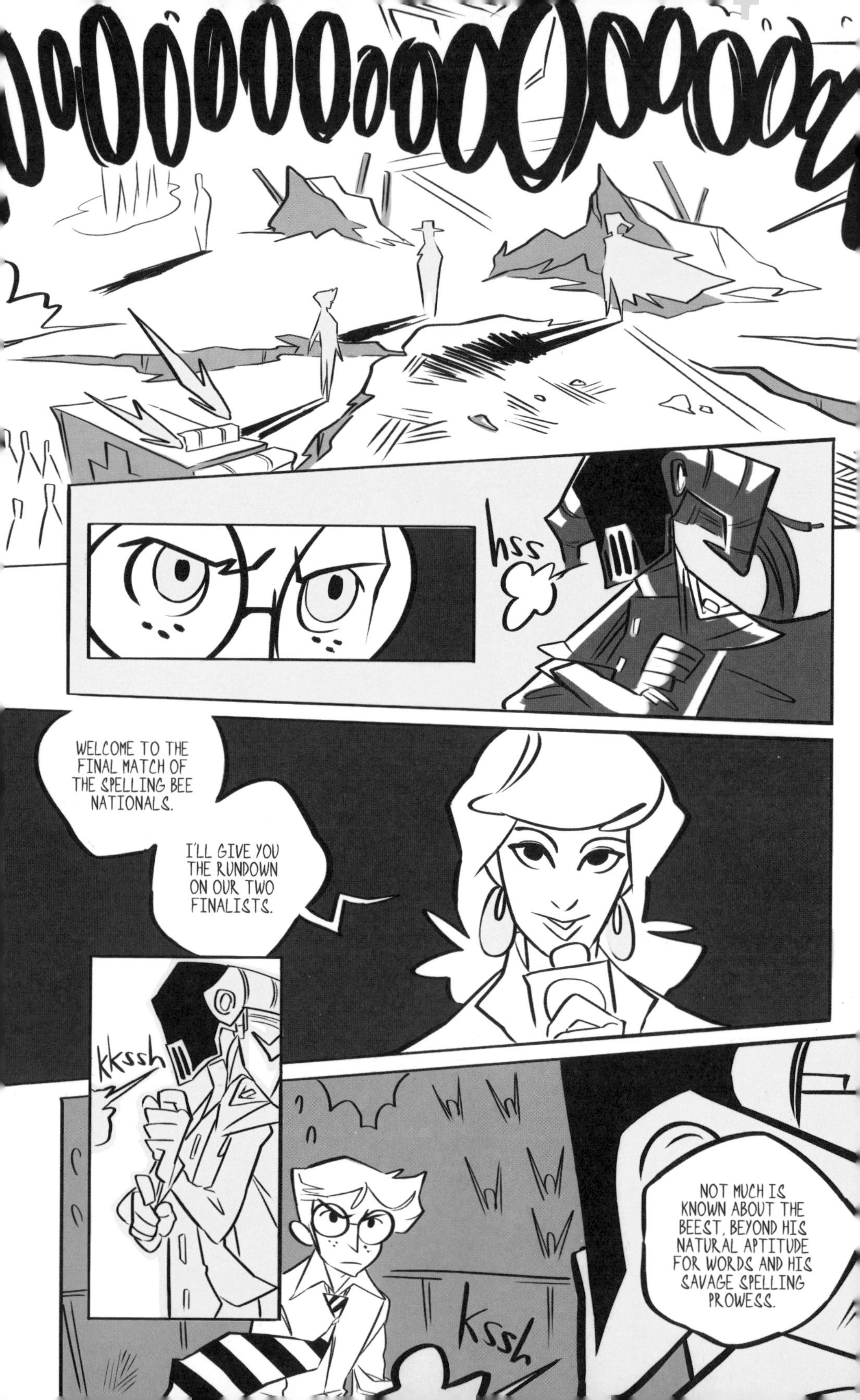
OOOOOOOOOOOOOOOO
hss
WELCOME TO THE FINAL MATCH OF THE SPELLING BEE NATIONALS.
I'LL GIVE YOU THE RUNDOWN ON OUR TWO FINALISTS.
kkssh
kssh
NOT MUCH IS KNOWN ABOUT THE BEEST, BEYOND HIS NATURAL APTITUDE FOR WORDS AND HIS SAVAGE SPELLING PROWESS.

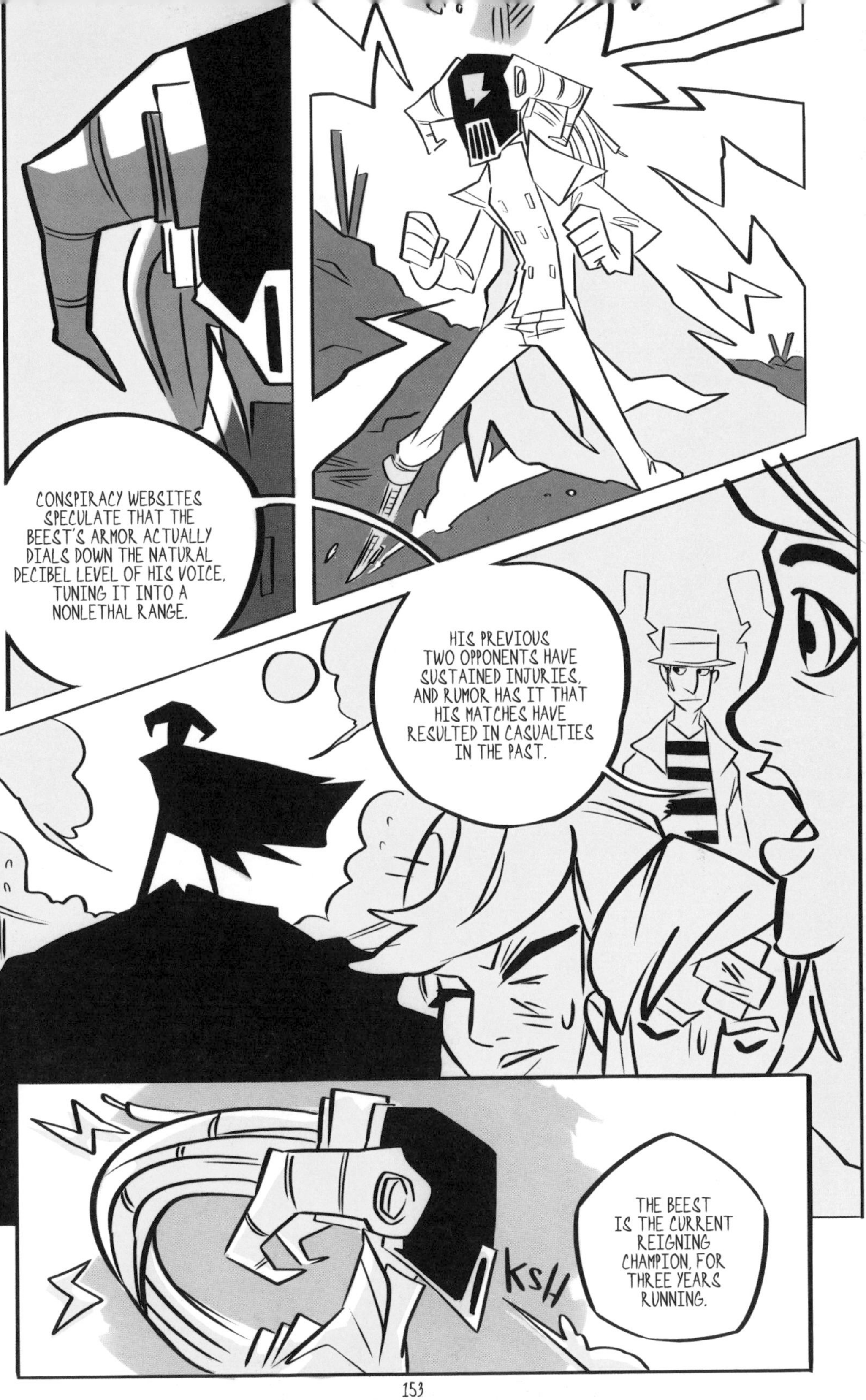
CONSPIRACY WEBSITES SPECULATE THAT THE BEEST'S ARMOR ACTUALLY DIALS DOWN THE NATURAL DECIBEL LEVEL OF HIS VOICE, TUNING IT INTO A NONLETHAL RANGE.
HIS PREVIOUS TWO OPPONENTS HAVE SUSTAINED INJURIES, AND RUMOR HAS IT THAT HIS MATCHES HAVE RESULTED IN CASUALTIES IN THE PAST.
KSH
THE BEEST IS THE CURRENT REIGNING CHAMPION, FOR THREE YEARS RUNNING.

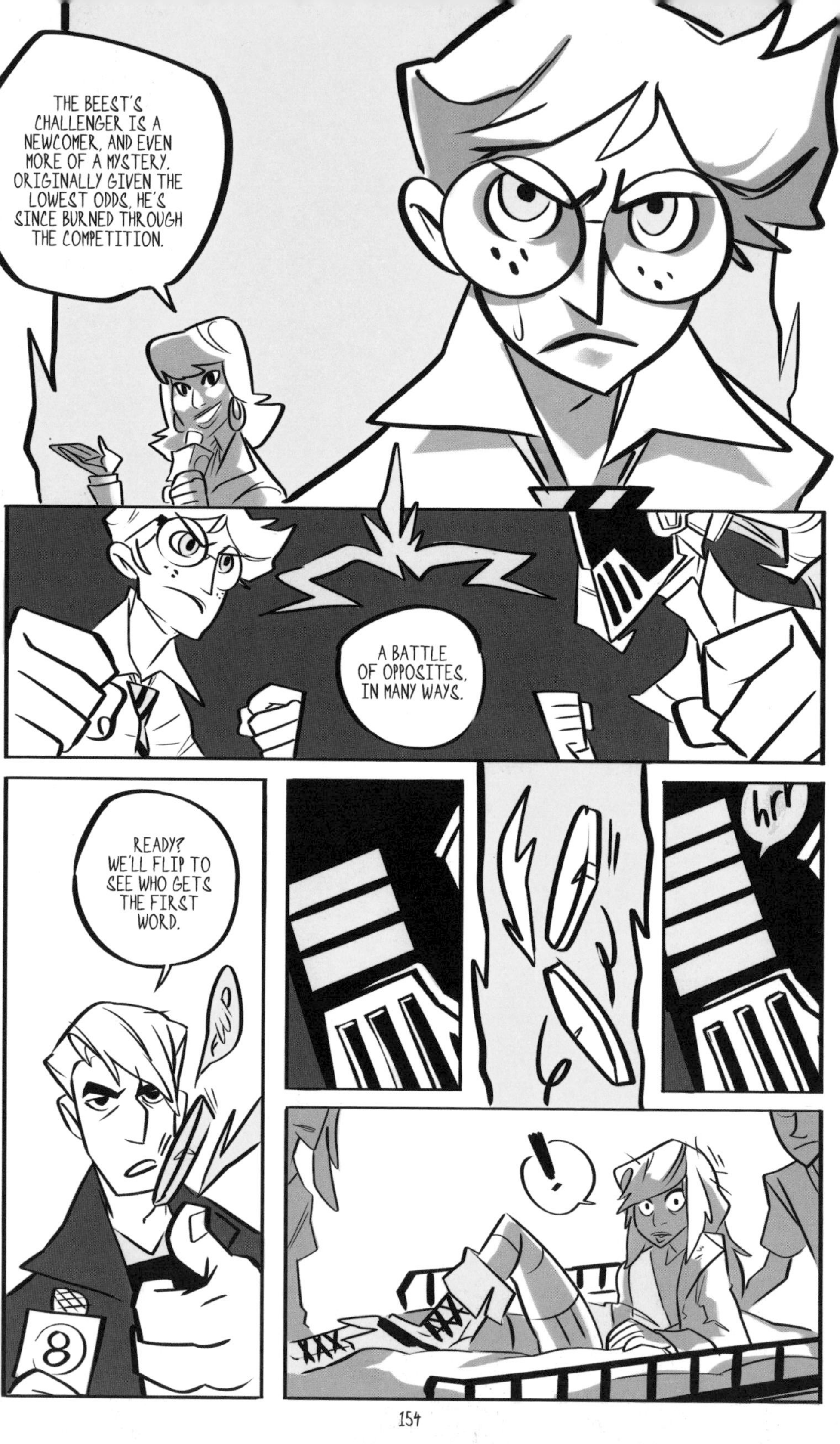
THE BEEST'S CHALLENGER IS A NEWCOMER, AND EVEN MORE OF A MYSTERY. ORIGINALLY GIVEN THE LOWEST ODDS, HE'S SINCE BURNED THROUGH THE COMPETITION.
A BATTLE OF OPPOSITES, IN MANY WAYS.
READY? WE'LL FLIP TO SEE WHO GETS THE FIRST WORD.
FWP
8
hrr
!

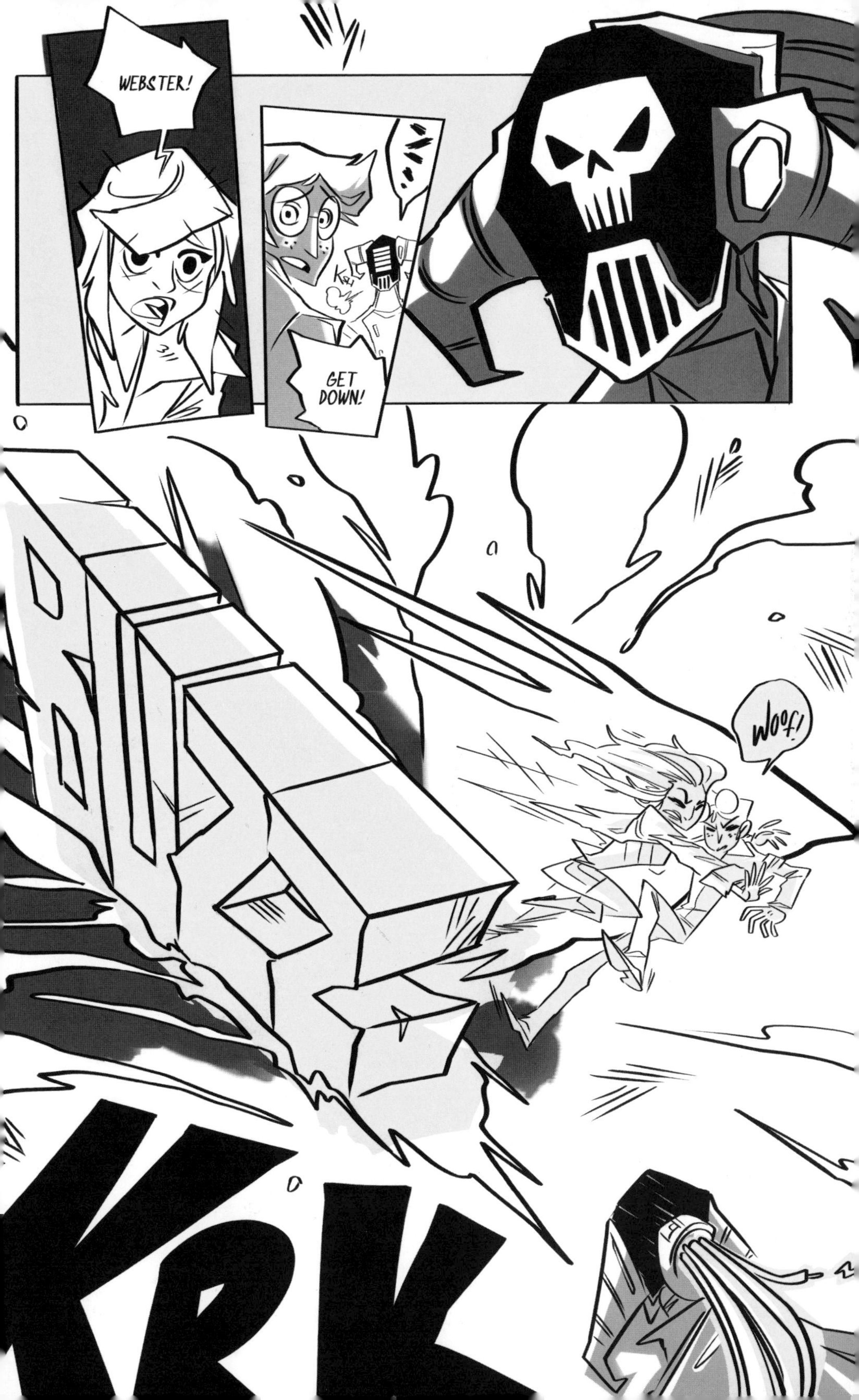
WEBSTER!
GET DOWN!
Woof!
KRK

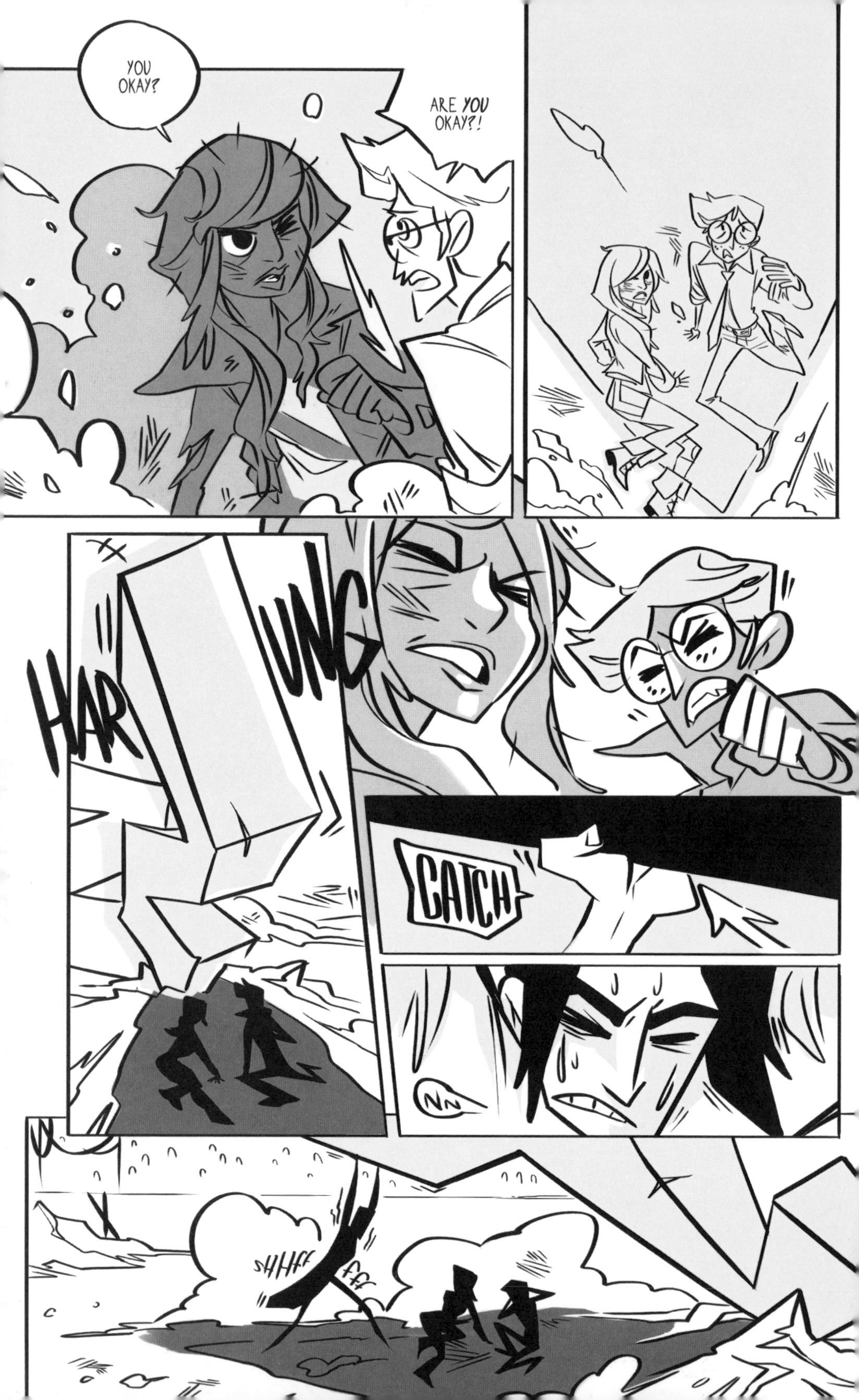
YOU OKAY?
ARE YOU OKAY?!
HAR
UNG
CATCH
NN
SHHFF
FFF

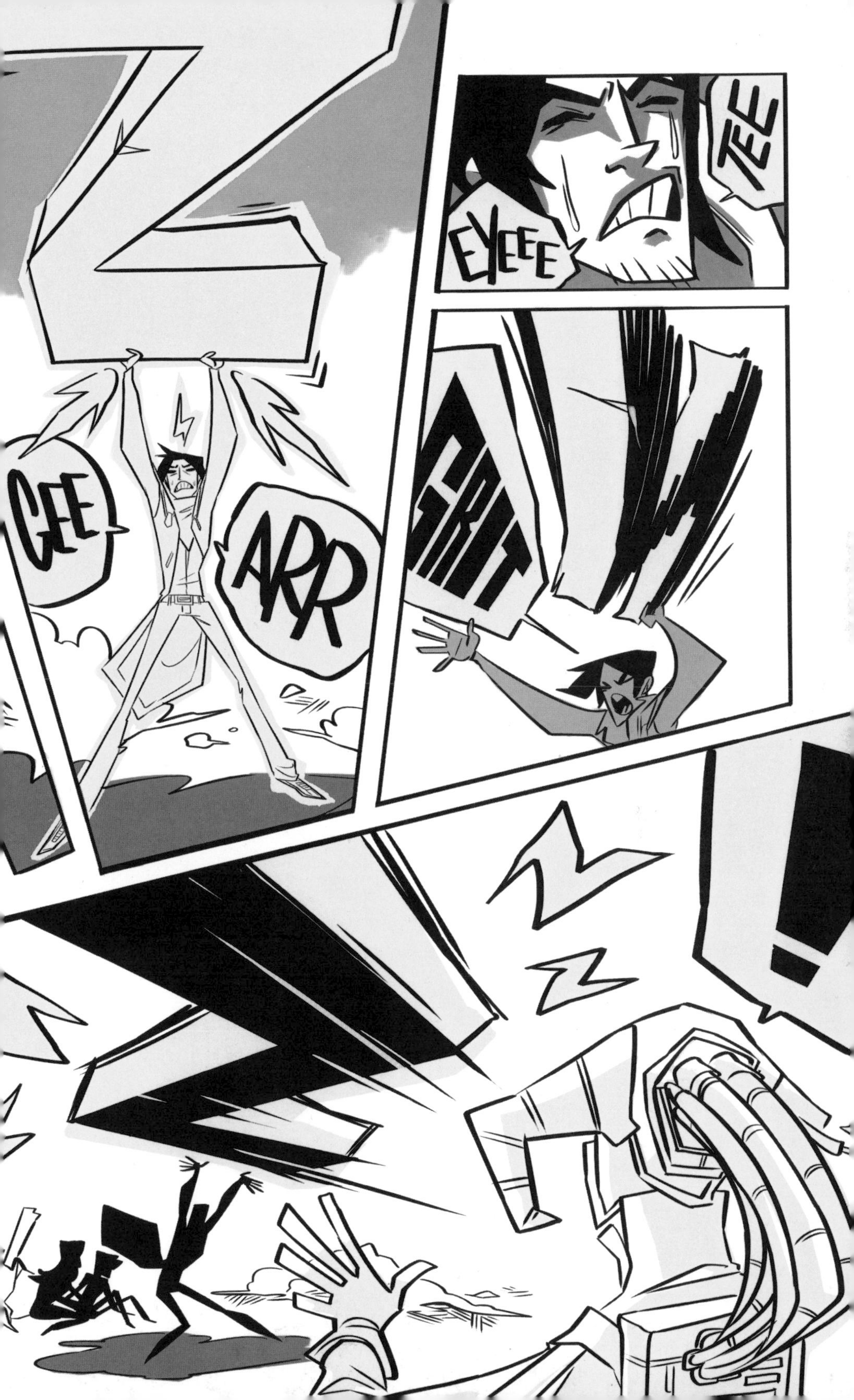
GEE
ARR
EYEEE
TEE
GRRT
!

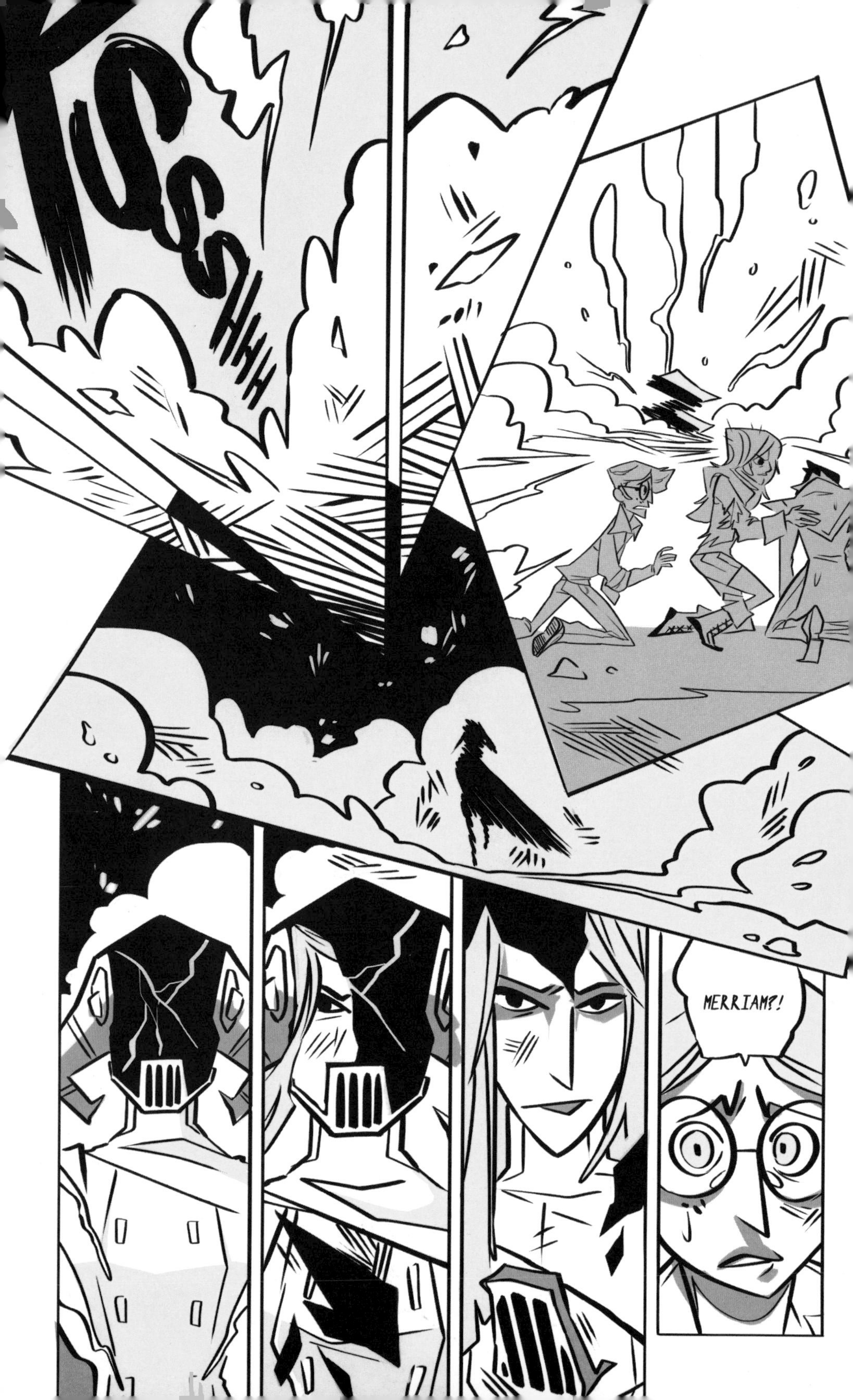
MERRIAM?!

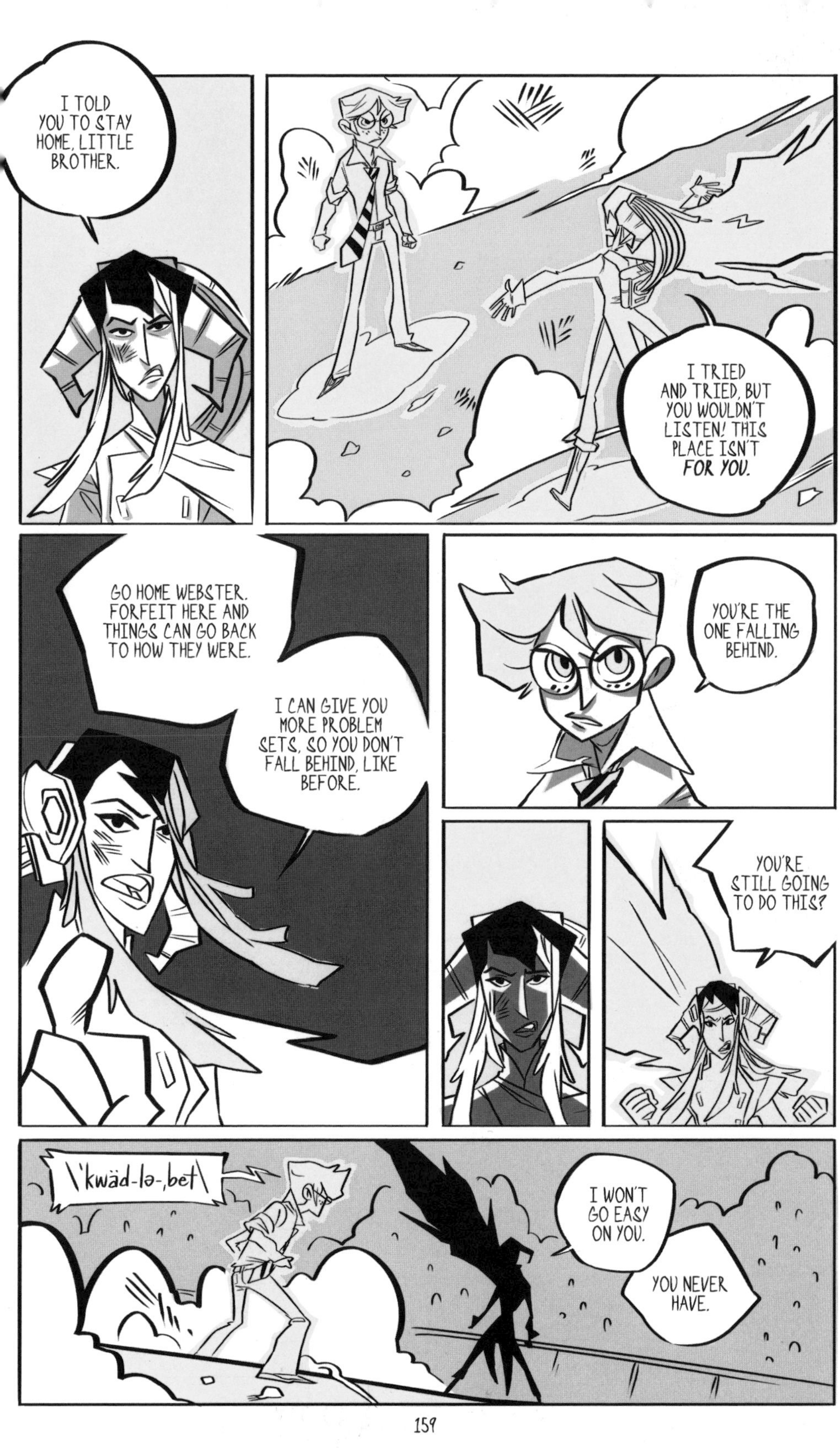
I TOLD YOU TO STAY HOME, LITTLE BROTHER.
I TRIED AND TRIED, BUT YOU WOULDN'T LISTEN! THIS PLACE ISN'T FOR YOU.
GO HOME WEBSTER. FORFEIT HERE AND THINGS CAN GO BACK TO HOW THEY WERE.
I CAN GIVE YOU MORE PROBLEM SETS, SO YOU DON'T FALL BEHIND, LIKE BEFORE.
YOU'RE THE ONE FALLING BEHIND.
YOU'RE STILL GOING TO DO THIS?
\ˈkwäd-lə-ˌbet\
I WON'T GO EASY ON YOU.
YOU NEVER HAVE.

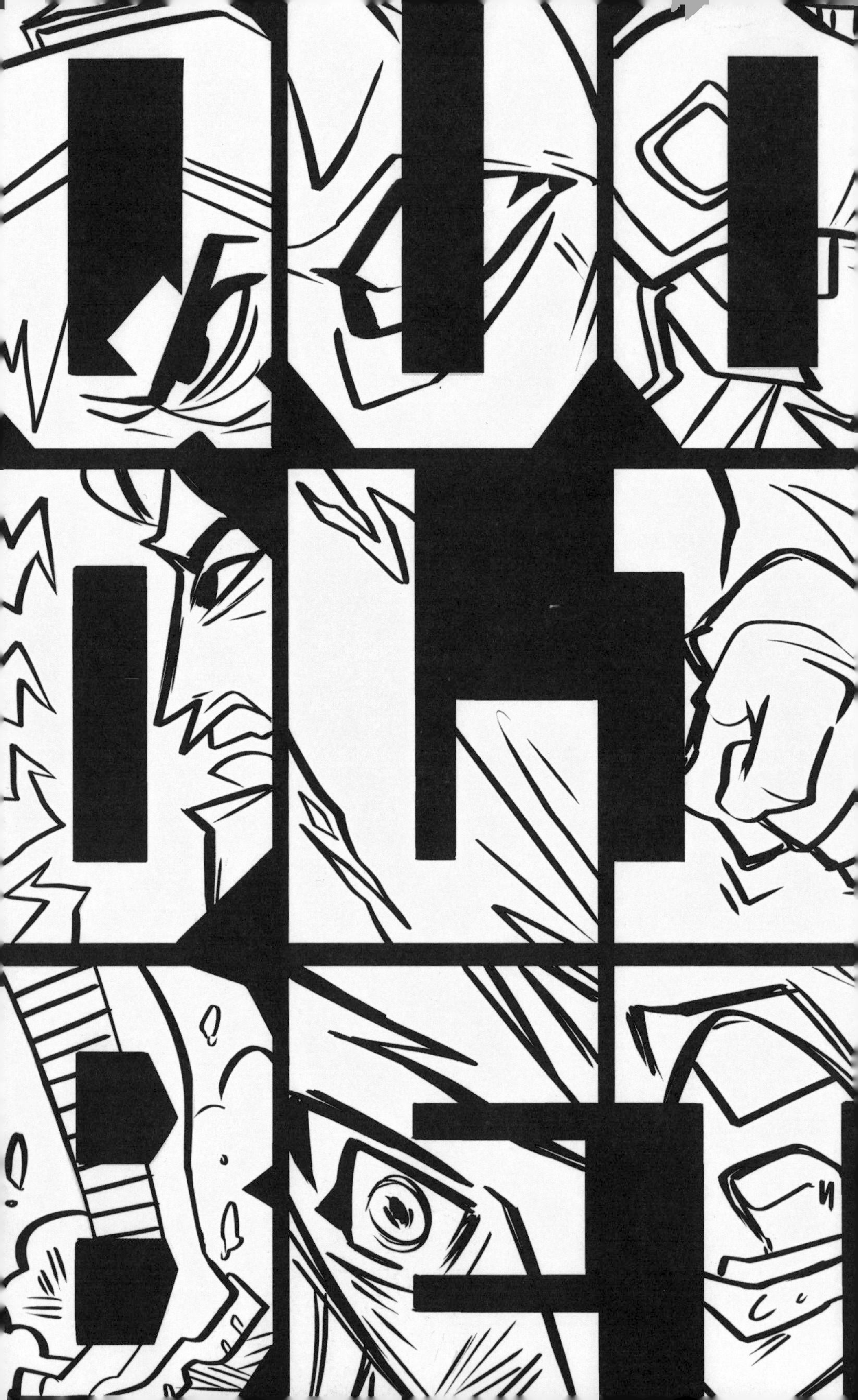

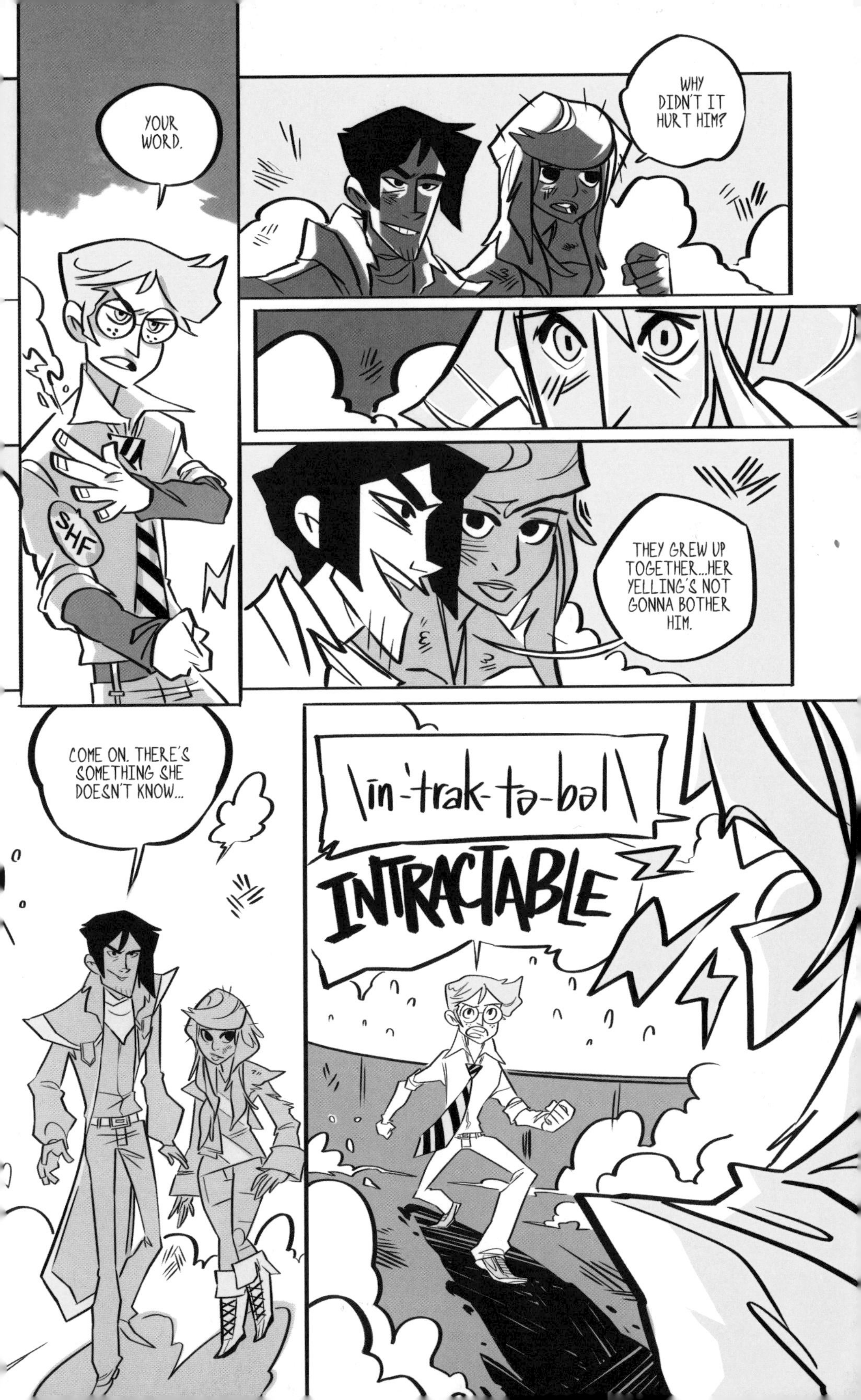
YOUR WORD.
WHY DIDN'T IT HURT HIM?
THEY GREW UP TOGETHER...HER YELLING'S NOT GONNA BOTHER HIM.
COME ON. THERE'S SOMETHING SHE DOESN'T KNOW...
\in-'trak-tə-bəl\
INTRACTABLE

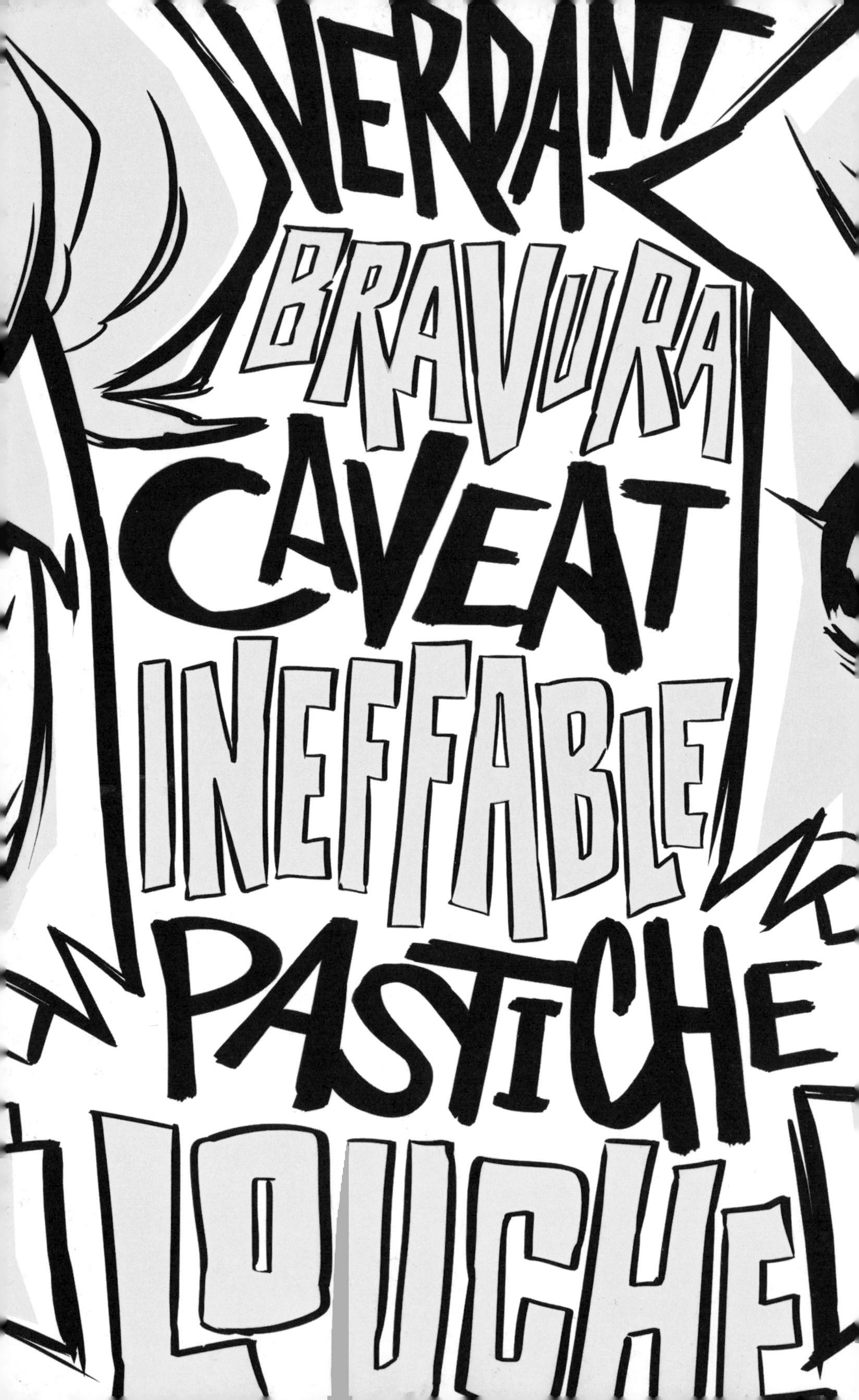
VERDANT
BRAVURA
CAVEAT
INEFFABLE
PASTICHE
LOUCHE

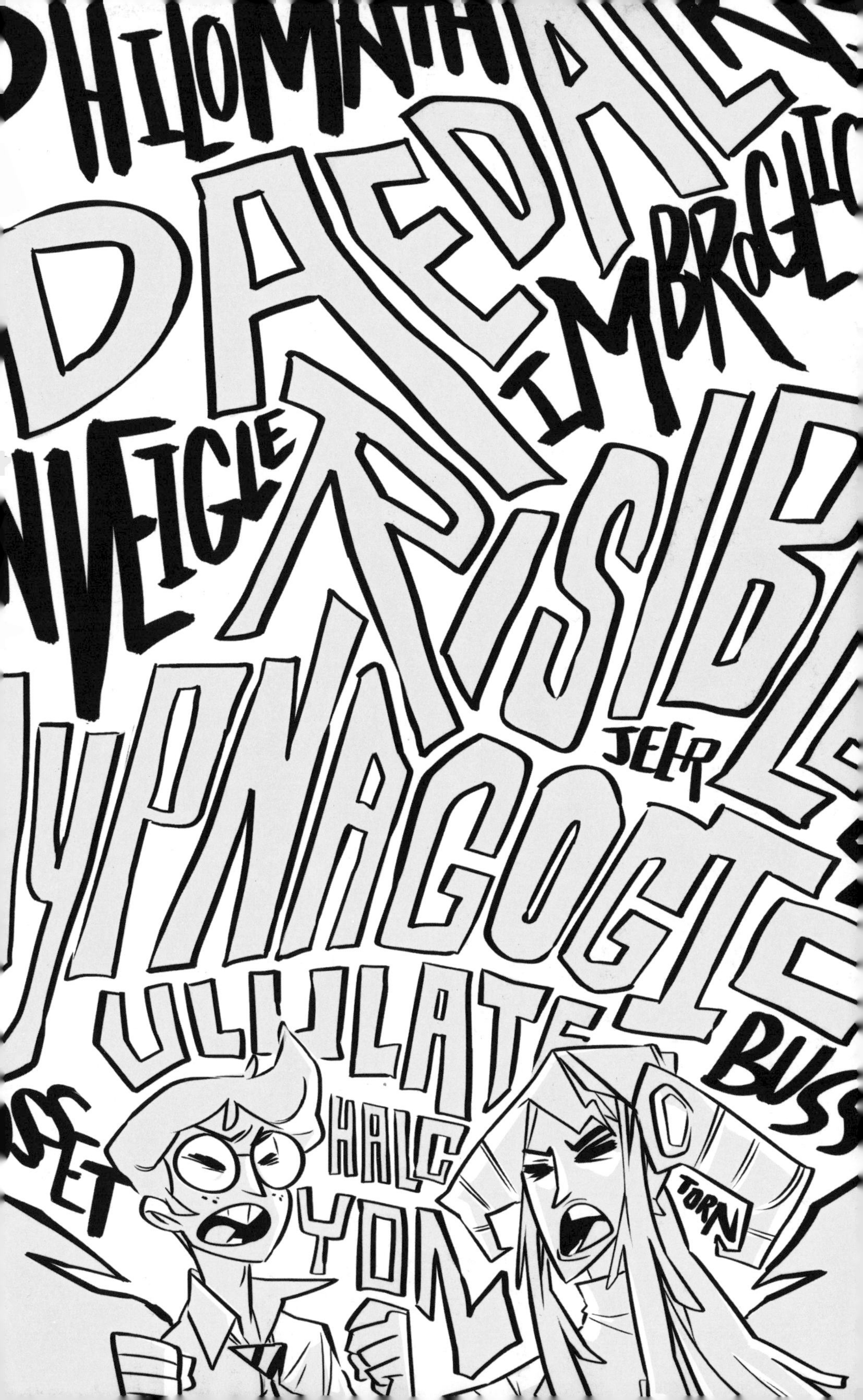
DAEDAL
JEER
ULULATE
HALCYON
TORN
BUSS

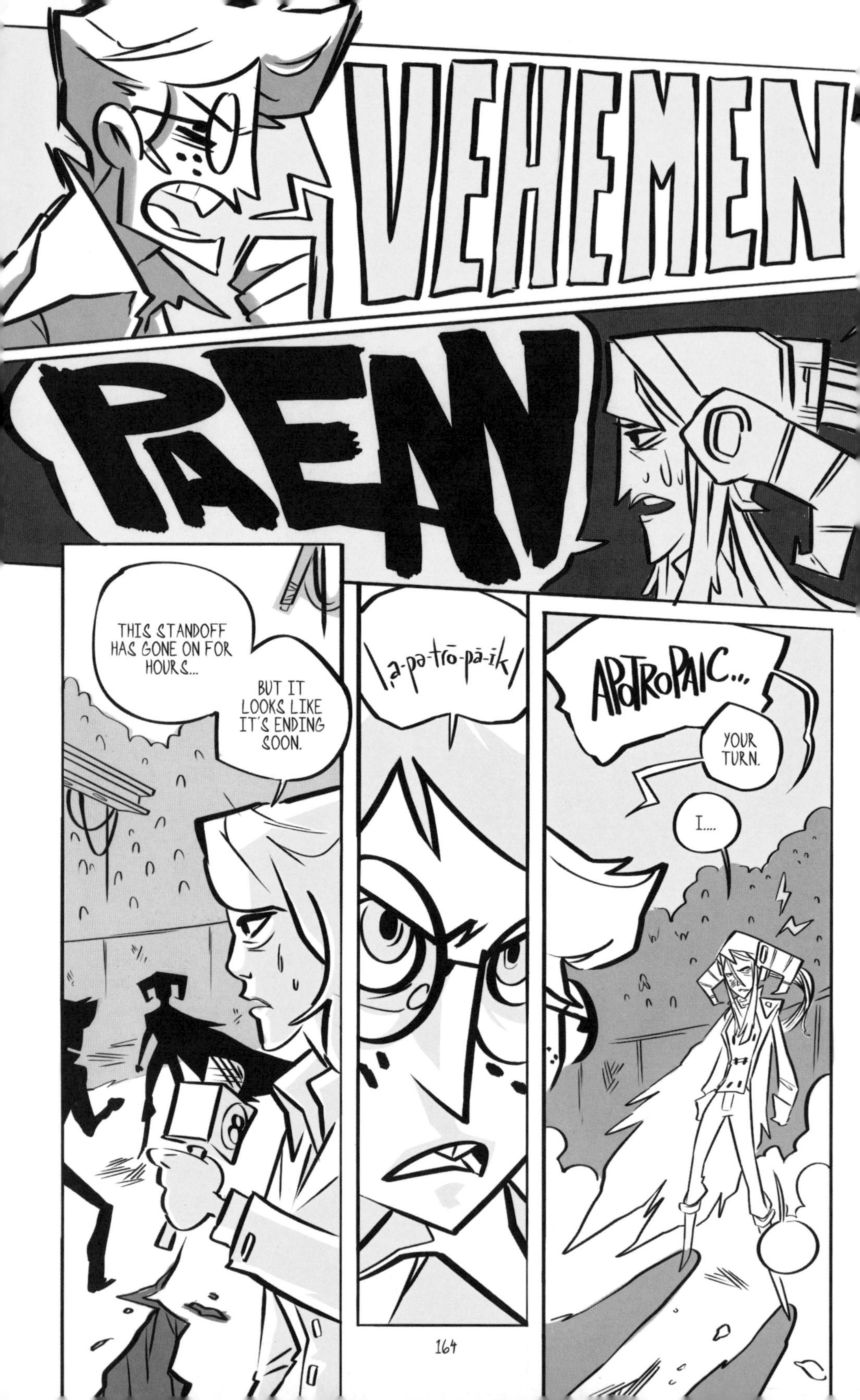
VEHEMENT
PAEAN
THIS STANDOFF HAS GONE ON FOR HOURS...
BUT IT LOOKS LIKE IT'S ENDING SOON.
\a-pa-trō-pā-ik\
APOTROPAIC...
YOUR TURN.
I....

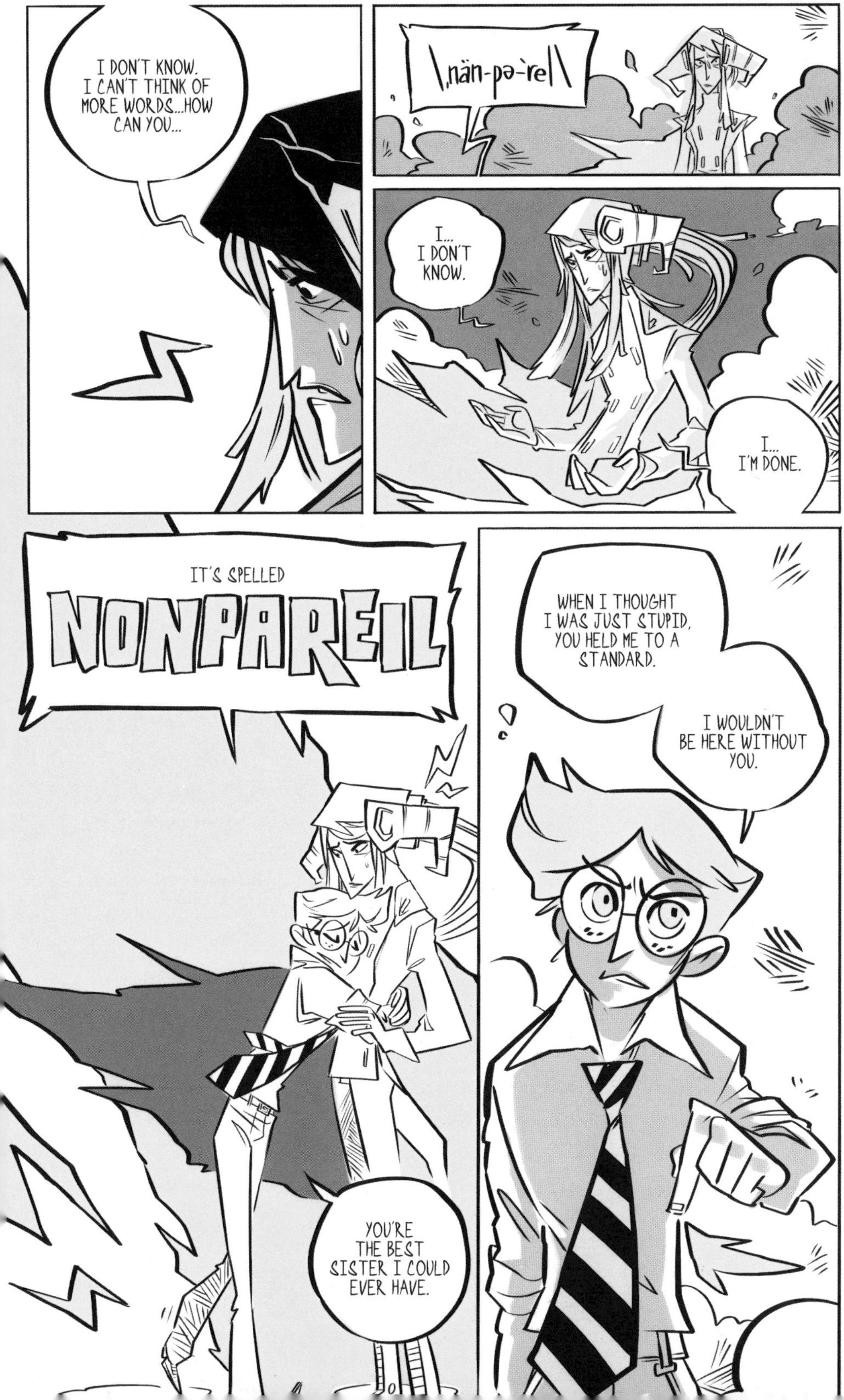
I DON'T KNOW. I CAN'T THINK OF MORE WORDS...HOW CAN YOU...
\ˌnän-pə-ˈrel\
I... I DON'T KNOW.
I... I'M DONE.
IT'S SPELLED NONPAREIL
YOU'RE THE BEST SISTER I COULD EVER HAVE.
WHEN I THOUGHT I WAS JUST STUPID, YOU HELD ME TO A STANDARD.
I WOULDN'T BE HERE WITHOUT YOU.

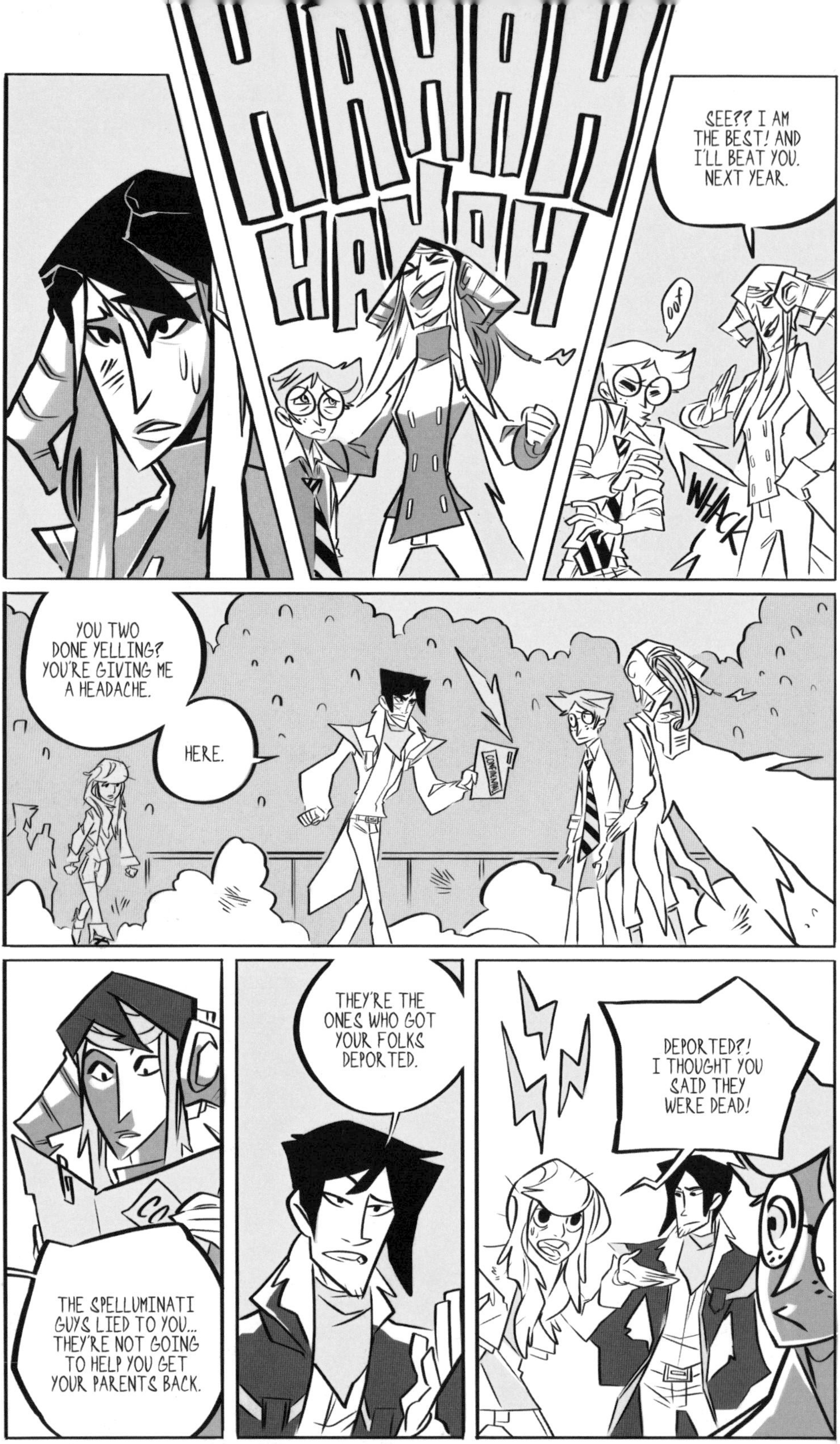
HAHAH HAHAH
SEE?? I AM THE BEST! AND I'LL BEAT YOU. NEXT YEAR.
oof
WHACK
YOU TWO DONE YELLING? YOU'RE GIVING ME A HEADACHE.
HERE.
THE SPELLUMINATI GUYS LIED TO YOU... THEY'RE NOT GOING TO HELP YOU GET YOUR PARENTS BACK.
THEY'RE THE ONES WHO GOT YOUR FOLKS DEPORTED.
DEPORTED?! I THOUGHT YOU SAID THEY WERE DEAD!

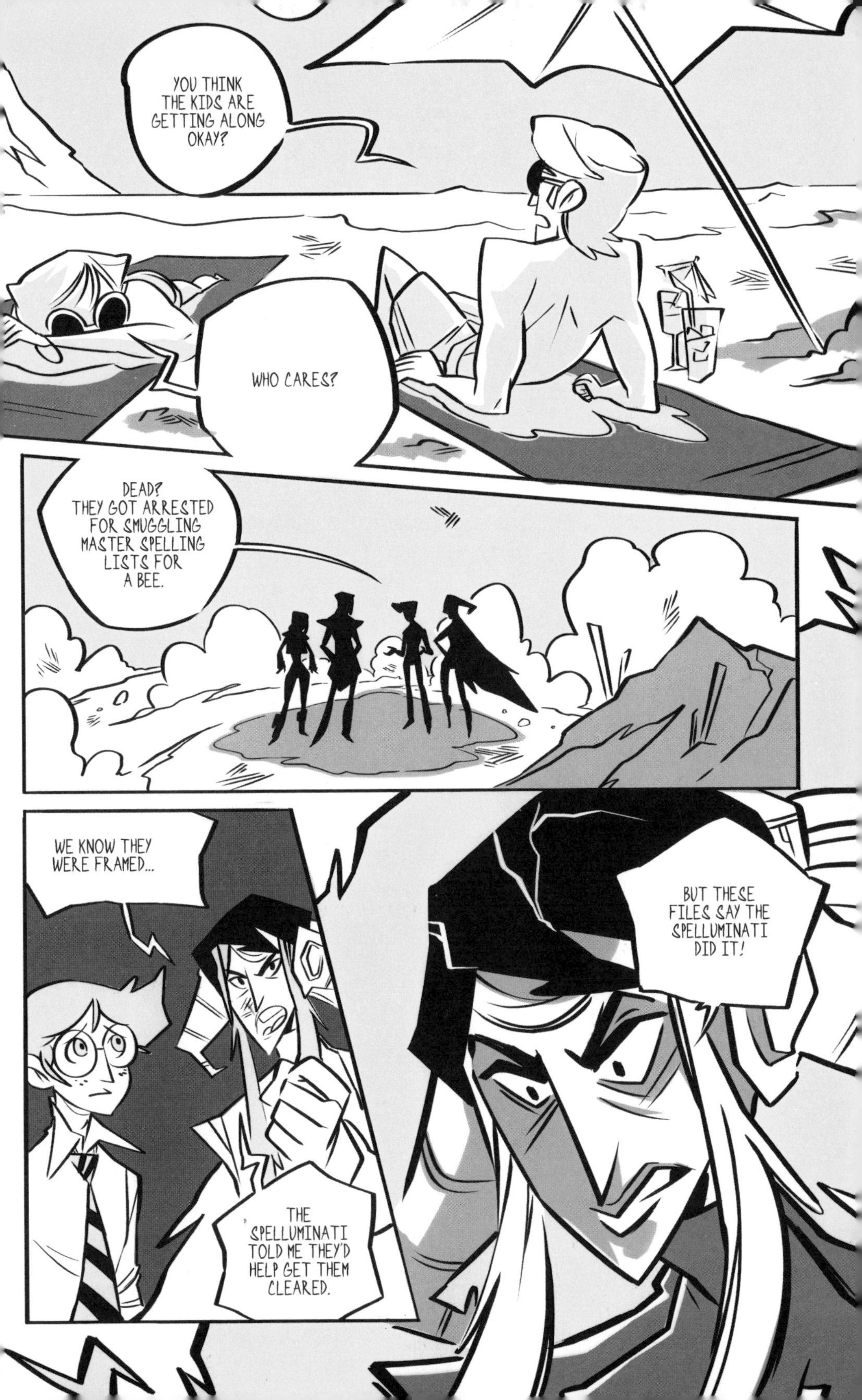
YOU THINK THE KIDS ARE GETTING ALONG OKAY?
WHO CARES?
DEAD? THEY GOT ARRESTED FOR SMUGGLING MASTER SPELLING LISTS FOR A BEE.
WE KNOW THEY WERE FRAMED...
THE SPELLUMINATI TOLD ME THEY'D HELP GET THEM CLEARED.
BUT THESE FILES SAY THE SPELLUMINATI DID IT!

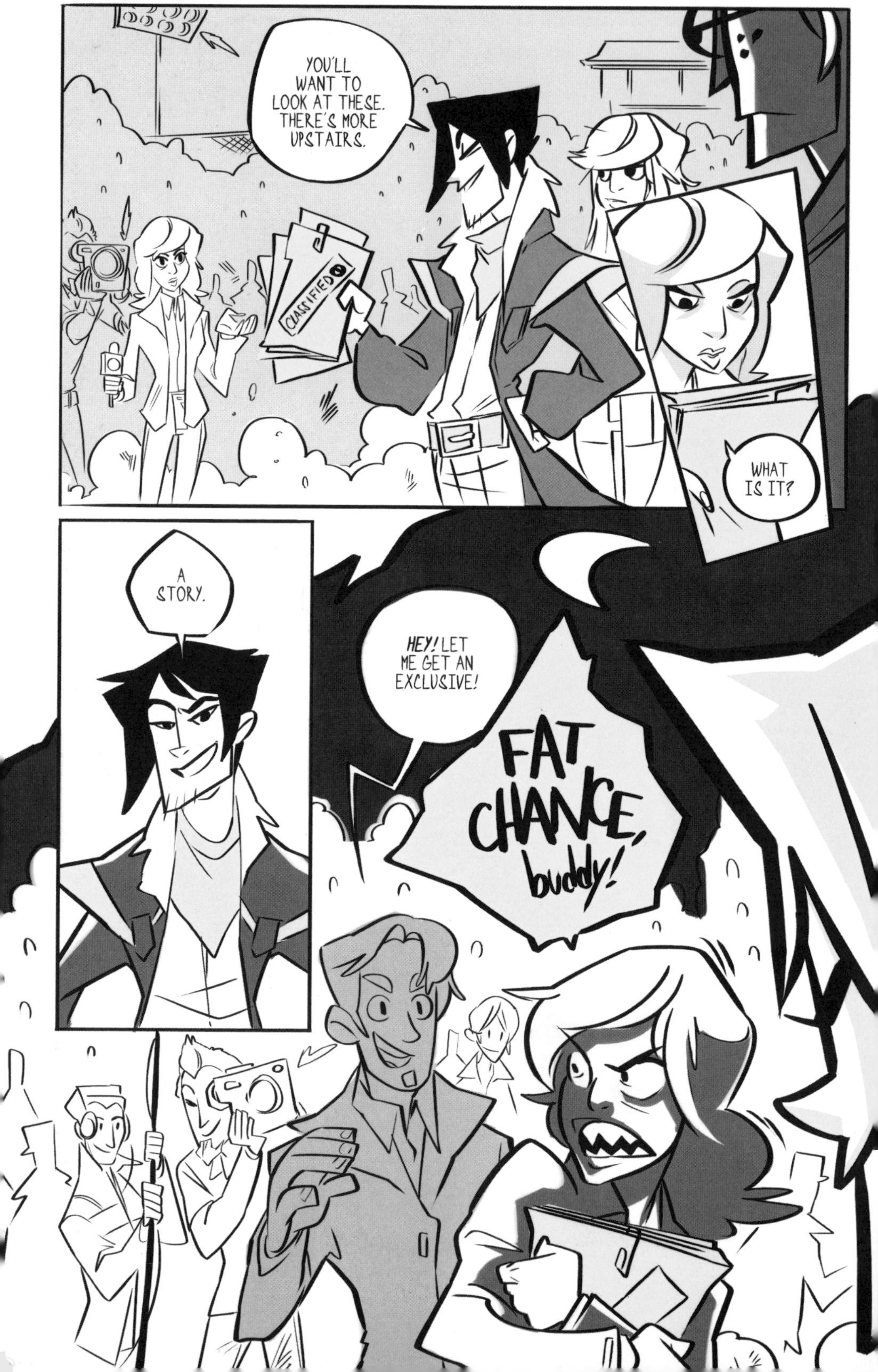
YOU'LL WANT TO LOOK AT THESE. THERE'S MORE UPSTAIRS.
CLASSIFIED
WHAT IS IT?
A STORY.
HEY! LET ME GET AN EXCLUSIVE!
FAT CHANCE, buddy!

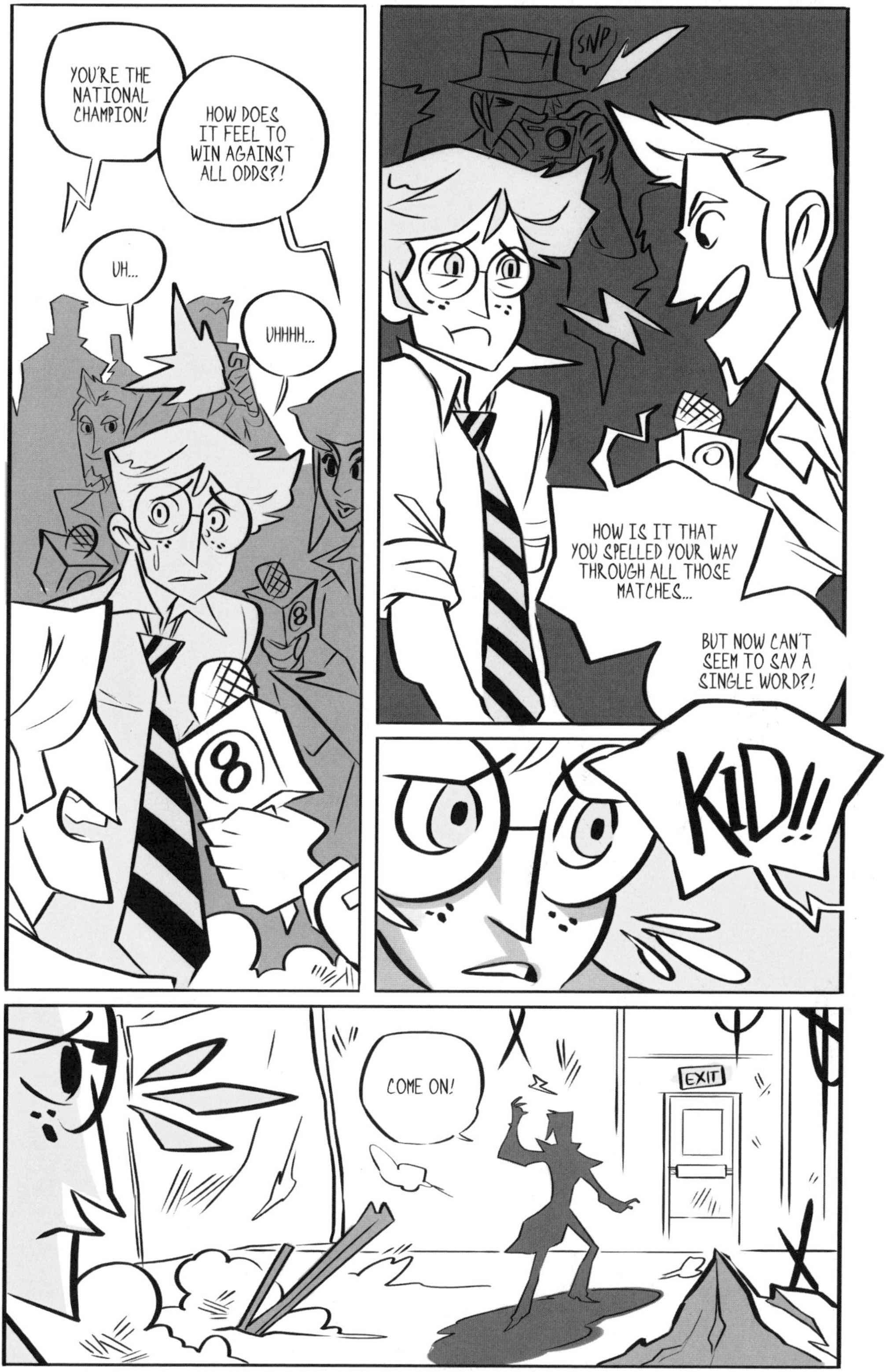
YOU'RE THE NATIONAL CHAMPION!
HOW DOES IT FEEL TO WIN AGAINST ALL ODDS?!
UH...
UHHHH...
SNP
HOW IS IT THAT YOU SPELLED YOUR WAY THROUGH ALL THOSE MATCHES...
BUT NOW CAN'T SEEM TO SAY A SINGLE WORD?!
KID!!
COME ON!
EXIT

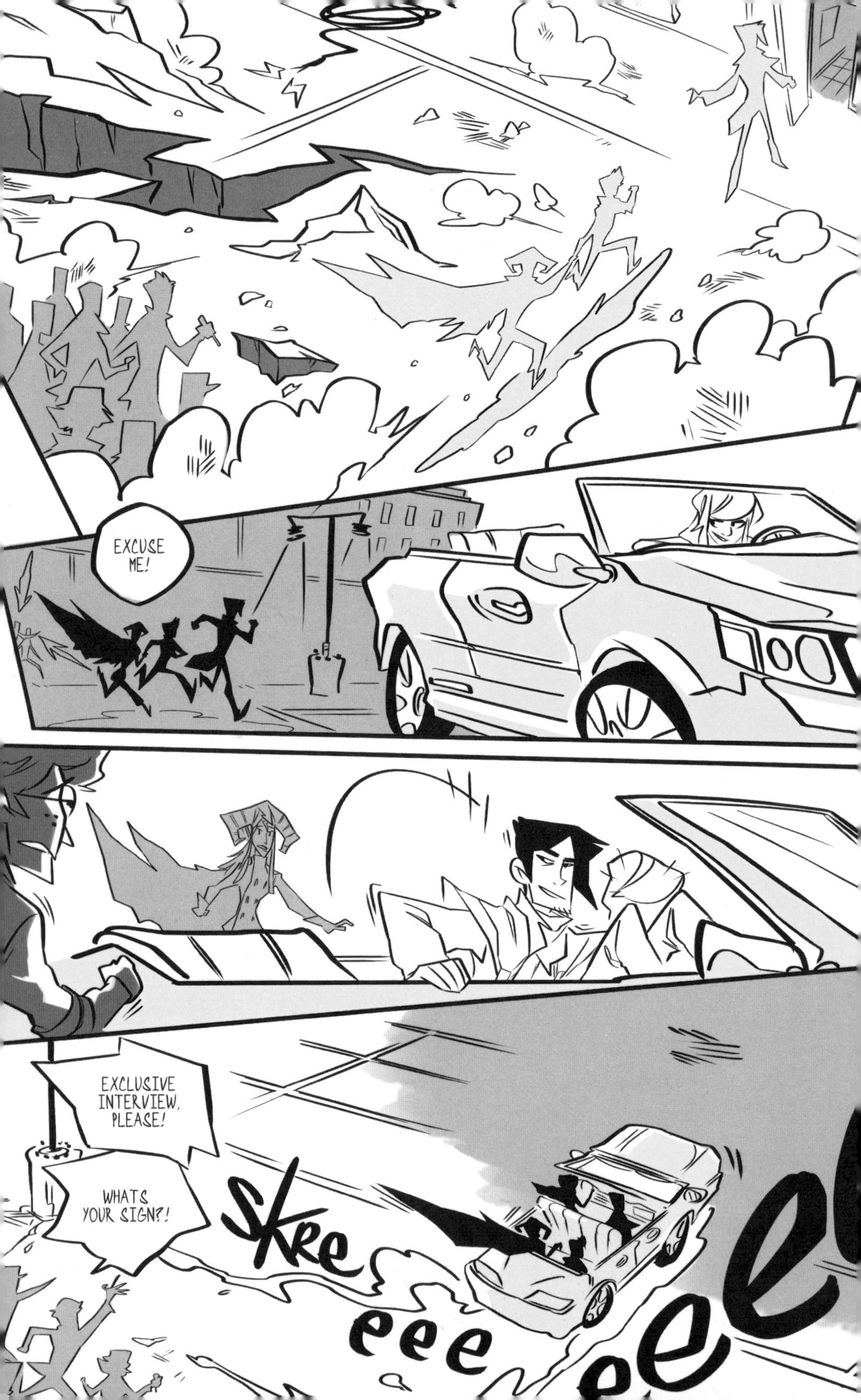
EXCUSE ME!
EXCLUSIVE INTERVIEW, PLEASE!
WHATS YOUR SIGN?!
SKREeeeeeeee

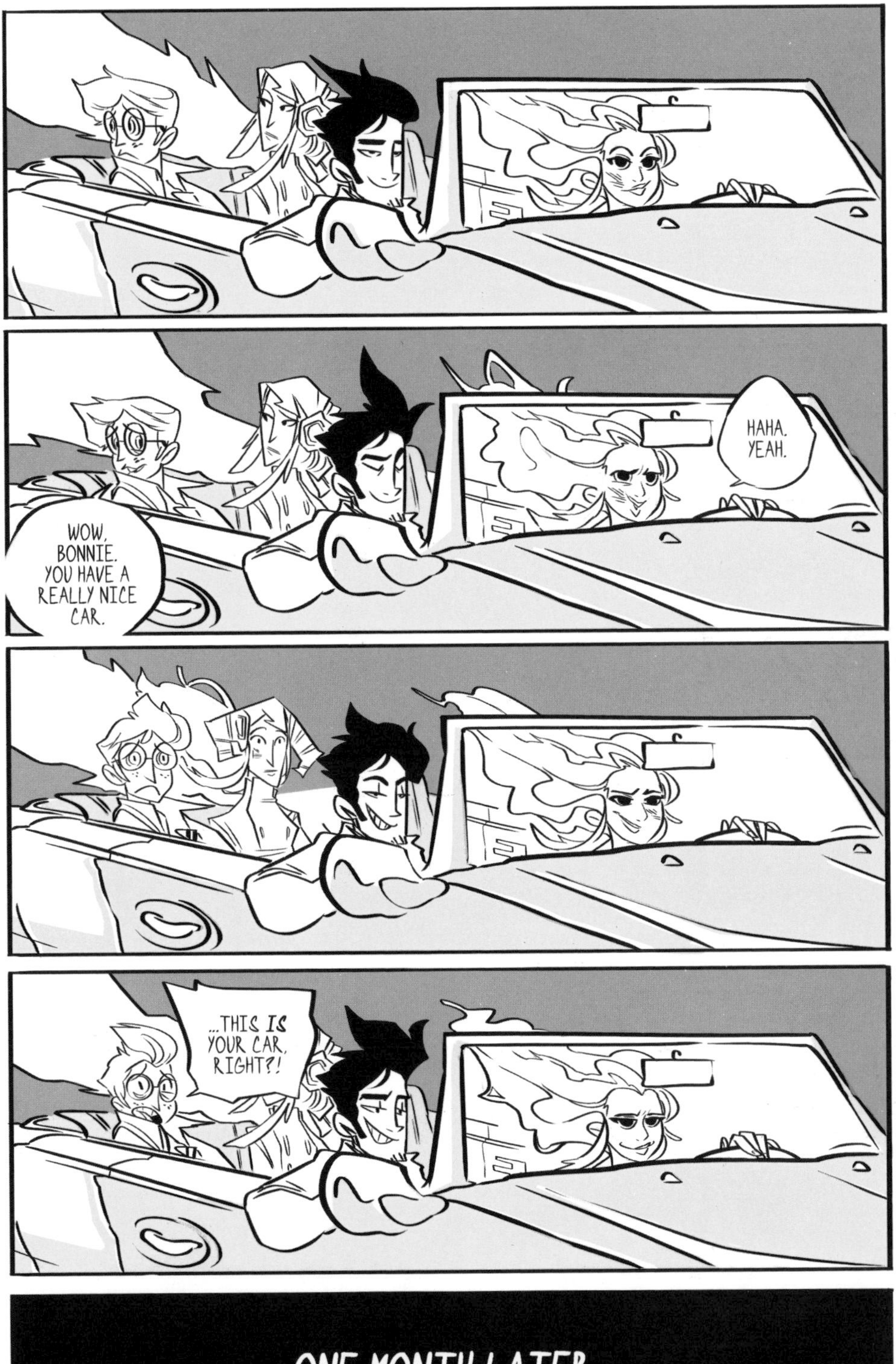
WOW, BONNIE. YOU HAVE A REALLY NICE CAR.
HAHA. YEAH.
...THIS *IS* YOUR CAR, RIGHT?!
ONE MONTH LATER

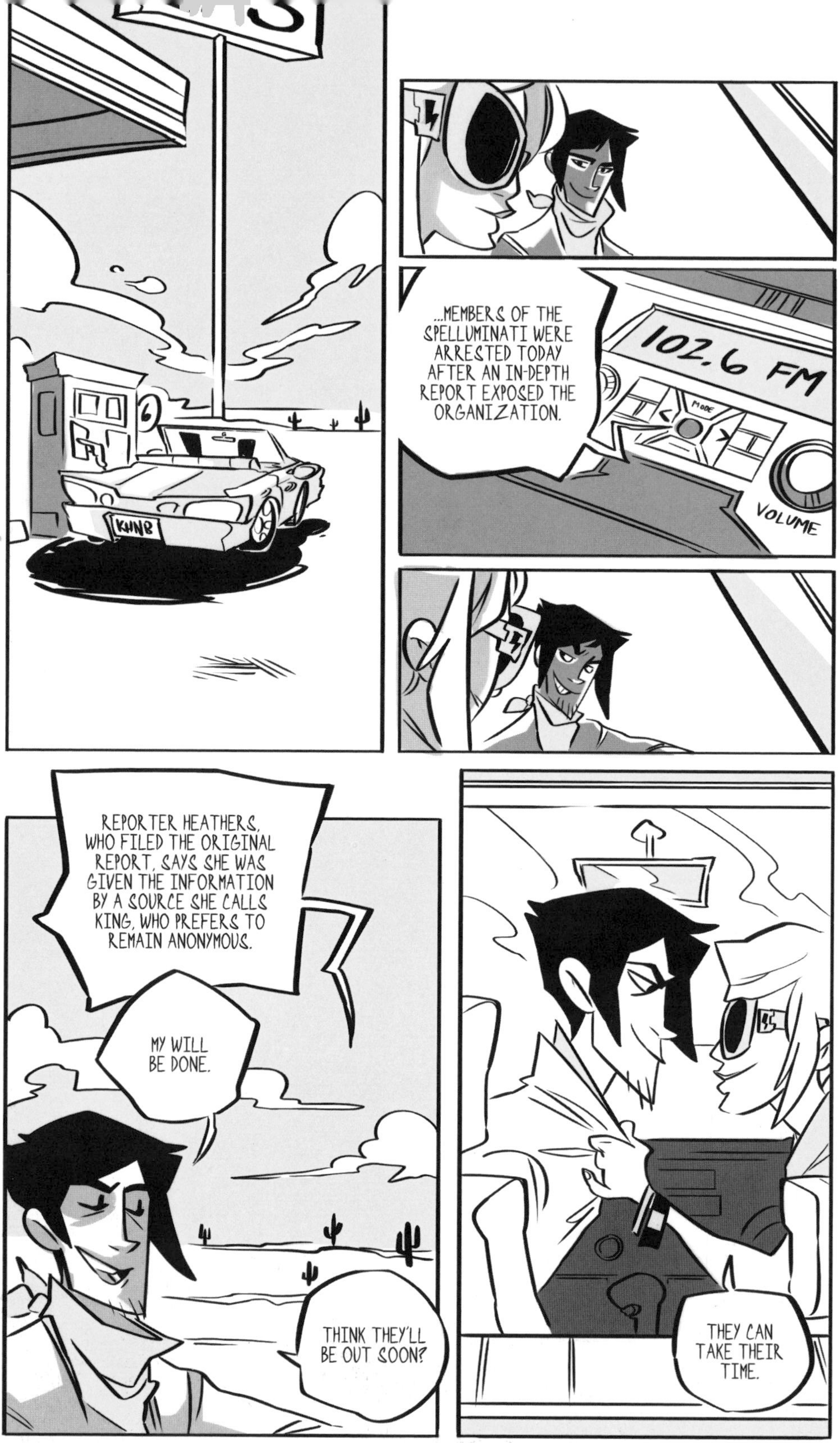
...MEMBERS OF THE SPELLUMINATI WERE ARRESTED TODAY AFTER AN IN-DEPTH REPORT EXPOSED THE ORGANIZATION.
102.6 FM
MODE
VOLUME
REPORTER HEATHERS, WHO FILED THE ORIGINAL REPORT, SAYS SHE WAS GIVEN THE INFORMATION BY A SOURCE SHE CALLS KING, WHO PREFERS TO REMAIN ANONYMOUS.
MY WILL BE DONE.
THINK THEY'LL BE OUT SOON?
THEY CAN TAKE THEIR TIME.

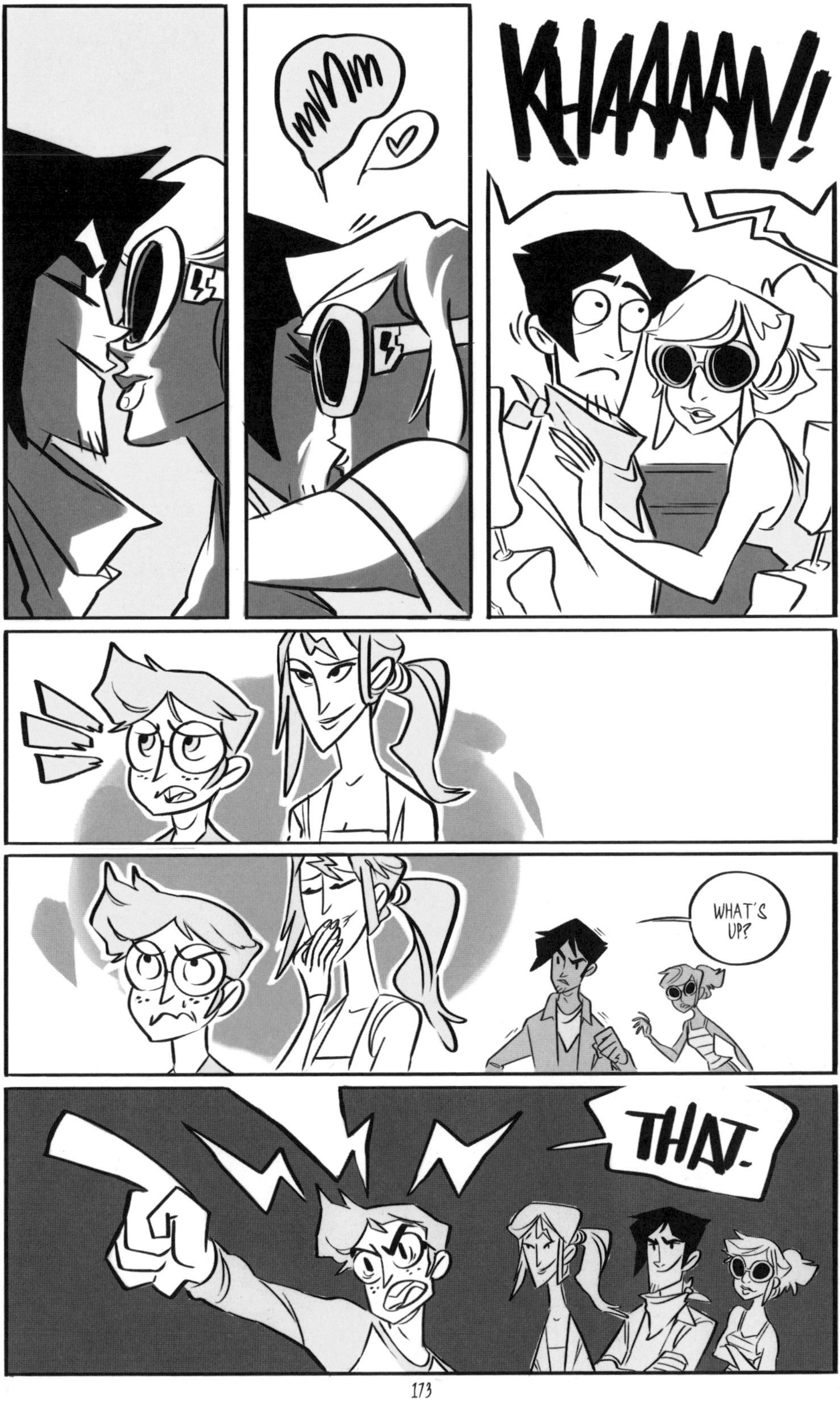
mMm
KHAAAAN!
WHAT'S UP?
THAT-

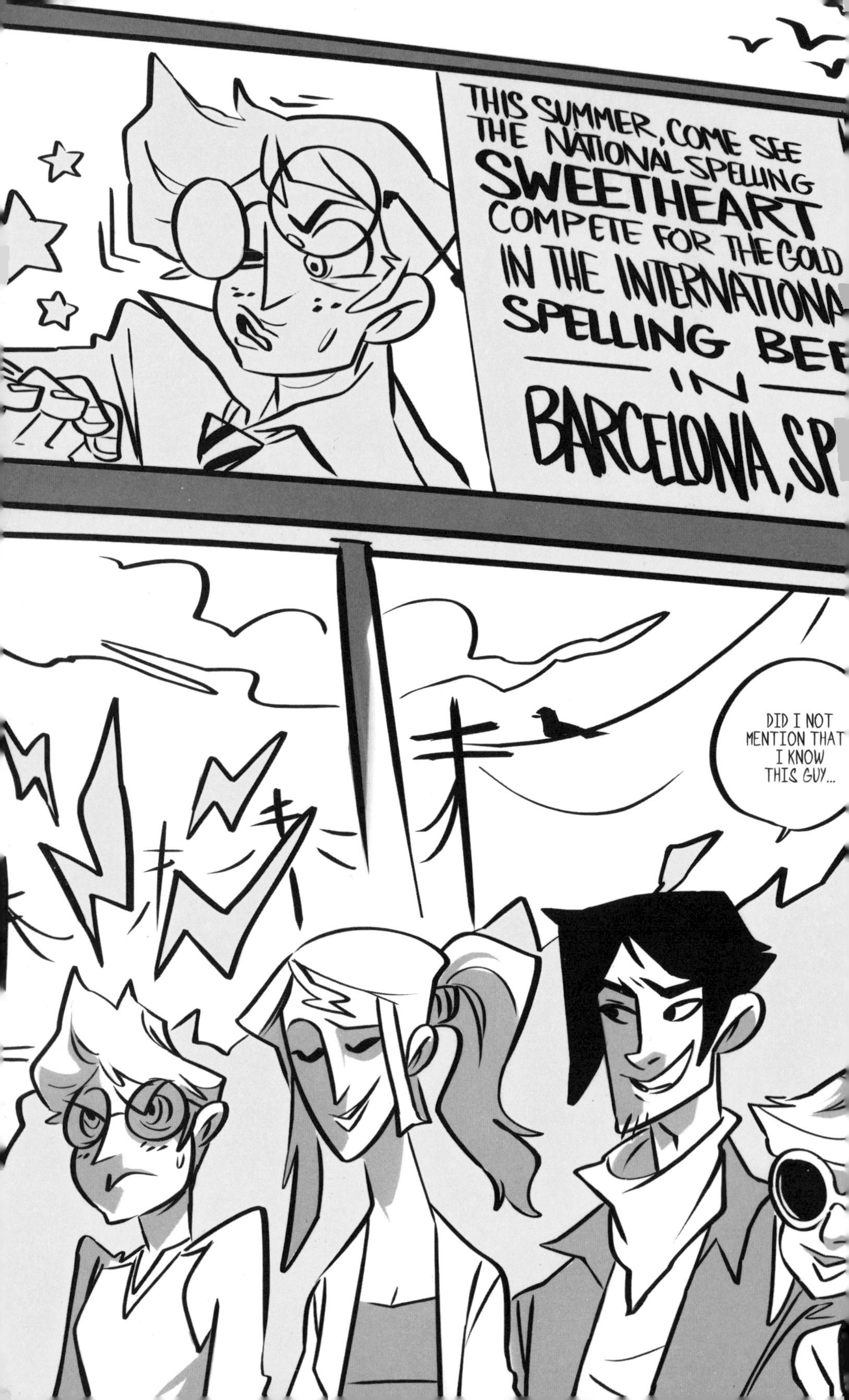
THIS SUMMER, COME SEE THE NATIONAL SPELLING
SWEETHEART
COMPETE FOR THE GOLD IN THE INTERNATIONA
SPELLING BEE
IN
BARCELONA, SP
DID I NOT MENTION THAT I KNOW THIS GUY...

end.

Ananth Panagariya is an author who has written
for Oni Press, BOOM!, Dark Horse and others.
He has self-published several books, including
three collections of the twice-weekly webcomic
Johnny Wander (drawn by Yuko Ota, available for
free online at johnnywander.com).

You can find him on twitter as @ananthymous.

He's eating ice cream... right... now...

Once a week, **Tessa Stone** climbs
down from her haven in the treetops
to do something other than comics.
Then she slowly disappears back into
the canopy, because drawing and
writing are what she likes to do best.